ASSASSIN'S OBSESSION

LUCY MONROE

LUCY MONROE LLC

Assassin's Obsession

by Lucy Monroe

1st Printing October 2024 Lucy Monroe LLC

DEDICATION

For all the avid mafia romance readers who love an unhinged hero and a downtrodden heroine that never gives up. This one is for you!

With special recognition for longtime reader, Kathleen Brigagliano, whose name I borrowed for Candi (though I changed the spelling a wee bit). Thank you!

Italian Mafia Hierarchy*
Godfather of Cosa Nostra: Severu De Luca
Head Enforcer/Assassin: Angelo Caruso
(Also known as Angel of Death)

Cosa Nostra Territories
New York: Five Families

Bonanno (Queens), Colombo (Bronx), Gambino (Staten Island), Genovese (Manhattan), and Lucchese (Brooklyn): each founding mafia is led by a don who could be from any of the families loyal to them.

New York Genovese family
Don/Boss: Miceli De Luca
(Also known as The Genovese and King of New York)
Underboss: Allessio Greco
Consigliere: Big Sal De Luca
Capos: Domenico Bianchi, Salvatore De Luca, Tomasso Marino, Niccolo Costa, Dario Ricci, Stefano Bianchi
Las Vegas
Don/Boss: Patrizio Mancini
Underboss: Raffaele Mancini
Detroit
Don/Boss: Pietro Russo
Boston
Don/Boss: Lombard
The Cosa Nostra is known as the Lombardi Family, despite the Americanized name for the don's family.
New England
Chicago aka The Outfit

* All names and positions are fictional or used in a fictional capacity, a product of the author's imagination, loosely based on La Cosa Nostra structure in America.

PROLOGUE

The Spring Before Severu De Luca Becomes Godfather

CANDI

One of the bold lookers is ogling my tits and ass.

Like he's been doing all night, he leers at me, trying to get my attention. I don't eye-flirt with bold lookers. It's too easy for their interest to tip over into action. So, I've been ignoring him.

Only, that's easier to do on stage. I'm not on the pole right now. I'm on the floor doing lap dances for extra tips. Tips I need for the new hydrotherapy they want to try with my mom.

"Hey, Candi. You taste as sweet as your name? I bet your pussy tastes like sugar, huh?" The bold looker's fingers slide over my ass cheek, heading toward my no-go zone.

My whole body tenses and I have to remind myself, I cannot brain the guy. I hate this stuff, but it happens. And if I react the way I want to, I get fired. So, I don't.

Ignoring his crass words, I shift sideways fast, moving out of range of the grasping fingers.

The guy I'm dancing for isn't looking at my tits anymore. His gaze is locked on his friend behind me.

Crap. What is the perv up to now?

I spin around to see, and all the air expels from my lungs.

A guy wearing an expensive suit and black latex gloves has the bold looker by the scruff of his neck. With the face of a fallen angel and death in his eyes, he meets my gaze and nods.

Like he's saying hello, but without words?

I'm not sure. But I nod back.

He starts dragging the bold looker toward the back exit. A bunch of guys in suits come out of nowhere and chase after him, yelling his name.

Angelo.

Needing a better look at my savior, I abandon my lap dance customer and follow right behind them. I'm as fast in stilettos as these guys are in their shiny dress shoes and I reach the alley right behind them.

Just in time to see Angelo drive his knife through the hand of the guy who tried to cop a feel. The man screams and starts begging.

Showing no mercy, Angelo twists the knife, saying something I can't hear.

The bold looker's scream turns into high pitched sobs.

One of the suit guys says, "Calm down, Angelo, man. He gets the message. No touching the stripper."

"Dancer. She's a fucking dancer." Angelo glares at his friend.

I'm pretty sure I fall a little in love right then. I *am* a dancer. Yes, I strip too, but I dance while I'm doing it with moves most athletes would find impossible to keep doing for an entire shift on the stage.

My ovaries definitely explode and for the first time ever at work, I soak my G-string with arousal.

I must make a sound because Angelo's piercing gaze snaps to me.

Staring back, no words come out of my mouth.

"You're scaring *the dancer*," one of his other friends claims, emphasizing the last two words.

I'm not scared. Not of Angelo.

It's my reaction to the violence he's perpetuating on my behalf. Ashamed of how turned on I am right now while another human being is wailing in agony, I spin on my six-inch heel and rush back into the club.

I don't see Angelo again, but sometimes, I feel the constant tension in my spine relax and I realize he's in the club.

Watching.

I want to tell him thank you for what he did, but that makes me feel like a bad person. You shouldn't thank someone for skewering a man's hand, should you?

I definitely shouldn't get turned on thinking about it.

That's just wrong.

But no one has ever protected me like that. Mom would if she could, but with her arthritis, sometimes she can't get around without her chair or walker.

She's sure not throwing a guy up against a brick wall and stabbing him in the hand.

CHAPTER 1

The Summer Before Severu De Luca Becomes Godfather

ANGELO

I'm itchy under my skin.

I haven't seen Candi in four days and it's pissing me off.

Flicking my gaze up to the security camera in the corner of the holding cell where Miceli and I are interrogating the member of a gang foolish enough to encroach on our territory, I nod to myself. Yeah, that'll work.

A camera outside her door. Maybe one inside her apartment. Her mom is always home.

Which is not the obstacle some people think it is.

It's time I met my obsession's family, even if it's as the apartment building's new maintenance guy.

"What has you smiling, you psycho?" Miceli asks from the other side of our guest.

"None of your fucking business." I kick the dealer so eager to sell his shit on the streets of Manhattan. "Not this asshole."

All yelled out, the *stronzo* grunts in pain.

Miceli squats down beside him, grabs his hair and yanks his head up. "You are alive for one reason. You take a message to your homeboys. Stay the fuck off our streets. The next one of you we find in our territory, for any fucking reason, even if it's to visit your sick grandma, ends up in the soup."

Our enemies know what that means, but I spell it out for him anyway. "Once we dump your body in the soup, you don't exist. Not even as a trace of DNA to leave behind."

~ ~ ~

Pitiful Princess smells like booze, pussy, sweat and disinfectant when I walk in.

I haven't been here since Wednesday and rage rolls through me. I want to gouge out the eyes of every fucking asshole ogling my girl.

That would piss off the boss, though. Severu doesn't want undue attention brought to the family right now. More importantly, Candi would be upset.

The customers are safe as long as they don't touch her.

Like the *stronzo* who will never have full use of his left hand again. I would have cut it off, but *she* came into the alley. Candi saw me playing with my prey, looked at me like I was a monster, and ran away.

I am a monster, but I'm not so depraved I will purposefully terrify the woman I plan to spend the rest of my life with.

If she found out later that I had cut the dick's hand off, she would never get past her fear of me. And that would make living together awkward.

So, I let him go.

After beating the shit out of him and warning him to get his ass out of the city if he wanted to keep breathing.

He blubbered about his job and family, but in the end, he saw reason. You don't need a job or miss your family when you're dead.

Without taking my eyes off the pure beauty undulating around the pole, I take my usual seat in the shadows. A minute later, one of the cocktail servers puts an unopened bottle of fizzy mineral water in front of me.

Ignoring the glass she placed beside it on the table, I take out a sanitizing wipe laced with a reacting agent that will change color if it comes into contact with several classes of drugs. I wipe down the bottle, check the wipe is still white and then twist off the lid before taking a sip.

A brand not served to customers, the bottle is from my own private reserve behind the bar.

Aware of all the ways to kill a man, because I've employed most of them, I don't drink or eat in public places unless I have personally vetted the kitchen and waitstaff.

In this case, I've had a little chat with all the bartenders and they know better than to allow anyone access to my stash of mineral water. I prefer a slice of lime and to drink my water chilled over ice, but those components provide too many opportunities for the resourceful.

Unless I get it myself, or have one of my men do it.

When I'm here, I'm too busy watching my girl to bother.

It's Saturday and that means I get to see her luscious tits bare except for the pasties she puts over her perfect nipples.

If she didn't use the pasties and keep her G-string on, I'd have to burn the club down, with all the customers inside.

Candi strips during the last set before she joins the other dancers working the floor. When the familiar music starts, men start throwing dollar bills on the stage. Cheap assed bozos.

I tip five hundred every night I'm in. I'd give her more, but there's no need. Soon enough she'll be living under my roof, eating my food and wearing the clothes I bought her.

There's a whole closetful in the house I got for us to live in on Long Island.

As soon as Severu becomes godfather and I know it's safe to, I'm packing her and her family up and moving them in. She wouldn't be happy if I tried to leave her mom and sister behind, even though neither of them is related to her by blood.

They're important to Candi. She dances here to support them, but soon she won't have to worry about that either.

I sip my mineral water, daydreaming about the life we'll have together once I tell her who I am and who she is to me. I'll be the only one who gets to see those generous tits bounce as she dances around the pole.

Her dance studio at the house has one, along with a chair for me to sit in while I watch her.

Candi looks toward the table in the shadows where I always sit as she unhooks her bralette and lets it slide down her arms. Is she hoping I'm here? Is that move just for me?

It must be.

We are two halves of the same whole. I am the darkness. She is the light. We were separated in the ether before our souls came to earth to inhabit these bodies.

We've never spoken a single word to each other, but we don't have to.

We're soulmates.

My cock grows so fucking hard as Candi drops the bralette to the stage. My fingers fist and release with the need to squeeze those gorgeous melons.

The miniscule skirt comes next, revealing the rhinestone studded G-string covering her pussy lips.

I ordered her one made with pure silk and diamonds because nothing less should cover my treasure.

She tosses a kiss over her shoulder before exiting the stage. Her tits will be covered again when she comes onto the floor. Anticipation thrums through my blood waiting for her to reappear.

When she does, she's wearing an outfit I've never seen before. The gold braid gathers in the nearly sheer white nighty under her generous breasts, the flowy skirt barely reaching the tops of her thighs.

My mouth goes dry at how beautiful Candi looks, but it's the small set of wings made from iridescent feathers peeking over her shoulders that makes my heart pound.

She's an angel.

Is that for me? Her Angel of Death. Now that she's seen me stab a man's hand, she must have asked around about who I am.

And she's dressed like an angel for me.

I nearly come in my pants thinking about it. I'm on my feet before I'm aware of moving, but I manage to stop myself moving out of the shadows.

I don't like how close the customers are to Candi as she moves between the tables. If I go to her, I'll kill the man offering her a roll of twenties for a lap dance.

Asshole.

But I have to let my girl do her thing.

For a little longer anyway.

The club is packed with bodies and I remain standing so I can watch my girl dance. She's moving her body sensually and smiling at her lap dance customer, but the smile doesn't reach her eyes.

Because she's not dancing for him. My girl loves to dance, but she doesn't love dancing for men perving on her body.

That's why I know she isn't going to mind quitting here.

Once I make her mine, no other man gets to see that sweet ass move like that.

I might have to kill the man she's dancing in front of right now. The way he's looking at her pisses me off.

I'll do it away from the club. Disappear him.

No body. No crime.

I don't leave other evidence behind. That should be circumspect enough to make Severu happy.

CHAPTER 2

CANDI

Tonight, the club is packed and the customers are riled up.

Since Bianca left, the club has hired some new dancers. One is on tonight and in her last two sets, she stripped down to a G-string so tiny it doesn't even cover her pussy lips. She's still on the stage and the punters are horny.

I like that word. Punter. I got it from one of my mom's British crime shows. It's better than calling the customers johns because that implies I do sex acts with them for money. I don't.

The sour smell of sweat assaults my nostrils and it's all I can do to keep the fake smile fixed on my face. A guy wearing a cheap suit, which is a step above the usual attire in here, waves me over with a roll of twenties.

The other men at his table are dressed like him and all wear similar expressions too. They think they're flirting with the wild side coming to a strip club and offering money for a lap dance.

"Twenty-five for ten minutes. No contact." I always spell it out beforehand.

He nods and peels off two twenties before laying them on the table. "Make it good and you can have both."

I don't roll my eyes. I want the forty bucks, but seriously? Make it good?

Shaking my barely clothed body within a foot of him will have him coming in his underwear. He's that guy.

Ignoring the music playing over the club's sound system, I start dancing to the soundtrack in my head.

I'm cupping my breasts and twerking my ass when suddenly harsh fingers dig into my hips.

Yanked backward, I nearly trip, but I've been dancing four nights a week in six-inch heels for three years. It takes more than pulling me off balance to make me fall.

Wanting those meaty hands off my body, I jerk forward, but the fingers dig in and I end up on polyester clad thighs. "Come here, baby. I'll give you a hundred to sit on my lap for a minute."

An unimpressive, but intrusive hardon presses against my naked backside as the guy wraps one arm around my waist and grinds up against me. My elbow flies backward but it barely connects before sliding off his chest because of the angle.

The man laughs. "You're a feisty little bitch, aren't you?"

This time, I throw my head backward but he shifts avoiding the headbutt. I miss his chin, but I hit his neck and that at least elicits a grunt from him.

Where's the bouncer?

If Gino is watching, he'll wave security away. He wants me working the backrooms and for all I know he put this guy up to this. To break me in.

But I am not letting some disgusting perv come against my ass. Even if it means getting fired.

The angle's wrong for me to hit the guy's instep with my stiletto heel too, so I lift my foot and grab my shoe. Holding it by the toe, I bring the heel against the side of his leg as hard as I can.

He yells in pain and his grip loosens. I surge forward and land on my knees. Someone kicks me in the backside and I go sprawling, losing my grip on my makeshift weapon and getting way too close and personal with the floor. They mop every night, but in between?

The risk of coming into contact with body fluids is high enough to have me scrambling to my feet. One foot is still in its shoe and I have to cant one knee to compensate.

Before I can get away, that same meaty fist grabs my arm, fingers digging in so hard I cry out in pain.

"Let her go." The tone is deadly, the timber loud enough to be heard over the music.

I can't see who spoke, but I know it's not the bouncer. Not that voice.

Latex slides between my arm and the fingers gripping it. Then there's an audible pop and the creep who tried to use me as a living sex doll screams in pain.

When his grip loosens I jerk away and this time he lets me go.

I spin to face him and my savior.

It's Angelo, the guy who skewered the hand of the guy that tried to touch me a couple of months ago.

He has this jerk's finger bent back at an impossible angle, but his eyes aren't on the now crying man. They're on me.

His black latex covered hand is gentle when he touches my bicep and the angry red marks that reveal where my captor's hand gripped me. "You alright, *dolcezza*?"

I don't speak either Italian or Sicilian fluently like my bestie, Bianca, but I'm pretty sure the dangerous man just called me sweetheart.

Which doesn't mean anything. Right? Lots of people use endearments like that. Only, Angelo doesn't look like the kind of guy to throw them around. But he just did. Directed at me.

Not that I think it means sweetheart like, girlfriend material. If anything, he's using it like you would to a kid or a friend.

But we've never even met officially.

Watching him skewer a man's hand in the alley isn't like being introduced, is it?

"I'm okay." Skeeved out and shaky, and tomorrow I'll have finger shaped bruises on my arm, but I'll live.

If the creep had managed to get off while rubbing against me, I'd be crying right now though. I know I would. And that makes me furious.

Because it's taking every bit of my self-control to hold back the angry and scared tears right now. I hate that I'm this scared.

I'm not a powerless teenager living with a predator anymore. I'm a grown assed woman who supports my family.

But the man now cradling his hand against his chest while he sobs took away my sense of power in a matter of seconds.

I reach down and grab my other shoe before walloping his other leg. Hard. "No contact means no touching, asshole."

"We all got that now," the guy who offered forty for a no contact lap dance says.

I notice the money's no longer on the table. Did he offer it to lure me into a vulnerable position for his friend?

"You should have gotten that when I said it five minutes ago," I snap, in no mood to play nice.

Angelo's handsome face twists in a scowl, which he turns on the guy who is doing enough crying for both of us. "You hurt her."

"I didn't mean to," the perv blubbers.

Yeah, right. "Not true. You took what I didn't want to give and would have taken more if you could get away with it."

"You're a stripper for Christ's sake. That's what you're here for." This little bit of wisdom is from one of the other office drones sitting at the table.

I spin to face him, to admonish him for saying the one curse word my mom would wash my mouth out for, as much as for being a total asshole. Only, his face drains of color before I can even get my mouth open to blast him.

Looking back over my shoulder, I see that it's now my accoster's whole hand hanging at an odd angle from the wrist. He's dangling limply from Angelo's hold, passed out from the pain.

"She's a dancer," Angelo says with pure menace. "Apologize for your mistake."

"Fuck you. You can't get away with this." The guy who just claimed being a dancer makes me fair game for whatever the punters here want is brave with a table between him and Angelo. "Let Ronnie go!"

My laughter shocks everyone at the table.

I shake my head at them. "You all really are stupid, aren't you?"

"What's that supposed to mean?" my original lap dance customer asks.

"It means that if you don't want to end up missing a hand, like your friend here," Angelo answers before I can. "After you apologize to her, you'll get your asses out of this fucking club, and you will never come back."

If I were them, I'd be pissing myself with fear, so I'm not at all surprised every single one of the group stands up and mumbles an apology to me before sidling around the opposite side of the table from Angelo and their friend.

The creep wakes up with a woozy moan while his buddies are trying to get away from him and Angelo. "Need the hospital," he slurs.

One of his braver, or more ridiculously foolish, friends steps toward them. "I'll take you."

"Pick him up in the alley behind the club in fifteen minutes." Angelo's words crack like a whip. "I'm not done with him."

"No, please, I'm sorry!" Ronnie implores Angelo from his knees.

"Apologize to her, not me."

The man who called me a bitch begs me with his eyes. "I'm sorry, okay? Call off your guard dog. Please!"

I shake my head. I have no power over Angelo. And even if I did? I wouldn't tell him to leave the guy alone. Why should I?

No one told my attacker to let me go. Not one of his friends said, "Hey, that's not cool."

No, they all laughed and watched us like we were putting on a show for them. That show lasted less than a minute before Angelo stepped in, but it was long enough for one of them to show some decency.

None of them did.

"Go to hell," I say.

Angelo's mouth quirks in an almost smile, his pale gray eyes reflecting approval of my words.

Then he looks away from me and he's pure retribution again. "You will never bother Candi again."

"We're never coming back here, don't worry." The guy who offered to take my attacker, who has become Angelo's victim, to the hospital says this like it's a hardship for the club that they aren't ever coming back.

And not an order they don't dare refuse.

"If you see her anywhere in New York, you will avoid her like she's got the plague and breathing the same air as her will cause your death." Angelo pauses. "Because it will."

For the second time ever, I soak my G-string as a shudder of arousal works its way up from my bare feet to the top of my head, leaving pleasure firing along all my neuroreceptors in its wake.

Angelo's jaw goes taut, like he knows what's happening to me. "Get dressed and go home."

My heart twinges at the rejection couched in consideration.

I shake my head. "I still have two hours of my shift."

"I'll square it with Ugo." Angelo mentions the GM, not Gino, his assistant.

I swallow and nod, too turned on by this show of protectiveness to speak.

Then without another look in my direction, Angelo yanks the man who attacked me to his feet and drags him toward the back of the club. The guy's friends go the opposite way, toward the front exit.

I wouldn't lay odds they'll be picking him up in the alley like Angelo told them to.

CHAPTER 3

ANGELO

W alking away from my girl when she's turned on only increases my rage at the man in my hold.

If not for him, I could be in the club watching Candi. But he had to ruin tonight for both her and me.

I shove him through the door to the back. A john steps out into the hall, takes one look at me and rushes back into the room he came out of.

"Angelo, you can't kill that guy." Nerissa hustles past me and turns to face me.

Ugo's right behind her, but he's looking like he wants to be anywhere but here.

"I'm not going to kill him." Losing a hand is final, not fatal. "I'll even put a tourniquet on his arm so he doesn't bleed out before his friends can get Ronnie here to an ER."

I told them to pick him up in the alley and if they don't abandon him, he'll be fine. Mostly.

Ronnie starts struggling again. "Don't let him take me out there and beat me up. He already broke my hand. I'm going to sue this place!"

"I'm serious." Nerissa steps to block the hallway more completely. "You know things are tense right now."

"Nerissa, I respect that you have the balls to try to stand in my way." I can count the people on one hand that would stand up to me with such cool.

Salvatore De Luca's sister and second-in-command has balls of steel.

"Good. Let him go and we can keep respecting each other."

Ugo is inching along the wall, like he's looking for a door to duck into. Salvatore needs a better GM for this place.

"This piece of shit assaulted one of the dancers in your club. I am taking care of the problem for you."

Nerissa gives the *stronzo* in the cheap suit an icy glare. "I'll take care of it."

I shake my head. "No can do. He touched Candi and that made it personal."

"Did you start dating?" Ugo asks, his voice an octave above his normal pitch.

What kind of made man is he?

"She's mine. That's all you need to know."

"You're claiming her?" Nerissa asks carefully.

"I am."

"Does she know that?"

"Not yet. Like you said, the timing is bad right now." Our don is angling to be the next godfather when Don Caruso dies.

Things are dangerous for anyone connected closely to the De Lucas right now. As the Genovese head enforcer and assassin, I take my orders directly from Severu De Luca. You can't get much more connected than that.

I'm not painting a bullseye on Candi's back by claiming her before the dust settles and our enemies are flushed into the light and eliminated. "I expect my claim to stay between us."

Nerissa jerks her chin in agreement and Ugo nods vigorously.

"Good. Now get the fuck out of my way." I don't bother to threaten either of them.

I don't have to. I take my orders directly from the don. No capo's second has the authority to get in my way, much less a made man with no rank.

"You promised not to kill him," Nerissa says without moving.

It wasn't a promise, but I jerk my head in acknowledgement anyway.

"Okay, but fuck, Death. Cutting a man's hand off is going to draw attention that our don doesn't want."

"No, it won't." I know what I'm doing.

Out of patience, I shove the guy squawking about suing the club and Nerissa and every employee who ever worked here toward the back exit.

Nerissa steps aside and lets us pass. "It better not, Angelo. What's going on at the top is more important than either of us."

"Agreed." But it's not more important than Candi's safety.

"Keep your lesson for Ronnie away from the club," she spells out.

I was going to take care of this situation in the alley and leave the *stronzo* to the tender mercy of his friends, but Nerissa has a point.

Better to take him to one of the spots I use when The Box is not expedient. Fuck. I need a car for that. As I open the back door, I voice command my phone to text Derian.

Death: *Need a work car in the alley behind Pitiful Princess.*

The ping from Derian's reply sounds as I open the back door.

Derian: *On it, boss.*

Tossing the pissant into the alley where he falls and rolls toward the dumpster, I register that the light in the alley closest to the backdoor is out and the streetlight above the dumpster is broken.

On instant alert, I scan my surroundings. My guard does not drop when I don't see anyone. This might be an alley behind a strip club in Lower Manhattan, but despite what the deed shows, it's owned by a capo in the Genovese Family.

And Salvatore keeps his properties up. There are no broken streetlights behind his clubs to act as an invitation to street thugs trying to peddle their shit on our territory.

Tuning out the moans from Candi's attacker, I open my senses to the sounds and smells around me. The swoosh of rubber on pavement from the avenue at the end of the alley gets filtered out. The scent of stale piss and garbage masks other smells and it's noxious.

I frown.

Candi walks down this alley every night to get home.

Making a note to text Nerissa and tell her to get the street sweeper down here, I move my head infinitesimally to the right and then to the left.

A shadow of movement on the left has me pulling my gun and spinning to face it. I prefer my knife, but guns are more efficient in situations like this.

The shadow detaches itself from the wall beside the dumpster, a deep rumble issuing from deep in its chest.

A dog.

Huge and black, it reminds me of the Cane Corso mastiff my grandparents had when I was a kid.

Fiercely loyal, that dog gave its life trying to protect my nonno from the scum who robbed him coming out of the hospital where my nonna lay dying after a massive stroke.

Nonna's heart gave out completely when she heard the news her husband of 62 years had been murdered and their dog was dead.

Some people said nonno and nonna dying on the same day was poetic. They loved each other so much.

I called it fucking unacceptable and tracked down every member of that bullshit gang before exterminating them like the cockroaches they were.

They were the first ones to lose their hands to my knife.

Severu's father, Don Enzo, insisted I join the Army after what he called my undisciplined killing spree. He said the Army would instill the much needed discipline in me. They did. And they trained me for my future career.

Killing people.

Favoring one of its back legs, the dog nevertheless takes up an assertive stance in front of the dumpster.

Is he protecting someone?

"Whoever the fuck you are, get your ass out here."

Another shape steps away from the dumpster, right in front of the dog. "You'll have to shoot me before you kill the dog."

"Who are you?" I ask, noticing that my prey is trying to crawl away.

Ronnie's headed toward the end of the alley that's blocked by another building. I'm not worried he's going to get away, so I ignore him and focus on the old man barely visible in the dim light of the alley.

"You the one who knocked out the streetlight?"

His ratty clothes and unkempt hair indicate he's living rough, but he stands straight and looks me in the eye. "The dog wouldn't sleep when it was on. Kept jumping at shit."

"He's limping. Does he need a vet?"

"Probably, but if I take him in, they'll scan his chip and return him to his people."

"And that is a bad thing?"

"Yep."

Something about the old man is familiar to me. The way he stands with a ramrod straight spine, his head fixed forward? That's pure military. But that's not the familiarity pricking at my brain.

"Why?" I ask.

"His owner is the reason he's limping."

"How do you know that?" I wouldn't, and don't, give the owner the benefit of the doubt either, but maybe the old man saw something.

"They was walking in Central Park and the dog went running after something. Probably a damned squirrel. He's big, but I doubt he's more than a year old. Still thinks he's a puppy."

If he's that young, he still is a puppy, no matter how big he is. "You an expert on Cane Corsos?" I ask.

"Knew a man who preferred them for his guard dogs."

I nod. It's a popular breed for that. My nonno wasn't the only man who grew up in Little Italy that thought so. Descended from the original breed to protect Roman emperors, the Cane Corso is the most popular breed of guard dog among *la famiglia*.

Wanting to know how the dog got injured, I ask, "What happened when he chased the squirrel?"

"The wife was holding the leash and he pulled her right off her feet, she slid into muddy grass face first. Was fucking funny. Until her asshole husband starts screaming at the dog and kicking him."

"You step in?" I ask. Not sure why.

Most people wouldn't.

"Yeah. Told him he should have been holding the leash in the first place. Wasn't the dog's fault he was too big for the woman to control."

I nod. The dog must weigh over a hundred pounds.

"Won't repeat what he said about Mars, but privileged little shit told me if I thought he was such a great dog, I could take care of him."

Something stutters in my chest. "That his name? Mars?"

Nonno's Cane Corso was named Mars. It's a popular dog name, but it gives me a jolt anyway.

"Not according to the tag I took off him. The yuppie couple called him Bentley Beauregard von Simmons. He answers just fine to Mars."

I shake my head. "He deserved to be rescued from the name alone. He's fucking Italian, not German."

"That's what I thought. They could have at least used an Italian car name and *di* instead of *von*."

"Mars is better."

"That it is." The old man points toward the back of the alley. "That guy you brought out here with you is going to escape through the vegan restaurant's kitchen."

CHAPTER 4

ANGELO

Turning my head, I see he's right and holster my gun before jogging after Ronnie. I snag the back of his collar and frog march him back to Mars and the old man.

Double fuck. The dog needs a vet, but his owner will no doubt deny giving him to the old guy when the vet calls to tell him Mars is in the clinic.

Ronnie's begging again. I shake him. "Shut the fuck up, unless you want to lose your tongue right along with your hand."

I need to think.

He shuts up.

The old man's lips twist in a sneer. "Not a lot of fight in that one, is there?"

"Nah."

"Known a lot of suits like him. Too many," he grumbles. "You need help with him?"

"Do I look like I need help?"

The old man deflates, mumbling, "No, 'course not."

I don't feel guilt. It's not a thing.

But there's a weird feeling in my chest right now and I don't like it.

"He touched my woman. It's personal." I don't explain myself either, but I guess tonight I do.

"She one of the dancers inside?"

"She is."

"That's a tough way to make your living. Those ladies work their asses off, and no one should be touching them without their permission." Calling Ronnie a nasty name in Italian, the old guy spits at his feet.

"What's your name?" I ask.

"Friends call me Boomer."

No. That's one coincidence too many, but this guy cannot be *that* Boomer. The son of an old friend of my nonno's, *that* Boomer wasn't made. He was career Army.

Lots of dogs named Mars though. Lots of men who go by Boomer, especially former military.

I dismiss the similarities and ask, "You got any urges to go to the cops with what you've seen tonight?"

My gut says *no*, but I always verify.

"Naw. Even if I didn't think that *stronzo* deserves what's coming to him, I'm smart enough to know better than to go against the Cosa Nostra Hangman."

"I haven't heard that name in a long time." Hangman worked for Don Matteo, the first De Luca don. Just like my nonno. "Hangman is dead."

"I guess he would be. He was a lot older than me. Thought hangman was the job though."

"You knew Hangman?" How does Boomer know I have the same job for Severu as Hangman did for Don Matteo?

Do I look like an assassin? It's probably something in the eyes. Like a lack of a soul.

"I did." Boomer coughs and pounds his own chest to get his breath back. "Back in the day, he ran with my cousin."

"Your cousin was *la famiglia*?"

Fuck, these coincidences are getting too big to ignore.

"Our dads were loyal Genovese soldiers."

"Then what the fuck are you doing sleeping behind a titty bar?" If he's who I think he is, he should have plenty of money.

His dad wasn't just a loyal soldier, he was a smart one. At least that's what my nonno always said.

"My dad was Cosa Nostra. I'm not. I didn't want to be a soldier in the Cosa Nostra, so I enlisted to serve my country. To be a soldier with honor." His mouth twists like that belief is a sour memory.

"Your dad disapproved of your decision?" Disowning a child for not taking the oath had been the least violent response by men of that generation.

And it would explain Boomer's current circumstances. Every one of Don Matteo's crew were old school, just like my nonno. If nonno had been around when the time came, he would have beaten me bloody if I'd refused to take the oath.

Never a chance of that though, even if it got delayed by Don Enzo's order that I go into the Army to learn discipline. I mustered out in time to pledge my allegiance to him and serve as his personal enforcer for two years before his death.

"Told my dad I didn't want his dirty money. Thought a life like his was the worst one I could live." Boomer looks around the alleyway and shrugs. "Guess I was wrong."

Like my nonno, Boomer's dad is gone. Unlike nonno, Boomer's father died peacefully in his sleep in his retirement bungalow in Florida the year before last.

"You talk to your ma?" I'm guessing not, if he's living rough like this.

"She don't need a son like me. She's got three that did their duty by the family."

"One of them is in the graveyard with your pop." Got shanked in prison doing a stint for aggravated assault.

Boomer nods. "But he died in the line of duty. *Like I should have.*" He mutters the last under his breath.

"Wasn't his duty to get caught." Was fucking sloppy is what it was.

Some of the old guard are too arrogant to be smart, like that asshole Lorenzo Ricci. Worst capo under Severu. He's going down soon though.

"There are a lot of prisons that don't have cement walls." Boomer looks off into the distance, seeing a place that isn't the alley behind Pitiful Princess. "A lot of ways to die that don't include getting shanked by another prisoner."

I can't argue that. "Do you want to die?"

"No one has asked me that in a long time."

Not sure why the fuck I'm asking it now, but I don't ask it again. I just wait for his answer.

He looks at me and then he shakes his head. "No, I don't want to die. I've been off the booze for almost a year, but I am still working to get back on my feet. Lost my job though when I had to leave the shelter to take care of Mars."

The dog woofs his approval, his bark a deep bass tone.

"What kind of work did they have you doing?" It wouldn't be what the Army trained him for, that's for damn sure.

"Took their computer training so I could stand behind the counter and take orders at McDonalds. With most customers using the kiosk menus, not sure how long that job was going to last anyway."

"What did you do in the Army?"

"What they trained me for."

The Army trains for all sorts, but delivered in that tone, he was trained like I was. To kill. "You get into special forces?"

"What is this, a job interview?" Ronnie asks with too much attitude for a man on the way to losing a hand.

I glare down at him. "Shut the fuck up."

"Just let me go."

"He's a whiny bitch, ain't he?"

"Calling Ronnie a bitch is an insult to Mars' dam."

"True." Boomer turns to look at Mars. "Sorry, buddy. No offense meant."

"You're a bum and you think you're better than me?" Ronnie snarks with bravado he's shouldn't be feeling. "You're nothing but shit on my shoe."

I clock Ronnie and he drops like a bag of rocks.

"You going to tell management me and Mars are back here?" Boomer asks.

"Your offer to help with that pile of shit still good?" I ask instead of answering.

Boomer straightens. "Yes."

"Bring Mars. We'll get him checked out." Without the dog being returned to his former piece-of-shit owner.

Headlights shine in the alley, flipping on and off in a pattern I train my guys to use. Derian's here.

Making a *proceed* motion with my hand, I don't have to tell Boomer to grab his stuff. He's not leaving it in the alley to get taken by someone else.

He disappears into the shadows by the dumpster as the nondescript black SUV, plates registered to a shell corporation, pulls to a stop.

Mars barks at the headlights. I give a firm command to sit and approach him with a confident posture, my hand out. He sits, showing that puppy, or not, he's had some training. It also shows that his animal instincts identify me as the alpha here.

As they should.

No one in this alley is as deadly.

Mars sniffs my hand as I talk softly to him. "That's a good boy."

Derian pops out of the driver's side and his cousin, Mario, exits from the front passenger seat.

Like me, my next in command, Derian Parisi, is from one of the old Sicilian families on his dad's side. However, his mother is a smart lady from Haiti, who keeps all the Parisi men in line, Mario included.

A couple of inches shorter than my six-foot-two, Derian is a good four inches taller than his cousin. Both men have the muscles, strength and agility that comes from the training regime all of my crew are required to follow.

Mars breaks training to move in front of me, growling.

Interesting.

You know how they say dogs pick their people? This dog just picked me, and I'm okay with that. Every family should have a pet and soon I'll have a family living with me on Long Island.

Mars will have to get some extra training though, to make sure he's socialized for children and a woman who spends a great deal of her time in a wheelchair. Cane Corsicas are extremely territorial and can be aggressive. Traits I admire and identify with.

Nonno believed they made the best family guard dogs though, once they were properly trained.

That's something Boomer can do, because it looks like we're sharing custody of a dog. He'll have to come work for me. Taking care of my dog has to be better than standing behind the cash register at a fast food joint.

I drop to my haunches and lay my hand on Mars' neck. "It's okay, boy. They're friends."

Jerking my head, I indicate to my men they should come forward. Derian comes first, giving Mars a wary glance. I grab his wrist and direct it toward Mars, letting the dog sniff while repeating the word *friend* in both English and Sicilian. *Amicu.*

I do the same for Mario.

Mars stops growling, but he maintains an attitude of vigilance. Just like I do.

"Bind him and toss him in the cargo hold." I indicate the unconscious Ronnie.

Neither of my men ask what's going on but immediately get to work, slapping duct tape over Ronnie's mouth when he wakes up and starts squawking. They must have pulled on his broken wrist when zip-tying him.

Oops. My bad.

But that's what I'm good at. Being bad.

The pain he's feeling right now is only a taste of what tonight holds for him.

Boomer comes out from behind the dumpster carrying a neatly rolled sleeping bag with tattered edges and wearing a backpack that has seen better days.

"Get in the back with Mars." I throw the keys to my bike to Mario and tell him where I'm parked. "Take it back to my place."

Mario nods and trots back down the alley, toward the street.

Derian tosses me the key fob for the SUV and I get in behind the wheel. My men know I don't ride in cars. I drive them. When I'm not on my bike.

Severu says I have control issues.

But the man working to take over as Godfather of the Cosa Nostra doesn't have any room to talk. At least I don't want to control the whole damned *famiglia* in North America.

CHAPTER 5

CANDI

Mom and Cookie are watching *She's Gotta Have It* when I let myself into the apartment.

"Isn't that a little old for her?" I ask mom, dropping my backpack on the floor by the door.

Mom shrugs her good should philosophically. "She's eleven going on forty."

"Aren't you a little old to be leaving your stuff lying around?" Cookie snarks.

Knowing that as the older sister, it's my job to set a good example, I stifle a tired sigh. "Yeah, I am."

Grabbing the backpack, I trudge to the bedroom we share to hang it on the hook on my side of the room. And then I just plop down to sit on the edge of my bed, letting my body and mind decompress from what happened tonight.

I've been running on nerve driven autopilot since Angelo dismissed me. When I left, I didn't care if he squared things with Ugo, or not. I couldn't stay after what that lech tried to do.

I know I'm lucky that this kind of thing doesn't happen more often, but every time it does, I question my life choices. I know we need the money I make at Pitiful Princess. There's no other job I can get that will pay me nearly as much.

Despite my hands off rules, I'm one of the top earning dancers. Maybe because of it. Men always want what they can't have.

So do women, I guess. I sure wish I could quit and find a job teaching in a community program, or something. But that's just a pipe dream.

One reality ground into dust a long time ago.

Dancing is pure joy for me. But I cannot make enough working at a dance studio to support my foster mom and sister.

My path is set, whether I like it or not, but Cookie's isn't.

Diamond Miller, aka Cookie, and I don't share a drop of DNA. What we do share is a foster mom who loves us like we are her own. The hub of our three-person family, Mira Czabok, took Cookie in first. My sister's birth mom died just like mine, but unlike me, Cookie was only a year old at the time and was placed immediately with our mom.

Cookie's birth mom and Mira had been friends. They'd prepared for what would happen when Ms. Miller died. Because money has always been tight for mom and it wasn't any better for Cookie's biological mom, the two women worked with social services to get mom approved for fostering.

Mrs. Miller wrote a letter of intent to designate mom as Cookie's guardian after her death, but didn't name her that in a will. With all of Mrs. Miller's family still living in Nigeria and her dead husband having no family at all, Cookie's social worker was more than willing to deal with the red tape to place my sister in mom's home.

She was, and still is, one of the good ones. This allows Cookie to get medical and dental insurance through the state, like I did when I was in the system.

My mom was more of a dreamer than Mrs. Miller. Bonbon was a dancer like me, but unlike me, she offered extracurriculars. I guess she was one of my sperm donor's favorites. She thought when she got pregnant, he would divorce the wife he didn't love and marry her. But that's not how Stefano Bianchi works.

He's a traditional mafioso through-and-through. He doesn't believe in divorce and he already had two sons. He had no interest in claiming me.

Mom loved me. I know that. But unfortunately, she was still fantasizing a version of my sperm donor where he played the hero when she died. She told me he'd come for me. That he'd promised to take care of me.

That didn't happen. Within hours of her death, a full-fledged ward of the state, I was placed in a group home. The sperm donor didn't even come to her funeral, much less make arrangements for the daughter he'd never once acknowledged.

Things got ugly in my last foster home and that's when I ended up with mom as a temporary emergency placement that turned permanent.

Mira Czabok might have debilitating arthritis that stops her from working fulltime, but she's fierce. She made sure I stayed just like she made sure Cookie was never moved to a different placement. Mira studied the ins and out of the social services system so intently, she knew more than the case worker who was supposed to be my advocate.

Which is why I will always take care of her, just like she took care of me. I aged out of care a long time ago, but mom never made me leave. She says I'm her kid.

She would've adopted me but didn't have the money for the paperwork and the lawyer. She's my mom no matter what the documents say. And my sister is more my sister than my brothers by blood.

They'll never acknowledge me any more than our father has. My last name is Brigliano not Bianchi and that's the way it will always be.

Pushing away thoughts of the past both distant and recent, I toe off my shoes and change my clothes. The thin tank top and sleep shorts I put on are more comfortable than the hoodie and baggy jeans I wear as a uniform to ride the subway.

The shorts have been washed so many times they're bordering on threadbare and super soft. Perfect.

When I come back out to the living room, mom and Cookie are once again engrossed in the movie.

Relieved I don't have to talk right now, I settle on the sofa beside my sister and steal the popcorn bowl from her lap.

Instead of complaining, Cookie gives me a guilty look. "Sorry I gave you crap about leaving your backpack on the floor."

Tugging on one of Cookie's many braids, I say, "Don't sweat it kid. You were right. Leaving stuff on the floor only makes it harder for mom to get around when she has to use her chair."

"Yeah, but I could have got it for you."

"Why would you?" I ask and grin. "You looking for nomination for the world's best sister award? Trust me, you already got it in the bag."

"You're such a dork." But Cookie's smiling when she turns back to watch the not so age-appropriate movie for an eleven-year-old.

A few minutes later, mom says, "You're home early." There's concern in her tone that she doesn't put into words.

"Nothing bad," I lie. "They just didn't need me tonight."

"But Saturdays are best for tips. Why did they send you home?" Cookie asks, sounding as worried as mom.

Should my eleven year old sister know tips at the strip club are best on Saturday nights? Probably not. But we don't lie to each other in our family and she's too damn smart not to know what I do for a living.

That doesn't mean she should be worrying about my tips. "Don't twist yourself into a pretzel over money, kid. That's my job."

"Actually, it's my job," mom claims.

"It's both our jobs," I soothe her. "I'm a grown woman and taking care of my family is a privilege."

Mom's smile is gentle, the ever-present pain shadowing her eyes. "The foundation is providing a monthly stipend now. Maybe you can take some more Saturdays off."

Mom knows that Saturdays are the nights I do the routine with the least amount of clothes on at the end of it. The tips are worth it, but she'll probably never be comfortable with me being an exotic dancer.

She never criticizes me though. Mom knows I dance at a strip club for a living because it's one of the few legitimate jobs in New York that doesn't require a college degree and pays enough to cover the bills for my little family.

I'm a good dancer, but I don't do it because I love having men's eyes on me and she knows it. I'm good at projecting sex on six-inch stilettos, but that part of me got destroyed in the foster home before I landed with Mom.

Or at least I thought it did.

Before meeting Angelo.

My ovaries dance with more verve than I do when he's around. Not that either me, or my ovaries would know what to do if he returned our interest.

I don't date. My cherry is still sitting on top of my ladybits sundae.

If the guys at Pitiful Princess knew that personal little secret, they'd never leave me alone. I would be the prize they insist on claiming.

"Did you find out if the stipend is temporary or a long term thing?" Waiting for mom to answer, I munch on a handful of popcorn, reveling in the forbidden buttery goodness.

Not that there's any real butter on the kernels popped in a microwave bag, but it's still a treat I shouldn't indulge in.

I got hired for my generous curves and ability to move them, but management has made it clear that if my waistline expands, I'm out.

Fair? No. Life? Yes.

"Petra said that it will last at least a year and is renewable."

"That's great." It's not guaranteed security, but it gives us a year to build up mom's emergency medical fund.

"It's enough to allow you to cut down to two nights a week and start taking more classes at the community college."

I take one a term when we have the funds to cover my tuition, but I'm not planning to take any more for a while. I haven't told mom that, but we need to save money for Cookie's education. Come hell, or high water, my little sister is going to college and living out her dreams.

We need the foundation money to pay bills, so I can save my income to make that possible. Mom knows it, but she wants things to be different.

"I've got tonight off. That's all I need right now," I finally say when her expectant expression doesn't shift.

"Maybe Petra can find me another foundation grant," Mom says, but her eyes don't reflect the hope of her words.

When mom's disability caseworker came to her a few weeks ago and told her that she was the recipient of a grant that covered specialized treatment not covered by our state insurance including visits twice a week from an in home nurse, we celebrated with ice cream.

When Petra showed up last week with what she said was going to be a monthly stipend check, mom insisted on going out to dinner and inviting Petra to join us. The three of us hadn't eaten in a restaurant in two years.

Mostly because of money, but also because mom hardly leaves the apartment.

The private foundation that doesn't share data on its recipients with the state is a huge blessing. Mom has to be careful applying for aid through the state because it could interfere with her custody of Cookie.

We can't let the caseworkers know just how limited in mobility mom really is, or they'd take Cookie away for sure. They'd do it legally and with all the right words that don't imply ableist thinking, but they'd still do it.

And it would still be ableist as hell.

Not that we'd have any way of proving that, or the money to hire a lawyer to fight a custody battle with the state.

Because mom is a foster parent, not Cookie's legal guardian. She and Ms. Miller set it up that way so that mom could get money to help raise Cookie, neither of them knowing how bad mom's arthritis would get.

Seven more years and it won't matter.

That's what I tell myself on nights like tonight. Seven more years.

Then mom can file for disability income, Cookie can go off to college and I can quit shaking my tits and ass at the Pitiful Princess.

CHAPTER 6

ANGELO

The drive to my dark site across the Hudson in New Jersey will take less than twenty minutes. Plenty of time to ask Boomer questions.

Sounding bemused after the first couple, Boomer says, "That handsy perv was right, this *is* a job interview."

"You need to hire somebody, boss?" Derian gives me the side-eye.

As my next in command, he's the first pass for new hires, which usually come from within Cosa Nostra ranks. Because we are an elite crew with a job description that requires a level of loyalty that can't be measured on brief acquaintance.

But I'm not looking for another member for my enforcer crew.

"There was a time I might have been useful to you in the business," Boomer says. "But I'm not as fast as I used to be and I haven't shot a gun in over three years."

"You'll have to practice," I say. "No one on my staff is incapable of defending themselves."

"Even your housekeeper?"

"Don't have one." But that will have to change when I move to Long Island.

"You'll be taking care of my dog and helping with his training." I will attend enough of the classes so the Cane Corsica doesn't forget who his alpha is, but I don't have time for the extensive training he's going to need.

"You've got a dog?" Boomer asks. "What breed is he?"

"You got a dog, boss?" Shock tinges Derian's voice.

"Yeah. Adopted him tonight."

"You mean Mars?" Boomer's quick to catch on.

"Yep."

"But he belongs to that asshole who kicked him."

"Not anymore." I'll be paying a visit to Mars' former owner to make sure he understands that there are no more dogs in his future.

I've killed men for less than kicking a dog.

"You want me to dog sit?" Boomer asks. "I don't want no charity. I make my own way."

"Good. I'm not a charitable guy."

Derian coughs. "Got that right."

I'm not offended. It's the truth.

I pay my men well, but it's not generosity. They put their lives on the line to earn it. Just like I do.

Before Candi, there was no one I wanted to do nice things for. I'm loyal to Severu, but that's not the same. He doesn't need me to take care of him.

The only person I want to look after is Candi. I do the same for her mom and sister because they are part of her. "We'll share custody of the dog, but you'll have to live on my estate for that. You might as well work for me too. Mars has to be acclimated to being with a family. I want him in special training sessions daily."

"You got a family? Don't take this the wrong way, but you don't seem the type."

I turn down a darkened side street without using my blinker. "Nothing to be offended by. My family don't live with me yet. I'm moving my woman, her mom and her sister into my place in a couple of months."

Everything has to be ready for them.

"You don't know me from Adam. How are you going to trust me to train Mars right?"

"You fuck up and I'll kill you."

"The boss don't kill easy," Derian pipes up.

Again, truth.

"I figured as much with him having Hangman's job and all, but it still feels like a lot to take on faith and he doesn't strike me as a fool."

"Don't worry. The boss knows *avan ou monte bwa, gade si ou ka desann li*."

Boomer frowns. "That's not Italian."

"Nah, it's one of my mamma's sayings. She's the smart one in the family."

"What does it mean?"

"Death knows he needs to know the details before committing to something. He'll have you investigated by our people. If something comes back hinky, he won't give you the chance to fuck up."

"Only thing hinky about my past is what my government had me do in the name of patriotism. Killing is one thing. Killing innocents is another." Boomer's voice is heavy with regret.

I shrug. "Innocence is in the eye of the beholder."

My don's enemies are guilty because they are his enemies. Doesn't matter if they've ever done anything deserving of death. If they are a risk to Severu and his family? They're charged and guilty in my book.

"You ever done any gardening?" I ask Boomer, thinking I can kill two birds with one stone.

Get someone to take care of the dog and put in a small vegetable garden for Candi.

I've got a service for maintaining the property, but this is different. She keeps a container garden on their tiny stoop. It's not much and she's told her little sister she wishes she had a garden plot, but the waitlist for a community plot nearby is too long.

Yes, I'm listening in on her conversations with her sister before they go to sleep at night. How else am I supposed to get to know my family?

"Where would I garden in the city?" Boomer asks.

"I bought a house for me and my family on Long Island. Need someone to put in a vegetable garden." I still remember nonna's and how she liked to spend time in it.

She went out there to cool off after she and nonno had words. Candi's going to need that kind of place too.

I'm bound to piss her off because despite my name, I'm more devil than angel.

CHAPTER 7

CANDI

"The boss wants a word." Nina, one of the cocktail waitresses who makes a habit of kissing Gino's ass, waits expectantly.

Like I'm going to stop getting ready and rush off to talk to the jerk-off assistant manager right this second.

Not happening.

I'm on in fifteen minutes and I still have to apply my false eyelashes. My least favorite part of doing my makeup for the stage, I always leave it for last.

"Did you hear me?" Nina demands.

I hold my breath as I get the second eyelash affixed to my eyelid.

Only when it's in place, do I reply. "Yes."

"He's not going to be happy with you making him wait," Nina says in dour warning.

Rolling my eyes, I turn from the mirror. "Unlike you, Nina, I don't spend my time here trying to make Gino happy."

Kissing up to the smarmy assistant manager might be worth it to the cocktail waitress to get preferential treatment in the schedule and backroom access, but I'd rather find another club to dance in than kiss up to that jerk.

I'm thinking about leaving regardless. Gino is putting pressure on both me and Bianca to offer extracurriculars. Not content with the extra cut he's taking out of our tips, our boss wants us to earn him a percentage of the more lucrative backroom business.

We're the only two dancers who don't and if Bianca gets the job at Amuni, I'm out of here.

"Maybe you should." Nina gives me a smug look. "He's your boss, Candi."

"Leave her alone, Nina. Candi is the only dancer who makes as many tips as I do." Piper, the OG dancer glares at Nina. "Unlike your replaceable ass, Gino isn't going to fire her if she doesn't hang off his dick."

"Whatever. I'll tell him I gave you the message," Nina huffs. "Don't blame me if he's pissed."

I don't roll my eyes again, but I want to. As long as I refuse to sell my ass so he can get a cut of the proceeds, Gino is going to be pissed at me. And I'm more than okay with that.

"He's in his office, if you're interested," is Nina's parting shot.

It's Ugo's office, but if Gino is playing top dog, the GM must not be in. Ugo was a better assistant manager than general manager, that's for sure.

He didn't care about the welfare of the dancers or club staff, but he sure as heck never tried to push me into selling my ass either. He respected our boundaries and no way would he let employees suck his dick for a better schedule.

Doesn't make him a hero though, because he's letting his assistant manager get away with it.

With ten minutes before I have to be onstage, I hotfoot it to Gino's office. Being a Wednesday night, the club's only about half filled.

I knock on the door and wait for an answer, not out of respect for Gino, but because both my biological and foster moms raised me right. I only had Bonbon until I was ten years old, but she was a good mom and Mira is the best.

"Come in," Gino yells after making me wait nearly a minute.

Opening the door, I see one of the other cocktail waitresses rising from her knees as she swipes at her mouth. Smirking at me, like blowing the boss is some kind of badge of honor, she leaves.

Poor Nina might be out in the cold when it comes to next week's schedule.

I stop about midway to the desk. "Nina said you wanted to see me?"

"I'm sorry for what happened last Saturday. You will be paid for a full night even though you left early and without a word to me." The words say one thing, his disgusted expression says another.

Someone else is behind this apology. Ugo? Maybe he cares more about the dancers than I thought.

But that last dig was pure Gino.

"Angelo said he would square it."

"Angelo Caruso is a customer, not management."

"Okay." If Gino's waiting for me to say I'm sorry about leaving on Saturday, he'll be disappointed.

"Have you thought any more about taking on more responsibilities?"

That's what he calls selling my ass and mouth. *Taking on more responsibilities*. What a joke.

"I'm fine with the *responsibilities* I have."

Gino narrows his eyes but he just flicks his hand toward the door, dismissing me.

I don't linger.

The bouncer who was in charge of the floor last week steps in front of me on my way back to the main room. "Hey, Candi. You got a second?"

He's got a black eye and busted lip that are at least a few days old. Did things get rowdy Saturday after I left? None of the dancers have said anything.

So, probably not. Gossip spreads like an STD without a condom around here.

"I'm due on in a couple."

"Won't take long. Listen." He pauses, then shakes his head. "I'm really sorry about Saturday. I should have got to you before Mr. Caruso. I was closer."

"Then why didn't you?" I ask.

"Gino waved me off. He doesn't like me interfering with the dancers and clients."

"Isn't that your job?" It's looking more and more like I'm going to have to find a different one soon.

"It should be."

"Meaning it's not?"

"Not since Gino took over." He touches his split lip. "But I'll be doing it for you from here on out."

"Why?"

"Because Gino can just fire me. Angelo Caruso can cut off my hands."

"Cut off your hands?" I gasp. "What do you mean?"

"What do you think he did to Ronnie?" The bouncer frowns, looking scared. "Never mind. Forget I said anything. Just don't worry about being safe on the floor, Ms. Candi. I got your back."

"You should have all our backs." Mira would be proud of the scold.

I sound just like her.

"Yeah, I should." He squares his shoulders. "Gino's not my boss. Ugo is."

I don't need the reminder, but maybe he does.

"Okay, well, good." He nods and turns to walk away, favoring his left leg.

Did Angelo beat him up for not doing his job?

After the way he broke Ronnie's wrist, it's entirely possible.

I reach backstage with seconds to spare, but the girls are huddled in a circle talking and I'm as addicted to gossip as the next dancer.

I rush over. "What's going on?"

"Bianca quit without notice. She's not coming in tonight."

"She got the job?" I don't do a thing to stifle my delight at the prospect.

Piper nods. "I guess. All I know is she's not coming back."

A grin takes over my face. "Good."

With Bianca gone, there's nothing holding me to this club.

"Listen, girlie, don't you go looking for another club to dance in," Piper says, like she's reading my mind. "Gino's not going to force you to offer extracurriculars. I'll make sure of it."

We all know that Piper has connections with the mafia that owns this place. What those connections are is unclear, but when someone needs to talk to management, she's the one to do it.

No one knows about *my* relationship with the Genovese. My biological father made sure of that long before my mom, his former mistress, died.

"If Gino doesn't want the same thing happening to him as it did to Ronnie, he'll back off," one of the other dancers says.

"It's true then?" I ask. "Angelo cut off his hand?"

Piper nods. "It's true all right. I've got a friend who works the ER. She confirmed it."

"Is he in jail?" I ask, more concerned for my dark savior than the perv who assaulted me.

"Are you kidding?" Piper shakes her head. "Ronnie told the ER it was a home improvement accident. No way is he ratting out the Genovese Mafia's top enforcer."

Something weird pings inside me when I learn who Angelo is. And it's not revulsion.

"It had to be him. My customer came rushing back into the room after we finished. I thought he wanted more." She makes a face that the others share sympathetically. Some johns get clingy.

Not that I've experienced, but the other dancer's talk.

"Only he didn't want anything to do with me. He was trying to hide from something in the hall. I cracked the door to see what was going on and overheard Mr. Caruso talking to Ugo and the big boss, Nerissa De Luca. He was saying something about not killing Ronnie and just cutting off his hand."

She gives me a pitying look. "I'm sorry, Candi."

The other dancers look at me with equal concern.

Only I'm not worried.

"That's all kinds of messed up," another dancer says.

I don't say anything. I think I'm messed up too. Because the only thing I feel toward Angelo Caruso is gratitude.

"Candi, that's you," one of the dancers yells and I realize we're already 16 bars into my intro music.

I rush onto the stage and leap up onto my pole with an exuberance I haven't felt in a long time, whipping my hair and smiling at the punters.

Angelo Caruso cut off a man's hand for touching me.

CHAPTER 8

ANGELO

"Stay, Angelo." Severu's order comes just as I'm about to leave his office after a meeting with his underboss, Miceli, one of his capos and the consigliere, Big Sal.

I step aside to let the others leave and once they are gone, I shut the door and face my boss. And wait.

Severu De Luca is only three years older than me, making him the youngest don in the Cosa Nostra right now. But nothing about him screams youth. We lose that air when we get made.

I'm not sure either me or my boss ever had it to begin with.

There's no family relationship between us going back at least four generations, but both our families started out in Sicily.

Related, or not, we have the same black hair, olive skin tone and Roman nose. At six-feet-four-inches, Severu tops me by two inches, but we're both taller than the average Sicilian male.

He has the typical dark eyes of our forefathers, but mine are gray. Some say they glow almost silver just before I kill someone.

After a full minute of frowning silence, my boss says, "Explain to me why my top enforcer cut off a man's hand when the Genovese made men are under strict instructions to stay under the radar right now."

"I didn't draw any attention." He knows me better than that.

"You cut off his hand!" Severu barks.

"I took care of it away from the club." Go me for not going with my initial plan to do it in the alley.

Severu doesn't look impressed with mine and Nerissa's solution. "You cut off his fucking hand."

"He deserved it and I didn't kill him." I even made sure he got to the ER. I can be reasonable.

"For touching a dancer giving him a lap dance?"

"She wasn't dancing for that douche and Candi has a strict no-touching policy."

"Candi." Severu says the name like he's tasting it for a bad flavor. "The stripper."

"Exotic dancer." She doesn't strip naked.

Not ever. She might drop everything but pasties and thong, but the ripe nipples that tip her bountiful tits are for my eyes only.

I saw them for the first time the other day when she came back into the bedroom after her shower and dropped her towel before I had a chance to look away. She usually gets dressed in the bathroom. I still don't know what made that day different, but I was as close as I've ever been to coming in my pants.

I've been obsessed with trying to guess what color those delicious looking peaks are ever since. Soon, I'll find out.

Unfortunately, the cameras I installed only have a black-and-white feed. I went for quality of picture under a range of lighting over color definition. The image is excellent, even when the room is dark. A good choice, it's angled toward her bed so I can watch her sleep.

I'm not a pervert. When her little sister is in the room hanging out, or getting ready for bed, I turn that camera feed off and only listen to the audio until after the kid falls asleep.

Then I turn it back on and watch Candi's beautiful, heart shaped face as it relaxes in somnolence. I always turn the feed off again before I go to bed myself.

After her sister leaves for school, I turn it back on and follow my new favorite routine. Watching my Candi pleasure herself under the covers before getting up and getting ready for the day.

Her pleasure belongs to me, just like mine belongs to her.

"Now is not the time to get fixated on your latest fuck." Severu's harsh tone breaks into the reel playing in my head.

"I haven't fucked her." It's not safe. Not yet.

He gives me an impatient frown. "Then do it and move on."

But I shake my head. "She's it for me, boss."

Fucking Candi is not going to a be a one-and-done for me. She's my future.

"What the hell does that mean?"

"She's my forever woman." One day, we'll get married.

Candi will be such a beautiful bride.

Severu's eyes widen before they narrow. "Better than anyone else, you realize how precarious things are right now. How much danger our families are in."

"That's why I'm not claiming her yet." I don't want a target on her.

"You don't think cutting off that asshole's hand is going to clue our enemies into how important she is to you?"

"Maybe, but it had to be done." Other men need to know she's off limits.

"So, then claim her and get her out of the club."

"Not yet." There's knowing. And there's *knowing*.

Right now, she's a dancer I protect, but no one outside a very small circle knows why. Once I publicly claim her, she becomes my Achilles heel. Not that I'll be like that asshole Achilles and leave my vulnerability unprotected.

Human armor protects as well as some demigod's magic dipping sauce. And it's under my control.

Candi will never come to harm on my watch.

"I've got two of my team on her at all times." And I watch over her more than she, or anyone else knows. "But she's safer with me staying in the background for now."

"Does she have any inkling you're coming for her when things settle down?" Severu's look questions my sanity, but his words don't.

I'll take it.

I know my approach to life isn't like everyone else's, but that's why I'm so good at what I do. I see the way forward to reach my goals and I don't hesitate to take it, whatever the cost.

"She saw me skewer a man's hand for trying to touch her and by now, she's probably heard about Ronnie. I figure yes."

"And she isn't running?"

"Why would she run? I'm protecting her. You would do the same if some *stronzo* tried to touch Catalina."

The death that lives in my heart is reflected in Severu's cold brown gaze. "Catalina is my wife."

"And one day, Candi will be mine." Her real name is Kathleen.

Cookie's social worker calls her Kath, but Candi never introduces herself that way and the people she's closest to call her Candi.

I'm one of those people. Whether she knows it yet, or not.

Sighing, Severu shakes his head. "Angelo, you need to let this go. She's not in the life and you don't know if she can be trusted with our secrets."

"What secrets? You don't think the dancers at Pitiful Princess know their club is owned by the mafia? For fuck's sake they probably work there because of the extra protection."

"That's not the point."

"No, the point is, she's mine."

"And if I ordered you to back off?"

"Don't." For the first time in my life as a made man, I don't know if I would follow orders. Not if those orders were to walk away from Candi.

I'll protect *la famiglia* with my life and serve it with the death of others, but I won't give up Candi for the mistaken belief that she's a danger to the family.

"She's that important to you?" Severu asks in disbelief. "And you don't even fuck her?"

I shrug. "When you know, you know."

One day I'll lay claim to Candi's body, but I've already claimed the most important thing.

Her life.

Something flashes across my boss's face and he sighs again. "At least you're listening to your instincts."

"Like you didn't at first with Catalina."

He shrugs, but we both know the truth.

Severu thought he wanted something he didn't. When most of us knew all along that Catalina was the best woman for him.

CHAPTER 9

CANDI

The club is packed for the Pitiful Princess's Halloween Party.

The 31st is next Thursday, but Saturday is our busiest night, so that means the big bash is tonight.

But we've been playing up the costumes and spooky vibes for the last week and that will continue through next weekend. Never say club management doesn't know how to exploit a holiday.

Our spotlights have orange filters over them and the floor is lit with blacklights that make all the white elements of everyone's costumes glow. Most of the dancers and waitstaff are wearing white pasties, thongs or makeup that draws attention to their butts and boobs.

Fake cobwebs and glittery vampire bats festoon the purple velvet curtains that separate the backstage from the front. The Halloween decorations make a discordant note with the Persian palace vibe of the club, but what are you going to do?

It's Halloween, Pitiful Princess style. Which means there are more dancers working tonight than any other night of the year except New Years Eve.

A lot of us wear costumes all year long, so I'm not sure what it is about the big Halloween party that makes it such a popular night, but there's a line waiting to get in that's twice as long as normal.

Maybe the customers like being able to dress up themselves. A surprising number show up in Halloween costumes, from something as simple as a baseball cap and carrying a ball glove, to really elaborate ensembles. Two themes prevail for dancer and customer alike.

Sex and sin.

All the nurses are naughty and a lot of the men have something stuffed in the front to make a noticeable bulge. No way are that many average guys sporting a fat ten inches in the skin tight bottoms of their batman costumes.

"That costume is banging," Piper says from beside me.

We're both doing our last makeup touches before going out on stage.

I smile at her in the mirror. "Thanks."

I'm wearing a white angel costume with gold trim tonight. It will look golden-orange under the lights on the stage and glow bright with a blue tint when I'm working the floor, highlighting my assets, and leaving the rest of me in shadow.

The skirt of the two-shoulder toga barely covers my ass, but I only wear the tiny toga dress for the first part of my set. Once it comes off, I'll be left in a thong and a bra made of satin and fine white mesh. Wider than usual, the straps are artfully designed folds of white satin. Crisscrossing right above my boobs, they keep the illusion of the toga I'll strip off at the end.

They also outline each globe like a neon sign, making the girls look even bigger than they really are. The nearly transparent white mesh covering them will glow for the punters without hiding the glittery white pasties on my nipples. Those will glow even brighter because of their opacity, giving the customers the sense they are getting a peek at my nipples.

The small white wings will stand out in the crowd but won't get in my way when I walk between tables working the room later. That's always good for extra tips and I need them just like the next girl. Tonight should bring in more tips than all the other nights this week combined.

"You've got a thing for dressing like an angel," Piper teases. "Anything to do with your stalker being named Angelo?"

Stalker. As if.

I shrug.

"The customers like an angel with big tatas," one of the other dancer's says. "Makes them feel naughty for lusting after her."

"I'm surprised that gold angel costume doesn't bring back bad memories," Piper opines. "I burned my biker chick outfit after that backroom group lap dance that went wrong a couple years back."

By *went wrong* Piper means the attack left her hollow eyed and too banged up to dance for two weeks. Just another example of people believing that workers in the sex industry give up their rights to safety, much less to say the word *no*.

Humanity sucks sometimes.

Bianca doesn't though. She's fighting for all of us to be protected in ways a lot of strip clubs wouldn't even consider. Doesn't matter to her if the dancers provide extra curriculars, or not, either.

They all get health insurance and paid sick leave now. When they're out sick more than one shift, with a doctor's note to back it up, they don't have to pay the nightly fee for using the backrooms either. They used to have to pay it whether they were here, or not.

The bouncers are now trained to put the safety of the dancers and waitstaff ahead of a positive customer experience.

Grateful for the changes in the club since my bestie took over talent management, I answer Piper's question about wearing my gold angel outfit. "When I wear it, I remember a man I'd barely met rushing across a crowded club to help me."

Just thinking about Angelo's speed and intensity now makes me wet like dancing for the punters with all their lust-filled gazes stuck on me never does.

And yeah, I do wear the angel costumes because they make me think of him. But that, I'm not saying out loud.

Piper tsks but she doesn't say anything in reply.

I take one last look in the mirror before turning away. "That wasn't the first time I was assaulted on the floor, but it was the first time someone besides another employee stepped in."

Piper gives two high kicks to test the adhesion of the body tape holding her six-inch heels on. "You couldn't rely on the bouncers under Gino's watch, that's for sure."

"Amen to that, sister," the other dancer says as she joins us at the curtain.

The music volume goes up a few decibels and Jessie Ware's *What's Your Pleasure* starts to play. That's my cue and I strut out onto the stage, playing to the customers along the way to my pole.

I have to step down off the center stage and walk six feet to the private stage with a single pole that I'm on tonight. I'm tense with awareness crossing those six feet of space on the main floor, but I hide my tension with a slinky glide up the steps to my platform.

As the whir of the retracting stairway sounds, removing easy access to the stage for customers, I let out a breath. During the other dancer's music, I go through a placeholder routine I choreographed a long time ago and use at least once a week.

It's a little tease and a lot of jiggle, but I don't do the moves that garner the most attention because this is not my spotlight.

My muscles relax, making every move easier and more fluid. For a second, I think it's the familiarity of the music that has the tension draining from my body.

But then I realize the truth. He's here.

I can't see him, but I feel his eyes on me.

Angelo Caruso.

I know who he is now. *What* he is.

They call him the Angel of Death and he's the top enforcer and assassin for the new Cosa Nostra godfather. Not that any of us are supposed to know that, but Piper told me.

She told me to keep my trap shut about it too because knowing too much about the mafia can get you killed. Only she said I should know who he is so I can make an informed decision.

I'm not sure what I'm supposed to decide about though.

Angelo's only ever spoken a handful of words to me.

It's not like we're dating, or something. Not even if I memorized every single one of those words.

You alright, dolcezza?

Get dressed and go home.

I'll square it with Ugo.

Angelo's position in the mafia doesn't make any difference to me. He'd have to come out of the shadows and talk to me for there to be even a hope of that.

According to Piper, when he saved me from Ronnie, Angelo was still the top enforcer for the Don of the Genovese. The same one of New York's Five Families my sperm donor serves.

That and a fiver will get me a cup of coffee at the corner diner.

I guess Angelo got a promotion of sorts when his boss became the new Godfather of the Cosa Nostra in America and Angelo kept his position as top enforcer for Don Severu De Luca. Now, he's the godfather's top enforcer, not just a don's.

Discovering he's the deadliest assassin in New York doesn't change how safe I feel when Angelo is in the club. If anything, it makes me feel more secure.

Because to me, he's not the Angel of Death but my guardian angel. The scariest guy in the New York underworld is the only man that makes me feel protected.

He always sits in the darkest corner reserved for what passes for VIPs at Pitiful Princess. In all the time since that night when Ronnie tried to molest me, I haven't once laid eyes on Angelo. Even though he's at the club most nights I work.

Even if Piper and the other girls weren't so quick to tell me, I would know he's there.

My body reacts with atavistic instincts when he's around, relaxing, knowing on a visceral level I can't explain that no one will touch me. That I'm safe.

My lizard brain, always on high alert when I'm at work, or anywhere besides home alone with my mom and sister, settles down when Angelo is nearby. That's how I know he's here now. Because when he's not, I spend my time on the stage tense and wary.

I learned to hide the fear in my first foster home when I figured out that some kids and even some adults in the system thrive on the distress of others. The skill is a handy one to have in my profession. Strippers are pros at coming off brash, confident and sexy.

But I'm not the only one who has to pretend when stepping out on the stage. If you look really hard, you can see it in the eyes.

The punters aren't looking into my eyes though, are they?

When my best friend, Bianca, used to dance here, it was better. We had each other's backs. But then she hooked up with Salvatore De Luca and got put in charge of talent management.

Although she has more power to protect me and the other dancers from an employer's position now, she only comes into the club a couple of times a week. Usually early, before things get really busy and I can't always leave mom and Cookie then.

So, I see a lot less of my bestie than I used to.

Piper's a casual friend, like a lot of the other dancers, but no one has my back like Bianca did.

Except, now Angelo does.

Does he know that the moment he arrives, I stop thinking about any of the other patrons? Probably not.

I don't know what this thing is between him and me. I'm pretty sure he's not into me like I'm into him, even if he's here almost every night I dance. Maybe I remind him of his sister, or his mom, or something.

But he's quickly become the only patron that matters to me. The only man I *want* looking at my nearly naked body.

My job means anyone who pays the cover charge gets to see that, but it's not the same as wanting it.

Even if he never comes out of the shadows to interact with me, Angelo haunts my thoughts everyday while I crush on him like I never did the boys in school as a teenager.

The idea of letting them touch me scared me. Even before that last foster home before I came to live with mom and Cookie.

Maybe that's why I can crush on Angelo. The distance he keeps makes my infatuation safe.

Angelo is the sexiest man I've ever seen and the only one I have ever wanted to touch me intimately.

At least in my dreams, I do.

I'm not sure that would translate into real life.

Because he's over the top protective of me without making any sort of moves on me. I'm grateful. I really am. And I know it's greedy to want more.

I remind myself of that even when I touch myself in bed thinking about him.

I've never had much of a sex drive. But since that first night I saw him skewer a guy's hand for trying to touch me, I get horny a lot more. And it's always from thinking about Angelo.

As soon as Cookie leaves for school and mom is busy elsewhere in the apartment, my hand slides between my thighs while I fantasize about Angelo Caruso until I have to bite my pillow to muffle the scream from my climax.

Angelo might be here every night doing business for the mafia and him being in the VIP area when I dance is just a coincidence. That's more likely than him crushing on me like I'm fixated on him.

Because he doesn't come anywhere near me. Not for a dance, not even to talk. He sends tips through the bartenders though. So, even if he's not here for me, he pays attention to me.

One of the bartenders tried to shortchange me my tips and she was gone the next day. Like completely ghosted. She didn't show up for work that night, didn't answer her cell phone when the manager called, trying to track her down, and never came in for her final paycheck.

We heard from one of the dancers who used to hang out with her that she left New York. The state, not just the city.

No one has tried to skim my tips since.

When everything was going down with Gino trying to force me and Bianca to do extracurriculars, a secret part of me hoped Angelo would hear about it and set Gino straight like he did that guy whose hand he skewered.

I didn't want to have to find a new club to dance in, but Gino really tried to mess me over and things were getting desperate. Turns out, Bianca told her new boyfriend what was happening, and he fired Gino before I had to quit my job.

I'm pretty sure that Angelo did something to my old boss anyway and that same secret part of me is glad. People whisper about how the smarmy assistant manager disappeared, and they don't mean that he up and left the city.

It's on brand for the Angel of Death.

He goes all in when it comes to making a point about my personal space.

No matter why he's protecting me, I have a serious lady boner for Death.

He's not even a decade older than me, so it's not daddy issues. No matter what the psychologists might think, I got over having a sperm donor rather than a father a long time ago.

It's the issue of feeling safe and I've spent most of my life not feeling that way. Even after coming to live with mom in the tiny apartment filled with love if not a bunch of material things.

So, now, I dance for the only man in the room I want to think about, my body flowing through the special routine I created just for him. I pretended I was choreographing a routine to do for my boyfriend, Angelo's handsome face and deadly stare my secret inspiration.

No other man could star in my fantasies like my warrior angel. Fantasies are all I will ever have of Angelo. His distance has made that abundantly obvious.

But I'll take fantasies of my warrior angel over dates with anyone else.

No one can compare to him and the safety I feel in his presence. Lately that feeling of safety has even been expanded to when I am home. His presence is that powerful in my mind.

It's almost as if he is watching me. Sometimes, I feel like he's in the room with me.

Piper's music fades and then the sensual thrum of *Closer* by Nine Inch Nails starts to play. An orange spotlight bathes me in its glow, and I move into a spin that takes me up the pole.

Perfect for my new routine, the beat reverberates through my body practically leading me into my spins and pole splits. If the lyrics get me hot pretending they are about me and a certain mafioso, no one else has to know.

Doing the splits against the pole, I spin around with my hair flying behind me. Tonight, it is not up in a ponytail, but loose. Instead of straightening it, I left it to fall in soft waves around my face. My dark hair and sexy outfit might make most people have less than angelic thoughts, but dancing is like being in heaven for me.

And I stay there through my whole spotlight set.

I remove my outer toga after a lot of teasing midway through the last song. The orange spotlight goes off and the customers shout their disappointment. But then I'm bathed in a blacklight spot, making all the bits that are meant to glow.

Is it my imagination, or are Angelo's eyes burning into me?

Holding myself on the pole with my thighs, I face his shadowed corner and cup my breasts in offering.

Money showers onto the stage around the bottom of the pole, but I barely notice it as I try to see Angelo's form through the gloom.

I can't of course. It's always shadowed in the VIP area, but tonight, with the blacklights the only illumination on the floor, it's stygian.

I finish my set to raucous applause and raunchy shouts, money falling like confetti on the stage around me. Picking it up, I'm riding the high of a perfect performance.

The Pitiful Princess may not be a musical on Broadway, but getting the choreography right for every bar of music feels awesome all the same.

Coming down off the stage, goosebumps form on my arms.

The sensation of Angelo watching me is even heavier than normal. Did he enjoy my new routine? Did he like when I stripped down to a sheer bra, pasties, my thong and glittery white wings?

Or is my body nothing more than the vessel of whatever person he is pretending to protect? Are his fantasies as active as mine, but with someone else playing the central role?

Even if he pretends I'm someone else, I wish he would request a lap dance. But he never does.

So, I'm not sure why my stiletto clad feet are moving me toward the darkness I always stay away from.

CHAPTER 10

ANGELO

My phone rings with a tone exclusive to one person.

My mother.

I'm tempted to ignore the call because I don't want to miss even a moment of Candi's set, but I answer. Severu and I have been waiting to see if Perla would reach out looking for information on behalf of her father, the Sicilian godfather.

I swipe to answer and the phone connects immediately to the earbud I wear constantly, but I still have to lift it close to my face to be heard on the other end through my mask. "What do you want Perla?"

"That is no way to answer the phone to your mother," she scolds me.

I don't bother to reply to the rebuke. She and I both know I don't care what she thinks of my actions. And I have no intention of engaging in pleasantries with this woman.

"I'm coming to New York. I would like to see you. Your stepfather has never met you, and he'd like to."

"I doubt that very much." She and Barone, husband number three and don over Calabria, a territory in Southern Italy, have been married for four years.

"Then you are mistaken. You are my son, regardless of how you wish to see yourself."

"I am not the one who decided not to be family."

"You didn't want to come to Sicily with me. What was I supposed to do, force you?" she asks in a tone meant to make me feel guilty.

"Haven't you figured out by now that playing victim with me is useless?"

"I would have thought that now you have a girlfriend, you would be more in touch with your emotions. You can't tell me the little stripper is fine with that dead eyed stare you're so good at."

Cold seeps into my limbs. Despite all my precautions and not claiming her yet, she knows about Candi. Which means the godfather does too.

"My life and anyone in it is of no concern to you," I warn her.

"How can you say that? Your grandfather and I are your only living relatives." Which means she knows that Henrico is dead.

Or strongly suspects it.

Don Caruso approved the hit, but that doesn't mean his Italian counterpart was happy with the plans they'd made for the succession being derailed.

Apparently, Don Caruso never told Don Messino that he planned to back Severu as the next godfather in America.

"Don Messino made it clear he considered me no family of his over twenty years ago." He was ashamed of the child he considered defective, telling my mother it was probably the IVF that made me the way I was.

Not a stellar human being, or particularly intelligent.

"I don't have time to get into old history right now," Perla dismisses. "We'll be in New York in two weeks. I expect you to make time to see me and meet with your stepfather."

"Send me your schedule." I make no promises, because she is not a priority for me.

Even if finding out what her father is planning is.

Frankly, I have more reliable spies in Sicily already.

CANDI

Uncertainty adds fizz to the bubbles of anticipation rising inside me. Buoyed up by it and performing a perfect set, I walk straight into the VIP area.

Except for Angelo, the men who sit here believe they can touch the dancers however they want. It's an unspoken rule, but the dancers who go into the VIP area are open to doing special favors in the backroom, or right there at the table.

I'm not, but Angelo is there and the past months have proven he's not coming out. If I want to see him, I have to go in.

Why my craving for him is so unmanageable tonight of all nights, I don't know and honestly don't care. I just want a glimpse. Then I'll leave.

That's what I tell myself, but I'm not sure I believe it.

Unafraid, I maneuver through the darkness covered in the certainty that Angelo won't allow anyone to touch me unless I give them permission.

Would he let a man I gave the go ahead to touch me? The fantasy of him being so protective he wouldn't even allow that sends inappropriate arousal zinging along my nerve ending.

That thought should definitely not turn me on.

But it does. A lot.

Despite my certainty of the mafioso's protection, I weave between the tables, using my tried and true techniques to avoid being touched.

Only, they aren't necessary. None of the men sitting at these tables even leer at me as I walk by.

Because of Angelo. I'm sure of it.

When I see him, at first my heart thunders in my chest. His face is painted like a death skull. The blacklight giving the impression that the skull is floating in the air above the table, its empty eye sockets watching me approach.

I'm only a couple of feet away when I can make out a hooded cowl and muscular body encased in unrelenting black. Angelo is eerily still as I approach his table.

I could doubt my certainty that it's him, but I don't. I can't see his eyes, but I can feel them on me. Just like I always do.

As I get closer to the table, the panic I should have been feeling all along hits me out of nowhere.

Do I really want to risk destroying the status quo? If I disgust him, he might stop protecting me. Do I want to take a chance of that happening? What if he rejects me completely and I'm left standing like a fool amidst men who will be eager to take what he doesn't want?

The questions swirl in my head as I stop in front of him, my body rooted to the spot. None of my fears can overcome this uncontrollable fascination.

My heart is beating so hard, it hurts. I'm supposed to be confident, a dancer who knows her place. I should cock my hip and ask if he wants anything, letting my fingertip play along my bottom lip.

But I can't get a single sound past the golf ball lodged in my throat.

It's been longer than six months since Angelo skewered a man's hand for me and over three months since he dealt with Ronnie.

What if the sensation of him watching me all that time is a figment of my imagination? And if it's not, there's a reason he's never come out of the shadows to talk to me.

Right?

Why didn't I think of that *before* I let my ovaries do the walking?

"What are you doing back here?" he demands in a tone so cold it gives my heart frostbite.

But relief pours through me too. That feeling? Not my imagination. If there was any doubt in my mind that the man dressed as the Angel of Death is Angelo, that doubt is gone now.

The connection between us is real.

He might be wearing skull face-pai...no wait, it's not makeup, but a mask fitted as close as skin to his face. But it's too smooth and the mouth doesn't move when he talks.

Also, I can't see the whites of his eyes and face paint wouldn't be able to hide that, no matter how well done it is. The black holes must be some kind of mesh he can see through though.

"Do you want a dance?" Did those words really just come out of my mouth?

Angelo surges to his feet and my frost-bitten heart starts to sink. He's going to leave. Whatever his reason for watching and watching over me, it's not because he wants me.

His head jerks in a nod toward the other side of the main floor. "In the back."

That beleaguered organ in my chest stutters.

"In the back?" I squeak, sounding more like a scared little doe than a woman who has spent the last four years stripping for a living.

He waves his hand in a hurry up and get moving action.

But the back? That's where all the extra curriculars happen. I don't work those rooms. He must know that, but his air of expectancy says otherwise.

"I uh...I don't work the back," I manage to get out.

"I'm not going to ask you to fuck me. But if you want to dance for me, it's not going to be in front of anyone else."

Little does he know I dance for him in front of a room full of customers every time I'm on the stage. But the opportunity to do it in private, with no one else watching, makes my heart sing.

Turning, I wave my hand in a come-on motion and start back the way I came. He doesn't say another word, but I know he is there and my steps don't falter as I bypass grabby hands and tables filled with men shouting for me to come over.

When we reach the door to the back, there's a bouncer guarding it. Another new policy implemented by Bianca. He looks at me in concern. "You leaving early? If somebody accosted you..."

His words trail off as shock that quickly turns to horror covers his face. He noticed Angelo behind me.

The bouncer looks between me and Angelo, the horror not abating from his features. "You want a room? With *him*?"

No time for cold feet now. I nod firmly. "Yes. Is the Pasha's Den open?"

"Yes." The bouncer gives Angelo a wary look, and then looks behind him, like he expects someone else to show up.

It's then that I realize the bouncer does not recognize the mafia enforcer, despite his costume being literally the Angel of Death.

CHAPTER 11

ANGELO

The room Candi leads me into is straight out of an Arabian nights fantasy.

Candi indicates a spice orange, velvet, three-section sofa that covers the entire ornately carved back wall and part of the two walls on either side. "Why don't you take a seat?"

Stalking forward, I shove aside a bunch of silk pillows and sit down in the center.

I don't know what I'm doing back here with her. She doesn't know who I am. This mask doesn't even show the color of my eyes.

Thought it was appropriate for tonight. Death at a Halloween party. Mask, or no mask, I'm the Angel of Death year-round though.

It's nice to have one night where the real me is on the outside, the monster there for everyone to see.

And it's the monster that Candi offered a lap dance to. Which pisses me off. Because she didn't offer it to *me*, but came strolling into the VIP area and offered her pretty body and sexy moves to a stranger.

Sure, she's one of the top earning lap dancers, despite her no touch rule. But it's that no touch rule that keeps the customers at Pitiful Princess breathing.

So why the hell did she venture into the VIP area tonight? She knows the rules. Customers who are looking for more sit there. They are handsy sons of bitches too.

The dancers and cocktail waitresses who serve that section encourage it, because they're looking for the extra money selling extracurriculars provides.

Candi doesn't go back there. Not ever.

What the hell happened tonight? Did she decide to start offering her ass up for sale? Fury rages through me. That is not happening.

If she needs more money, the foundation will increase her mother's monthly stipend. Since the foundation is me, news of the increase will be given to her mother tomorrow.

No way in hell am I allowing her to offer extracurriculars to other men. Not that she seemed eager to come back here with me until I promised I didn't want to fuck her.

What if she's looking to start giving lap dances with a happy ending or blowjobs?

Seeing red, a low growl rumbles through my chest.

No way in hell is her mouth going on anyone's dick but mine. My men already know not to let the customers touch her when I'm not around to take care of it, but I'll remind them that their continued presence among the living depends on it.

"Did you enjoy my set tonight?" she asks in a sultry voice.

My teeth grind together, and I bite out, "Yes."

Wearing my mask, I planned to approach Candi without her knowing who I am. Flirt with danger. Enjoy a lap dance.

But not like this.

Not after she came into the VIP section.

When she came down off her stage and started walking toward the darkest area in the club, I stayed put, waiting to see what she would do.

And fucking lucky for her and the other *stronzos* sitting at the tables in the shadows, she approached me first.

Not that any of them were fool enough to even look at her with intent. That area is reserved for men in the life and mostly in the Genovese Family. They all know who I am, and they all know that I don't want anyone touching her.

No one knows why because I haven't taken her to my bed and they all know that too. I made sure of it.

I would have claimed her right after the dons kissed Severu's ring, but there's unrest in Sicily. The godfather in the old country has his panties in a wad because our new North American godfather isn't from one of the traditional ruling families.

There are plenty in the Sicilian mafia that think the De Lucas are upstarts since Severu's grandfather only became a don because of how many leaders got put in the slammer in the 70s and 80s by the RICO act.

A behind-the-scenes money man, he proved himself to the Five Families with his ruthlessness and ability to rebuild under the FED's radar.

Things are different in the old country. And those differences are getting on my nerves.

I want Candi in my house and in my bed. Pretty soon those hidebound *stronzos* are going to find out that annoying death isn't good for their life expectancy.

It's time for a change in leadership in Sicily. I'm just waiting for Severu to give me the go ahead, but right now he insists we play nice. Build bridges, not battles, or some such shit.

He says his grandfather brought the doubters around and he will too.

Yeah, I don't see it.

"Chair or bar?" Candi asks.

"Bar." My voice is hoarse from the strain my rage is putting on the muscles in my throat.

Just the fact she knows the bar is an option in these rooms pisses me off. She doesn't work back here.

But her friends do and I bet they talk about it. It better be that, and not that she's been doing her research in preparation for bringing customers back here.

Candi presses a button in the wall near the door and a bar lowers from the ceiling.

She seems mesmerized by its descent, but I'm looking to see if there are streaks of left over fluids on it. I don't see anything but that's not a guarantee.

"You need to wipe that down with sanitizer before you start." A shudder rolls through me at the thought of Candi's skin touching a pole covered in other people's germs.

"The dancers sanitize it before it goes back into the ceiling," she assures me.

I shake my head. "Better safe than sorry."

Before each set, cleaners come on stage and sanitize the poles for the ones getting new dancers, but there's no one here to watch and make sure the dancers are as fastidious on their own.

Her mouth twists in a grimace, but she grabs a spray bottle and paper towels out of a decorative chest. She doesn't half-ass it, but cleans the pole thoroughly.

"Satisfied?" she asks with a hand cocked on one hip.

I jerk my head in affirmative.

She smiles. "Good."

After she does something by the door, *Closer* by Nine Inch Nails starts to play. It's the song she danced to onstage.

And one on my playlist for working out. It makes me think of her.

Someone else might think it's funny that we both gravitate toward an industrial rock band that started before either of us was born. But to me, it's just proof we're meant to be together.

My eyes are glued to her as she dances her new routine just for me. My boner is so hard, its probably pressing a permanent indent in my leather pants.

We didn't negotiate how long she would dance for me, and neither of us says anything as the next song on her list begins to play.

Leaning back against the pole, her tits lifted like perfectly round melons lifted toward heaven, she reaches behind her. Then her bra straps go slack.

My breath stutters in my chest when she grips the front of her bra.

Candi pulls the mesh away from her body, revealing the soft, flawless skin of her breasts. The bra flutters to the floor and I have to swallow against my suddenly constricted throat.

My throat's not the only thing constricted. My cock is trapped in leather and drooling with the need to be let out. I curl my hands into fists to stop myself from opening my fly and taking myself in hand.

Candi notices and her eyes flare with satisfaction.

She likes turning me on.

But it's not me, she's turning on, is it? As far as she knows, it's some rando she brought back here.

Fuck.

Moving away from the pole, Candi slinks toward me, every curve of her gorgeous body moving with sinuous grace. She dances closer and closer until her tassel covered nipples swing in front of my face, the creamy skin of her tits making me salivate with the need to taste.

"Is this what you want?" she purrs.

I swallow and have to clear my throat before I answer. "Yes."

I fucking want her naked, that tiny triangle of white silk that makes up her G-string gone, the pasties peeled away from her nipples. Nothing but Candi flavored skin for me to taste and touch.

But I promised not to fuck her and if I get her naked, I'm not sure I can keep that promise.

Reaching for one of my hands, she pulls it toward her. "If you take off your gloves, you can feel me."

There's no holding back the groan her invitation pulls out of me.

"You want me to touch you?" I ask, to be sure.

"Yes."

Fury fights with desire.

Desire wins. This is my woman. And whether she knows the man she's inviting to touch her perfect flesh is me, or not, I'm the only one that ever will.

I peel one of the gloves from my hand and pause. I'm not putting it on this sofa when I have to put it back on later. Of course, tonight is the one time I'm not wearing my cargo pants with extra gloves in one of the pockets.

Sitting here I can feel the DNA of others crawling over my skin despite the barrier of my clothes.

Candi puts her hand out. "Give it to me."

I do before removing the other glove and doing the same.

She walks over to the chest and takes out a new paper towel before laying it on top and then putting the gloves on top. She's so fucking perfect for me.

Her strut is confident as she walks back across the room, but there's no mistaking the nerves reflected in her eyes, the vulnerable way she bites her bottom lip, the way her long nails curl into her palms.

She doesn't stop until she's right in front of me though, her body undulating to the music.

The air grows sultry with want around us, the vulnerability replaced by desire in her gaze. There's a pulse pounding in her neck to match the one thundering in my chest.

She wants this.

I fist my hands on my thighs to stop myself from reaching for her. She's not ready for my hands on her, no matter what she says. But she will be.

Leaning back on the couch, I spread my legs to give her room to dance between them and then beckon her with a backward jerk of my head.

Her pupils dilate with excitement as she steps forward, bending at the waist so her gorgeous tits sway in front of me. Then she spins around, her arms lifting so her hands can slide under the silky brown hair. She lifts it away from her nape, giving me an unfettered view of her curvy ass as it jiggles with her movements.

Nothing about Candi is fake. Not her tits. Not her ass and when that bountiful flesh shimmies in front of me, all I want is to touch. Who she believes I am be damned.

Then she steps forward and bends down, giving me a glimpse of naked pussy lips barely contained by a thin strip of white satin.

She's wet and the satin clings to her lips, hinting at the slit I want to bury my cock in.

The sound that comes from my throat is pure frustrated need.

Her hands slide around her ankles from the inside, the grip holding her in place as she whips her hair in a move I've seen a thousand times from other dancers. But with her, it's always different.

Fantasies of jacking myself off with her long ponytail morph into burying my hands in her long locks as I fuck her mouth.

I groan. "You're so fucking sexy, Candi."

She straightens and looks at me over her shoulder. "I'm glad you think so."

Are those words for me, or for the stranger she agreed to give a private lap dance?

Shoving the irritating thought aside, my eyes devour the sight of this beautiful woman moving so sensually for my eyes only.

The song playing goes into a staccato beat and she spins back, kicking her leg high, swinging her stiletto covered foot in an arc over me.

The music shifts to Nine Inch Nails again and she moves into a familiar pose she does on the bar, but there's no bar there to support her.

Candi repeats the moves she did against the bar in the air right in front of me. Her hand holding her leg up in a vertical split as she spins, her hair flying around her. I'd like to see the men I train in hand-to-hand combat with show that kind of core strength and agility.

As the music reaches one of its crescendos, she drops to her haunches, offering me her tits like she did on the bar.

I know it was just part of her act. I'm not that far gone, I do realize that even when it feels like she's dancing for me, I'm sharing her with a room full of other guys slavering in lust over her.

But as she shimmies her ass and shakes her tits, undulating her body with sensual abandon, it feels like this dance was designed for me.

It's not true. She designed this dance for the guy she was willing to take into the backroom.

When her next set of moves brings her onto the sofa, straddling my hip, but not touching it, my desire is back to warring with rage at the thought of her doing this for another man.

She grabs my wrist and lifts my hand to the side of her generous tit. Her skin is every bit as soft as I dreamed it would be and for a second I am completely lost in the sensation of touching her for the first time.

Her eyes meet mine, her pupils blown, like she is as sexually excited as me.

Or... "Are you high?" That would explain a lot.

Candi falters in her attempt to slide my hand down her body and stares at me. "What did you just say?"

"I think someone put GHB in your water, Candi. This isn't you."

"What do you mean it's not me? This is what I do. "

"You don't come into the backrooms for anyone."

She stares at me as if she doesn't understand my words, and it convinces me even more that someone slipped a roofie in her drink. I'll kill the son of a bitch but right now I need to make sure she's safe.

Ignoring the need raging through my body, I grab her by the waist and lift her away from me. "You need to go home, Candi. You're not safe with your decision-making impaired like this."

Neither are the men she could invite into the backroom after me. Them I don't care about.

Her I do.

Even knowing I have to let her go, my fingers reflexively squeeze the soft skin under my hands.

But she's not looking at me with sexy need anymore.

Dark eyes narrowed in a glare that would kill if it was a bullet, she yanks on my wrists, trying to dislodge my hold. "I'm not high and you don't get to make me feel bad for doing what *you* pretended to want."

"I don't pretend shit."

"Right. Why did you come back here with me?" she demands.

"Because I wasn't letting you offer what you were offering to me to someone else," I tell her honestly. "Fuck, Candi, who would drug you?"

"For the last time, I'm not drugged." She shoves at me.

I step back because she's clearly distressed.

"I know exactly what I'm doing. Do you think I could dance like that..." She waves her hand toward the bar. "If I was under the influence of GHB or K?"

"Don't try to tell me dancers never work high."

She shakes her head, kicks her leg up into another split and spins with smooth strength that gives lie to the idea that she is high. Dropping her leg, she cocks her hip. "If I was impaired, I never would have been able to keep my hold on the pole doing that, much less do it standing."

"Then what the hell is going on?" I demand. "You don't take men into the backroom."

"It's none of your business if I do." She stomps away to grab her sheer bra and jerks it on with short movements.

She's so magnificent when she's angry, I almost miss her next words in my lusty haze. She's not impaired and my body is telling me to take what she's offering.

But she's not offering it anymore.

If those stilettos were the knives they're named for, I'd be bleeding right now.

"If you didn't want to watch me dance, you could have just said no." Her voice is choked with emotion. "You don't have to be an asshole about it."

Her angry tread takes her to the door and she jerks on the handle to open it.

But then she stops and looks back over her shoulder at me. "I don't know why you protected me like you did those two times, but consider the dance payment. I'll square it with management."

The fuck she will, but I let her leave, a weird feeling fizzing in my chest. Happiness.

Candi, my woman, knew who I was all along.

CHAPTER 12

CANDI

M y back aches. My feet throb. As I open the door to the back alley, weariness drags at me like cement blocks chained to the back of my kicks.

I'm always tired when I finish a shift, but this is something different. This doesn't just go bone deep, I'm weary to my soul.

I know it's because of Angelo's rejection.

He didn't even have the decency to leave the club after. I could feel his eyes on me for two more hours before he left.

So. Proof positive, he's not there to mack on me, but for mafia business. Knowing he only wanted the private lap dance because he was *once again* looking after me doesn't help.

Especially after he left me a freaking $1000 tip with the head bartender.

I told him he didn't have to pay for the dance. I offered to pay for my time in the backroom, but management asked if I planned to do more private lap dances. When I said no, Nerissa De Luca gave me a free pass.

It could be because I'm friends with her sister-in-law, but I don't think so. She had a look of pity on her face. Everyone knows I took Angelo to the backroom and they all assume it didn't go well for me.

They're right. Darn it.

I wish I could afford to reject his pity payment, but I can't. And it makes me cranky.

Sometimes it feels like I don't have any control over my life.

My head down, I watch the damp pavement in front of my feet. I've stepped into nasty surprises left behind by both animals and humans. Never again.

I'm concentrating on avoiding a puddle of something I'm happy to leave unidentified in my brain, so I don't realize I'm not alone at first. I'm about a third of the way down the alley when I register a noise.

The scrape of shoe leather on pavement.

A whimper. "Please. I'll get the money."

"Times up." The words aren't spoken with any particular menace, the bored tone making the message more chilling.

Dread in my gut, my head snaps up as I freeze in place. No one has noticed me yet, which only tonight right? Usually the street at the end of the alley would be quiet this time of night, but right now it's still noisy with party revelers.

We usually close at 2 am, but it's already three and I just finished my last set.

Two hulking forms loom over a kneeling man. The one behind him is holding him in place by his shoulders.

They're close to the wall opposite to the club's back entrance, but not visible to the street because the dumpsters are between them and the mouth of the alley. Where I need to go.

"You owe our boss and he's out of patience." The man in front backhands the kneeling man. "He said to take it out of your hide."

Why do I think he's not talking about giving the deadbeat debtor a beatdown despite the smack?

My instincts are sending up danger flares for real though and I slowly start moving backward, grateful I changed into rubber soled kicks before leaving for the night.

Not that I would walk to the train in my six-inch heels regardless.

"You already beat me up. You can't squeeze blood out of a stone."

The stupidity of this guy stops me in my tracks for a second in sheer amazement. Even I know you don't taunt the big guys you owe money to in a deserted alley. Mostly deserted.

I'm here, but I'm not jumping into whatever this is. If it were a kid, or one of the other girls, or something, I'd take my chances. But I'm not putting my neck on the line for someone delulu enough to think he can renege on a debt to guys like that.

"I guess we'll just have to squeeze the blood directly from the source then," the guy in front says in the same bored tone.

This is going nowhere good. I take another silent step backward.

"No! I can't pay if I'm dead." The kneeling guy sounds smug, like he really thinks this argument is going to save him.

"You were never gonna pay anyway. You've been bragging about taking a beating. *Not going to pay until I'm damn good and ready.* That sound familiar to you?"

Oh, man, I really don't want to be hearing this. Can you say *witness to a crime?*

"We don't need losers like you giving our other customers ideas about paying their debts in broken bones instead of cold cash." This is from the guy behind the kneeling man.

He doesn't sound nearly as bored. He sounds pissed.

"At least dead you're useful as a lesson to others."

Oh, shit!

I spin around and run as fast and quietly as I can toward the backdoor. The sound of my feet landing against the wet pavement are thunderclaps in my ears.

"What the..." The guy behind me isn't making any effort to muffle the sound of his footsteps.

The clack of dress shoes smacking the rain soaked street grows closer and closer.

I reach the backdoor of the club and yank on the handle, but it's locked. My brain knows it automatically locks behind you when you go out, unless you prop it open. My terror demands I keep yanking with one hand while pounding on it with another.

A heavy hand lands on my shoulder and yanks me backward. I scream, hoping someone inside the club will hear.

The guy's other hand smacks over my mouth, muffling me. "Be quiet."

The scent of cordite fills my nostrils. How many deadbeat debtors has this guy already shot tonight? Terror courses through me, reinvigorating my limbs. And ignoring his advice, I kick backwards, twisting and trying to get away.

The guy shifts his hold on me so his forearm is a tight bar across my chest. "You're only making things worse for yourself."

I recognize that voice. It's one of the club regulars.

Barely old enough to drink, Freddy's got a thing for Piper. He pays for a trip to the backroom a couple of times a week and his prolific tips are enough to let her know she's got his number.

Not that tipping means a guy's hung up on you.

Gah! Why am I still thinking about Angelo when I'm about to die for being in the wrong place at the wrong time?

Knowing Freddy is the man holding me doesn't give me comfort. He and his friends are mafia. I don't know if they're Genovese, like Angelo and my sperm donor, but they've got that made man attitude.

Cold and soulless.

The door cracks open and hope makes me double down on my struggles.

Pressing his hand so hard against my mouth, my teeth cut the inside of my lip, he barks, "Get lost. There's nothing to see here."

And the door shuts again. Just like that.

I don't even know who was on the other side. They didn't step out into the alley to check who was pounding on the door even. And I don't really blame them.

Looking is just asking for trouble. But I doubt anyone's calling the cops either. If I recognize the guy holding me, they probably do too.

The mafia doesn't take kindly to snitches and they don't leave witnesses.

The only one who's going to save me, is me.

I bite hard on the fleshy part of Freddy's hand. The coppery taste of blood lets me know I broke skin. Good.

Take that, asshole.

"Son of a bitch!" Freddy pulls his maimed appendage out of the reach of my teeth and his other arm loosens just enough.

Jerking away, I drop low, and breaking out of his hold completely, run toward the mouth of the alley.

"Catch her," the older guy still standing over their intended victim yells.

My arms and knees pumping, I sprint with all I've got. I don't waste breath screaming again, I'm set on one goal. Getting to the street.

But then, silhouetted against the light from the street, two more large human shapes come into the alley. They head toward me at a jog and my heart sinks.

Backup has arrived for the guys intent on killing the deadbeat debtor and my goose is cooked.

With a burst of terror driven adrenalin, I sprint at an angle, hoping to avoid their long arms by scooting close to the brick outer wall of the club.

"Don't let her past!" The guy who's doing nothing to chase me down shouts.

The two men spread out, making it harder to avoid getting caught by them. The alley is narrow, but not so narrow I won't try it.

I duck down and try running right between them. I think I'm going to make it when I'm lifted clean off my feet by an arm around my waist.

"Help me!" I scream, hoping I'm close enough to the mouth of the alley to be heard over the street noise. "Call 911!"

"Shh, Ms. Candi. Don't hold her so tight, Derian."

"She's a wildcat, Mario. If I let go, who knows what she'll do." He looks down at me and grumps, like he's feeling put upon. "We're not going to hurt you."

Ms. Candi? Not going to hurt me? Who are these goons?

"I don't believe you. *Help!*" My shout has less oomph because the hold around my middle is making it hard to fill my lungs.

Then I do the only thing I can think of, knowing it's probably the most ridiculous claim I'll ever make. "If you hurt me Angelo Caruso will cut off your hands."

"He wouldn't stop at our hands if harm came to you because of us, trust me," the guy my captor called Mario says in enthusiastic agreement.

"Then let me go."

"No can do. Those two work for somebody else," Mario explains. "We let you run, and they follow. Maybe not now, but later. We let that happen and we might as well order our own gravestones."

"You don't got yours ordered?" Derian asks. "Better to have shit like that taken care of and not leave it to your grieving mamma."

"Cut the crap and hand over the stripper," Mr. Give-a-Lot-of-Orders-and-Do-Nothing says. "She's seen too much."

"You looking to lose a hand, *stronzo*?" Mario asks.

Oh, I know what *stronzo* means. Bianca uses it a lot. Derian just called the murderous goon an asshole.

"Or worse," Derian says in warning, his voice low. "*Bat chen an tann mèt li.*"

"What the fuck did you just say to me?"

"Literally? Beat the dog, wait for its master. It means that if you touch Ms. Candi, you'll have to deal with Death."

"I'm nobody's dog and your boss is *not* my master," I grouse.

"No offense intended. It's one of my mamma's sayings." He sounds like he thinks that anything his mom says can't be bad.

That kind of reverence for his mother makes him referring to me as a dog owned by a master almost forgivable. Apparently, he didn't mean it literally. It's like one of those old-timey sayings everybody knows the meaning of, but doesn't actually make sense in literal translation.

"Last guy that really pissed our boss off over Ms. Candi ended up with both hands sawed off and choking on his own dick before being tossed in the soup," Mario says with unmistakable approval.

These two don't just revere their mothers, they have some hero worship going on where Angelo is concerned. That shouldn't give them points in my book, but it does.

"Ronnie didn't die," I point out. He lost his hand, but he's still alive.

"That perv didn't piss Angelo off as much as your old boss," Mario offers with way too much candor to be good for me.

He wouldn't be this forthcoming if he and Derian planned to let me go, would he?

Shit. My goose isn't just cooked. It's spit-roasted without lube.

But if Angelo did *that* to the man who tried to force me to start selling my body, he isn't going to be okay with his underlings hurting me either. Will he?

"Death ain't going to do shit when our boss approves the hit." It's Do-Nothing putting his nose in again.

"Our boss is a capo," Freddy says, like that should impress the other men. "Gino's right. He'll approve the collateral hit. You know the rules. We don't leave witnesses."

Gino? Are you kidding me? This jerk's name is the same as my dead boss? Why are all the Gino's I meet assholes? If this one kills me, Angelo will probably disappear him like he did the smarmy ex-assistant-manager that tried to coerce me and Bianca into turning tricks.

That isn't going to miraculously bring me back to life though.

Which is the only thing keeping my hysteria at bay. Derian and Mario aren't going to kill me, but they've got to have some plan for keeping me silent. Probably threatening my family.

A pit forms in my stomach, and I remind myself that life is never perfect. But even if I don't get happy endings, since I'll never say a word to anyone about what I know, my sister and mom are safe.

Me, not so much.

Gino twists a silencer onto his gun, getting ready to follow through on his murderous intentions.

Derian chuckles. "You're just now putting a silencer on your weapon?"

"Death would have our asses for being so sloppy," Mario says.

They think this is funny? I'm about to be murdered and they're making jokes?

"Yeah, well the rest of us don't spend all our time killing. But since you work for Death, you're good at disposing bodies. You can take care of hers." Gino swings the gun toward me like a pointer. "And the cretin here too once we've offed him. Do your part for the family."

The humor disappears like a puff of smoke in a conjurer's trick. We once had a dancer who did magic tricks on stage during her sets. She was popular, because instead of pulling stuff out of a top hat, she pulled it from between her balloon-like breasts.

What is wrong with me? Why am I thinking about Lola when I'm about to lose my life and leave my mom and sister to fend for themselves?

In the short time my brain is off on its tangent, the air around us has gone so icy, I expect my breath to puff in little clouds when I exhale.

"You think the godfather's soldiers need to do more for *la famiglia*?" Derian's voice sounds like it was forged in the depths of hell.

Appropriate for a guy who apparently works for the Angel of Death.

Suddenly there is a gun in Mario's hand, silencer already attached.

The weapon isn't pointed at me though. It's pointed at Gino. Surprised offense washes over his face and I want to gag.

He really thinks he's all that, but seriously?

Angel of Death. Plus godfather. He did the math and came up with his ABCs.

"Ain't nobody in the Genovese *Familia* with more clout than Death except our new fucking don. Miceli De Luca is the only made man in the Family we would even consider listening to about countermanding an order from our boss. And the don would never revoke an order from Death."

"Just because you work for the godfather's pet serial killer doesn't give you any jurisdiction over us," Gino huffs. "Put that fucking gun away before I call my boss."

"Aww, he's going to tell his dad on us," Mario singsongs to Derian. "I'd pit our papà against his any day."

"He's right." Derian pauses long enough for Freddy to relax and a smug smirk to form on Gino's face. "We *are* the best at disappearing bodies. We sure as hell can dispose of these two jamooks."

Freddy takes a wary step away from his cohort, drawing a clear distinction between the two of them.

Not super loyal, but also not stupid.

I'm not part of the mafia, but one thing I've discovered about Angelo is that no one wants to mess with Death.

And lucky me. Even if he doesn't want me the way I want him, Angelo Caruso has me under his protection.

"You're not going to waste your brothers over a piece of stripper tail," Gino announces like he's really not getting the memo.

"That's exotic dancer to you, asshole." Yep, that's my mouth writing checks I don't have the gun, or ability to use it, to cash.

But hey, the guy holding me in what feels like a much less nefarious grip does.

"Shut up, bitch this has nothing to do with you," Gino says snidely. "The men are talking."

Unexpectedly fury boils up inside me at his supercilious attitude. I've dealt with more demeaning jerks than him, but after the last fifteen minutes, his words hit me on the raw.

"Just shoot him already. He's a misogynistic, murdering waste of good Italian tailoring." I may live paycheck to paycheck, but I'm a New York girl, through and through.

I know my designers and that jerk is wearing Armani, or a very good knockoff of it.

Did I really just tell a man to shoot someone else? There must be something in me from my sperm donor's gene pool, because I'm not apologizing.

And I'm for sure not taking it back.

Not that Mario gives me the chance. There's the sound of a loud sneeze and then a dark hole appears in the center of Gino's forehead.

He crumbles to the ground as my heart thuds in shock.

"Why did you do that?" I practically shriek.

"You said to shoot him," Mario says, like *that* matters.

Derian adds, "He called you a bitch."

"So have a hundred other people."

"I wouldn't give their names to Death if you want them to keep breathing," Mario says like that's the rational takeaway from this.

"He's not even here!"

"But we are."

There's nothing to say to that undeniable reality.

Watching our exchange like it's a tennis match, Freddy puts his hands up in surrender. "I didn't say nothing."

"So, it wasn't you that suggested your boss *the capo* could override Death's order of protection on Candi here?" Derian taunts.

"I didn't mean nothing by that. How was I to know that Death put her off-limits?"

"You hang around the club. I've seen you," I say, not willing to just forgive and forget he wanted to kill me.

"I apologize, Candi. I spoke out of turn, and I never should have grabbed you back there."

I must be sick, because I get a thrill out of Freddy's debasement and abject apology. And I feel nothing but relief the other guy is dead.

Gino would have killed me without blinking an eye.

"That a good enough apology, Ms. Candi?" Derian asks.

I glare at Freddy, not sure it is. He wanted to kill me. He *would have* killed me. "You had to know who I am when you chased me down."

"I thought Death was done with you. The way you avoided each other after you took him to the backroom. Piper figures you didn't put out and it pissed him off?" He says it like a question.

As if I'm going to tell him my private business.

Mario swears. "The boss isn't going to like hearing people are speculating Candi's not under his protection anymore."

"I don't think that's going to be a problem after tonight," Derian says.

Because of their rescue of me? It does send a pretty strong message.

"Call your boss and tell him Death takes responsibility for the witness."

Something shivers up my spine at those words. What does it mean when a mafia assassin *takes responsibility for you*? I don't think it means these guys are just going to let me go on my merry way.

Have I jumped straight out of the sizzling frying pan into the gasoline drenched bonfire?

Freddy nods and pulls his cell phone out of his pocket.

"Put it on speaker," Derian orders.

"Yeah no," Freddy shakes his head. "You know it's not safe to use the speaker when talking business."

Mario scoffs, "You weren't worried about being overheard when you were talking about capping Angelo's woman."

Angelo's woman? What the heck is that supposed to mean? His woman who reminds him of someone he wants to protect maybe.

"You're not exactly worried about it yourself."

Derian releases me, but with him and Mario so close, I'm not going anywhere.

He pinches the bridge of his nose and sighs. "The difference is we already reconned this alley for listening devices and cameras earlier tonight."

"That doesn't mean there's nothing at my boss's end," Freddy says, proving he would make the perfect himbo. Pretty to look at but not a lot going on between his ears.

"Do I tell him, or will you?" Mario asks.

But it's kneeling guy who says patronizingly, "What are you? Stupid? Putting your boss on speaker ain't got nothing to do with what gets heard at his end."

Freddy grimaces and I almost feel sorry for him. Except, *willing to kill me.*

"Doesn't matter. Don't mean I want you listening in on my phone call," Freddy says belligerently.

Mario sites Freddy down the barrel of his gun. "Do what Derian says or I shoot you and we make the call."

Freddy glares, but he makes a production of calling his boss and then putting it on speaker while it's dialing.

"Is it done?" a harsh voice asks without saying hello, or anything else.

"Not yet." Freddy pauses. "There's a complication..."

"What kind of complication?" his boss asks in a tone that would make me worried about keeping my job.

In the mafia, I don't think that means just getting fired either.

"Well, first...this broad came out into the alley where we had the mark on his knees, ready to do what you ordered."

"Yeah, so?"

"She overheard too much to let her go." Freddy gives me an apologetic look.

Now he's sorry?

"So, take care of it."

Take care of it. *Kill her*, he means. Jerk.

I cross my arms over my chest and glare around the group of men. "I'm not disposable."

"Is that her? Why the fuck is she still breathing?" his boss demands.

"About that—"

"Let me talk to Gino. He should have been the one to call me."

Freddy tugs at his shirt collar. "Uh, you can't, Mr. Bianchi."

The other man slips into Italian, but I don't care that I can't understand what he's saying. Only one thing registers: the name of the man on the other end of the line. There's only one capo by that name in the Genovese Family.

Stefano Bianchi. The sperm donor.

My biological father.

I tune back into the phone call as Freddy says, "Gino got on the wrong side of Death's crew."

Stefano barks a single word that triggers a torrent of them out of Freddy's mouth.

"Derian and Mario showed up when I was chasing after the strip..." Freddy looks at me. "Dancer. They said we couldn't waste her and Gino didn't like hearing that. He, uh, he called her a bitch and she says, just shoot him already and Mario did."

"Mario shot one of my men?" Stefano asks in shocked fury. "Where?"

"In the alley, boss." Freddy groans, realizing before Stefano starts yelling that wasn't what the capo meant. "In the head. Gino's not coming home tonight."

I expect an explosion, but there are several long seconds of tense silence. I don't know about Freddy, but I can hear Stefano's absolute rage coming through loud and clear in it.

Then Stefano says, "Let me talk to Derian."

Freddy looks around like he's hoping for some kind of deliverance, but there's nothing but the drizzle of Fall rain.

"He can hear you, Mr. Bianchi. I got you on speaker."

The Italian that erupts out of my sperm donor's mouth is too vicious to be anything but a lot of cursing.

"They told me I had to," Freddy whines.

Stefano's Italian is voluble.

"I know who my boss is, but..."

I don't know why Freddy isn't replying in Italian, but at least I'm getting his half of the conversation.

Maybe he understands the language, but is crap at speaking it. I'm that way with Polish because of my mom.

"In the alley behind Pitiful Princess," Freddy says in response to a question from Stefano.

Derian frowns during Stefano's next barked Italian then says, "That won't be necessary Mr. Bianchi. We'll take care of the body."

Stefano speaks again furiously.

"Take it up with Death if you want to give him a proper burial." Derian doesn't sound worried that Mario killed someone who worked for the capo.

"*Qual è il nome del ballerino?*" Stefano asks without addressing Derian's words.

I recognize enough words with my rudimentary Italian to know what he just asked. *What is the name of the woman?*

"My name is Kathleen Brigliano," I say with unexpected emotion in my voice. They are the first words I have ever spoken to my sperm donor. "You knew my mother as Bonbon."

I don't bother giving him her legal name because I doubt he ever cared enough to find out what it was. She was the stripper he fucked, not the love of his life.

Does he even know mine?

I don't know if the fact I carry his blood will carry any weight with him. But right now, *I* need him to know that his goons threatened his daughter's life and that *I* know who *he* is.

Tonight, my father ordered my death. And now he knows that I know he did that. He might not have known it was me he so cavalierly consigned to an early grave, but it's still true. And that matters.

"Bianchi knows your mom?" Mario asks like he knows there's something more to it than what I have said.

"He knew her. She died when I was ten."

"I'm sorry for your loss." Mario's words ring with unexpected sincerity.

"Thank you."

"I didn't...I don't..." The mafia capo's voice is uncertain, his words saying nothing, even if he's speaking English now.

He might not know my name, but he knows I exist. Mommy told him.

Looking directly at Freddy, I say, "Your boss is my sperm donor."

I might be *his* secret, but my existence is not *my* secret to keep.

Freddy blanches. "Fuck me."

"He ordered you to kill me. I think you're in the clear." Do I sound bitter?

I'm not. Would it have been good to have a dad who cared about me? Sure, but despite everything, I'm fine now.

It doesn't make any difference to me if everyone in the Genovese Family knows Stefano Bianchi donated sperm to my existence.

That fact doesn't change the truth he has never been my father.

CHAPTER 13

ANGELO

My smart watch buzzes with a notification from the secure text app designed by Dominic's crew. His hackers are better than anyone the FEDs have on *their* payroll. That means we can communicate freely on it.

Doesn't mean we do. But we could.

The buzz pattern tells me it's Mario or Derian. Both are on Candi's detail tonight and now's the time she heads home from the club. I'd be there to watch over her...hell, I wouldn't have left in the first place, but Severu is meeting with the Godfather of the Night, head of the Greek mafia on the East Coast.

Having two such powerful men in the criminal underworld meeting means next level security. That means I'm here, protecting my godfather's back.

When the Council of Nine meet next year, it's going to be Defcon One level security measures.

Tonight's top secret meeting is more Defcon 3. But as the godfather's top enforcer, there's no way I'm not here. I don't just make sure Severu's orders are carried out; I guarantee his safety.

And still, I surreptitiously flip my wrist over and tap the screen's central biometrics scanner so I can read the message that just came in. Because it's about Candi.

Mario: *Ran into a river.*

When I read those words, I maintain my security vigilance, but tune out the voices of the two men talking.

River is our codeword for moderate trouble. *Flood* means rescue is needed, but even a *stream's* worth of trouble when Mario's texting while on my woman's security detail is too much.

A second text comes in shortly after the first. Part of the app's security is that texts are permanently deleted three seconds after being read or received in the already opened app. So, we keep them short.

Mario: *La Barbarina has bad timing.*

This, I know. Her decision to make a move on me tonight sucked timing wise, no matter how delicious it was. Even if it was safe to let the world see who and what she is to me, there was no way I could skip this meeting.

And once I get my sweet dancer under me, I'm not leaving her until I've slaked us both. That's not going to happen in the backroom of Pitiful Princess in the few hours I had before I needed to be here.

But that dance? Was fire.

She is every bit as skilled as the 18th century Italian ballerina *La Barbarina* and hell of a lot sexier. Which is why it's my codename with my men for her.

Mario: *There's a guy on the course that didn't pay fees to play.*

Mario: *He got caught in a sand trap.*

Some schmuck didn't pay his debt to a Family business and Candi witnessed him getting a beating? Not good.

Mario: *La Barbarina tried to get out of their way so they could play the 18th hole.*

Fuck me. Take not good and give it a shot of steroids. My girl witnessed the start of a hit and tried to run? Why the hell were Capo Bianchi's men planning to execute someone in the alley behind the club though?

You take someone to a black site for shit like that.

If you don't have your own, you take them to The Box. Every Genovese capo has access to the subterranean rooms of the Oscuro building used for interrogations and executions.

Does the capo know his cousin is that stupid?

Mario: *CB's guys want to play her at the 18th hole.*

The fuck they are going to kill my woman.

With a quick hand signal, I bring two of my men to take over my spot at Severu's back. I don't leave the room, but step aside and pull my phone from my pocket.

Death: *You better play the 18th hole with them first.*

Mario: *I got a hole-in-one on the 18th playing against G.*

A head shot, execution style? Nice. But G? Then it clicks. Fucking Gino Bianchi, no less. A leader of one of Capo Stephan Bianchi's collection crews who also happens to be one of his distant cousins.

But the *stronzo* wanted to off my woman? Fuck that. He's lucky he died so easy.

If Mario capped him, he had it coming.

Candi's old boss was a Gino too. I'm never letting another man by that name within breathing distance of her again. Who knows what the next one might try to do to her?

Gino Bianchi got mercy he didn't deserve. If I'd gotten him to my black site, he would have hurt and begged for mercy twenty-four hours for every minute Candi feared for her life before I finally ended his miserable existence.

Threatening my woman's life is a capital offense, but I still need to get the hit sanctioned by Miceli before I can go to her. Especially considering his distant family connection to the capo, not to mention Aria De Luca, Severu and Miceli's mother.

Death: *Other player?*

Mario: *Sitting this round out.*

Not a threat then. If he were, he'd be dead too. Doesn't mean he'll survive the night though.

I hold grudges and everyone in the Family knows I have a protection order on Candi. If they don't, that's their problem and if they act out of that ignorance, then I make it mine.

And my solution for dealing with problems like that isn't quick and it's not merciful.

Death: *Gate-crasher?*

Mario: *Contemplating the sand trap.*

Still alive? That's good. It means Candi didn't actually witness a hit, but things between us just got a lot more complicated. Even with Gino Bianchi's hit sanctioned, she still witnessed a beat down and threat to murder.

Excitement pours through me as I realize the curvy dancer is safer with me than on her own now.

My men are going to bring me the best pre-Halloween treat, the only Candi I want to eat.

My phone buzzes again.

Mario: *CB is La Barbarina's father.*

Mario's shock saturates those five words. Mine matches it. What the ever loving fuck?

How did Candi end up in foster care in the first place and having to dance for a living to support herself and her mom and sister if her dad is a capo in the Genovese Family?

Bianchi is old school, and it's obvious Candi is the result of one of his affairs, but he's still an asshole. You don't abandon family.

That's a lesson my mom didn't learn either. Another thing my perfect woman and I have in common.

Mario: *CB wants his golfer to bring La Barbarina to his private course.*

Like hell that is going to happen. There's only one place Candi is going tonight.

Our new home.

Death: *Take her to the Long Island course.*

Death: *Send men to keep her two caddies in the game.*

I don't trust Bianchi not to use her mom and sister as leverage against her.

Satisfaction fills me that I assigned my top men to watch over Candi when I left the club tonight. I trust all my men, but Derian and Mario don't back down. Not even to a capo.

There's a chain-of-command in the Cosa Nostra. Just like in the military. But you can't run a crew of enforcers when they're afraid of offending someone higher on the food chain than them. Enforcers have to stand outside the chain of command while respecting the one within their team's ranks.

That's how I operated during my years of military service and it kept me and my men alive deep in enemy territory. The same standards make it possible to do my job as Severu's top soldier among *la famiglia*.

My men are taught to do the same. They respect me as their boss and Severu as mine, but they ignore the political jockeying for position among the capos and other high ranking made men.

As it should be.

The men who get caught up in it don't stay on my team.

Even so, Derian and Mario are the least likely among them to let a capo push them around.

CHAPTER 14

CANDI

"Kath?" Stefano's voice is hoarse.

"My friends, call me Candi. You can call me Kathleen if you have to call me anything."

He clears his throat noisily while everyone in the alley stares at me like I flubbed my choreography and ended up on my ass on the stage.

Rolling my eyes, I shrug. "What? You've never seen a stripper whose the illegitimate daughter of one of your capos? Considering how many of them screw around in the backrooms, I find that hard to believe."

"Don't talk about yourself that way," Stefano barks.

"I'm not talking about myself any particular way," I deny. "I'm talking about men like you. I'm not the one with anything to be ashamed about in this scenario."

Regardless of the terminology, I know what I am and I'm not ashamed of it. I'm a stripper. So what? It's an honest way to make a living. At least I don't beat people up and kill them over bad debts for a living.

Mario whistles. "She's got some balls. Talking to a capo like that."

I glare at him. "Doesn't take any extra bravery to tell someone the truth."

"It does when the truth can get you hurt." This from the unhelpful peanut gallery named Freddy.

"Why doesn't anyone admire my courage in standing up to you fuckers?" The guy still kneeling on the ground asks, aggrieved.

"Nobody asked for your opinion." Freddy kicks the guy who falls forward on his face.

I shudder in sympathy.

If I didn't know, he was going to die. I would think that was the worst thing that could happen to him tonight. Despite the street cleaners suddenly coming through here on a regular, the last place I'd want to be right now is face down in the wet muck.

If it's not a stray dog leaving his mark, it's the rats. And don't get me started on people thinking alleys are a great place to piss, or worse, when they don't want to bother looking for a bathroom.

"Bring her here to me," Stefano orders.

"Not going to happen." Derian sounds pretty certain of himself.

I appreciate that he does not want to let Freddy take me away, but I'm not feeling all that positive about what comes next. I'm still a witness. This is still a mafia thing.

"*Lei è mia figlia. Verrà da me.*"

The only word I recognize in Stefano's words is daughter, but the arrogance in his tone is a universal language.

"She may be your biological daughter, but you're not the one who put a protection order on her. That would be my boss. Don't think being a capo will save you from his wrath if you violate it."

"I am not going to harm my daughter," Stefano says in English, exasperation ringing in his tone.

I guess he uses English so I can understand the words. Like that will make me feel all warm and fuzzy toward him. As if. No chance am I letting his henchman take me anywhere.

My mom made the mistake of believing Stefano Bianchi once when he said he would protect me.

I never will.

My past shows just how empty those promises are when uttered by the untrustworthy capo.

But there's a weird sensation in my chest.

After all but ignoring my existence for twenty-four years, Stefano called me daughter for the first time. In both Italian and English.

Whatever is going on in my chest, I refuse to be moved.

"First you order my execution and now you're ordering your goon to kidnap me? That's father of the year stuff right there." I make no effort to tone down the snark.

"I didn't know it was you."

"Is that supposed to make me feel better about the fact that my sperm donor ordered the death of a perfectly innocent person tonight?"

"Hey, I'm innocent too!" Mr. Bad-Debt has righted himself into a sitting position.

Guess his knees were getting sore from kneeling.

Freddy smacks him on the back of the head. "I told you to shut your trap."

Stefano's sigh is heavy. "Bonbon never understood about mafia business either."

"Don't you say her name. You don't have the right. Mommy believed your lies. She thought you were something. But I know the truth."

"Kathleen, you don't understand. You were just a child."

"A kid never once held by her dad. While your sons were living safe in your mansion on Long Island, mom was turning tricks in the backroom to keep us in a single room, rat infested building. She was there for me. She took care of me."

"Kathleen," he says sharply, like he has the right to reprimand me.

I ignore the interruption. "But you?" I ask with all the disgust I feel. "You're nothing, Stefano Bianchi. You were nothing but a john sloppy with the condoms. And you are nothing, *nothing*," I repeat with fervor. "Nothing to me."

"Did I say balls?" Mario asks, his tone filled with awe. "That's pure pussy power right there."

"What's that supposed to mean?" I demand. Is he calling me a bitch?

Derian says, "Balls can only make babies. Pussies can push them out into the world."

"Yeah. Balls? They're the weakest spot on a guy's body. Pussies are tough as hell," Mario adds.

"Shit, I never thought of that," Freddy says.

"Enough!" Stefano barks. "If you mention my daughter's pussy again, I'll cut your tongues out."

"They weren't talking about my ladybits, they were complimenting me on my strength. Keep up."

Mario licks the tip of his glove covered finger and makes a sizzle sound. "Tsss..."

Done with this conversation and ready for this night to be over, I turn to Derian. "As fun as this is, I need to get home. Can I go now?"

I don't assume I can just leave. I figure there's at least one round of threats about keeping my lips zipped before they'll let me go.

There is a glimmer of something that looks like pity in the made man's eyes. "You know that's not going to happen."

"You said you wouldn't hurt me," I remind him.

"We are not going to hurt you. We're going to keep you safe." As improbable as it should be, the voice of the man who just murdered one of his cohorts rings with truth.

Derian and Mario are *not* going to hurt me. At all. And sometime during the conversation with Stefano, Derian's hold on me relaxed. He's growing complacent, thinking I'm not going anywhere.

Because I'm talking to them like all of this is normal?

Too bad for him, my guard hasn't dropped once. Taking advantage of the loosened hold, I launch forward with the strength of my dancer's legs and sprint toward the mouth of the alley again.

"Hey!" Mario's voice rings after me.

Derian doesn't say anything, but I know it's the sound of his shoes hitting pavement behind me. I increase the length of my strides, running as fast as I can. I'm a dancer. Every muscle in my body is strong, but my core and legs are next level.

I can *pas de bourrée couru* across a stage in seconds. Using a longer stride, I'm even faster as I speed toward the street.

Unfortunately, apparently, made men trained to be on Angelo's crew are also fast. The sound of Derian's feet getting closer spurs me into a burst of even more speed. My foot hits the pavement of the sidewalk just as a hard arm comes around my stomach.

If I had the core muscles of a regular person, his hold and my momentum would knock the wind out of me. I don't. It doesn't. And I scream as loud as I can.

Not a single head of the early morning revelers turns toward me. One man dressed as a ghoul veers into the street to avoid walking near me.

Derian's not going to hurt me, but I'm not under the same compunction when it comes to him. I send an elbow straight into his side and swing my legs forward to gain momentum before kicking backward.

I hit his shins so hard with the heel of my tennis shoes, pain jars up my own legs.

"Fuck," he grunts.

But he doesn't let me go. I don't give up. I throw my head back, trying to connect with his chin. Anticipating the move, he shuffles me downward by shifting his hold on me to his other arm across my collarbone.

His fingertips dig into my shoulder as my head connects harmlessly with his chest. Harmless to him. Pain radiates through the back of my head.

"Stop that. You're going to hurt yourself."

"Let me go!" This time when I yell, a group of people turn their heads.

"You okay, lady?" a youthful voice asks.

"Say yes if you don't want that kid and his friends to end up collateral damage," Derian says in a tone that sends chills through me.

Damn it. No way am I going to let that happen. And somehow my kidnapper knows it.

"I'm fine," I yell. "My boyfriend is an asshole, but he won't hurt me."

"Fuck, don't call me your boyfriend."

"You don't want to be known as a stripper's boyfriend, don't try to kidnap one."

"What I don't want is to die," he says fervently.

"Right, as if being my boyfriend is a terminal disease."

"Trust me, it would be. Death cut off the hand of a man who touched you. What do you think he would do to a man claiming you?"

"Claiming me? What are we, living in the Middle Ages? Nobody is claiming me."

"I wouldn't count on that."

"You can count on something. If you don't let me go, I'm going to maim you." It's an empty threat, because cutting off limbs is not my thing.

But to give credence to my words, I dig my long, pointed fingernails into the skin of his wrist.

"Fuck. I'd let you go if I could. Trust me on that." He spins us around and heads back into the alley. "Get the duct tape, Mario. "

Terror rushes through me. They might have an aversion to hurting me, but there's a lot of ways to cause me harm without physically hurting me.

And being helpless to prevent those things is so not on my agenda tonight.

"Don't you dare," I shout at Mario.

"Hey, I've got some right here." Again, help from the peanut gallery that can just keep his mouth darn mouth shut.

Freddy.

I'm going to tell Piper to cut him off.

The asshole.

The tape glints dully silver in the illumination cast by the streetlights.

Our alley is one of the few in the city that has them. I always assumed that was because the club was owned by the mafia, but they didn't get installed until early this year.

Mario unrolls several inches from the roll and then holding it up at both ends, approaches me.

"Help, I'm being kidnapped. Call 911." Shouting those words over and over again at the top of my lungs, I thrash wildly, kicking and hitting with everything in me.

I believe Derian will kill witnesses, but someone can call the cops without showing their face in the alley.

"There's a dead guy here, shot by one of my kidnappers!" Murder might elicit more help than a kidnapping.

Derian's hand clamps over my mouth as he manages to trap my flailing limbs against my sides with his other arm. "Hurry the fuck up, Mario."

When Mario tries to grab my legs, I kick him in the face and he staggers back. Score one for the power of a dancer's quads.

Freddy jumps into the fray, grabbing one of my ankles with both his hands and forcing it toward the other one that Mario is now keeping immobile. Once Freddy is hugging my lower calves, the only movement I can manage is tipping my pelvis.

"Keep your face away from her body if you want to keep the eyes in your head," Mario growls at Derian, who immediately turns his head aside.

I would roll my eyes at the ridiculousness, but I'm too angry. I squirm, making it as hard as I can for Mario to get the tape around my thighs. He doesn't just wrap it once either. He takes the roll around again and again, going down several inches and making it impossible to break the restraint.

Even for a woman with the strength in her upper legs that I have.

"Move your hold. I need to get her ankles," the kidnapping jerk tells Freddy.

Freddy obeys and I take immediate advantage, kicking out with my lower legs. My knees can still bend, but there's not enough power behind the blow to do any damage.

Mario doesn't even grunt.

"Make sure the tape doesn't touch skin," Derian instructs while keeping my arms pinned and my mouth covered.

I bite him like I did Freddy, but unlike the younger man, even drawing blood doesn't make Derian move his hand away.

"You're something else, Ms. Candi. I don't know if I envy the boss, or feel sorry for him."

If Angelo is the reason this is happening to me, he should definitely feel sorry for the other man because I'm going to steal one of his knives and stab him with it.

Mario straightens after giving my calves the same treatment as my thighs. But not even a millimeter of the duct tape reaches past the hem on my jeans to press against bare skin.

"We need to gag her next," Derian mutters. "She's proving to be some kind of cannibal."

"She bite you too?" Freddy asks with glee. "Hurt like a bitch when she did it to me."

Derian doesn't answer, but blood from his wound is making his hand slick on my face and I'm able to yank my head to the side. "Serves you both right. I hope your hands get infected and fall off."

"Yeah, you better get the bites disinfected. The human mouth has more than six billion bacteria," Mario says. "Some scientists estimate it's as high as twenty billion."

"You been watching the science channel again?" Derian's hand drops away from my face since I'm not screaming.

Mario shrugs. "It's interesting." He looks at Freddy. "Give me your tie."

Neither he, nor Derian, is wearing one. Mario is dressed like how you think a mafioso would, in a suit and shiny dress shoes. But the guys that work for Angelo both wear clothes I wouldn't be surprised to see on soldiers in a dark ops unit.

Yes, I watch television too. Not the science channel, like Mario, but I learn things.

"What about me?" The metallic taste of blood makes me feel nauseous. "I've got both Mario and Derian's blood in my mouth. I'm going to have to do a full course of doxy-PEP."

"Shit. Death ain't going to like that," Mario mutters, reaching toward me with the tie.

I rear my head back.

"Wait," Derian orders. "You got a clean pocket square on you?"

Mario nods. "Course I do. I was raised just like you were."

"You guys carry handkerchiefs?" Freddy asks mockingly. "What kind of mamma's boys are you fuckers?"

"The kind that can kneecap you here in the alley and leave you for the rats to find." Suddenly the hand that isn't holding his crisp white handkerchief is filled with a gun already tipped with a silencer.

Is that the one he shot Gino with? Must be. He's not going to carry around two guns with silencers on them, is he?

The thoughts are bouncing around my brain like ping pong balls at a national tournament.

"Put that away and use your kerchief as a barrier between Ms. Candi's mouth and the tie. Who knows the last time he washed it?"

"Hey, I'm not a slob. I get my ties cleaned whenever I spill somethin' on 'em."

"Yeah, you're real fastidious," Derian mocks. "Death don't want your dirty neck sweat in Ms. Candi's mouth."

I would laugh at the ridiculous exchange, but I'm too busy trying to avoid Mario's attempt to gag me, my jaw locked tight and my lips sealed.

"Don't make it so tight that it hurts her," Derian orders.

"You don't gotta tell me not to hurt her. I like my hands where they are just fine."

"You don't have to do this," I say in desperation, my head turning side to side to avoid Mario's questing hands. "I won't tell anyone. I promise on my mom and sister's lives. Just let me go home."

"Don't worry about your ma and sis," Mario says. "They're being watched over too. Death ain't going to let harm come to them."

At the thought of my mom and sister being *watched over* by the mafia, I scream with frustration.

The second the pad of clean cotton pushes into my mouth, I regret giving into my anger.

"Hurry up, Mario. If someone calls the cops, that's going to be another headache we don't need tonight." Derian doesn't sound worried. Just annoyed.

Mario quickly fixes my gag in place with Freddy's tie. When I smell the sweat Derian mentioned, I'm glad Mario put the clean handkerchief in first. Not that I'm going to thank either of them for it.

Once I get free, I'm going to show them something and it isn't going to be my gratitude.

Now that I'm gagged, Derian pulls the sleeves of my oversized hoodie down over my hands and then crosses the left over the right and tapes them to my body like a straitjacket.

Unlike a straitjacket, the armholes on my hoodie are large enough to pull my arms out of without unzipping it. Not sure what that will buy me, though.

But knowing I'm not completely trapped helps keep a total meltdown at bay.

Mario tosses the roll of duct tape to Freddy, who immediately binds the bad debtor's hands behind his back. When the guy starts yelling, Freddy slaps a piece of duct tape over his mouth.

That's going to hurt coming off.

But probably not as much as whatever else Freddy and my father have planned for him tonight.

"I'll get the car." Freddy trots off, leaving his prisoner on the ground.

"Bring the SUV around," Derian tells Mario. "After all the screaming, it's just asking for trouble taking her out on the street."

Mario salutes Derian and disappears out of the mouth of the alley.

Never mind that I'm covered with enough duct tape to make me look like a silver mummy, it's my screaming they're worried about. Any other night, the tape would be a giant attention-drawing red flag, but with so many people dressed up for the Halloween parties happening tonight? Not so much.

It feels like only a few seconds have passed before I hear the purr of an SUV coming down the alley.

Derian's hold on me keeps be upright and at his side, facing away from the street. Surprised by the lack of light, I turn my head to see the SUV backing toward us, the backup lights casting a dim glow along the wet pavement.

Once the SUV stops, even those disappear. When the liftgate begins to rise, no interior lights show either.

A dark shape hops out of the driver's side and trots to the back and leans inside the opening. Derian carries me to the passenger side and puts me in the back seat of the SUV, using the seatbelt to trap me in place.

As soon as he shuts the door, I start wiggling my arms upward, stretching the hoodie fabric until, my arms are free of the sleeves and I can unzip it from the inside. Tearing Freddy's tie off, I throw it on the seat and spit out the handkerchief already wet with my saliva.

Gross.

I start working on my legs, but it only takes a few seconds to realize there are too many layers of duct tape stuck on each other to rip it. I'm still searching for the start to peel it away when the door on the driver's side opens.

"Shit! She's loose, Derian!"

This time when they truss me up, they do something with the tape that makes it impossible for me to get my arms out.

"Don't start screaming and we'll leave the gag off," Derian says.

Glaring, I refuse to answer, but I don't start shouting either. They're being careful not to hurt me, but they're also determined not to let me go.

Having the ability to call for help if I get the opportunity is my only chance at getting away. It might be slim odds, but I'm not giving them up.

I occupy myself watching two professional killers clean up the scene of their crime. Mario snaps open a body bag and lays it beside Gino, rolling the dead man into it with quick efficiency.

"Get your spent bullet so we can toss it in with the body," Derian instructs as bright headlights illuminate the alley.

Freddy is back.

"Bet you fifty I can find my brass in less than fifteen seconds," Mario says to me with a wink, proving he and probably Derian too, is aware I'm watching them.

My witness to the mob's crimes status just keeps getting more and more pronounced.

Derian shakes his head. "Don't take that bet, Miz Candi. You'll lose your fifty."

Despite the conditions in the alley, I don't doubt Derian's words.

"No bet," I mutter.

More bright headlights illuminate the alley, and I whip my head around to see a car pull to a stop close to the front bumper of the SUV.

Freddy leaves the headlights glowing when he jumps out of the car.

I'm not surprised when Derian barks, "Turn off the lights and leave the car running."

Freddy obeys without arguing. When he comes around the back of the SUV, Mario repeats his offer of a bet to the younger made man.

Freddy stares at him and laughs. "I'll take that bet. This alley is full of crap and without the Merc's headlights it's too dark."

"To be that young and naïve again," Derian says with fake sorrow.

Mario turns on a high-powered pen light and walks forward in a straight line without looking to the left or right.

Five seconds later, he bends down and picks something up, then holds it open palm out toward Freddy. "Got it."

"Impossible!" Freddy squawks. "No way is that your bullet."

Mario shines his penlight onto his palm, where a smashed piece of metal gleams dully. "I know my bullet trajectories."

"Gross," I mutter. "There's blood and brain matter on that."

I can't believe he just picked it up like that doesn't matter.

Who am I kidding? These guys probably touch brain matter and blood on a regular basis. But it's still gross.

At least he's wearing gloves.

Mario shrugs. "If I left it behind, Death would cut off my hand just for being stupid."

"You realize it's not normal to talk about your boss cutting off people's hands, don't you?" I snark, squirming in my seat in silent protest.

Mario shrugs. "It is for us."

"Yeah, I don't envy you working for Death. " Freddy sounds entirely sincere in that sentiment.

"Open your trunk," Derian orders my father's soldier.

Looking relieved, Freddy is quick to obey. "Thanks for letting me take Gino back to the boss."

"You're taking him and your bad debtor over there to The Box."

"The Box?" Freddy asks with alarm. "Why?"

"Because our boss said to and unless you want to get on his bad side, you'll listen to him."

"But Mr. Bianchi will kill me."

"Nah. He already lost one guy tonight," Mario says consolingly. "He's not going to fire you."

"There's a lot he can do to me to make me regret disobeying him," Freddy replies.

"Yeah, but do you really think it's worse than what Death will do?"

CHAPTER 15

ANGELO

A n electric current of anticipation buzzes under my skin.

She's going to be here soon.

My forever starts tonight. Ahead of schedule, but that can't be helped. Candi witnessed something she shouldn't and now she's more at risk away from me than with me.

I've had fun with our courtship, but the darkness inside me that's drawn to her light is fucking glad.

I've already doubled security on the property and the number of men watching her mom and sister's apartment. We'll move them to the mansion soon, but waking my future mother-in-law in the middle of the night to drag her out of her home doesn't seem like the way to start our relationship off right.

Mario: *Three minutes out. Warning. La Barbarina is pissed at how the game is playing out.*

A grin pulls at my lips.

My little dancer is angry. Not afraid. Angry.

So perfect for me.

Forcing myself to wait in the living room for her arrival, I stand at the window, tossing my knife high, catching it and then walking it over my fingers before flipping it over my thumb and doing it all over again. I've done this so many times, I don't have to look at my knife anymore.

I've only been home for a few minutes because I was in Manhattan too, but I keep my eyes fixed on the frustratingly empty drive.

My leg muscles tense with the need to pace, but I remain in place, my only movement the small flicks of my hand manipulating my knife.

Finally, the gates begin to slide open and then Derian pulls through in his SUV. It takes both him and Mario to get her out of the truck even though she's wrapped in what looks like half a roll of duct tape.

Her mouth is moving, but the double pained bullet resistant glass doesn't allow sound through. They disappear through the front door and I turn away from the window, walking rapidly across the living room to the partially open door.

I hear her before I see her.

"Put me down, you overgrown ape!" That's not mere anger; that's pure fury in her dulcet tones.

Interesting.

My men's voices aren't loud enough to make out individual words, but their placating tones can't be missed.

When they're right outside the door, I hear Mario. "She wasn't this mouthy in the car."

"That was before she managed to get her gag off the second time," Derian says.

Frazzled is a new tone for him.

Mario grunts. "At least she didn't get the jacket off after we retaped it."

"You two can admire my Houdini-like skills another time," Candi says acerbically. "You need to let me go!"

"No can do." Mario says with exaggerated patience, like that's not the first time he's had to say the words.

"You know this isn't necessary, damn it. I won't go to the cops." Pleading bleeds into her tone.

I don't like it. Candi should never feel the need to beg.

"Sure, Ms. Candi, I believe you, but will your dad?" Derian asks.

"Don't call him that. He's not a father to me, much less a dad." The pain I hear in her voice bothers me more than the near begging.

Should I kill Stefano Bianchi? His neglect hurt Candi and for that, he has to pay. With his life?

The judge is still deliberating on that one. The judge being me. Killing a capo in my own Family isn't something even I treat lightly.

And there's the small chance it would upset Candi. She may profess to despise him, but she's got a tender heart. Too tender to leave to the mercies of a man like Stefano Bianchi.

"You're safer with us." Mario's long-suffering tone says he's repeated *this* more than once too.

Her scoff is loud. "Right. You've got me wrapped up in duct tape like a mummy, taken me on a long ride out of the City against my will. I thought you were going to kill me and dump the body," she complains.

"We don't dump bodies on Long Island," Derian informs her.

The sound of frustration Candi makes sends a zing of arousal straight to my cock.

"You brought me here against my will, which is called kidnapping by the way—"

"My men didn't kidnap you." I step into the hall, cutting her off before she can launch into another tirade. "They brought you home."

Candi's sulfuric glare zeros in on me. Her usually smooth and shiny long brown hair is in a mess of snarls around her head. A smear of dried blood taints her chin. I pull a sanitizing wipe from my pocket and tear the small foil packet open.

"You should not have left blood on her skin." I gently rub away the dried blood with the alcohol pad.

Mario texted me that she bit both Freddy and Derian. Which made me proud, but I've got a course of doxy-PEP ready for her. Lucky for her we keep it on hand. Blood borne pathogens are a risk in our line of work. No matter how careful you are, sometimes blood spray gets into your mouth or eyes.

Our protocols for dealing with that when it happens means Derian's not going to give her anything, but I don't know what kind of safety procedures Bianchi's soldiers are supposed to adhere to.

Even if I did, I wouldn't trust them. Not when he runs such a sloppy crew. She wouldn't have witnessed anything if they'd been doing their job right.

"This swanky mansion on Long Island is not my home."

"It is now." Maybe I could have broken that more gently.

My poor dancer's face turns red as a tomato and a wordless scream of frustration erupts from her beautiful lips. Doubling her efforts to get out of my men's hold, she squirms like a fish on a hook.

"I don't care if you're the world's best assassin," she yells at me. "I'm not letting you keep me here, away from my family."

I give Derian a look meant to warn. With the way her legs are taped together, and her hoodie has been turned into a straitjacket, even her dancer's balance won't keep her upright if they let her go. And if she falls, Candi won't be the only one pissed.

Showing why they are number one and number two on my crew, Derian and Mario keep their hold on Candi without touching any part of her skin.

The duct tape wrapping job is more evidence of their superior thinking skills. There's no way she's getting out of the bonds, but no rough ropes or zip ties are rubbing against her tender flesh either.

I step forward and lift the squirming woman into my arms. Derian and Mario release her with clear relief.

With a heave backward, she tries to throw herself away from me.

I have to grab her close to stop her from falling to the marble tiled floor. She feels so right in my arms, I close my eyes to savor the moment.

Finally.

Leaning down, I inhale deeply and saturate my olfactory senses with her delicious scent. Spiced by the sweat of her efforts to get away tonight, it sends arousal roaring through me.

"Let me go." Her words are a plea entirely different than the one she made to my men.

My cock hardens painfully.

She tries to twist away again, straining her bound muscles.

"Stop that." I squeeze her more tightly to me. "You're going to fall and give yourself a skull fracture."

Should we have carpeting in here? I'll ask what she thinks when she's in a better mood.

A sound comes out of her a lot like the one my nonna's old fashioned kettle use to make when it came to a boil on the stovetop. "Someone is going to end up with a skull fracture and it's not going to be me. Let. Me. Go!"

"*Di m kisa ou renmen, ma di ou ki moun ou ye.*" Derian gives Candi a look of respect, his words echoing in my head. *Tell me who you love, and I'll tell you who you are.* "You keep her, boss. She's as strong as my mamma, that one."

Without acknowledging Derian's words because of course I'm keeping her, I look at Mario. "Her phone."

He pulls it out of his pocket and offers it to me. "Here you go, boss."

I release Candi's legs and put my arm around her middle, with her facing away from me so I have a free hand to take the phone. She immediately starts trying to kick me with her heels and gets more than one solid hit in before I manage to get the phone into my own pocket.

Regretting not putting her in a fireman's hold to begin with, I rectify my mistake and dismiss my men with an inclination of my head.

Enjoying Candi's inventive invective and threats, I carry her into the room I just came out of.

Give my entire arsenal of weapons to the gun buyback program? My woman knows how to hit where it hurts. The fact that her threat shows how well she knows me warms me.

Ignoring threats and insults, I reluctantly let her go to set her on the couch closest to the fireplace. "A hoodie is not a warm enough jacket for this weather."

Reaching over, I press a hidden button in the wall near the mantle and the gas fire springs to life. Warm air gently blows from the vent at the bottom and I shift the ottoman so that when I sit down to face Candi, I'm not blocking it from reaching her.

"It's not winter yet." She squirms into a more upright position. "What business is it of yours what kind of jacket I wear anyway?"

She's not ready for an honest answer to that question, so I shrug. "Just stating an opinion."

"Well, keep your opinions to yourself. You're not my parent and even if you were, I'm years past being a child."

Grazie a Dio. The thoughts I have about her are not remotely kid friendly.

Candi squeezes her eyes shut and scrunches up her face. "I can't believe I'm talking about clothes with my kidnapper."

"I'm not your kidnapper."

Her eyes pop open again, filled with ire. "What would you call it?"

"I'm your man." Keeping the truth back isn't doing her any favors.

"You should talk to your doctor about getting meds for those delusions of yours."

"It is fact, not fantasy." If any other man tries to claim her, he will die.

"You can't be *my* man! We aren't dating. Before tonight we'd spoken maybe two sentences to each other."

"I've spent several nights a week with you for the past year, I'd say that constitutes dating." That's more time than I spend with any other person.

She stares at me like I've lost the plot. "You came to my club to conduct your mafia business while I danced. That's *not* a date."

"I wasn't there for business." That the darkened VIP section is a good place to get certain things done is inconsequential. "I was there for you."

"Well, I wasn't there for you." A flicker in her pretty brown eyes says something about that is a lie.

"Weren't you?" I push.

Heat darkens her cheeks again, but it feels more like embarrassment than anger. What does she have to be embarrassed about?

"I was working. You were working. *Not a date*," she emphasizes.

"You want romance?" Can I do romance? For Candi, I can try.

"From my stalker-slash-kidnapper? I don't think so!" She wriggles against her bonds.

My girl's not a quitter.

"I watch over you."

CHAPTER 16

ANGELO

"That's the definition of stalking," she gripes then narrows her eyes in thought. "A year, really?"

"What can I say?" My fingers ache with the need to touch her, but I hold myself back. She needs time to adjust. "It was love at first sight."

They say sociopaths latch on quickly when it comes to finding that special someone and she's definitely mine.

"That's a myth."

"Agree to disagree." I wink at her.

"Well, if you really did love me, I definitely wouldn't be trussed up like this," she accuses.

While I disagree, that's easy enough to fix. "Do you want me to remove your bindings?"

"Of course I do!" The look she gives me questions my intelligence.

It's not an expression I'm used to having directed at me. No one else would dare. But Candi can dare anything she wants with me.

I pull out my knife, flipping it into the air and catching it with the forward edge up. "Your wish is my command, *amate*."

"What are you doing?" She rears backward, but she's against the couch with nowhere to go.

I position my knife to slice through the denim and tape on her right pantleg. "What I said I would. Now stay still."

"Just cut through the tape where it holds my legs together. Or unwind it, or something!"

"I will always endeavor to give you what you want," I promise her. "How I give it to you..." I shrug.

"You're going to cut me!"

"I won't." Tossing my knife, I keep my gaze locked to hers, catching it in an icepick grip, before launching it into the air again. "I'm very good with knives."

She gasps. "Stop that. You're going to drop it and one of us is going to end up bleeding."

"Never happen," I scoff. My knife is an extension of my hand at this point.

Sometimes I don't even realize I have it out until someone says something.

"Yeah, well, stop it anyway."

I catch my knife and keep it in my hand this time. Look at me listening to her express her needs. The book I read on building strong relationships said that's an important trait in a good partner.

Giving time is another. I definitely give her that. If I'm not with her in the club, I'm watching her on the cameras I installed in her apartment.

I've got this boyfriend thing in the bag.

"You're going to ruin my jeans," she gripes, her brows puckered adorably. "I've only got two pairs baggy enough to wear on the subway."

I make a point of looking at the amount of duct tape wrapped around them and then back at her.

"Don't give me that look," she mutters. "You could peel the tape away." She huffs out a sigh. "At least you could try."

I start slicing up the pantleg, the denim and duct tape giving way to my knife's sharp blade with ease. "Waste of time."

"And you would know that how?"

"In my line of work, there are many situations that duct tape is preferable to zip ties."

The longer the tape stays against fabric, the more residue it leaves behind. Warm conditions only make it worse. Since Candi is not shivering, I assume her ride in the SUV wasn't a cold one.

"Your work as an assassin?" Curiosity eclipses her anger for a second. She's wants to get to know me.

That deserves a reward, so I answer the question with a nod. Some made men hide their mafia lives from their wives. I will never be one of them.

Reaching the top of her thigh, I hold my knife between my teeth so I have both hands to maneuver Candi onto her back.

She squeaks—again adorable—but doesn't fight me.

"You're doing a good job of not moving," I praise her as I finish cutting the denim over her pelvis.

"What are you doing now?" Her voice is sharp, but she doesn't move.

I hum with approval at her self-control. "Finishing what you asked me to do."

My knife cuts through the waistband of her jeans and the denim falls to one side.

"Well, one leg is free anyway." She lifts said leg, bending and stretching it.

Mesmerized by what I can see of her beautiful flesh, as I always am, I forget momentarily about the other leg. But when she tries to sit up, I remember.

"Stay there. I still have the other one to do before your legs are free."

"You could have started with my hoodie, and I could have removed my jeans myself," she grouses. "Didn't they teach you anything about efficiency in Made Man school?"

I smile at her little joke, that's truer than she knows. Half the men in our ranks trained as soldiers in one branch of the military or other. Only a few went into Special Forces like me, but the mafia has a long tradition of getting Uncle Sam to pay for our soldier's weapons and hand-to-hand combat training.

And smart leaders like Severu and his father before him, add to that training. It's not called made man school, but it amounts to the same thing.

"Well, get on with it," she grouses.

"Shh. Don't rush me." Running my hand down her still denim clad leg, I say, "I'm enjoying unwrapping my gift."

"Your goons might have taped me up like a package, but I'm *not* your present," she huffs. "Anyway, it's almost Halloween, not Christmas."

I cock my head to one side in thought and nod in agreement. "You in our home for the first time is the best Halloween treat ever."

"Spare me the Candi for Halloween jokes. Besides, it's not Halloween yet."

Technically, she may be right. It's the early hours of the morning of the 27th, but that doesn't make her presence any less of a treat.

"You're cute when you're grumpy." I finish cutting through her left pantleg and waistband.

"I'm not grumpy, I'm furious." Her scowl has a definite pout cast to it though. "And it's not cute."

Tapping her nose, because I can't help myself, I say what I've been thinking since she started her Grumpy Cat routine, "Adorable then."

Her body tenses and I slam my hands down onto her thighs just in time to stop her from doing me damage with a well-aimed knee. "None of that now. You want me to remove the rest of your bindings, don't you, *piccola gatta?*"

My spitting little cat.

She honest-to-god hisses, but subsides. "Yes."

Plans for my demise burn brightly in her eyes while she waits for me to cut her hoodie off of her.

Lightness bubbles through the dark haze of need for violence that is my constant companion, dissipating it so much I can feel an emotion I have only recently become familiar with.

Delight.

Since that first night I watched Candi dance, I have learned what it means to feel both that. And joy.

Thinking about her warms the cold places in my soul, but I only ever feel actual joy and fucking delight when we are together.

I pull the jeans away from her body, bemused by what I find underneath them. I thought the shorts were a kind of underwear. But there's no waistband I can see.

"Stop staring at my bodysuit."

"But how do you go to the bathroom?" The black Lycra that covers the tops of her thighs and goes up her torso under her t-shirt and hoodie has no access for that basic function.

"I don't need to pee on the train and I take it off when I get home."

My combat readiness trained mind puts the pieces together instantly. And the reason for her wearing the bodysuit fills me with fury.

"If someone attacked me, they couldn't just yank my jeans off and..." She pauses before finally saying. "Hurt me."

By hurt she means force penetrative sex on her. Rape.

But wearing her bodysuit means an attacker would have to completely undress her to do it. Which takes time a lot of opportunists wouldn't risk. Unless the asshole had a knife to cut access.

Just the thought of anyone pulling a knife on her in threat makes a red haze of rage cloud my vision.

Cazzo. "That never would have happened," I grit out. "My men have been watching over you when I can't since the first night I saw you."

"Well, I didn't know that, did I? And also, you do realize how creepy that sounds, don't you?"

"Being protected is not creepy." It's necessary, especially in our world.

Whether she realizes it, or not. Though the bodysuit she wears under her clothes says she's very aware of the danger she faces on the streets of New York.

Knowing why she feels a particular need to protect herself like that ratchets my fury up to homicidal levels. If her former foster father wasn't already dead, I would have killed him the minute I found out what happened.

"Uh, you look angry." For the first time tonight, I hear fear in Candi's voice.

That snaps my focus back into place faster than anything else could. "My wrath is for anyone who would try to harm you, Candi. *I* never will."

"Me being here against my will says otherwise." One perfectly sculpted brow lifts in challenge.

I shrug. "Circumstances did not allow me to woo you as I planned."

"Woo? What am I, a Victorian maiden?"

"If you were, I'd be in trouble. I'm no one's idea of a gentleman." Not even by modern standards.

"Yeah, well, guys who consider themselves gentlemen sat by and did nothing when Ronnie tried to use my body to get off."

CHAPTER 17

CANDI

Angelo goes still above me, the rage he just banked back to burning in his eyes like the infernos of hell.

Only now, I know it's not directed at me.

"That's what he was doing?" he asks in a deadly quiet tone.

"Uh, yeah." He couldn't tell? "Why did you come tearing across the club to rescue me if you didn't know he was doing that?"

"He was touching you. They're not allowed to touch."

They're not allowed to touch. They who? The punters. Who else could it be?

That should freak me out, right? Why don't those words freak me out?

Another question: why aren't I more scared?

Do I really believe a man who has been *stalking* me for *a year* and who has cut off men's hands for touching me won't ever turn that level of crazy on me?

The truth is this whole night, I should have been a lot more afraid than I have been. Yes, I had a few bad moments when Freddy was chasing me in the alley, but mostly? I've been frustrated and angry.

Angelo's guys kidnapped me. That, at the very least, should have terrified me. They taped me up, completely taking away my freedom.

It should have triggered memories I've spent every day since coming to live with Cookie and mom trying to forget. But it didn't. It just made me mad.

Once I got my gag off, I yelled at them like they were inept busboys spilling drinks on my stage.

Then he was there and instead of reacting in any kind of way that made sense, my ladybits, which apparently did *not* get the memo about being kidnapped, started dancing to a club techno beat.

He took me in his arms and the most ridiculous sense of peace washed over me. Go me for hiding it from him, but seriously? Even now, I'm lying here on the sofa, letting him cut my clothes off like a little lamb happy to be sheered for spring.

Okay, I really need to stop watching documentaries about rural America.

A little lamb? Really?

I can't even work up a real sense of dread as he slices through the fabric of my hoodie and the umpteen layers of duct tape Derian and Mario had to use to immobilize me.

I'm a little proud of that. Also? I don't mind how relieved they were when Angelo showed up.

That'll teach them to kidnap a former foster kid. We're tough.

But something's gone wonky with the instincts for survival honed in the foster care system. I don't feel threatened by Angelo. Him calling this place *our* home just feels too ridiculous to take seriously.

Whatever his plans are for tonight – and it's looking like some kind of weird role play where we actually have a relationship – come tomorrow, I'll be back in the small apartment I share with mom and Cookie.

One good thing will come from this unbelievable night. I'll get Angelo Caruso out of my system. Being kidnapped on his behalf is bound to curtail my fascination with him. Right?

If I'm lucky (and he is too), I'll finally punch my V card too. Yes, I am seriously considering having sex with the unhinged mafioso.

Not that I'm going to make it easy on him. Whatever weird fantasy he's got playing in his head, having his guys kidnap me is not okay. Even if they did save me from becoming collateral damage to my sperm donor's mafia business.

"This is so not okay," I say out loud both for his benefit and mine. "Listen Angelo, you can't go around kidnapping women."

"I am not attached to women. I am attached to you." He finishes the last cut on my hoodie with a flourish and pulls the now tattered garment from my body.

I push him away and surprisingly, he goes. Not far, but he sits on the sofa beside me instead of hovering over me.

Scooting into a sitting position, I roll my eyes with well-honed sarcasm. "Lucky me."

If part of my brain actually believes the words I just uttered and maybe even a little bit of my heart, I'm not about to admit it. That my inner romantic preens under the attention of this dangerous man says more about my psychopathy than his.

"You're going to have to let me go back home." Eventually.

After—my thoughts are interrupted by a jaw cracking yawn, tonight's adrenaline starting to wear off.

He leans forward, earnestness in every line of his superbly sculpted made man body. "This is your home."

"I'm pretty sure it's not. My home is an apartment in Queens with my mom and sister."

"That was your home," he dismisses. "Now you live here."

Does he really think it works like that? He can just say it is true and suddenly it is? Probably in his world stuff *does* work that way. Who is going to argue with Death?

But I'm not part of his world.

I'm just a normal person and I don't live in a mansion with enough security to protect the president. "You can't make that decision for me. Where I live is my choice."

It has been since I turned eighteen and the state foster care system lost authority to tell me where I could live. No one, not even Death, can take me away from my family.

"We belong together. If you can't see that right now, I'll help you." Angelo's tone is so freaking complacent.

"That." I shake my finger at him. "That right there, Angelo. Saying that is *not okay*. You can't convince me that I belong with you as if it's a done deal."

"You are the soul that was ripped from me at birth."

"Don't say stuff like that." Because it touches my heart in places I was sure atrophied a long time ago.

He grabs my hand and pulls it to his lips, kissing my palm. "There's no light inside of me, but when I am with you, your luminance *surrounds* me."

"I might wear an angel costume to dance, but I'm not one." Not even close. My mafia assassin needs a reality check. "Angels don't shake their tits and ass for tips."

Angelo grins savagely. "When you are born to be a denizen of hell, you recognize someone who isn't. Call yourself what you want, *amate*, but your brilliance isn't tarnished by dancing on a stage."

"So, let's say I did agree to date you, you'd have no problem with my dancing?" I pull my knees to my chest, crossing my arms over my shins and wait for the inevitable hurtful answer.

"I would prefer you spend your time finishing college because that's important to you."

I knew it. No matter what he says, my job *is* a problem for him. Look how he reacted tonight...or last night rather. Whatever.

"You might have forgotten how you reacted to my private dance, but I haven't."

"I thought you didn't know who I was and were offering to let some stranger touch you."

"You thought I was high," I condemn. "And anyway, what business is it of yours if I do start offering extra curriculars?"

"Keeping you safe, even from yourself, is my job." He runs his glove-covered fingertip along the line of where my forearms touch.

Ignoring the pleasure sparking along my nerve endings, I frown. "I'm pretty sure it's not."

"It is and if you want to keep dancing at Pitiful Princess, I won't try to stop you, but I will keep watching over you."

"Stalking me you mean?" Does he mean it?

If I were to agree to his ridiculous idea that we should be dating, would he really be okay with me continuing to dance?

You didn't think dating him was such a ridiculous idea before, my inner voice singsongs. Which was also before he had his guys kidnap me, I remind myself.

Self is not impressed.

"Call it what you want." The shrug in his voice says it doesn't bother him even a little to be called a stalker. "We were born to be together."

"That's more of that love-at-first-sight crap. I already told you, I don't believe in it." My fascination with him may have reached the point of obsession, but that's not love. "I can't believe you do either. You have to know that there's no such thing as soulmates."

"Before I saw you for the first time, I would have agreed with you. But before I met you, I believed I would never bring a woman into my life. Now I know we were both wrong. Because you are my soulmate."

I shove my tender heart into my shoes. "Angelo, it doesn't work that way."

"It does if we say it does," he assures me.

Why are those words so tempting?

"We implies both of us, right?" I ask.

Brows furrowed, his gray gaze fills with wariness. "Yes."

"We implies I agree with you and I don't." I ignore the constriction in my chest at those words.

Okay, I'm stupidly reluctant to steal his phone and call the police to tell them I have been kidnapped. Maybe I do trust him not to harm me in a way that makes no logical sense.

But no way am I in love with him. I didn't even know he was watching me for most of the year.

And no way do I believe he loves me. He can't. "You stayed in the shadows, how was I supposed to get to know you? How could you think you know me well enough to love me?"

"The connection of two souls does not require the kind of surface knowledge that will inevitably come with time."

What is he, the Cosa Nostra's love guru?

I don't think so. "Can't you hear how bizarre that sounds? Angelo, that's not the way relationships work."

"My parents married less than a month after their first meeting."

"So, I have them to blame for your belief in love at first sight?" My own parents were anything but poster children for the idea.

My mom fell in love with my sperm donor, but he never saw her as anything but his side piece, if that.

Angelo grimaces. "Not exactly."

My interest piqued despite the exhaustion dragging more heavily at me with every passing second, I ask, "Why not exactly?"

"They were promised to each other for 10 years as a political alliance. They were not soulmates like us."

"Then why use them as an example?"

"Because in my world, arranged marriages between virtual strangers *is* commonplace. Some couples fall in love. Others don't."

"Okay, that's weird." Though I bet my sperm donor's wife is the other half of a strategic alliance.

If he loved her, he wouldn't have cheated on her.

"Not in our world."

"There is no *our* world," I remind him.

"We both live in it. That makes it ours."

I shake my head. "You can't decide that for me."

"It was decided for you when Stefano Bianchi fucked your mother and got her pregnant. You are a daughter of the Cosa Nostra."

"Yeah, no. My sperm donor and his random affiliations have nothing to do with my life."

Angelo smiles at me. Again. This guy. Shouldn't Death be the cynical one between us?

"There's nothing random about his connection to *la famiglia* or yours either," he explains patiently. "Cosa Nostra blood runs in your veins. You are under our protection."

"It didn't feel like protection tonight when my sperm donor told Freddy to off me." It was such a cruel thing to do, which only increases my disdain for Stefano Bianchi.

What if it had been another dancer who came into the alley when I did? What if it had been Piper? Would Freddy's crush on her have saved her? What if it was one of the dancers that didn't have a connection to any of the guys in that alley? Would she be dead right now?

The very thought nauseates me.

Knowing about how Angelo exacted retribution against Ronnie and Gino, not to mention that guy whose hand he skewered, and really who knows how many more men tried to touch me over the year that Angelo was watching me?

None of that bothers me like knowing my sperm donor would have ordered the death of an innocent woman. Someone who, even if she's not my friend is someone who didn't deserve to die tonight.

"Do you want me to kill him?" Angelo asks with a little too much enthusiasm.

"No. I'm not Stefano. I don't order people's deaths without a care to the people they leave behind." Okay, I did do that earlier, but not on purpose.

How was I supposed to know Mario would take my words literally, much less act on them?

I'm not riddled with guilt about it though. Not after Gino was so intent on killing me. He dismissed my life as worthless because I saw something I shouldn't. And whose fault was that? I wasn't the one doing criminal business in an alley used by more than one business open until the wee hours.

But Gino decided I would pay the price for his poor planning. Just like Stefano Bianchi before he found out who the witness was.

Not that I trust him to have given up on the idea of offing me. It would take care of two problems for him. My existence as his biological child and as a witness to criminal dealings related to him.

Regardless, whatever this is going on between me and Angelo, I have no doubt that if I said, yes, Death would claim another soul. Unlike my ignorance with Mario, I *know* that and I'm not about to act on it.

I might not feel any real guilt about Gino's death, either of the Gino's deaths if I'm honest with myself, but that doesn't mean I'm going to order another execution.

Their own predatory actions cost both men their lives. That's not on me.

I guess that viewpoint is evidence of Stefano's DNA showing in my character. Mommy was never that pragmatic about hurting others. She was the true romantic, believing Stefano Bianchi was Richard Gere to her Julia Roberts.

But Mommy's life wasn't a scene out of *Pretty Woman*. Not ever.

"You sure?" Angelo presses.

"Positive." I might carry Stefano's DNA but that doesn't make me a carbon copy of him.

If I put Stefano in Angelo's crosshairs, that *is* on me. And it's not a reality I'm willing to live with.

"I had a feeling you'd say that." His disappointment is real.

"Wouldn't you get in trouble if you killed a capo?" There's got to be a rule against that kind of thing.

Angelo shrugs. "I'm an assassin. I know how to make it look like an accident."

"You're too arrogant to hide it from your boss and you can't tell me the godfather would be okay with you killing one of his capos."

"Although technically, every member of the Cosa Nostra belongs to the godfather, Miceli De Luca is Stefano's don," Angelo informs me apropos of nothing.

"Why take the risk though?" I ask, smothering another yawn.

"You know why."

"That *love at first sight* and *you're the soul I never had* schmaltz might work on another woman." Especially when a guy as sexy as Angelo says it.

Even I want to melt into a silly puddle of goo around him. But I've seen too much. Been through too much. I'm not swallowing his claim to love me when I'm still all but a stranger to him.

Strangers hop into bed together all the time. They don't fall in love across a crowded strip club.

"You can't love me if you don't know me," I continue. "People might get married without love in *your* world but they don't fall in love at the altar."

"We know each other, *amate*."

"You don't know the important things about me. I don't know the important stuff about you." And I'm going to keep reminding him of that until he gets it through his gorgeous, thick head.

"Don't we?" The look he gives me sends an arrow of want straight to my core.

I shake my head, trying to dislodge the thoughts and feelings I should be too exhausted to experience right now. "If you knew me, you'd know that I don't like being threatened. Or held down. I especially hate being trapped."

Just because I didn't react to the whole duct taping thing like I would have expected doesn't change that truth about me. Or that he allowed it to happen to me without knowing the risk he was taking with my mental wellbeing.

"And yet you're not hysterical." He brushes his fingertip down my cheek. "Not a single tear has fallen from your beautiful brown eyes."

"I'm not a crier." My first foster placement taught me that crying was a weakness that, at best, got you sent out of the room and taunted by the other kids.

You learn early to protect yourself in the system, or it eats you alive. I didn't get eaten. Not even by my last foster father.

"You will cry when you need to when you are with me," he says, like it's a rule. "You will always be safe to show your emotions when I am there."

How can he know what I'm thinking? Or has Angelo had his own experience of learning to hide vulnerability? I can't imagine Death was ever helpless. But little Angelo? Maybe his vulnerability is where Death came from.

"Whatever. Me not crying tonight doesn't change what happened, or your part in it."

"I would not change my part in it. You are alive because of the protection order I put on you."

I can't argue that point because deep down, I know he's right. "Still doesn't mean you really know me, or that we're somehow meant for each other."

"You demanded to be let go, but you didn't beg for your life," Angelo says with undisguised admiration.

"You didn't hear me in the alley. I begged for Derian and Mario to let me go." And I'm not ashamed of that.

If the choice is death or begging? I'm going to plead for my life. I can't leave my mom and Cookie unprotected.

"They didn't listen." And I'll make them regret the duct tape and gag someday.

Somehow.

"They were under orders."

Unimpressed, I rolled my eyes. "I care because?"

Angelo laughs. "You give me joy, Candi Brigliano."

"My name is Kathleen." Not that I want him to use it, but Candi is the name my family calls me.

Angelo is not my family. Besides, right now, I'm seriously annoyed by the mafia assassin.

"Which you never use. The only person who calls you Kath is the social worker."

"It's creepy that you know that."

"Is it? I should know everything about you—"

I put my hand up, stopping him. "Don't start with the soulmate stuff again. And if you knew as much as you think you do about me, you never would have had your men tie me up."

Which was the point I was trying to make before he derailed me.

"I did not tell them to tie you up."

"Right. You just told them to bring me to you and since I wasn't going to come along like a dog on a leash, they trussed me up like a Thanksgiving turkey."

"You should not stuff the turkey," he informs me like *that's* the important thing he got out of my rant. "It increases the risk of food poisoning."

"So not what we are talking about right now."

"What are we talking about?" he asks, lifting me into his lap.

I let him.

Just kill me now because clearly, I have joined the ranks of too stupid to live characters in every horror novel ever. But a big part of me wants to curl up against Angelo's broad chest and forget the stress of the night and my life.

Deep inside, I *know* he'll keep me safe. Which is probably why getting taped up didn't bother me like it would have if someone else had done it. Derian and Mario are under Angelo's orders and their boss would cut off their hands for hurting me.

They even said so.

"Knowing the important stuff about each other," I remind him.

"The most important thing about you is that you are mine." His hand slides between my long sleeved t-shirt and my bodysuit, pressing against my back. "I will always protect you."

CHAPTER 18

CANDI

"What would you do if I bought into your delusion and believed all the stuff that comes out of your mouth?" I have no trouble believing he wants my body and even less trouble admitting I want his too.

But no way can he really want me, Candi Brigliano, the real woman with all my baggage and history, not the fantasy dancing the pole on a stage.

"Celebrate," he says with complete earnestness.

Shut up heart, we are not that naive. "Well, it's not going to happen."

"You're not afraid of me."

I don't say anything because that is not a lie, no matter how last girl standing in a horror movie that makes me.

"Salvatore's guy had to sedate Bianca to get her back to his place," he says, mentioning my best friend and the capo she's now married to. "Derian didn't need to do that with you."

"If that's your measure of success, your bar is set too low." I do nothing to curb the sarcasm rolling off me. "That fact does not earn you, or your men, a gold star. If Derian or Mario *had* drugged me, they'd be facing way worse payback than what I'm planning."

"We are so well matched," he croons.

I roll my eyes. "Because I'm planning to make them pay? A penchant for payback is not a romantic thing to have in common."

"Agree to disagree."

I squash the smile trying to curve my lips upward. This guy. "So, this kidnapping thing is somehow normal in your world? Like your stranger marriages?"

"*Arranged* marriages. And no, not really. Severu blackmailed Catalina into marrying him. Miceli signed a blood contract with Róise after Boss Shaughnessy offered her as guarantor of an alliance," he muses. "No, kidnapping is pretty rare actually."

"Is that supposed to make me feel special?"

"You are special. You're my person."

Maybe if I ignore him, he'll stop saying stuff like that. Arguing hasn't done the trick.

"I terrify most people just by breathing in the same vicinity as them," he informs me, like it's some kind of secret.

Newsflash. It's not.

"Tell me something I don't know." I mean, his punishment for breaking the no-touch rule is to cut off hands. "You're a scary guy."

"But not to you." His voice just oozes satisfaction.

Not sure what I'm going to say, because I can't really deny it, can I? I open my mouth to reply, but a yawn cracks my jaw instead.

Angelo hops to his feet with me still in his arms. "You need your rest."

"I wish. This is fun and all," I say with exhaustion blunted sarcasm. "But my mom and sister will be worried sick if I don't go home tonight."

And if we aren't going to do the nasty, I have no legitimate reason to stay. Most people would question my thought process for thinking sex with my kidnapper would be one.

But they don't live in my head. Only I do.

And tired, or not, I really wish we were going to have sex.

"I had Mario text them from your phone." Angelo leans down to turn off the gas fire, barely jostling me.

"No way is my mom going to believe that text is from me." We have our own way of communicating through text. "She's probably already called the cops."

Mom expects certain abbreviations from me. And when I text after work, there's a code word I use to prove it's me and I'm not texting under duress.

Carrying me out of the living room, Angelo says, "Pull your phone out of my pocket and check for yourself."

"That sounds like the beginning of a cheesy pickup line."

His laughter makes me smile. Who knew a deadly assassin could sound so *joyful*. Apparently, that's what I give him.

Which, if I let myself believe it, is a heady thought.

Me, Candi Brigliano, exotic dancer still working to get my associates degree, makes the deadliest man in New York happy.

"Which pocket?" I ask.

"The right one."

Reaching for my phone is too physically awkward to be sexy, even when my fingers brush along an erection of impressive proportions.

Angelo sucks in his breath and stops dead in the middle of the hall, which is really more like a hotel lobby. It even has a grand marble staircase wider at the bottom than at the top with decorative rails going up both sides.

I guess rich people call this a foyer. I call it big enough to hold our whole apartment.

"Fuck, *amate*." He closes his eyes, like he's trying to regain his control.

Pretending his instant reaction to me isn't the absolute catnip it is to my kitty, I fish my phone from his pocket. I might do a little extra touching along the rigid length than necessary.

I can't drum up even a little surprise or self-condemnation when instead of trying to dial 911, I actually do what Angelo says and check the text stream with my mom.

Every text is more unbelievable than the last.

Stunned by how Mario not only uses my abbreviations but the code word too, I look up at Angelo. "How?"

"I watch over you."

"But the code word...we only talk about that in the apartment."

His smile is like a naughty boy getting caught as he nods in agreement.

How? He's got my apartment bugged?

Unsure how I feel about that and fully aware that my first reaction isn't absolute dismay, I say, "Mario told my mom I was going home with you."

"And she was neither surprised, nor upset by that news." Angelo doesn't even try to hide how pleased he is by that.

If he's been listening in on our conversations, he knows I've been talking about him to her for weeks. Mom's one of the reasons I ventured into the VIP section to ask if the mafioso wanted a lap dance.

She says I need to go for it.

Of course, she doesn't know he's in the Cosa Nostra, or that he's cut men's hands off on my behalf. She wouldn't get it.

All she knows is that he's not like the other punters and I really, really, really wanted him to ask me out.

So, she buys the story Mario sells in the text stream that's supposed to be from me like it's a 50% off sale in the meat department.

"Mario told her that it's late, so I'm staying over at your place." He'd even sent a picture of the mansion with me in front of it.

I have no idea how he managed that feat of doctored photography, but it worked. Mom is not worried at all. Mario-me even told her to go to bed and get some sleep, just like I would have done, if I really had been staying over with a guy I wanted to get to know better.

Like that's ever happened before.

Mom's last text makes my heart squeeze in my chest.

Mom: *He must be something really special to have made it past your barriers of mistrust where men are concerned. I'm so happy for you, honey. But you tell him if he hurts you, he'll have me to answer to.*

Mom uses the voice to text function because of her arthritis and I can hear her voice in my head as I read the words.

"Am I?" Angelo asks.

I look up from my phone. "Are you what?"

"Something really special."

"According to you, you're my soulmate," I remind him.

He leans down and presses his forehead to mine. "I want to know what I am according to *you*."

"You know," I grumble. "You were listening."

He lifts his head so our eyes can meet. "Does that bother you?"

"Would it matter if it did?" That it doesn't is definitely a me problem. "I know you've been stalking me, but Mario's ability to impersonate me is next level."

"I told him what to say in the texts." Angelo makes it sound like that's the most normal thing in the world.

It's not.

"But how did *you* know what to say?" I press.

I mean, there's stalking and there's *stalking*. Right?

He starts toward the stairs, showing no strain from carrying me. "You leave your phone in your locker when you dance."

I don't ask how he got into the locker or the phone. A semi-decent lockpick would open the locker and my phone is an off-brand piece of crap that's at least five generations old. It would be a piece of cake for a guy like him.

"Okay, but how did you know that I've talked about you to my mom and sister?" Will he admit to bugging the apartment?

He squeezes me tighter, like he thinks I'm going to leap from his arms. "Do you really want the answer to that?"

"Yes," I say firmly. "I want to know."

Apparently being stalked and kidnapped is not a dealbreaker for me. Because I am in possession of my phone, but making no effort to call 911 while he carries me upstairs. To the guest room?

Not sure if I want the answer to be *yes*, or *no* to that.

"I have camera feeds inside your apartment and out in the hallway."

Camera feeds? As in he has been *watching* me not merely listening? He said he watched me, but I didn't think he meant it like that.

"Uh, that's clinical grade obsession right there."

"Maybe, but you've figured out by now my brain doesn't work like other people's." It's not a question.

And he's right. No way would your average person think dismember-
ment a reasonable reaction to a punter overstepping.

"I think my brain has a twist too," I admit. "Ronnie would never have
had to pay for his assault on me. Now, maybe he'll think twice about trying
to molest another woman."

"He won't have long to do that thinking." Angelo's voice drips menace.

"What do you mean?"

"He didn't just touch you. He tried to rape you."

"Most people wouldn't see it that way."

"I'm not most people." He stops on the landing.

It's not some small patch of carpet at the top of the wide marble staircase.
No, it's a whole other room, with chairs and flowers in a vase on the table
against the wall that runs between two open hallways.

Does this place have wings like some medieval castle? "Killing people
must pay well."

"Generational wealth, but yeah, it pays pretty well when your boss is the
godfather."

Generational wealth? Who is this guy? And why is he so obsessed with
me?

Focusing on something besides my sudden attack of insecurity, I say,
"Those cameras would have to have sound for you to know all the things
you do."

Which are in a word, embarrassing. I say stuff to my mom and sister I
wouldn't even admit to Bianca. She's got no clue about my crush on the
mafia assassin. Mom and Cookie are the only two people on the planet that
get to see the softer side I hide under my prickly exterior.

"Yes."

I fist his shirt. "Now is not the time to clam up on me. How did you get
cameras into my apartment?"

CHAPTER 19

CANDI

Angelo carries me down the hallway on the right, his footsteps making no sound on the lush carpet. "I impersonated building maintenance."

"You're the guy that came around and fixed all of the things mom's been complaining about to the super for years?" My mind spins with all the work he did to hide his real reason for being there.

We now have decent water pressure in the bathroom, and there are brand new mobility rails to help mom in the shower and on and off the toilet.

All four burners on the stove work again and there's no pan under the kitchen sink to catch the slow leak anymore. Because it's gone.

All the dings in the walls have been patched up and painted over. I thought it was a miracle our cheap building superintendent coughed up the cash for all the repairs.

Now, I know he didn't.

The apartment looks better than it has since I moved in as a terrified fifteen-year-old.

There was no miracle. Only Angelo Caruso masquerading as a maintenance guy.

Mom described the guy as past retirement. She'd said she felt bad about him having to get down on the floor for some of the work, but he'd insisted on fixing everything.

Angelo nods. "Spending time fixing stuff around the apartment was a good way to get to know your mom."

"Why did you want to get to know her?" I ask.

"Because one day she'll be my mother-in-law."

My brain officially shorts out.

"That's it. Don't say another word. If mom and Cookie really aren't stressed out about my disappearance..." And the text stream says they aren't. "Then I want that bedroom you had Mario tell my mom I was going to sleep in."

All ideas of getting lucky tonight with Angelo are buried under the avalanche of thoughts spinning through my brain.

How am I supposed to respond to the knowledge that his stalking wasn't the cute kind where he came in to watch me dance every night, but *stalking* that led to him impersonating maintenance so he could put cameras with sound inside my home.

Now, he's talking about us getting married someday. And of all the things he's said tonight, that's the one I really can't parse.

"Whatever you want, *piccola gatta*."

"What does that mean?" I've got a good idea about *amate* and am not even going to think about that one.

"Little cat."

"Because you want inside my pussy?" I ask.

Stepping through an open set of double doors, he guffaws. "Good one *amate*, but no. Sometimes, you remind me of a hissing, spitting kitten."

He allows my legs to drop and holds onto me until I'm standing in front of him, stupefied. "I remind you of a cat?"

"Yes. I want to pet you and make you purr."

"Cheesy." The wet patch on my bodysuit at the apex of my thighs doesn't agree with that description, but that's between me, my ladybits and the Lycra.

Releasing me, Angelo turns and steps toward the open doors. I bite back the sound of protest that wants out. That is *not* disappointment I feel that he's listening to me about letting me sleep.

When he shuts the doors with him on the inside, relief battles instant anxiety. When do I tell him I've never done this before?

Do I have to tell him why? That's not required, is it?

Angelo presses his palm against something on the wall to the right of the door. Something whirs and then a wall begins to descend from the ceiling, covering the double doors.

"Uh, what is that about?" I should be afraid he's locking me in with him, but we've already established that the caution part of my brain is on the fritz where he's concerned. "What if there's a fire?"

At least my inner safety bunny poked her head out of her hole to acknowledge that danger. She's not a total lost cause.

"This room is fireproof, unless the fire starts in here."

"That's very..." Over the top. Villain in his evil lair ish. "Fire safety first of you."

"Our bedroom and both Cookie and Mira's bedrooms in the other wing are also saferooms. The walls, ceilings and floors are impenetrable and there are emergency rations in the secondary closet."

Cookie and Mira's bedrooms in the other wing? Secondary closet? What the heck is that? Cookie and I use pegs on the wall to hang things up. Mom has a closet in her bedroom, but I have a feeling the *secondary closet* in here is bigger.

"What are you, Batman? Don't tell me there's a secret cave under this pile of rocks with super cool crime-fighting technology." Still not acknowledging the *Cookie and Mira's bedrooms* comment. "And you actually have freakin' wings in this house? How very Bridgerton of you."

"Since I am a criminal, there is no crime fighting tech in the basement, or anywhere else in the mansion. There is an armory though and another saferoom kitted out like an apartment."

"Wow, you are really ready for a siege."

"I will always make sure my family is protected."

"I'm making a rule. No more comments about me being your family. And definitely not another word about my mom and sister moving in if you want to share that bed with me." I wave my arm toward the giant bed covered in silver gray bedding with teal accents.

Angelo's gray eyes go molten and he mimes zipping his lips.

CHAPTER 20

ANGELO

I can't believe Candi just agreed to share our bed with me. I expected her to argue about it and was prepared to make myself a bed on the floor.

Not to leave, of course, but I doubt she'd expect me to. We belong together and I think under her Grumpy Cat cynicism she knows it.

Candi's disheveled appearance reminds me that there is something we need to do before living out one of the many fantasies that have played over and over again in my head for the last year.

"Come on, *amate*. I think you're going to like the bathroom." Taking her soft, smaller hand in mine I lead her into the bathroom.

Just like the bedroom, the designer used teal in the décor because I told her to. It's Candi's favorite color. Will she notice the intentional mix of teal and gray? The color of my eyes paired with the color that she likes best is a reflection of our connection.

Of our lives entwined.

I thought about telling the designer to use the rich chocolate brown of Candi's eyes as the other accent color. But that shade of brown belongs to me. Not the staff that makes the bed, or the cleaners who vacuum under it.

Just me. Does that make me a little obsessed? Maybe, but I'm a sociopath and she's my person. That means I'm possessive about everything personal related to Candi.

"What do you think?" I can't help asking.

I've been waiting months to share the home I bought and furnished for her with *la mia piccola gatta*.

She takes a second to look at the double sink vanity made with a space for her to sit and do her hair and makeup. Her gaze slides to the walk-in shower with teal frosted glass surround and the oversized tub that we can bathe in together. It has jets that are placed specifically to soothe sore leg and back muscles because of her dancing.

Whether, or not, she continues to work at Pitiful Princess, my Candi loves to dance. If it is up to me, she will always have an outlet for that.

"Do you want me to buy you a dance studio?" Would she enjoy teaching dance?

She's working on a degree in business, but that could apply to lots of stuff. It doesn't have to mean she hopes to have her own studio one day.

One thing I've never heard her talk about to her mom or sister is Candi's plans for the future.

She gives me that deer in the headlights look again, like when I mentioned her mom and sister's room in the other wing. "Uh, I don't know how to answer that."

"Yes, or no works for me. Or you need to think about it." The book I read on relationships said that some people are used to snap decisions (that would be me) and others need time to consider all the angles.

Candi might be like that.

She winces. "Can we focus on the here and now?"

So, the idea of a dance studio is like her mom and sister moving in with us. Something she has to get used to. "Sure, *piccola gatta*."

She makes a choked sound, and I realize she's caught an image of herself in the mirror.

Her hands fly to her head and she tries to smooth down the tangled brown strands. "Why didn't you tell me I was such a mess?"

Is that a real question? The look on her face says it is.

"I will never tell you that. You are always beautiful to me. You could shave your head, dress in trash bags, and I would still think you're beautiful." I hope she doesn't shave her head though.

Her hair is a curtain of dark silk that I itch to take my gloves off and run my fingers through. Maybe when she's got less of other people's sweat and germs from the alley in it.

"Yeah. No. Not about to wear a trash bag like a rain poncho."

Endlessly intrigued by her, I ask, "Did someone make you do that?"

"My mom didn't *make* me. She did it to keep me dry. When there's no money for a raincoat, a trash bag with holes cut for your neck and arms works."

She and her mom lived in poverty while her father, the capo, lived a life of luxury with the family he acknowledged. I really want to kill Stefano Bianchi.

"Anyway, I've been growing my hair out since I moved in with mom and Cookie and I'm not about to cut it off now."

She must get it trimmed though because when her luxurious hair isn't tangled up around her head, it reaches just past the middle of her back. It would cover her ass if she'd been growing it that long and never trimmed it.

Besides, it always looks smooth and healthy. I wonder if one of the other girls cuts it for her. Candi doesn't spend money on herself if she can help it.

That's something that's going to change. She will never have to do without so her mom and sister have what they need again. I will make sure they *all* have everything they want now that they are my family too.

"Why since then?" Every little thing about Candi fascinates me.

"Mom was the first foster parent who didn't force me to cut it to make it easier to manage." Candi makes air quotes when she says *easier to manage*. "There is no way I'm cutting it unless I don't have a choice."

"You will always have a choice." I'll make sure of it.

She grimaces. "Do you have a brush, or something?"

I point toward the side of the vanity that is hers. "Check in there."

Eager to see her response to my attempt to get her all the same things she has at home, but better when I can, I watch as she pulls open the top drawer. The breath exhales from her mouth in a small gasp when she sees what's inside.

Beautiful brown eyes gleaming with interest, she opens one of the eye shadow palettes. "It's never been used."

"Of course not. It's yours." I can't help brushing her hair back from her shoulder just to touch her. "I know you like that brand. But you hardly ever buy it."

"That's because it's so expensive." She stares up at me, her expression disbelieving. "All of this is for me?"

"Everything on that side of the vanity is for you."

She swallows. "Okay, not addressing that right now."

She opens the drawer below and gasps again, this time a little louder. That drawer is filled with the things she needs to style her hair. High-end versions of her favorite hair products, along with the best blow dryer and straightener on the market.

I consulted with one of the top hair stylists in New York. His receptionist tried to tell me I couldn't get an appointment for at least six months. Once we got that straightened out, he was happy to consult with me on what to get Candi.

Or, you know, happy to keep the fingers he needed to keep doing his job. He even offered to cut my hair.

But I don't let people touch me that I don't know.

That might be a problem. Not for me, but I don't want people to touch Candi that I haven't vetted either. What if she wants to go to a hairstylist? Or get a massage?

Hard no on that one. Even if it's a woman.

Maybe I should watch some YouTube videos on how to do it.

All of the potential situations that might necessitate Candi being touched by a stranger land hard, one on top of the other. Doctors appointments. Getting blood drawn.

Despite her reserved nature, my boss's wife is going to want to hug Candi when they meet. Catalina's not a stranger, but I still don't like it.

And there's Candi's friends. Bianca. Piper. The other dancers. She's going to want to keep them in her life and spend time with them.

Forcing the spiraling thoughts away, I focus on the way Candi touches each item in the drawer like it's precious. Nothing, not even my need to protect her is going get in the way of enjoying our first night together in our home.

"Would you like to take a shower first?" I look at the bath. "Or maybe we could use the tub and you'll let me wash your hair."

I don't care if it makes me strange, but I have fantasies of washing my woman's beautiful, long hair. Of taking care of her and pampering her in the way she deserves.

She spends so much time taking care of other people. Her mom. Her sister. The other dancers, though I doubt they realize how she lobbies on their behalf with her bestie and their advocate in *la famiglia*, Bianca De Luca.

Candi stares at me, her eyes wide. "You want to wash my hair?

"Yes."

"No one has done that, not since mommy died." Her expression is blank, not telling me anything about how that makes her feel.

"Will you let me? "

She bites her lip and nods. "Yes, but can we do it in the shower? I don't want to soak in water cloudy with shampoo and conditioner from my hair."

"Good thinking." Since I don't take baths, I wouldn't have thought of that.

I start stripping my clothes off, piling my weapons in the specialty drawer in the vanity for that purpose. There's another drawer just like it in the nightstand on my side of the bed.

Candi's eyes are wide again as she watches the collection of knives and guns go into the drawer. "Wow. I would never have guessed you had that many weapons on you."

"That's the idea." Leaving one of my guns on top of the counter, I close the drawer and press the pad that sets the biometric lock.

The house and our bedroom are as safe as I can make them, but not having a weapon accessible would be as unthinkable as cutting off my own trigger finger.

I remove my boots and stack them side by side on the shoe rack that folds out from the wall. They can remain there until the morning, or I can put them in the closet with my others. Either way, no one will trip over them and knock them askew.

The fold-down shoe rack is part of my accommodation for living with another person.

After removing my shirt, I fold it and place it in the laundry hamper built into the vanity.

Unstrapping the ultralightweight body armor I require my entire crew to wear at all times, I let my eyes roam over *mia amate*. "You're not getting undressed."

She shakes her head, like she's trying to gather her thoughts and pulls the long sleeved t-shirt over her head, revealing the bodysuit underneath.

"You need warmer clothes." And better ones, but I don't say that out loud.

All of my clothes are made with silk or impact resistant materials, if not a blend of both. The strongest natural fiber on the planet, using silk is not an indulgence, but a necessity in my line of work.

The clothing hanging in Candi's side of the closet is made with the same high-end fabrics, but it's a hell of a lot prettier than my wardrobe of black t-shirts and cargo pants, augmented with a few bullet proof black suits for when Severu wants me to look the part.

She grimaces. "My clothes are fine. Stop sounding like my mom, or the shower isn't going to be nearly as sexy as I'm anticipating."

Her words run through me like an electric current. Shower and sexy being the ones that stand out.

It only takes me seconds to remove my body armor, adjust the straps for easy access without dangling messily, and lay it parallel to my gun on the counter. Grabbing the back of the neck of my undershirt, I quickly yank it over my head and fold it for the laundry hamper as well, not taking as much care as usual to make sure the rectangle of fabric is symmetrical on all sides.

Forcing myself not to grab it back out of the hamper, I notice that Candi has stopped moving again. Her eyes don't have that far away, zoned out look now. She's staring at me, but it's not how I dispose of my dirty clothes that has her mesmerized.

Her mouth parted slightly, her pretty brown gaze is stuck firmly on my chest.

I don't mind this reverse in our usual situation and flex my pectorals for her. Candi licks her lips, sending blood surging through my already hard cock.

Taking my time, I remove my black cargo pants, sliding them over the erection straining against my boxers. She makes a sexy little sound as I push the impact resistant fabric down my thighs.

"You're beautiful." she says, her voice filled with awe.

"No one has ever called me beautiful before." She can call me whatever she wants, but it feels strange.

Leaving my boxers on I drop to kneel in front of her and begin untying her shoes. "Here let me get these off you."

Lifting her foot for me to pull off her tennis shoe and the no-show sock she's wearing under it, reveals an unmistakable wet spot in the crotch of the bodysuit.

Head bent down, the scent of her arousal surrounds me, almost destroying my self-control.

Candi wants me. Maybe even as much as I want her.

She lifts her other foot, reminding me what I'm supposed to be doing. For the first time in memory, my hands tremble as I take off her other shoe and sock.

I have to control the slavering beast inside me, or I'm going to fuck her up against the wall without giving her the care I promised myself I would.

Forcing myself to complete my task, I fold her socks together and put them in the laundry hamper.

"Hey, I'm going to need those to wear home tomorrow."

I ignore that comment like she's been trying to ignore mine about her moving in and put her tennis shoes next to my boots on the shoe rack. Her dancer's feet are so much smaller than mine.

Turning back to her, I try to figure out how to remove the bodysuit thing. "How do we get this off you?"

Not averse to grabbing one of my knives from the weapons drawer and cutting the awful thing to shreds, I run my hands up the outside of her thighs.

Candi shudders. "The neck hole stretches."

"Never wear this again." The Lycra smashes her gorgeous, round tits into one amorphous curve. "It hides your body."

"A. That's the idea. B. You don't get to dictate my wardrobe choices." The heat in her eyes makes her defiant frown less convincing.

"I don't like the way it hides you from *me*."

"Haven't you gotten your fill of seeing my body?"

My brows draw together in confusion. "Is that a trick question? I could look at you all day long, every day for the next century and still not get my fill."

"Oh," she breathes out, like I surprised her.

How is that a surprise? I've been obsessed with her for a year.

She grabs the neckline at her shoulder and stretches it so the Lycra can slide down her upper arm. "I don't want to hide my body from *you*."

"Good." We'd have a hell of a problem if she did.

Candi pulls her left arm free without exposing her luscious tits, but her nipples are pressing against the stretchy fabric now.

One of the first things I noticed about Candi was how dancing the pole didn't turn her on. She did a good job faking it, but she was just going through the motions.

Stripping for me turns her on though.

And in turn that makes me hotter than I already am. Fuck. We are not going to make it into the shower at this rate.

Candi pulls her right arm out of the bodysuit and then pushes the Lycra down, allowing her generous breasts to bounce free.

All the air leaves my lungs in a whoosh.

Nipples the color of raspberry sorbet, dark pink and luscious, drawn tight into rigid peaks make my mouth water.

I want to touch, but keep my mitts where they are as she continues to push the stretchy fabric down her body until it bunches right above my hands.

"Help me?" she invites.

I take over and push the bodysuit down to her ankles with a lot more speed less finesse. She steps out of it, kicking it aside.

My need to put it in the hamper is only a twinge compared to the other needs she provokes in me. To taste and touch. To fuck and pleasure. To claim.

Her perfectly smooth, puffy pussy lips are bisected by a slit glistening at the edges with her juices. My head leans forward to taste before I realize what I'm doing and I jerk it back.

"Fuck, *amate*, I want to taste you, but that will have to wait."

"Why?" she asks breathlessly.

"Because if I touch your pussy now, I will not cherish you the way you deserve." And my Candi deserves everything good. "Are your inner lips the same raspberry as your nipples?"

She widens her stance just a little. "Why don't you check and find out?"

My groan is loud and not at all exaggerated.

Surging to my feet, I step back, away from temptation. "You are playing with fire, *piccola gatta*."

Crossing her arms under her tits, putting them on display in a way she cannot be unaware of, she gives me a heavy-lidded smile. "Are you going to take off your gloves or do you shower with them on too?"

"You know I do not wear them all the time." Just most of the time. "You got me to take them off at the club earlier."

"That didn't last very long." She pouts up at me.

"I won't put them back on until we leave the bedroom," I promise.

She cocks one eyebrow. "That implies you're going to take them off now."

In answer I peel my gloves off, placing them precisely on top of my body armor.

Her gaze flicks to the counter with my things on it and then back to me. "You're very particular about where things go."

"Does that bother you?" There's no point in denying a truth I cannot change.

Everything has its place. Including me. I belong in the Cosa Nostra.

Including Candi. She belongs with me

CHAPTER 21

CANDI

D oes it bother me that the man who is about to become my lover clearly has at least a touch of OCD?

"No," I reply honestly. "Everything at home has a designated place when it's not in use."

We don't fold our dirty clothes, but the one-bedroom apartment is pretty small for three people. Mom's bedroom used to be the dining nook connected to the kitchen. It's only cordoned off with a curtain, which makes things easier when she needs more help getting in and out of bed.

So, the need to keep a path clear for her wheelchair isn't the only reason we keep stuff put away. If we didn't, none of us would have the room to move around.

Angelo's hands fist and unfist at his sides, fascinating me.

It's only the second time I've seen them without the black gloves, and the first was a matter of hours ago.

With his propensity for covering them, I would expect Angelo's hands to be pale. But they aren't. He has the swarthy complexion a lot of people identify with Sicilians. Only, just like the rest of Italy and Europe, Sicilians run the gamut from pale as marble to looking like they have a perpetual tan.

Like Angelo.

My skin prickles with the need to be touched by those hands.

"The way you're looking at me is not helping my self-control," he grits out and shoves his black knit boxers down his legs.

My breath catches as his large, veiny cock springs upward to curve toward his stomach.

I may not have had sex before, but I've seen enough blowjobs given in the public areas of the club to know he's bigger than average and the level of rigidness is not normal.

"Are you always that turned on when I dance?" I can't help asking.

"Sometimes."

"Why not all the time?" pops out before I have a chance to stop it.

"Some nights you look tired, and I want you to be able to go home and rest, but I know you won't."

Even though I'm almost naked and undulating on a pole, seeing me work when I'm tired does not turn him on. That should not hit me as hard in the feels as it does.

He squeezes the base of his hardon in what looks like a painful grip. "If you keep looking at me like that, we are never going to make it into the shower."

"You keep saying that like it's a threat. You're the one who wants a shower so bad." But not without reason, I have to admit.

I'm crusted in dried sweat from all of the running and stress adrenaline.

The fact a guy like him is struggling so hard to keep his hands off me in this condition does more for my libido than a hundred punters chanting, "Take it off!"

He takes a step toward me, but stops, an inner war reflected in his stormy gray eyes. "I want to wash your hair."

I only have to glance at myself in the mirror that covers the entire wall behind the vanity to know why.

With a wry grimace, I put my hands up self-consciously to touch the matted tangles of my hair. "I'm nobody's fantasy right now."

I really should wash it and at least try to get the tangles out. If I don't, mom will insist on using her homemade recipe for detangler and I'll end up smelling like apple cider vinegar.

Besides, there was blood on my face when I got here. Angelo cleaned it off, but *I'll* feel better after washing my face, brushing my teeth and gargling with antiseptic mouthwash. Something I'm sure he keeps on hand.

"You are always my fantasy." He runs his hand up and down his erection. "Isn't that obvious?"

Swallowing to bring moisture to my suddenly dry throat, I nod.

Precum forms pearlescent beads on the tip of his erection and he spreads it over the hard column. "I want to wash every inch of your beautiful skin so I can lick it after."

A shudder works its way from the bottom of my feet up to the top of my head. "Sounds like fun."

"I think so too." He prowls another step nearer bringing the earthy scent of his body and arousal with him. "First my hands will get the privilege of touching you and then my tongue will get to taste you."

I'm 100% behind that plan. "I can't decide if I should make sure I'm freshly showered the next time we do this, or not, because both the touching and the tasting sound amazing."

Because no way is this a one off. I may not be able to wrap my head around what *he* thinks this is, but the feelings I have for him are too big to be satisfied with a single night, or day as the case may be, in his bed.

If only it were just the sex, that would be easier to figure out, but I like being around him and he's the only man I've ever known to make me feel safe.

Angelo reaches past me, his arm brushing against my breasts and I suck in a startled breath but I don't pull away.

"I'm only turning on the water, *amate*." He does something behind me and it sounds like raindrops start falling from the ceiling to patter against the tile floor at the bottom of the shower.

Turning to see, my butt slides along his thigh. Electricity arcs between us and for a second the air is suspended in my chest.

Then two showerheads about four feet up the wall and on opposite sides of the enclosure begin to spit out a cascade of water, startling me into breathing again.

Steam fills the glass enclosure too quickly to be the result of the water alone and sure enough there are vents on the floor emitting gentle puffs of steam, filling the air with the scent of mint and eucalyptus.

I have never once in my life been in such a luxurious shower. "Washing at home is going to feel like taking a spit bath after this."

"Then I guess it's a good thing this is now your home."

I shove my arm up and smack his chest with the back of my hand. "What did we say?"

His chuckle is the only acknowledgement I get to my words. Then he nudges me forward.

Out of habit, I put my hand out to check the temperature of the water. It's deliciously warm, but not too hot.

Angelo's hands settle on my shoulders, his thumbs kneading the base of my neck. "It won't change temperature no matter how long we take."

Trying hard not to melt into a puddle of goo from the neck massage, I ask, "Why's that, magic?"

I wouldn't find that impossible to believe with this man. There's definitely some kind of magic in the way my muscles are relaxing under his touch.

"It's hooked up to its own instant hot water heater. Just as the showers in your..." He stops talking and kisses the top of my head. "But I won't mention that right now."

Reluctantly, because the massage will end, I turn to face him. Pleased with himself, he's smiling like he expects a gold star for remembering my moratorium on talking about my mom and sister moving into the mansion.

If I had one, I might give it to him, but all I can do is return his smile with one of my own.

That seems to be all he needs because gray eyes that can give a glacier a run for its money for coldness light up. "You are so beautiful when you smile, *amate.*"

I don't know how to reply to that. Men don't tell me my smile is beautiful. That's not what they're looking at when they see me.

Angelo traces around my mouth before swiping his thumb across my bottom lip. "The first thing I noticed about you were these perfectly luscious lips curved so prettily in a smile."

"Now I know you're lying," I tease with an underlying sense of truth. "No way did you notice my face before my body when I was practically naked."

I'm billed as voluptuous. Which means I've got banging curves the customers show a lot of appreciation for. Men drool over my big boobs and butt and according to Piper, they fantasize all sorts of things they want to do with them that I never want to know about.

"I do not lie to you," Angelo says with conviction. "First, it was your lips and then it was your eyes."

"Were you daydreaming about blowjobs?" I tease as I step backward into the warm rain he calls a shower. "But I don't get how my eyes caught your attention."

He follows me, not allowing any distance to form between us. "I didn't fantasize about you wrapping those luscious lips around my cock until the third night I watched you dance, but your eyes mesmerized me."

At least he admits to thinking about it, which makes me more likely to believe him about being *mesmerized* by my eyes.

Warm water patters onto my head in droplets, not the steady stream coming from the wall mounted showerheads. I didn't even know water could be made to do that with no clouds involved.

Hot water from the showerhead in the wall washes over my sweat encrusted body. And I close my eyes turning my face up to the rainwater from the ceiling.

For long moments, I simply stand there, letting the water wash away the stress of the night and the wee hours of this morning.

The stress of what I perceived as rejection from Angelo after crushing on him so hard and offering myself on a platter.

The stress of nearly dying at the hands of my sperm donor's men.

The stress of being kidnapped by Mario and Derian.

Not to mention my near heart attack from worrying about my mom and my sister being upset enough to call the cops when I didn't come home after work.

All of it washes down the drain with the deliciously hot water.

"Isn't this a waste of water?" I ask without opening my eyes, not exactly wracked with guilt about it.

"All bathing and drinkable water waste gets recycled through an underground filtration system."

"Mom will approve."

"Good. I want her to like me."

That right there. Could he have said anything more perfect. My psychopath stalker wants my mom to like him.

Tipping my head forward again, I open my eyes and find Angelo intently watching me. Like my standing here under the water is just the most fascinating thing ever.

I step further into the shower but when I reach the center of the six-by-six foot enclosure, the water from above stops falling on me.

Curious about why, I look up and gasp. There's a silhouette of a dancer set in a circular piece of iridescent stone in the ceiling. She's wearing stripper heels and angel's wings.

Both the shape of the wings and her curves are very familiar. "That's me."

"It is."

"How? Why?" I shake my head. "Never mind."

Both answers are obvious. How? Angelo is seriously rich and money talks. Why? The man is also seriously obsessed with me.

"I like looking at you."

Even when it's an artistic representation of me. I get it.

"It's not a picture of my eyes," I tease.

"That's above the bed."

"What? No. Seriously?"

He nods, his gaze locked on me like I might disappear any second and he can't take the chance of that happening. Naked and locked in his safe-room bedroom, there's no chance of that.

But being the center of this man's attention is still a heady feeling.

"What's so interesting about my peepers anyway?" They're ordinary brown, like millions of other people have.

"Sometimes, when you dance, you're somewhere else in your mind." He traces my brow line with his forefinger, like he just can't *not* touch me. "That first night, your expression was that of an ethereal being transported to earth for mere mortals like myself to gaze upon."

"You're pretty poetic for a mafia hitman."

Something flashes in his fixated gaze. "Only when it comes to you." He searches my face, looking for something. "That doesn't bother you?"

"What?" I try to remember what we're talking about. I'm standing naked in the shower for the first time with a man; I can be forgiven for being a little distracted. "That you're a hitman?"

"I'm more than an assassin, but yes, that."

"It should, right? A good person wouldn't have a personal relationship with a criminal." I guess I'm not a good person because the only person I want to get involved with is him.

"Does that mean you don't want to be in a relationship with me?" His expression says that ship has sailed though. "Because you are the best person I know."

Why does he have to say stuff like that? "Most people wouldn't call a stripper a good person."

"Why not?"

Does he really not know? "Sex workers are considered morally corrupt." And I make my living in the sex industry.

"So are made men." He shrugs. "Makes sense. We kill to get made."

"Innocent people?" I ask, knowing I hope the answer is no.

"No. We're not street thugs. It's not about proving ourselves with a random act of violence. It's about proving our loyalty to *la famiglia* by protecting it. The Army required the same from me, but they didn't call it getting made."

"What did they call it?" Unable to help myself, I put my hand over a tattoo of the grim reaper on his chest.

This is how he sees himself.

His big hand settles over mine, pressing my fingers into his skin. "My job."

"Harsh."

He shrugs. "I learned what I needed to serve the Genovese and protected my country while I did it."

I get that. "I love to dance and doing it at the Pitiful Princess allows me to support my mom and sister while I do it. Even if other people think I should be happy to let them do without and get a so-called respectable job."

"Does that bother you?" He moves us so we're standing under the shower rain again.

"I grew a thick skin about being judged before I ever went into foster care." My mom was a stripper, and I wore trash bags as rain gear. Other kids *and* their parents judged me and mom plenty. "My experiences in the system only put callouses on that skin."

"Close your eyes. This shampoo isn't supposed to burn, but let's not take any chances." He pulls a bottle out of an alcove in the wall and squirts some liquid into his hand. "I have a list of people who hurt you. I want you to look at it and add names that are missing."

"Why?" I love the coconut and vanilla smell of the shampoo and wallow in it a little.

It smells like the stuff I buy from the discount grocery store, only the scents are pleasantly natural, not chemical.

"So I can kill them." The gentleness of his touch as he works the shampoo into my hair is at odds with the ruthless dismissal of human life in his words.

Yeah, that's not going to happen.

"Seeing you skewer that man's hand last Spring didn't upset me," I admit to my personal avenging angel. "It made me feel protected."

"Good."

"But I'm not going to make a list of people for you to hurt on my behalf and I'd prefer if you got rid of the one you've made."

He doesn't answer and I get the feeling that his list isn't going anywhere.

"Sometimes, when I dance, I pretend I'm at a theater, performing in a big stage production," I admit, to get his mind off killing people from my past.

The only one I would voluntarily put on that list is the foster father from my last placement before coming to live with mom. But he's already dead.

Some random mugger made the world safer for vulnerable girls by stabbing him to death a week after I was pulled from his home.

"What else do you fantasize about?" Strong fingers massage my scalp.

I groan my appreciation for how good that feels. "Some nights I like to remember how happy my birth mom was to come to the recital at the community center when I was five and I danced for her."

Running his fingers through my hair, Angelo helps the suds wash away. They're tear-free as advertised, but I keep my eyes closed. It's easier to share my private thoughts in the dark cocoon that creates around me.

My fantasies probably aren't what other people expect an exotic dancer to think about. I learned early that most people buy into the fantasy of the sexually charged woman who gets off on turning men on.

The customers are convinced every dancer on the stage and pole is picturing them in her mind as her body moves so sensually.

Dance can be a very sensual art and the act of moving my body like that can create a low buzz of arousal which adds to the sensuality. Some dancers do get turned on by all the lust-filled gazes locked on them. But for me, the punters only exist in my periphery.

Only one man has ever been different. "When I feel your eyes on me, I dance for you."

And it makes me wet.

The hands carefully rinsing out my hair go still. "You know when I'm there."

"When you walk into the club and start watching me, something inside me relaxes because I feel safe."

I risk opening my eyes to see what he thinks of that and get caught in a stare so intense it makes me shiver despite the warm water and steam.

"I keep you safe even when I'm not there," Angelo promises.

"Good to know." Pressing my water slick body against his, I trap his hard shaft between us. "But it's not the same."

"You get excited when you dance for me."

"I do."

"But you don't when I'm not there."

At the risk of making his head swell, I admit, "No, I don't."

Heat surges between us again, but Angelo doesn't give into it. He pours more shampoo on my hair as if he knows that long hair like mine needs a second wash almost every time.

Who am I kidding? He probably does know. He probably knows what size shoes and underwear I wear too.

"Your style of dance is like art. No one else's even comes close." He's just as careful and thorough this time around washing my long hair as the first.

"Thank you. I don't usually get compliments on my artistic style of dance."

"That's because the audience is too caught up in your beauty to notice."

"That's one way of putting it." The customers are too busy dreaming about what they want to do to my body to notice the art in how it moves.

Angelo maneuvers me closer to the wall of the shower and detaches the head cascading water in a steady stream. "I'm a man, *amate*. Seeing your tits makes me hard."

No surprise there.

"And I will never grow tired of looking at all your perfect curves." He stops like he's waiting for me to acknowledge that.

"Okay."

Lifting the showerhead, he begins a more thorough rinse of my hair. "But your ability to tell a story through dance is special. It makes me *feel* and that's not something I do often."

"What does that mean?" How does someone not feel?

"Emotions are the 2.7mm Kolibri in my arsenal for life."

"Uh, I'd probably know what that meant if I knew what a Kolibri is." It's a weapon. I got that much because that's what you keep in an arsenal.

"It's a small gun with very little impact power." He puts the showerhead back on the wall.

"Okay?" Then it clicks. "You're saying that you have emotions but they're weak."

"When I feel, that emotion isn't weak, but the impact emotions have on my life is very low because I feel so infrequently."

Is he saying he doesn't actually *feel* anything for me? Is obsession an emotion? I'm pretty sure it's not.

"You feel desire for me." The still hard penis between us is testament to that.

"Yes." He closes his eyes, almost like he's in pain. "And it's playing hell with my intentions right now."

"I thought psychopaths were all about getting their needs met, no matter what."

"You realize that as a made man, I am not going to visit a psychologist, right? I don't have a neat diagnosis for the way my brain is wired."

"Can you feel love?" He's already claimed to love me, but if he can't feel that emotion, it's a lie. And he promised he wouldn't lie to me. "Do you have a conscience?"

If he doesn't, it won't bother him to lie to me.

"Define a conscience. Do I feel guilt for killing the enemies of my family? No." He starts to spread conditioner onto my hair, the yummy scent of coconut intensifying. "Do I feel guilt for killing men or women who would destroy the people most important to me? No."

"That sounds like you don't have a conscience then." Which explains why he finds it so easy to cut a man's hand off for touching me, but not why he would do it.

"Do I feel something inside me that is acutely unpleasant when I see you unhappy? Yes." The angles of his handsome face are harsh with intensity. "Does the need to take care of your sister and mom spring from my need to take care of you? Yes."

My heart speeds up, because although he's answering the question about his conscience, what he's describing sounds a lot like an assassin's version of love. It's not going to be hearts and flowers with Angelo, but I'm not a hearts and flowers kind of girl.

Obsession works for me in a way that casual interest wouldn't.

Maybe knowing I'm his focus is what makes me feel safe.

"Is that a conscience?" He pulls me close and rubs his hands up and down my back, and then massages my bottom as the steam swirls around us. "Maybe not. But it's what happens when a man who has no soul finds one."

Unless my ability to read people has suddenly taken flight, he's not lying. For the first time, Angelo's assertion that I'm his reclaimed soul rings true. And it touches emotions that I do my best to protect but am well aware of having.

Angelo believes that I give him the equivalent of a conscience.

Maybe not a fully realized one. He couldn't be top enforcer for the Cosa Nostra godfather if he was squeamish about killing, or doing the other things he has to.

But the fact that Angelo cares about my mom and my sister's well-being is more important to me than his job title.

Yes, I'm aware that makes me a little bit like him. The people I care about are more important to me than the people who end up in Angelo's crosshairs. And one thing I'm certain of is that my family and friends, like Bianca and Piper, will never be there.

Because I am his soul.

And he won't hurt me, adding him to the list of three people I believe that of absolutely: Mom, Cookie and my best friend, Bianca De Luca.

"My conditioner has been in long enough." And I've waited long enough for what comes next.

Sex.

Angelo doesn't move, but his hands on my butt feel so good, it's hard to complain about that. "Xabat said to leave it in for at least three minutes. It has only been two and a half."

"I don't think thirty seconds is going to make or break the silkiness of my hair. My hair has done just fine with bargain shampoo and conditioner and no special hair masks all my life. We are not doing one more thing to put off sexy times."

He smiles patiently at my rant, which probably took the thirty seconds he wanted to wait anyway.

"Doesn't that hurt?" I point at his rigid erection, still leaking from the tip.

My nipples ache with pleasurable pain. I'm positive it wouldn't take more than brushing against them for me to have a mini-orgasm.

"I'm used to it being this way around you."

"You spend hours at the club like this?"

"Sometimes."

We already talked about that, but I was more interested in the fact that he wasn't always turned on than that he spent hours that way on other nights. "You mean you never went into the bathroom to rub one out?"

"No." His grimace of distaste says it all.

Right. The clean thing. "Why not go out to your car and take care of it?"

"That would have meant not watching you."

And he would rather sit there in painful arousal than stop watching me.

Before I can say another word a wolf's smile takes over his rugged features. "Time's up."

Was he freaking counting the seconds in his head?

"Good!" I'm ready to bend forward and dunk my head under the chest-high spray rather than wait for him to remove the showerhead from the wall again.

But he doesn't give me the chance. In a lightning fast move, the showerhead is in his hand again. He rinses my hair for the final time with a subtly different touch. Caressing my skull with sensual movements, my soon-to-be lover works the conditioner from my long tresses.

He replaces the showerhead and pumps some soap gel into his hands. "Now, it's time to wash you."

"How long is this going to take?" I make no effort to hide my sexual frustration, even as I can't take my eyes off his hands rubbing together to make a good lather.

Angelo's laughter is pure masculine appreciation for the condition he's gotten me in by washing my hair.

I don't care if he thinks he's the world's best lover and has mad skills for turning a shower into foreplay. I'll give him a plaque with that on it if he'll just get to the good stuff.

"Can we hurry this up?" I ask crankily. "Only, I'm ready for my first orgasm not engineered by my own hand."

He goes still in the act of running the soap over my shoulders and down my arms. "None of your other lovers has ever give you a climax?"

"I've never had another lover, so that would be a no."

His jaw works as his hands tighten on my upper arms. It doesn't hurt, but I'm not going anywhere.

"You've had boyfriends."

I don't bother asking how he knows that.

"In high school." I haven't dated since I graduated. "And they were more friends that were boys than boyfriends."

But like all my other school friends, I lost touch with the boys that took me to the prom and sat next to me at our school's sporting events. We always went in groups, and they were lucky if they got a short kiss goodnight.

"They didn't touch you?" Angelo's voice is tight, like he's trying to control those emotions he says don't rule his life.

Something sure seems to be *impacting* him right now.

"No. They were lucky if they got a kiss goodnight." I don't mention that I experimented with tongue kissing with my sophomore crush.

I have a feeling that will put him on Angelo's list. I'm learning how my sociopath's brain works.

"They never touched you here?" He cups my breasts, kneading them with deft fingers.

My knees go wobbly. "N...n...ooo..."

"They never saw the pretty pink raspberry of your nipples?" Angelo squeezes my breasts one last time before pinching both my nipples.

I was right, is the last coherent thought I have as my body crashes into an orgasm that cannot even sort of be described as mini.

When the sparkly bits recede from the edges of my vision, I'm in Angelo's arms being carried from the now silent walk-in shower.

CHAPTER 22

ANGELO

I can't believe my precious love has never had a climax with another person. Pride courses through me at the knowledge that my touch just sent her straight over the edge.

"I thought we had to get me clean before you know..."

"The pleasure of washing every inch of your skin will have to wait for another time." What the fuck was I thinking, believing I had the patience for it this time?

It took every iota of self-control honed by first my nonno, then the military and finally Enzo De Luca not to take Candi up against the shower wall, her hair sudsy with shampoo.

She's so damn sexy with water running over her body. I knew the rain shower was a good idea, but not how profoundly it would affect me to see water running in rivulets down her breasts.

If her first time had been up against the shower wall, I would have been furious with both of us.

"Why didn't you tell me you're a virgin?" I demand.

"Excuse me, stalker-boy, but I didn't realize we were dating. When was I supposed to announce that little tidbit? When you rejected me earlier tonight, or maybe you think it's something I should have in the intro package for my spotlight dances?"

"Fuck no!" I'd have to kill all the men in Pitiful Princess for hearing that.

The idea of killing the men who lust over her while she dances is growing on me.

I have no problem with Candi dancing, but letting the men live who have seen her do it is another matter entirely.

"Don't go getting any ideas of going on a rampage on the punters, Angelo. I never looked at them. None of them made me wet." She's rubbing her hand over my chest, her tone soothing.

I force the animalistic growling that's clearly worrying her to stop. "You can keep dancing," I promise her.

"Good, because that's how I make a living."

"But I can't promise not to kill the men who lust after you."

"Because you know I'm a virgin?"

Is that what tipped me over the edge? Maybe. "I'll need to remove some names from my kill list."

"I knew it! You wanted to kill the boys I dated because you thought we got jiggy with it."

Jiggy with it? "You need more friends in your own peer group."

She blushes adorably as I set her on her feet and hand her a towel to do that turban thing she does that soaks the water out of her long hair. These are specially designed to wrap with a narrow tail on one end.

Shaking it out, she stares at it. "What is this?"

"For your hair."

Understanding dawns quickly because Candi is smart.

Leaning forward, her bountiful tits swinging, she flips her hair over her head and uses the towel to deftly wrap it. Watching her do something she's done a thousand times before, but here in our home makes something go weirdly tight in my chest.

There's nothing odd about the effect seeing her backside and a glimpse of her pussy in the mirror has on my body.

When she straightens, I'm waiting with a heated towel to dry her.

"Anyway, that *is* from my peer group," she snarks, like there's no pause in our conversation.

"Is it?" I pat the moisture from the slope of her breasts, cupping each one in turn with my terry cloth covered hands as I dry the undersides. "I'm pretty sure that song came out when I was still in diapers and you're nearly a decade younger than me."

"Whatever. My peers said it." Huffy, she tries to grab the towel from me. "I can dry myself."

"But I want to do it."

Candi's hands settles on her hips and she glares up at me. "You can't always have your own way."

"Agreed. A healthy relationship is about give and take."

"You sound like you read that in a book."

I shrug. "I did."

"You read a book about how to get along with people?"

"I read a book about how to get along with *you*."

Who the fuck cares if I get along with other people? Some men with stunted emotions like mine are so good at pretending, they charm everyone. An assassin doesn't need to charm anyone and I don't try. Not even Candi.

I want...no, I *need* her to accept me as I am. When she said that watching me skewer that guy's hand didn't upset her, I thought my heart would burst out of my chest with the joy I only feel with her.

"If you'd actually approached me in the last year, instead of creepily watching me from afar, that might be romantic."

Note to self: orgasms make Candi snarky.

"I was protecting you."

"Yeah, yeah, yeah...watching over me." She snags a towel and starts drying my torso. "I got the memo the first time. It still would have been more romantic if you'd I don't know, *talked* to me."

I give myself a moment to revel in having her take care of me like this. It's not something I expected, but I like it.

"It wasn't safe for you for me to single you out like that." Forcing myself to give up the feel of her rubbing the towel over my skin, I kneel down to dry her legs.

She's a lot more careful than I am wicking the moisture from my hair, before sliding it down to rub over my shoulders. "Sure, because talking to me is so dangerous. I'm pretty sure you cutting the hands off of men who touch me singled me out."

"Not in the same way. That could be dismissed as one of my idiosyncrasies. Everyone in the Family knows I like to play with knives."

"That's one way of putting it." I don't have to see her roll her eyes with that tone in her voice.

"I don't flirt, Candi. I fuck women and I walk away. I don't talk to them." I look up at her, my palm resting against her now dry inner thigh. "If I had talked to you, my enemies would have known I have a weakness."

She narrows her eyes, like she's trying to read me. "Are you going to walk away after we have sex?"

"No." I'll tell her as many times as she needs to hear it. "You are my one and only. I'm yours."

"I get a say about that."

"You get all the say about whether you accept or reject me, but there will be no other man for you." If she fell in love with someone else, I want to think I would let her have her happiness.

But I am me. Chances are, I'd take him out.

The kill list I have to amend now that I know none of her boyfriends touched her is proof of that.

"That's not creepy at all."

"You don't sound scared by my brand of creepy," I observe.

She doesn't look it either.

"Nothing about you scares me." There's nothing but sincerity in her tone.

Just like earlier. Even Severu watches me with a wary eye sometimes, but Candi is not afraid of me.

As it should be.

Sliding my hand upward, I let my thumb brush over her slit. She moans.

"Have you played with toys here?" I press into her vaginal opening, finding it slick and hot.

"No," she moans. "Don't have toys."

I suppose sharing her room with the precocious Cookie means keeping everything in there G rated. Which means that no one and nothing has touched Candi's most intimate flesh.

My obsessed heart wants to sing the Hallelujah chorus right now.

So, I don't ask why no other men. That's obvious, even to me. What happened to Candi in her last foster home before moving in with Mira and Cookie traumatized her sexually.

"Did he...?" I ask. "You don't have to tell me anything, but I don't want to remind you of bad memories either."

I know some of what happened to her. I shouldn't, but I had Mario get access to her file. He's good at charisma and seduction when he needs to be. He sent the reports to me without reading them.

So, I'm the only one outside of her case worker, who knows what is in the now sealed report taken at the time of Candi's removal from the home. The account is sketchy, with very little detail, but the gist is there.

Her foster father tied her up on more than one occasion and fondled her breasts while he got off, threatening to hurt her if she told anyone.

Candi didn't tell her case worker, or her school counselor, having already seen how easily the system let kids down during the five years she'd been in foster care. But she took a chance and told a teacher she trusted, and that trust was not misplaced.

Lucky for Candi, the teacher was dating a prosecuting attorney for the State of New York. With him on her side, Candi's abuse did not get swept under the carpet.

She never spent another night in that foster home either. Her teacher's intervention and the mandatory therapy afterward didn't undo the damage that had already been done though.

Subsequent reports labeled Candi as untrusting and borderline antisocial.

I should have realized Candi would never let her high school boyfriends touch her intimately. The miracle is that she *wants* my touch.

"Nothing you do could be like him," she tells me with conviction. "Even if you tied my hands and touched me like he did, it wouldn't be the same." I'm her exception.

Because our souls are connected, whether she admits it or not.

CHAPTER 23

CANDI

I don't know why Angelo's fingers on me feel so different than my own, but everything I usually feel when I pleasure myself is magnified by about a hundred.

It's all so different.

Intense.

The whole soulmate idea is feeling less and less like a ridiculous fairytale.

I've never experienced the kind of overwhelming, instant attraction I had for Angelo that first night. And there's the sense of security I feel when he's around, not to mention how I crave his hands on me when even the accidental touch of other men makes my skin crawl.

Cookie, the budding scientist in our family, would probably say there's some kind of biology at play here.

All I know is, right now my body is on fire and it's all down to Angelo.

His thumb presses deeper inside me stretching my sensitive flesh. "You're so slick for me."

I don't know what that keening sound is that comes out of my throat, but it's a new one for me.

"Fuck, yes, *amate*. Tell me about your pleasure." Angelo abandons the towel he's using to dry me, letting it fall to the floor in a crumpled pile as he slides his other thumb right over my clitoris.

A thousand needles of prickling pleasure radiate out from the nerve-rich nub. My whimper might embarrass me if I wasn't so turned on.

"Feels so good," I moan.

His thumb swirls around my engorged clitoris and I shudder with ecstasy.

"Fuck," he breathes out.

"That's the idea," I try to joke, but my voice breaks on *idea* as he shifts his hand.

Suddenly, two fingers are inside me and both his thumbs rub up and down on either side of my pleasure nub. "You're going to come for me again."

The bliss arcing along my nerve endings says he's right. Past experience says it's unlikely.

No matter how turned on I am by thoughts of this man – and he's the only one to inspire sexual desire *after* I come – I can never bring myself to a second climax. I've given up in cranky frustration more than a few times since my inner sex goddess started fixating on Angelo.

"I've watched you try to come again and give up," he says, his lips against my neck.

That should freak me out, not turn me on more. "Stalker."

"Your stalker."

"Yeah, if you start stalking someone else, I'll take one of your knives and cut off your dick," I promise him. "I might have to drug you first, but I'll do it."

Rational? No.

True? Yes.

He growls and grabs the base of his erection. "Fuck, you're going to make me come."

"We're both messed up." But I can't work up any more self-disgust than I can abhorrence of him.

"We are what we are." He kisses me under my ear, sending a shiver through me. "And what we are is perfect for each other."

"I'm not a sociopath." Life might have twisted my outlook a little, but I definitely have a conscience.

I feel guilty every time mom goes to bed in pain from working too long on her computer so that I can work four nights a week and still take classes at the community college.

I worry about the other dancers who take clients into the backrooms because I don't trust men and I care about my friends.

But none of that makes my threat any less true.

"You're possessive." He gently bites my earlobe. "I like it."

Shivering from the feel of his teeth on my ear, I sway forward. Angelo shifts one arm around me, holding me against him as his fingers continue to send shards of bliss through my ladybits.

I wait with my anticipation in overdrive to see what comes next. I'm sure I should be doing something. Anything, but my limbs feel separated from my body as Angelo pushes pleasure into me with knowing fingers.

All I can do is watch and *feel* as his head moves down my chest. I expect him to take one of my nipples into his mouth. I've watched porn. That's the next step, right?

Only it's not.

When his mouth connects to my skin next, it's right between my breasts. His kiss, soft and reverent, sends butterfly wings fluttering inside my tummy. More friends come to join the first wave when he presses his lips against the top slope of each of my boobs, kissing them.

He does it over and over, open mouthed, the tip of his tongue flicking out to lick me until every inch of the girls are covered in his DNA.

"I knew you would taste sweet, my delicious Candi." He nips the underside of my breast.

A moan of pure want snakes out of me. For once, the joke about my name doesn't irritate me. I want to be sweet for him, but that admission is staying inside my head, where it belongs.

I'm not some sappy romantic.

What's left of rational thought takes flight when Angelo's lips latch around one of my nipples. At the same time his arm shifts and his middle finger slides between my butt cheeks.

My gasp turns into another wordless sound of need when his fingertip plays across my sphincter as his other fingers push deep inside my vagina.

The finger rubbing over that other hole is unexpected, but what really shocks me, is how good it feels. Who knew there were so many nerve endings there? Pleasure flutters along every one of them to my core.

He sucks, barely biting down on my nipple and presses just the tip of his finger past my tight ring of muscle as he thrusts in and out of my slick vagina while his thumb rubs over my clitoris.

My head tips back in a wordless scream as the second climax I doubted I could have contracts every muscle in my body in ecstasy.

Angelo draws out the pleasure, stimulating my nipple with his tongue, not his teeth and gentling the movements of his fingers. It's just enough to keep the ecstasy shimmering through in a series of aftershocks that would knock down my apartment building if they happened in Queens.

When my body goes limp, he catches me before I can fall and lifts me into his arms.

Intensifying my need to have Angelo inside me.

He carries me into the bedroom, rips the bedding back and lays me down on the bed. His handsome face is hard with lust, but his eyes look at me with wonder.

Like I'm the most amazing thing he's ever seen.

"Angelo..." I sigh, wanting to give him the same pleasure he gave me, but too spent to lift myself off the bed.

"What do you need, *amate*?"

"I want..." I sigh again, luxuriating in the fluffy pillow my head rests on and the feel of the soft sheets under me.

"Tell me."

"You. I want you inside me, but I don't know if I'll come again. I'm not even sure I can do much more than lie here." I'm a limp noodle.

His smile is wicked. "Relax, *piccola gatta*. I'll do all the work."

"Good." It's probably for the best anyway.

My experience with all this is nil.

"You trust me," he breathes, like it's some kind of miracle.

I wouldn't be here if I didn't. "You already knew that."

"I knew that here." He raps the side of his head with his knuckles. "But now it's settled here." He rubs his chest in a circle with his fist.

Yeah, we're both having all sorts of emotional revelations tonight. But he's a lot more willing to tell me about them than I am willing to return the favor.

Talking is overrated anyway.

I expect him to come down over me and do the deed, but of course he does something else. Picking up my leg at the ankle, he brings my foot to his mouth and starts doing what he promised to in the shower.

Even knowing we just stepped out of the shower, the fact he's licking the instep of my foot blows my mind.

It tickles, but it also sends waves of sluggish desire straight to my center. His mouth moves up the inside of my leg, kissing and nibbling as he goes. Stopping just above my knee, he sucks on my skin there, the sensation sharp and intense.

Ripples of delight radiate out from his mouth on my skin.

I don't know how long he does his vampire imitation, but when he lifts his head, he makes a noise of deep satisfaction. "I want to mark you everywhere."

Maneuvering up onto my elbows, I look down my body to see a red mark on my leg. "You gave me a hickey?"

"I prefer the term love bite."

People have preferred terms for stuff like this? Or maybe it's just Angelo? "Okay."

Regardless of what he wants to call it, I have an unexpected reaction to seeing his mark on my skin.

A sense of rightness washes over me. I sort of love knowing that tomorrow there will be something I can look at *on my body* that is proof of what's happening right now.

This connection between us is primal and my reaction to him marking my skin with *love bites* is just as primitive.

A long way from done, Angelo licks a path up the inside of my thigh. His hot tongue and soft bites sends arrows of ecstasy directly to the bullseye that is my still pulsing clitoris.

Pushing my thighs wide, he fixes his hot gaze on my most intimate flesh.

"You have such a pretty pussy. Puffy lips I fantasize about when you dance in your G-string, now on display just for me."

"Only for you." There's a reason the privacy panels on my G-strings are lined and made with fabrics that don't indent at my slit.

Other dancers wear thinner, clingy G-strings for the opposite effect.

"Only for me." He brushes one fingertip along my outer labia, barely touching me. "I want to take pictures so I can have a painting done."

A roll of laughter takes us both by surprise, but I shake my head. "No way are you going to take a picture." I pause and consider that. "Well, maybe a picture would be okay, but I am not letting you have some kind of portrait done of my ladybits."

"We'll see."

"Yes, we will." How is he going to be okay with something like that being done? "What are you going to do, kill the artist after it's finished?"

Angelo's level of possessiveness is definitely on the unhinged end of the spectrum.

He cocks his head, like he's thinking about it.

"No, just no."

"I'll do what I did for the portrait of your eyes and the mosaic of your silhouette in the shower. I hired artists in Eastern Europe with the under-standing they would destroy all source material upon completion of the artwork."

I gulp. "Why Eastern Europe?"

"It should be far enough away."

"For what?"

"For me to feel the need to kill them." He inhales deeply. "Your juices smell so good."

"I'm glad...not that I smell good down there, though that's good too..." I ramble when I never ramble. Only with this man. "I mean I'm glad you wanted to figure out a way not to kill people you hired to do you a service."

"It would be a waste of talent and when I'm ready to commission more likenesses of you, I would have to find someone just as good."

Self-interest for the win. "Now you want to have someone paint a picture of me down there? Where would you hang it?"

"My gun room. No one else has access," he says immediately, indicating this isn't the first time he's had this thought. "I'll have the artist who did your eyes. She caught your essence perfectly and is working on a series of your smiles now."

He looks up at the ceiling and my gaze follows his. He wasn't joking when he said my eyes were above the bed. There's a tryptic of paintings, all about two feet high by six feet wide.

Each painting shows a segment of my face up to my eyebrows and down to the top of the bridge of my nose.

My eyes.

In the top painting, it's clear I'm smiling. In the middle one my eyes are thoughtful. And in the bottom one I look angry. Those are the three emotions he chose to look at when he went to bed at night?

"Why one of me angry?"

"Because you're beautiful when you're pissed off."

"Says every romance hero ever."

"You read romance?" he asks.

"It's something to read." And sometimes getting lost in a fictional world is the only way to deal with the real one. "Mrs. Kowalski down the hall gives my mom a grocery bag of them once a month when she's done reading them."

Why are we talking about my reading habits right now? Oh, yeah. Because of the tryptic. The resemblance is unbelievable. It's so close it's like looking in a mirror.

The giant images of my eyes looking back at me are a little disconcerting, even more so the thought that Angelo lays in bed at night and looks up at me looking down on him. No wonder he felt like we were dating for the last year.

He's been totally obsessed with me. What happens when that obsession burns itself out?

What if I catch feelings and my sociopath is actually a psychopath and unable to return them despite his belief that his obsession is love.

"What does that look mean?" His finger slides inside of me.

"You don't expect me to answer when you're doing that." He can't.

"I could stop." He withdraws his finger. "Tell me."

"Go back to fingering me and I will," I bargain.

His grin tells me I fell right into his neatly laid trap.

"Do you really need to know my every thought?" I ask.

"Yes."

"You take the obsession and stalking thing to whole new level, don't you?"

His fingers push back inside me and he presses upward against something that makes me see stars. The good kind.

"Wha...what if I don't want to tell you?" I ask.

"Then don't tell me."

Is it really that easy? "Will you stop touching me if I don't?"

"Even I don't have that much self-control."

Something loosens that had gone tight inside me. "Good, because I don't want to be manipulated with sex."

"I will never do anything you don't want me to."

"So, you just assumed I wanted you to stalk me?" I ask with disbelief.

"You never said you didn't." His fingers slowly piston in and out of me, sparking what should be an impossible renewal of sexual need.

How? How does he make my body sing for him like this?

"If I asked you to stop watching me, would you?" I gasp out, turned on but needing an answer to this question.

He doesn't answer at first while a war rages in the depths of his gray eyes. Finally, he nods with a jerky movement of his head.

Considering his level of obsession, his answer should surprise me, but it doesn't. His promise never to hurt me means protecting me even from himself and I believe that promise.

"What happens when you develop a new obsession?" Not wanting to see his expression when I ask that, I let my torso fall back to the bed only to be confronted once again with my own eyes staring back at me.

He'll have to get a new bathroom ceiling for one.

"I am thirty-three years old, *amate*. You are the only person I have ever been obsessed by. I need you when I don't need anyone. Watching you sleep quiets the buzz in my head."

I don't ask what that buzzing is about. I'm not sure I want to know.

"No more heavy thoughts," I decide. "I'm about to have penetrative sex for the first time, I say we focus on that."

Because only time will prove the longevity of his obsession. The only question is: do I jump in with both feet, or try to stay safely on the shore?

CHAPTER 24

ANGELO

C andi asks what happens when I'm no longer obsessed with her. That only happens when I'm dead and even then, I'll haunt the halls of hell looking for a way back to her.

She says she wants to focus on the sex and I'm down with that. My cock is so engorged it hurts. Embracing the pain, I lean down between her thick thighs and let myself taste her from the source.

With the first lap of my tongue from her perineum up to her clit, I fucking almost come. She smells and tastes like *mine*.

How can she wonder if there will ever come a time that's not true? There won't.

There is no Angelo Caruso without Candi Brigliano. Not anymore.

Chasing more of her juices, my tongue delves into her opening with my fingers. It's a tight fit, but she's so damn wet, her virgin pussy lets me in.

"Angelo!" Her hands grip my hair and pull.

The pain is another reminder how perfect she is for me. Even when she says she'll lay back and let me do my thing, Candi can't help touching me.

I fucking love it.

"I need you, Angelo," she says fervently. "I need you inside me."

All in good time. But first...I lick my way up to her clit and circle the swollen bundle of nerves with the hardened tip of my tongue. Over and over until she's canting her hips in silent demand.

She wants to come a third time when she didn't believe she could come twice in a row.

I do this to her. I am the one she wants to share her body with in a way she's never shared it before.

Me. Not a normal guy with regular feelings and reactions. *Me.* Angelo Caruso. Angel of Death.

Candi's lover.

Her breaths are coming in harsh sobs and she's trying to guide my mouth to give her what she wants with her hold on my hair.

But I don't. Not yet.

Reaching up, I gently disentangle her fingers and lift my head. "Are you ready for me, *amate*?"

"I was ready in the shower," she grouses.

Fuck, do I love when she gets grumpy.

"Good." I prowl up her body, enjoying the hell out of the marks I left on her thighs and undersides of her beautiful tits.

I stop when the head of my cock presses against her opening. "Are you on birth control?"

"You don't know?" she asks with clear disbelief.

"You could have the shot, or an IUD. Women get birth control places other than their GP all the time."

She husks out a laugh. "Which tells me you've read my medical file."

"Is that a question?"

Her head moves restlessly side to side. "No. It's not. And yes, I am."

"For me?" I want to know.

How long has she been on it? What are the potential side effects of what she's using? Pushing the questions aside for later, I wait for her to answer.

"If I say yes, it'll give you a big head."

"That's not a no."

"Yes, who else? I guess you read my medical records before the whole skewer a guy in the alley thing because that's when I went on the pill. And I got it from my GP."

My face creases in a smile of joy. She got birth control *for me*. Because she knew, like I did, that we are meant to be.

With the last barrier addressed, I push the head of my cock inside her.

She tries to scoot backward and I clamp a hand on one of her hips. "You'll stretch, trust me."

"Yeah, that's another thing every romance hero says. Only I thought oversized dicks like yours were a figment of author imagination."

How does she make me laugh when I'm literally aching to thrust home? No matter where we live, this woman will always and forevermore be my home.

"Are you sure you've used that thing like this before?" she demands, then shakes her head. "Don't answer me. Homicidal is not a good look when you're getting impaled by a steel shaft masquerading as a penis for the first time."

I am the apex predator, ready to claim my mate. Every animal instinct says to thrust deep and hard. But I am more than an animal trained to kill, no matter what people believe.

I am a man. Her man.

"I'll fit," I promise her. "You need to trust me. I'll take it slow."

"I do trust you. You're the only man I could do this with," she says in a voice aching with vulnerability.

I am the only one who gets to see this side of my woman made tough by life's lessons.

Forcing my body to still, I cup her luscious breast, playing with the nipple in a way I have already learned turns her on. "Relax. Your body responds to mine like you were made just for me."

It's almost enough to make even a man like me believe in God.

"I was responding," she complains. "But you stopped before I could respond all the way."

"Because the next time you come, I will be inside you." And being on the verge of climax will make this first time easier.

Which is why I make sure to bring her back to the precipice again, the whole time the head of my cock the only part of me inside her.

Fuck, it's hard and I'm pretty sure I'm losing my mind by the time her tight vaginal walls loosen and I can start a shallow thrusting. Every thrust forward, I go a little deeper until I'm fully seated inside her.

My body is clamoring for me to fuck her raw but I stop moving altogether and savor the moment. I never believed sex could make two people one, but that is how I feel right now.

I'm connected so deeply with Candi, there is no ending to her and beginning of me, or vice versa.

"You're inside me." She gazes up at me with an expression in her dark eyes I've never seen before.

Completely open to me, there's no guarded look in her pretty brown irises.

"I'm inside you," I agree. Then I rub my fist over my heart. "And you are inside me."

She nods. It's not a verbal agreement but it's more than enough.

I start to move and her hips follow mine. We rock together, lost in the sensation of each other until the urgency builds to fever pitch for both of us.

Wanting to feel her come around my cock, I swivel my hips on every downward thrust, pressing my pelvic bone against her swollen clit.

She moans and gasps and watches me with an expression in her eyes I could not bear to share with another. Not even to have it painted.

"Please, Angelo, I need it. It's right there. I'm on the edge, but I can't come," she wails the last.

Her anguish shouldn't make me smile, but when she mewls like the cat I liken her to, I can't hold back the curve of my lips.

She's so far gone, she doesn't even notice.

"Don't worry, I've got you." Holding myself up with one hand, I slip the other off of her tit and slide it down between us.

And I press my thumb against the bundle of nerves that will tip her over the precipice.

Her vaginal walls contract around me like a vise just before she screams loud enough I'm glad this room is soundproof.

That sound is not for anyone else's ears.

It's my last thought before my own body goes off like a rocket pouring my essence inside her.

For the first time in my life, I wish it could take root and create a child.

Later, I think Candi is asleep when her fingertip traces the lines of black ink on my Grim Reaper tattoo. "You know how you said you're more than a hitman for the mafia? Well, you're more than Death to me too. You could break my heart, Angelo."

When I wake up from our post coital nap, her words are still ringing in my head. *You could break my heart.*

I've never been that to someone. The person who could break their heart. My mom couldn't leave me behind fast enough when she returned to Sicily.

Nonno and nonna cared about me.

Nonno never let the fact that he'd married my nonna after my biological grandfather died stand between us. He called me his grandson and his word was law.

Nonna found my lack of emotion difficult, but she claimed to love me all the same.

Nonno said my dad's family, the Carusos, were wrong. That I would make a fine made man one day and he would be proud to sponsor me into *la famiglia*.

But if I had died, or run away, it wouldn't have broken his or nonna's heart.

I don't inspire that sort of feeling in others.

Except Candi.

The sound of Candi's phone ringing breaks into my reverie. After a couple of rings, mine starts going off as well. There's only one number besides Candi's programmed to ring through my DND setting.

Severu De Luca's.

And I know why he's calling. I could have taken care of this last night, but that would have meant potentially being called to his office and taken away from Candi on her first night here.

That wasn't going to happen. I have no regrets.

Candi's phone stops ringing only to start again and she stirs beside me.

"Wass...that?" she slurs sleepily.

"Our phones." I lean over and grab both off the nightstand and hand Candi hers.

After inserting my bluetooth ear device, I connect the call. *"Sì?"*

Answering in Italian is my boss's clue there is someone in the room with me that I don't want to overhear me talking about business. It also tells him that person doesn't speak Italian.

If they did, I would call him Mr. De Luca, the code for non mafia present, or Don De Luca, the code for mafia I don't trust present.

"Miceli just called me," Severu says without preamble.

"Good for you. Maintaining a strong filial bond helps keep perspective for a man in a position of such power," I quote something Big Sal said in one of the meetings between Severu and Miceli after my boss became godfather.

Candi scoots off the bed and heads to the bathroom, her phone next to her ear. I'm only hearing one out of three words but it sounds like Mira is calling and whatever she's saying is causing Candi agitation.

"Enough of the sarcasm," Severu says regaining my attention. "Why is one of his capo's lodging a formal complaint against you?"

A formal complaint? What the fuck? "Because Stefano Bianchi is an asshole."

An even bigger one than I thought if he's lodging a complaint against me for Mario killing the man who wanted to off Candi. His fucking *daughter*.

"Less of one than some of the other NY capos. What's going on, Angelo? He claims your people interfered in a business venture and appropriated a piece of his capital after golfing to the 18th hole with one of his people."

Our phones are secure, that doesn't mean we get sloppy. When it comes to communication with our new godfather, that's even more important than usual.

"All true."

Severu's silence lasts five full seconds. "He's demanding restitution."

"Candi witnessed his men preparing to take a nonpayer out of the game. It was play him on the 18th or her."

"Managgia la miseria."

"Candi is also Bianchi's biological daughter." I don't hide important shit from my boss.

And if Candi won't let me kill him, Stefano being her bio dad is going to cause problems down the road. It's also not something we have a code for, but neither is it something I plan to keep under wraps.

If outing Bianchi as Candi's sperm donor will prevent him from demanding restitution, he can consider himself outed. My woman didn't hesitate to tell the made men in the alley last night.

No need to hide it for her sake.

"Gino was going to play the 18th hole with his boss's daughter? His own cousin?" Severu's voice could compete with a glacier for chill. "That is not how you treat family."

"Depends on who you consider your family, boss." I sure as hell don't consider my Caruso relatives family.

My dad was the last person with the same last name I counted in that group.

Severu grunts, knowing my story. "Your kid is your kid, regardless."

"Not what my mom thought," I remind him.

The De Lucas have the kind of closeknit family others envy. I never did because of that whole lack of emotions thing.

However, the day Severu asked me to continue in my role with him when he became the godfather, he also told me he considered me family. And family were the only people who could be trusted to be in the inner circle.

My phone buzzes several times, telling me there are texts from one or more of my men.

"The other day, you said she belongs to you. Is that still true?"

"There will never be a time that Candi does not belong to me."

"Then it is you who should be asking for restitution since Bianchi's men threatened to kill what belongs to you. Do you want to escalate this?"

"No."

Several seconds of silence greets my answer. "You're not usually a man to turn the other cheek."

"She doesn't think much of him as it is, but it would hurt Candi to find out that her sperm donor is seeking restitution after having tried to have her killed. I will not have her upset by Stefano or anyone else."

"Unfortunately, you are probably right. Women in this world carry the emotions we can't. However, Stefano Bianchi cannot get away with attempting to manipulate us."

That was Stefano's biggest mistake. Whether he sought restitution to have a hold over me or Severu, he will regret coming for someone in the godfather's inner circle.

"I promised Candi I wouldn't play the 18th hold with him."

"Noted." Meaning he understands that if the decision comes down to take Bianchi out, one of my team will do the actual killing. "We make compromises for the women we love."

"Yeah." Severu sure as hell made a big enough one for Catalina.

"Once my brother learns that Stefano is using the situation for leverage when it's his own daughter your guy played the 18th hole for, he'll take the necessary steps to remind his capo about our family's position on protecting one's children."

Since the first De Luca became Don of the Genovese, they have had an ironclad rule that none of the men in positions of power in their organization are allowed to harm their wives and children. Protecting them from harm is the other side of that principle.

Now that Severu is the godfather, that precept is being rolled out among all Five Families in New York and the other Cosa Nostra mafias in Las Vegas, Detroit, New England, Boston and The Outfit in Chicago.

The Las Vegas don already has the rule in place or Don Enzo would never have let Severu's sister marry the don's son and underboss.

There's been some grumbling out of Detroit and Boston, but no outright rebellion. It helps that they all know who will be dispatched to deal with insurrection.

Me.

And no one wants me showing up to clean house.

Do I wish I could be the one to impart that message on Severu's behalf to Bianchi? Yes.

Would I rather they were actions rather than words? Definitely.

But I promised Candi I wouldn't kill her father and if I see him right now that is exactly what I am going to do.

"Miceli said that you refused Bianchi entrance to your estate. Now I understand why."

When did Stefano Bianchi try to get access to my house? He's sure as hell not on the short list of people allowed on the estate without gaining approval from me or Derian.

Candi lives here now. That means my security can't have holes in it.

Since I wasn't contacted, Derian must have denied Bianchi entrance. I smile. That would have chafed his ego.

"I'll let Miceli know the full situation."

Severu De Luca is the godfather. For him to offer to discuss this with his brother on my behalf shows exactly what place I hold in his life.

An important one.

Which I appreciate more than ever before, now that I have a family to protect.

"Thank you. I need to get Candi settled in." And the rest of her things moved over from Queens, along with her mom and sister.

Neither do I have time or the patience to deal with Miceli's warped sense of humor.

"Not to mention your future mother-in-law and sister-in-law, now that they are at your estate." That warped humor? Runs in the family.

"The fuck you say?"

"Apparently, Bianchi brought them to the estate to see Candi but was refused entrance while they were given access."

That would have really pissed the capo off. Derian definitely deserves a bonus.

Wild-eyed, Candi comes tearing out of the bathroom. "My mom and sister are here. Here!" she yells like I didn't hear the first time. "They're demanding to see me. You gotta undo that room door thing before mom calls the cops. I need clothes! *Where are my clothes?"*

Her body jiggles enticingly as she rushes around the room, like her clothes will magically appear. I disengaged one of the room safety protocols so I could send them and mine from last night down the laundry chute already.

Along with the towels I left on the floor of the bathroom. Which I never do, but fuck if getting inside Candi wasn't more important than my need for order earlier.

"I've got to go," I tell my laughing boss who can clearly hear Candi's yelling. "Thanks for handling things with Miceli."

Ending the call, I point toward the closet. "You have clothes in there."

"What?" She shakes her head. "Never mind. I don't care why I have clothes here. I'm just glad I do because if I go downstairs in a towel or one of your shirts, mom is going to start swearing in Polish *and* she'll still probably call the cops."

That is something we'll have to educate Mira about. When you're part of the mafia, you don't call law enforcement. Ever. Which is one of the reasons I have the job I do.

Candi rushes to the closet while I read the messages that came in while I was talking to Severu.

Derian: *B visiting the in-laws.*

It wasn't sent priority so the message didn't make it past my DND settings. Derian made the call he could handle whatever was happening and apparently he did.

Derian: *In-laws going for a drive with B. M along for the ride. I'm in the mood to take a couple of friends for a drive too.*

Derian made sure that Mario rode in the car with Bianchi and Candi's family while he followed with two more of my men in his SUV.

Derian: *In-laws here at the estate. Mom is agitated.*

He waited until they got here to text me because Miceli isn't the only made man in our organization with a warped sense of humor.

The next message is from Mario.

Mario: *Better bring Ms. Candi down here, boss. Your m-i-l could give Derian's mamma a run for her money dressing down the men in this family.*

The Haitian firecracker has a reputation in *la famiglia* and no one messes with her, or her family. She's one of the few people I actually like.

A new message comes in.

Derian: *Do you want me to block cell phone service so Mrs. Czabok can't call the police?*

Shit. I rush into the closet and start throwing on clothes. As a concession to time, I only arm myself with four weapons.

"You seriously think you need a gun and three knives to meet with my mom and sister?" Candi demands, looking at me askance.

"I don't go anywhere unarmed."

Candi's eyes widen. "Even in your own home?"

I shrug. "I'll always be prepared to protect you."

"You don't have to protect me from my family." She shoves her feet into the ankle boots I knew would look beautiful on her.

"I know that. But you never know what else will happen. Bianchi tried to gain access to the property, using your mom and sister to do it." No matter how secure my property is, I don't drop my vigilance.

Ever.

"Stefano went to my mom?" Candi rushes over to the steel wall. "Get this thing open! It's worse than I thought."

I do something on my phone. "Put your hand on the pad with the red light above it."

Candi does as I tell her and her palm print gets entered in the system.

"Now type in your birthday, year included."

"That's not obvious at all." She taps in the numbers.

"It only works from this side of the wall. The code for the other side changes daily. Only you, me and Derian have access to it."

"I don't have access to squat."

"You do on your new phone."

"New phone?" She rushes out of the room as soon as the wall slides up and she can open the door. "Not important right now. Stopping mom from calling the police is."

CHAPTER 25

CANDI

Mira Czabok may have debilitating arthritis. She may sleep behind a curtain in the kitchen and be wearing her only pair of dress shoes she bought at Goodwill a decade ago.

But when she is in a temper, my mom is a queen.

There are seven guards milling around the foyer when I come tearing down the stairs, Angelo's shout to be careful only spurring me to go faster out of orneriness.

What does he think? I'm going to trip and fall in the first pair of designer boots ever to grace my feet?

The guards are all watching mom like she's a bomb about to explode and they don't know which wire to cut as she yells at them in a mixture of English and Polish, none of it particularly polite.

But the way she looks at them is a monarch getting a glimpse of unruly peasants.

They don't scare her at all. She's looking for her daughter and here I am.

I remember thinking she'd never cut a guy's hand off to protect me, but coming to Long Island in the company of a mafia capo to rescue me is pretty much the same thing.

"Mom! I'm right here," I yell in really bad Polish.

But it gets her attention, and she stops mid rant to turn her glare on me. "Young lady, do you have any idea what time it is?"

Considering the fact I didn't check the time on my phone before answering her call, the answer is *no*, but that doesn't feel like the right answer to give my irate mother.

I look to Cookie for help and like the stellar little sister she is, she pats mom on the back. "I told you she'd be fine. Just because she didn't answer her phone earlier and hasn't called even though it's almost dinner time doesn't mean she got kidnapped like her douchebag sperm donor said."

Almost dinner time? We eat at 6:30 pm every night so Cookie has time to do homework after school and to relax after dinner. Mom insists on keeping the same schedule on the weekends too.

Considering Angelo and I didn't go to sleep until nearly noon – because sex is fricken amazing and we woke up an hour after falling asleep the first time to do it all over again – that's not so bad.

Obviously, mom does not agree.

"Language, young lady!" Mom pats Cookie's shoulder to soften the rebuke.

Oh, we're both *young lady*. We're so in trouble right now.

Cookie tries to look repentant. "Sorry, I should have said douchebag *biological father*. My bad."

"Diamond Marie Miller!"

I appreciate Cookie taking the heat off me but I don't want her in trouble on my account. "I can't believe I slept that long. I'm really sorry, mom. I should have called earlier."

Mom turns her attention back on me. "You're an adult. You can stay out all night. You texted to say where you were going, but then Mr. Bianchi came by and he said things did not go the way you said they did in your text."

"When we got here, they wouldn't let him past the gates with us." How much Cookie enjoyed that is in her voice. "Mom wouldn't wait with him because she was worried about you, and I wasn't missing out on seeing this house. It's epic!"

I can't help smiling. Cookie's one of the few people that has that effect on me. Angelo is now one of the others. Not sure how mom is going to feel about that, but it is what it is.

"Let's go sit down in the living room." Mom's not in her wheelchair. She can walk, but the lines around her mouth say she's in pain.

"I'd like to talk to you alone, *without him*." Mom nods toward Angelo with her head.

Before I can reply to that, a big black dog comes running toward us.

"Mars!" Cookie drops to her knees and puts her arms out in welcome. The dog gallops toward her.

Terrified he'll eat her, I leap toward them, but Angelo lifts me up with an arm around my waist. "Don't startle the dog. He knows your scent, but he still has to get used to you."

I struggle against his hold. "That's my sister he's about to eat."

"He's not going to eat her."

Fortunately, the dog does not make a liar out of his human. He nuzzles Cookie, licking her face. My sister's giggles at the dog's attention are as carefree as I've ever heard her.

She hugs him and tells him all about how she got here in babytalk, calling him a good dog and her friend.

Cookie adores that dog.

Which raises the all-important question. How does she know him?

A gray haired man comes rushing after the dog, yelling it's name but skids to a stop when he sees Cookie and Mars loving on each other.

"That explains it." He looks past my shoulder at Angelo. "Sorry, boss. He got away from me. But I guess he scented Cookie."

"Looks like it," Angelo says wryly.

"You can let me down. I'm not going to scare your dog." Apparently being trussed up by Derian and Mario had more impact than I thought, because I do *not* like being immobilized again. "I swear if one more guy manhandles me this month, I'm going to stab him in the eye with a stiletto."

"Shoe or knife?" Angelo asks, his voice laced with eager curiosity.

"Keep holding me up like this and you'll find out," I promise.

His laughter no longer shocks me. Something about me makes the mafia assassin happy.

Speaking of happy, my sister and the dog are so delighted with each other, no one else registers. Mom, on the other hand, looks ready to find that stiletto and use it on somebody.

My best guess is Angelo, but she's pretty mad at me too.

After hugging me, like he can't help himself, Angelo releases me.

Mom is going to have to wait a minute.

Turing to face him, I demand, "How does my sister know your dog?"

"Cane Corsica's are excellent family guard dogs, but they are also territorial. It was imperative he learned to socialize with children and to see your sister as his friend and charge."

"That's the why, not the how." I don't bother asking why it was important to get the dog used to Cookie.

Angelo has this whole life for us planned out and in his head it was a done deal before we ever met.

Silly me, I'm starting to want to live in his dream.

Cookie looks up, her cheek wet from dog kisses and a big grin on her face. "Mr. Boomer brings Mars to my school twice a week. Me and two of my friends got picked out of the whole school to help socialize him, but I'm his favorite."

"Boomer takes your dog to my sister's school twice a week?" I practically shriek, which does in fact startle the dog.

Jumping in front of Cookie, Mars growls at me.

Angelo says something in Italian and makes a gesture with his hand.

The big black dog stops growling immediately and trots over to stand beside my kidnapper turned lover. That is such a weird thought outside of a romance novel.

Angelo reaches for me. "Give me your hand."

"Are you sure it's safe?" I give the dog a wary eye.

"I've been training him. You, your mom and your sister are his charges, but he only knows your sister and your mother's scents. He associates them with good things and his training to protect."

He's been training his dog to know and protect me and my family. Is there a word for super stalker?

"How does he know our scent?" I give my hand to Angelo.

He brings the dog closer with another hand gesture and guides the dog to sniff my hand while talking to it in Italian. The only word I catch is *amica*. Friend.

Mars snuffles my hand and then licks it.

"Can I pet him?" The dog seems like he wants pets, practically vibrating in eagerness to get closer, but he doesn't move without Angelo's permission.

"Of course."

I drop to my haunches and scratch the dog behind his ears. "You're beautiful, aren't you Mars? Just like your human, you're a warrior aren't you? Is that why they named you Mars?"

"You know me so well," Angelo says approvingly.

"Unless she's been hiding things from me and my daughter would not do that, she barely knows you at all." Mom's limps forward.

My heart plummets. I never should have let us stay standing so long.

Angelo notices my distress because apparently he notices everything about me and says, "Get Mrs. Czabok's chair, Boomer."

I don't know what he's talking about but less than thirty seconds later, the man called Boomer comes into the foyer riding a motorized chair. It's the most streamlined scooter I've ever seen.

We couldn't afford to get mom even a used clunky one, but I've drooled over the catalogues and I know this mobility device set Angelo back several thousand dollars.

"Sick!" Cookie shrieks. "Look at that, mom!"

Mom is looking and the longing in her eyes is painful to see. Unless someone has lived without mobility, they can never know what it feels like to lose it. Mom couldn't leave the apartment for six months when the elevator was broken a couple of years ago.

I can't help thinking that if Angelo had been around then I bet it would have been fixed within a day.

"Please sit down, Mrs. Czabok," Angelo tells her. "Boomer will show you how to operate it."

Mom lets Boomer help her onto the chair of the scooter.

When she's sitting comfortably on the dark red leather seat, she glares warningly at Angelo. "Don't think you're going to buy my approval with expensive gifts."

"I would not dream of it." Angelo sounds genuinely shocked by the idea. "But whatever I can do to make your life easier, I will."

"Because of my daughter?" Mom asks mistrustfully.

"Yes. What is important to her is important to me."

"I told you the douchebag was lying," Cookie pipes up.

"Use that word one more time and you lose TV privileges for a week."

Cookie mimes zipping her lips and it reminds me of Angelo earlier. I smile.

Those two are going to be a force to be reckoned with.

While Boomer is showing my mom how to maneuver the chair, I slide my hand in Angelo's and squeeze. "Thank you."

"You're welcome. I didn't intend to keep the scooter here, but Boomer was testing it out for manufacturer defects before I had the nurse give it to your mother."

"The nurse?" I look up at him. "You mean the in-home care nurse from the foundation Cookie's social worker found for us?"

Angelo nods. "She was going to tell your mother she'd been chosen to test the maneuverability of the company's latest model. In exchange, she would have gotten to keep the scooter."

"You know mom's nurse?"

The man who claims I am his soul looks at me like I'm not very bright. "She works for me."

"Excuse me for not knowing just how far you were willing to go for the title of Most Benevolent Stalker." And also, I thought the nurse worked for the foundation. Then it clicks. "You're the Foundation."

He shrugs.

Tears prick my eyes.

This man.

CHAPTER 26

CANDI

"I get you were worried because I didn't answer the phone, but what are you doing *here*? You knew I would call back." As soon as I woke up anyway.

Mom and I are alone in the living room while my sister plays with the dog in the yard outside the windows so we can see her.

She has an entourage of two guards and the older man, Boomer. Angelo is consulting with Derian and Mario, probably telling them how much to reveal about last night to my mom and sister.

Although it sounds like Stefano told them pretty much everything. That tattletale Freddy must have told him that Angelo's men had to tape me up like a mummy to get me to go with them.

Mom looks at me like she's trying to catalog injuries. "Your biological father came to see me."

"Cookie said that in the hall."

"Yes, well clearly you aren't a kidnap victim, but he didn't lie about everything, did he? Mr. Bianchi told me that Angelo works for the mafia and he would know."

"He's the top enforcer for the new godfather." Mom's never been part of the mafia life, but a New Yorker would have to be living under a rock not to know what that means.

"Why didn't you tell me that?"

The easy answer is because I didn't want her to worry, but mom doesn't want easy. She wants truth.

So, I give it to her. "I didn't want you to think it was like it was with mom and Stefano."

"How is it different?" Mom gives the look that says she thinks I don't have an answer for that. "You're a dancer like Bonbon was. He's in the mafia like Stefano."

"Both of those things are true, but they aren't everything."

"Stefano wouldn't have bought your grandmother a scooter to get around more easily, that's for sure."

Not that he ever met my grandmother, but then neither had I. Mommy grew up in and out of foster care until she ran away at fifteen. Her mom never got sober and died before I became an adult and might have gone looking for her.

If mommy ever knew who her dad was, she never mentioned it. I might have been only ten when she died, but she shared pretty much everything with me.

Some would say she was guilty of oversharing, but I would say she did her best. She loved me and tried like hell to be a better parent than her own mom.

"For starters, Angelo is not married to another woman. That's a pretty big difference. For another, Angelo is not paying me to have sex with him." I don't look down on my mom for turning tricks, but the fact my dad paid her for sex and treated her like a commodity even after she gave birth to his child?

That makes him the douchebag my sister called him.

"But you two *are* having sex?" Mom doesn't try to soft pedal the question.

It's not her way.

My answer is just as direct. "Yes. Not that it is any of your business because I *am* an adult."

She says a little prayer in Polish. "I am very worried for you, Kathleen."

Kathleen? Okay, this is serious. She's really worried.

I don't know how to fix that. All I can give her is the truth. "I have never felt as safe as I do when Angelo is nearby."

Not even when I'm at home, but I leave that left unsaid. Mom would understand it. It's hard to feel completely safe when you're a few busted locks away from a break-in.

I wonder if Angelo would be willing to install a steel door for the apartment? Even if he's serious about us all coming here to live, it can't happen overnight.

"How can that be?" mom asks, sounding bewildered. "He's a mafia enforcer. He's no better than a killer for hire."

"I am top enforcer for the godfather." So much for Angelo leaving me and my mom to talk privately.

Mom glares at him disapprovingly. "You said you would give us a few moments alone."

Angelo nods, his expression serious. "I thought that if you were going to discuss what Bianchi told you about me, I should be here."

To defend himself?

Mom looks at me like this should upset me. "Is this what you want from your life? A man who won't respect your boundaries?"

"It's not my boundaries he's imposing on. I didn't ask for time alone. *You* did." I had said I wanted Angelo to be here.

I've never liked the game of telephone and didn't want to play go-between with my mom and lover.

Lover.

I have a lover.

"I don't know why you are smiling right now, Kathleen. I'm worried for you," she says again.

"If I ask him to leave right now, he would go." I'm confident of that.

Mom gives Angelo that gimlet stare that always gets me and Cookie to tell the truth. "Is that true? When Candi asks you to go, are you going to leave us alone? "

"If Candi asked me to go, I will leave."

"But I'm not asking him to go," I tell my mom. "He can answer your questions better than I can."

"Can he tell me honestly you weren't kidnapped last night? That he's not using you for his own purposes. Mr. Bianchi seems to think you're in danger if you stay in New York."

"He would say that." Stefano has wanted me out of New York at least since I was eighteen and probably since my birth.

The one and only time I was approached by a representative of my father's happened after I turned eighteen and aged out of the system. Stefano offered to pay my tuition and living expenses for college, on one condition. I had to go to a university in another state.

If that was his idea of *taking care of me* like he promised mommy, it was a nonstarter. I couldn't leave mom and Cookie and turned the stipulation down.

I never told mom about the offer because she would have wanted me to go.

"Look, mom, we're both safe to say whatever we need to in front of Angelo. He won't get angry, no matter what that is. He's not going to hurt us." How do I know that?

That's a question I hope she doesn't ask, because the only answer I have is my heart trusts him. And that's way too lame to say out loud.

"You can say that about him?" Mom's derision hits me on the raw.

"Angelo isn't the one who ordered my death. In fact, if he hadn't declared me off limits, I wouldn't be alive right now. Yes, his men kidnapped me, *for my own safety*," I stress. "After they stopped one of Stefano's men from shooting me."

I'm still going to make them regret trussing me up, but that's neither here nor there. If Angelo and his men are going to be in my life then they have to learn I'm not a pushover.

Mom's face drains of color. "Someone was going to shoot you?"

"Gino was definitely going to kill me."

"Your old boss?" My mom asks with confusion.

I shake my head. "Another Gino. This one worked for Stefano and he was definitely going to pull that trigger."

"Worked for? Did Mr. Bianchi fire him for what he was going to do."

"Not likely."

"Then why are you using the past tense?"

"Because someone shot him before he could shoot me."

Mom gives Angelo a concerned glance. "Should you be telling me this? I'm assuming no police were involved in whatever happened."

"No police, but in the mafia, my people are as good as law enforcement." Angelo walks toward the door. "I'll order some tea and be right back."

"Who's going to make it?" I want to know.

"The housekeeper probably. I'll introduce you to all the staff and security later."

"That doesn't sound intimidating at all," I mutter under my breath.

Mom sighs. "I guess killing for the mafia pays well."

"That's what I said. He told me he inherited money too."

"Made by criminals, no doubt."

"Yeah, mom, like every other multimillionaire..." I look around the house, consider the staff comment and the size of Angelo's security force. "Or billionaire with squeaky clean ancestors who never took egregious advantage of anyone else. Legally, or not."

Mom sighs, knowing I have a point.

I lean forward and gently take mom's gnarled hands into mine. "I'll say whatever I need to in front of Angelo. And I want you to know that there's no danger for you speaking your mind in front of him too."

Maybe I should give mom and Cookie a chance to adjust, not that my sister seems to need one, but things are moving fast with Angelo and I *need* my mom to see what I see in him.

Because I want to be with him and I don't want to be at odds with her to do it. She's too important to me, but so is he.

Whether that makes sense, or not.

"The three safest people in New York are you, me and Cookie," I promise her.

"Not if he's the top enforcer for the godfather. The godfather comes first."

"First, while I augment security for Severu when I feel it is necessary, his head of security is responsible for the godfather's safety on a daily basis." With a considering look at mom, Angelo turns on the fire before fetching a fluffy throw from inside the square leather ottoman coffee table.

"Stop sneaking up on us," I grumble.

"There was no sneaking." He lays the throw over mom's lap. "Your mother saw me return."

Because the armchair she's sitting in has both a view of the door and the floor-to-ceiling windows, whereas where I'm sitting faces the windows directly.

"You walk really quietly."

"You'll get used to it." His eyes laugh at me as he settles onto the sofa beside me.

Memories of him cutting off my tape covered clothing play a montage in my brain. So, I almost miss my mother's grudging thank you.

But Mira Czabok taught me and Cookie manners and always led by example.

"Do you need anything else?" While Angelo's tone isn't exactly solicitous, the way he waits for my mom to answer shows it's not a perfunctory question either.

"I'm fine, thank you," mom replies politely, but her eyes hold no humor. She's not swayed that easily.

Angelo nods. "The tea will be here shortly."

I've got zero doubts that there will be green tea for mom and vanilla black tea for me. Not that I get to drink it that often, but it's my favorite and Angelo seems to know all my favorite things.

Does Angelo even drink tea?

"You said first," my mom prompts Angelo.

"Second, there will never come a time that it will be a choice between her safety and Severu's."

Mom frowns. "That's easy to say, but how can you be so sure?"

"Because if the situation arose, I would allow Derian's team to protect Severu, but would personally insure Candi's safety."

"How can I believe you?" Mom asks with a tremulous voice.

Now she's really pulling out the big guns. It's one thing when mom is angry, but when she acts all vulnerable?

I know she's doing her best to get me to agree to whatever she wants me to do. She's not one for showing weakness and allowing herself to do so always gets to me.

However, even though she catches me right in the feels, it doesn't always work. Like when she tried to get me to quit dancing at Pitiful Princess. It was the one way I could make enough money to support us and still go to school, so I refused to get a different job.

Just like then, the only way to reach my mom is to be as open as she is.

"Mom, I want you to meet my soulmate." I take Angelo's hand, and he immediately laces our fingers together. "This is Angelo Caruso."

CHAPTER 27

CANDI

Mom's mouth goes slack in stunned surprise.

Angelo is practically vibrating with that emotion he claims only I bring to him. Joy.

His hand squeezes mine. "You said it. You can't take it back."

"I don't want to." If that makes me as delusional as he is, at least we're living in that dream together.

"Candi, a man without a soul can't be your soulmate. I didn't want to have to tell you this, but Mr. Bianchi told me––"

"I don't care what my biological father has to say," I cut my mom off quick. "His opinions are of no value to me."

"It's not an opinion. It's a fact. Angelo Caruso is the nephew of the former godfather."

I look to Angelo for verification.

He nods.

"Even though he was more than ten years younger than his cousin, because of who Angelo's maternal grandfather is, he was supposed to become the next don in his family." Mom says the words like she's imparting a terrible secret.

I'm not appalled. But I am curious. "Why are you Severu's head enforcer? Is that a role for him to groom you to take over when you are older?"

I don't understand how the mafia works, but I watched the Godfather franchise, just like everyone else.

"No. I will never be don and Severu will be the godfather until his death many decades from now."

"Oh. So why does it matter?" I ask my mom. "I'd think you'd be happier he's not that high up in the hierarchy."

Angelo shifts his leg. Only a tiny bit, but there's something about what I just said that agitates him. What?

Mom doesn't notice. "Because of *why* at the age of ten those plans were abandoned."

"Why?" I ask Angelo, not mom.

"Both my grandfather and my uncle decided my cousin Henrico would make a better don and potential godfather after all."

"Tell her why," mom practically dares him.

He looks at me with his unfathomable gray gaze. "They considered my inability to emotionally connect with others too big a detriment."

Mom's expression isn't one of victory, but pity.

For me.

I don't feel pitiful though.

Knowing Angelo isn't expected to lead the mafia someday is more of a relief than anything. I would make a terrible godfather-ess. Is that even a word?

"If you were a don, we couldn't be together, could we?" I ask.

The mafia hierarchy is a lot like royalty, I guess. The higher you go, the less say the person involved has about who they marry and build a life with. At least, that's how it is in the movies.

"My position wouldn't matter. Once I saw you that first time, you became my future."

Comments like that are sounding less stalker-y and more romantic to me. Mom's expression says she definitely considers them on the stalker end of the spectrum though.

"You're missing the point, Kathleen. Two of the biggest criminals in the world thought your *soulmate* was too without conscience to be put in a position of leadership." Mom's voice is laced with both pity and frustration.

Something about that doesn't ring true though. Why would criminals care if their leader-in-training suffered from a conscience?

"What happened?" I ask Angelo.

"To understand the dynamic, I have to give you some background on my birth family."

"I'm listening." I smile to let him know I'm doing it with an open mind. Mom has enough walls up for both of us.

"My parents' marriage was arranged between two old and powerful Cosa Nostra families. Senior and Perla didn't love each other, but as a kid, that never bothered me."

"Because you didn't really get emotions to begin with," I guess.

"Right. I hadn't met you."

Mom makes a strangled sound, but I ignore her for the moment. This is too important for me to get sidetracked by her reaction.

"You didn't bond with either of your parents?" That would have been so lonely for him.

"No. The first person I connected with emotionally was my nonno and that was after my dad's death and my mom leaving me behind as a failed experiment in dynasty building."

"What does that mean?"

"Her father is the Sicilian godfather. Don Messino wanted an alliance with the American godfather, Don Caruso. He had two brothers. My dad and my uncle. Uncle Rico was the oldest, but he was already married to someone from the Lombardi Family."

"Who are they?"

"The Cosa Nostra mafia that runs Boston. His wife was related to the don's family and there was no way Uncle Rico would get away with killing or divorcing her."

This time, both mom and I give the same disturbed hum. He makes murder and divorce sound like pretty much the same thing and that's chilling.

"So, that left your dad."

"Senior agreed to marry Perla on the condition that their oldest son would become the next Luchesse don and eventual godfather. No one expected it to take nearly a dozen years and IVF for my mom to finally bear a living child."

"That poor woman." Mom shakes her head sadly. "IVF wasn't an option for Jakub and me. No money for it, but we tried for years to get pregnant."

"My mother's only interest in having a child was in the power it would give her as the mother of a future don and godfather. Until I went to live with my nonno and nonna, I was raised by nannies."

"Oh." Now Mom looks like she pities Angelo.

That's a step in the right direction, so I hope he doesn't say anything that might mitigate it. Like, he didn't really care because he never felt anything for her anyway.

What if he would have bonded with her emotionally if she'd been there to bond with? How different would Angelo's life have been?

"It was clear I was different from an early age and my cousin, Henrico, took every chance he could to point out how much to our uncle."

"The godfather?"

"Yes. My father was killed when I was ten. Without him alive to push his brother and my grandfather into sticking to the agreement, it was only a matter of time before they reneged."

"Because you were different?"

He shrugs. "You know that diagnosis I'll never get? Henrico convinced my uncle, Don Caruso that I'm a psychopath without loyalty. It didn't take much to convince my grandfather in Sicily of the same thing."

"But you were only ten years old!" They couldn't have diagnosed something like that at such a young age.

"There were no psychologists involved. Just me and my lack of connection to the adults around me." He looks at my mom for the first time since he started talking. "My parents fired my first nanny after I called her mamma. She is the only one I ever allowed myself to care about, because losing her hurt."

His tone reveals nothing of his emotions, but for him to admit that it had hurt is huge.

"Your parents were not good people," I mutter.

"I'm sorry you suffered that neglect," my mom says with sincerity. "But whether they made you like you are, or you were born this way, you are what you are."

"And what is that, mom?" I demand. "A man who *is* loyal. A man who is trusted by the *current* godfather so much he was made his top enforcer."

"Being trusted to kill people on demand is hardly a ringing endorsement for his character." Mom's words are harsh, but her tone lacks the conviction of earlier.

"He's more than just an assassin. Angelo has a lot more responsibilities than that." Okay, I might be exaggerating here a little because all I know is that Angelo told me he's more than a hired killer.

I'm not sure if that means he has more responsibilities or not. In fact, I don't honestly know what he meant by that at all.

But that doesn't stop me from standing up for him.

"Your daughter is right, Mrs. Czabok."

I love how Angelo pronounces mom's last name with a perfect Polish inflection. He cared enough to find out how and then practice it.

Doesn't that show he has depths other people don't see?

"I do have many responsibilities within the Cosa Nostra, especially now that my boss is the godfather."

"Like what? Are you trying to say you don't kill people for the mafia?" she asks, sounding almost hopeful.

"I do kill people," he disabuses her of the notion he doesn't immediately. "But protecting them is also part of my job. I am the ghost in the night our enemies fear, but I am also the man sent to dispatch justice on behalf of the innocent."

"What does that mean?" I ask because frankly that sounds more dangerous than the killing part.

"Do you think a mafia wife can go to the police when her husband is hurting her? What happens when an employee embezzles from the family businesses? Who enforces the laws that protect all members of *la famiglia* when not going to the police is the first rule everyone in the family learns?"

"What are you saying?" Mom asks point blank.

"An enforcer is a soldier. We enforce the laws. One of Severu's laws as a don was that none of the high-ranking officials in his organization could abuse their families."

"That should go without saying," mom says, unimpressed.

Angelo looks at her dispassionately. "What you might consider prosecution and punishment happen in 100% of discovered cases within the Genovese Family."

"Because of you?" This is so not what I expected Angelo's extra responsibilities to be.

"For those not directly under the don in the hierarchy, yes."

"But I thought..."

"In the last year, my team's remit has expanded to include assessment and intervention in domestic violence within the mafia."

"Oh. I don't know what that means."

"The don's enforcers have always been responsible for punishing those guilty of breaking our laws, but although protection of the family is a key precept of the mafia life, the accepted practice was that the don could not interfere in the domestic life of his made men."

"That's changed now?" I ask.

"Yes." Angelo doesn't sound like he cares either way, but knowing this is part of his job is making me seriously wonder how much of a morally gray superhero my mafia assassin is.

It never occurred to me that criminals have no access to the judicial system. Honestly, I never even thought about it. "What about divorce? I always heard that there's no divorce in the mafia."

"We won't be getting a divorce."

"See, this is exactly what I'm talking about!" My mom sounds upset again.

"I will not keep your daughter against her will," Angelo vows, even though last night he did just that.

Though if I'm honest with myself, once I got here, I didn't stay because I was forced to and he knew it. The man has studied me way too closely not to.

"Neither will I ever give her a reason to want to leave me," Angelo adds. "Candi's happiness is my priority. I will never harm her. I will always protect her and those she holds dearest."

My heart pounds in my chest with an unfamiliar emotion. It's both gratitude and an overwhelming sense of security, even stronger than anything I have known because of him. This isn't a promise to protect me while I hold his interest.

This is a vow for the future that I absolutely believe.

For the rest of his life, Angelo will be dedicated to keeping me safe and happy. I'll do the same for him. Because relationships go both ways. And as wild as it might have seemed to me yesterday, today I acknowledge Angelo Caruso and I are in a relationship.

One I didn't know about for almost a year and that's still weird, but a relationship all the same.

Is that love? I don't know.

It's definitely obsession but it's an obsession that will keep me safe and has the potential to make us both genuinely happy. I don't see the downside.

"So, if she wants you to quit killing people will you?" mom asks.

My heart squeezes in my chest because I don't know if I want the answer to that question. Worse, unlike what my mom clearly believes, I'm not sure I would ever ask my assassin to stop being one.

Angelo directs his answer to me, a flicker of apology in his gray eyes. "There's no quitting your job in the mafia."

"Mafia men retire," my mom counters.

"Do they?" Angelo asks.

"Considering you'd know the answer to that better than we would," I say wryly. "My guess is no."

And I'm not nearly as bothered by that as I probably should be. The look mom is giving me says she knows it.

My stomach sours at the thought of disappointing her, but we've never lived in a perfect world. Why can't we live in a safe one? One where I'm happy with a man who fascinates me in every way.

"To answer your initial question in relation to other married couples within the Cosa Nostra. If the legal risk to *la famiglia* is too great, the divorce cannot happen, but the don can and has ordered a separation."

"What does that entail?" I'm not thinking about me, but my friend Bianca, who married a capo in the mafia in August.

"That's case by case."

"Give me an example," I press.

"When we were kids, one of the capo's wives petitioned the don for a divorce. Her husband had shared too much about the business with her for divorce, but the don ordered the capo to provide financial support for her and their children to live without him outside the city."

"And she was okay with that?"

Angelo shrugs. "If you are raised in the life, you know that once you become part of the mafia through marriage or getting made, the only way out is death."

"You said you'll protect the people I hold dearest."

"Yes."

"Will you protect Bianca from Salvatore De Luca?"

"If it becomes necessary, yes." There's no hesitation in Angelo's words and I like that he doesn't try to tell me it will never be necessary.

Bianca is bananas for the guy and he seems equally, intensely smitten, but that doesn't mean I don't want an exit strategy for her just in case.

CHAPTER 28

ANGELO

C ookie and Mars come skating into the living room, and I'm not ashamed to admit I'm grateful for the interruption of the *heartfelt* discussion.

Communication might be important to a healthy relationship, but talking this much is giving me a headache.

The little girl stops abruptly in front of me. "I'm hungry. When's dinner?"

Surprised she has no hesitation about talking to me, I answer, "The housekeeper will have dinner on the table at 6:30."

That's the time they usually eat and I'm not about to mess with Mira's schedule for Cookie.

"Cool! What are we having?"

"Diamond Marie!" Mira admonishes. "Is that any way to behave as a guest in someone's home?"

"Sorry, Mr. Caruso. I shouldn't have asked what we're eating." She wiggles her brows at me where her mother can't see. "But if you wanted to tell me..."

Mira laughs and so does Candi.

I find my own lips trying to tilt upward. "It's Sunday. That means fava bean soup to start, stuffed manicotti and *arrosto* for the main course. Though I don't know if it's beef or pork."

"You have three dinners on Sunday?"

"Three courses to a single dinner. It's tradition." Nonna always insisted on a full Sunday dinner together, no matter what else nonno and I got up to during the rest of the week.

My new housekeeper is old school like nonna was and prepares the same, whether I'm here to eat it, or not.

"We didn't intend to descend on you for dinner," Mira says still looking at me like I'm the bug on the pin she's trying to figure out.

But maybe one that she doesn't want to squish under her shoe anymore. Progress.

"You are family. You cannot be an intrusion." That is something nonna used to say and that I genuinely believed I never would, much less the words about to come out of my mouth. "My home is your home. I hope one day, you will make it your home full-time."

"We get to live here?" Cookie's, black and pink braids fly around her head as she turns it side to side, looking at everything in the living room.

Candi spends three hours every few weeks box-braiding her sister's hair. I don't know where she learned how to do it, but she uses different colored yarn extensions each time and Cookie likes it.

There is always at least a week, but often longer in between taking out her braids and re-braiding her hair when Cookie wears her curls free.

My woman might use cheap, discount shit on her own hair, but she gets the stuff for Cookie's hair from a salon. Not an expensive one, but not a discount store either.

"No one said anything about us living here," Mira frowns at me.

Am I leveraging Cookie's enthusiasm for new experiences and her obvious enjoyment of our home to get my way? Yes.

Do I regret doing so? Not at all.

I want them living here where they will be safer and Candi will be happier for having them with her.

"Mr. Caruso did! If we're living here, will I call you Angelo?" she asks me excitedly.

"I would like it if you called me Angelo now. Or *fratello*."

"Is *fratello* your middle name?"

"It's Italian for brother."

Cookie's eyes go wide. "You're my brother?"

"I will be when I marry your sister." When that happens is up to Candi. That it will happen is a given. Soulmates do not live separate lives.

Mira gasps sharply, but Candi just laughs. "Angelo lives in his own little world, but you can call him *fratello* if you want to."

Which is as good as an agreement that one day we'll be married. I'll ask her of course. Every woman deserves a proposal story she can share with her children and grandchildren. Nonna said that too.

Her first husband was an arranged marriage but my Caruso grandfather still proposed. Nonno proposed three times before nonna said yes to her second marriage.

Candi gets *one*. With me. And she's the only woman I will ever marry.

"We'll discuss Angelo's delusions later," Mira says, using the same dry tone her daughter does sometimes. "You need to get washed up before dinner."

"I'll show you your rooms. They have en suite bathrooms," I inform them.

"And if I know Angelo, they have everything you could need to freshen up too," Candi says wryly before turning a concerned look on her mom. "If you want to lie down, I'll bring you a tray for dinner."

Mira straightens her spine. "That won't be necessary. I'll eat with the rest of you. And we don't need a guest room to wash our hands and faces for dinner."

"They're not guest rooms. They have been designed specifically for each of you," I assure my future mother-in-law.

She does not look comforted. "I don't think––"

"Oooh, I want to see!" Cookie bounces on the balls of her feet. "What color is it?"

"I'd like to see too." Candi grins at her sister. "I bet there's pink and orange in your room."

Cookie looks at me with wide eyes. "Those are my favorite colors. Did Candi tell you?"

"Yes." Technically, her comments to her sister that I listened to informed me of Cookie's favorite colors. "And I told the designer."

I'd also told her that Cookie's birth mother was from Nigeria and showed her a picture of the head wrap Cookie treasured and kept in its own box under the bed. The designer had sourced similar fabric for beanbags and the cloth covered headboard on Cookies bed.

The little girl's room is a riot of color that I could not live in, but emulates her side of the bedroom she and Candi share.

"Like you told the designer that Candi's favorite color is teal?" Cookie asks as I lead everyone toward the elevator.

"Yes."

"Is your favorite color gray?" Cookie wants to know.

I press the button to open the elevator doors hidden in the foyer wall. "I don't have a favorite color."

"It's the color of Angelo's eyes." Candi smiles up at me, sharing the knowledge of why I asked the designer to use those colors together.

"Woah, you have an elevator?" Cookie automatically steps back to the corner of the elevator making room for her mom's scooter. "Is that a rich people thing?"

"It's here to make the entire house accessible to your mom." I push the button to take us to the second floor.

Mira looks at me, startled. "You installed it for me?"

"Yes."

As the doors begin to close, Mars bounds inside and sits on his haunches next to Cookie. Boomer says my dog doesn't like the elevator and whines when he has to ride it. He's not whining now.

"I hope this elevator doesn't break down like the one in our building." Cookie gives Mars scritches behind his ears.

"I have it checked and serviced weekly."

Candi cocks her head to one side. "Um, isn't that a little excessive?"

"I clean my guns daily. Sometimes, twice a day."

Mira bursts out laughing, her expression untainted with wariness for the first time since she arrived. "Good to know my elevator warrants the same attention as your guns."

"If you want me to have it checked and serviced daily, I can," I offer, not sure what's so funny about cleaning my guns.

An improperly cleaned gun is the difference between life and death in my line of work.

"That won't be necessary. Once a week is plenty." She and Candi share a wry look.

I don't know what that's about either. Elevator maintenance isn't any more amusing than gun maintenance. Both are necessary tools that are dangerous when they don't work properly.

This not getting the joke is nothing new for me, but for the first time, I share special secret knowledge with someone too. *La mia piccolo gatta.* Like the gray and teal thing and how Candi's face shows her ecstasy when she comes. And now she knows I share that knowledge with her deepening the connection between us.

Candi slides her hand into mine as the elevator doors open. "Thank you for installing an elevator and making sure it'll never break down with my mom stuck inside."

"You're welcome."

We come to Cookie's room first.

She stops just inside the door and Candi gasps.

"It's like *maami's* headwrap," Cookie says reverently.

Candi stares up at me. "Where did you find the fabric to do that?"

"I gave a picture of it to the designer." I don't bother spelling out that I took it while going through their things one day when they were all out of the apartment so I could get to know them better.

"How long have you been working on this house?" Candi's hands curl around my forearms.

The sound of Mira and Cookie talking turns to a buzz in the background. "I bought it two weeks after I first saw you dance."

"This is more of that love at first sight stuff."

"You don't sound as dismissive of it today."

"How can I be?" She steps closer and speaks low for my ears only. "This isn't just obsession, it's consideration. You made space for me, my mom and my sister in your life."

"Of course." My life would be as empty as it was before I met her without the other half of my soul that allows me to feel.

"I felt a connection the first time I saw you too." She leans up and kisses the underside of my jaw before turning to her mom and sister.

Stunned by her casual affection and words, I stand back and watch. It's something I'm very good at.

"If we lived here, I could have friends over without bothering you and Candi," Cookie says to her mom.

Mira looks at me consideringly and then back at her youngest daughter. "Your friends don't bother us now and it would be hard for them to get here."

"You'll have a car and driver at your disposal going forward." And a security team, but I'll ease them into that over dinner. "The SUV kitted for the scooter will arrive next week."

Mira laughs with disbelief. "Careful, or I'm going to think it's my heart you're trying to win and not my daughter's."

"She *is* my heart." Nothing is too much if it means making her happy. "Taking care of you is an extension of caring for her."

"I'm beginning to see that. Mr. Bianchi was wrong about you, wasn't he?"

"No. I am the man he says I am, but with Candi, I am more."

"Candi isn't the reason you police your mafia friends."

They're not my friends, but I don't correct her. For once, I get the nuance of what she's saying.

"I am only glad I became more than the killer Don Enzo brought me into *la famiglia* to be." I don't believe Mira would ever accept my place in her daughter's life if I was just an assassin.

Severu gave me a purpose I didn't know I needed to be worthy of *la mia amate* in her mother's eyes.

Leaving Cookie in her room, Candi and I take Mira to hers across the hall.

"Your room is set up like a mother-in-law suite." She has her own open concept small kitchen, dining area, and sitting room, with a separate bedroom and bathroom.

"It's bigger than our apartment." Candi walks around the sitting room, touching things.

The big screen television mounted on the wall. The lift chair that will make it easier for Mira to get in and out of. The matching couch and armchair for her daughters and friends to use.

"There are no tight angles to make maneuvering her scooter difficult."

Mira disappears into her bedroom and Candi yanks me down to attack my lips with her own.

I don't know what brought this on, but I'm enjoying it too much to stop and ask.

"Eww...get a room, you two!"

At the sound of Cookie's voice, Candi breaks the kiss but doesn't move away. "You're sure you want an eleven-year-old living with you?"

"I like your sister."

Candi shakes her head, gives me another quick kiss and steps back. "What do you think, Cookie? Can you see yourself living here?"

"If you can talk mom into it." Cookie's expression sobers. "She's worried since the douche—"

"Mom told you not use that word," Candi interrupts her little sister. "I don't think any more highly of my sperm donor than you do, but you need to find a more eleven-year-old friendly way to say it around mom."

Cookie sighs. "Jerk works."

"So does mug and I guarantee he wouldn't like being called either," I tell her.

"Okay, okay, no more of the d-word," Cookie says with a long-suffering eyeroll.

"I'm glad to hear it." Mira comes back into the room.

"Is the bedroom alright?" I ask.

"Yes. In fact, I'm going to take Candi's suggestion to lie down for a while. I'm not really hungry." Her shoulders droop with fatigue and most likely pain. "It has been a long day."

Candi's face falls. "I'm sorry, mom."

"Don't be sorry for the actions of others. I wasn't worried about you until Mr. Bianchi showed up. And for goodness's sake, don't apologize for finding your soulmate, sweetheart. I always promised myself I would never put you through what my mother did to me when Jakub and I started dating."

Candi rushes over and gently lays one hand on her mother's shoulder. "You're the best mom. Don't ever believe any different."

"I'm the only one you've got, so I have to get it right," Mira says like she's said it many times before.

"Are we spending the night?" Cookie asks hopefully.

"Yes, I think we will. This old body isn't up to the trip home." Mira sighs. "I could really use one of those magical massages the therapist Petra sent me to gives."

Pulling out my phone, I send a message to the therapist. When I hired for Mira's care, he agreed to be on call for a situation just like this one.

"He'll be here within the hour," I tell Mira.

Mira stares at me. "I know you're a big time mafioso, but how are you getting my therapist to do a weekend house call?"

"It's his job."

"Somehow, I think there's more to it than that, young man, but thank you."

A weird warmth unfurls in my chest at her calling me young man.

CHAPTER 29

CANDI

"I noticed some clothes in the closet and drawers," Cookie says almost diffidently to Angelo as we leave mom's room.

"They're yours," Angelo answers the question my sister does not ask.

"So, I can change into some of them for dinner? Only this place is kind of fancy for what I'm wearing." Cookie indicates her favorite pair of jeans with a chunky belt and a short sweater that shows some midriff.

Middle school fashion is very exacting. Who cares about warmth when you're on trend?

But the thing is, this is one of Cookie's nicest outfits and she must have worn it to impress Angelo when she met him.

"You can wear whatever you want, Cookie. Those clothes are yours."

"Great!" Cookie turns to head back into her room. "I'll see you downstairs."

"Okay," Angelo replies. "But Cookie?"

She stops in the doorway and faces him. "Yeah?"

"You don't need to change if you don't want to. The house is just a house. You being comfortable here is what matters."

Which is why the sociopath had a bedroom designed specifically for her.

Emotion clogs my throat and I have to clear it to say, "You look great, little sis. As always."

"You have to say that. You're my sister and you love me." Cookie looks expectantly at Angelo.

For a second, I think he's going to miss the cue and then he winks. "Well, I'm practically your brother, but for what it's worth, I think you look great too. That's exactly the kind of outfit the personal shopper I hired told me was in style for girls your age."

"Yeah?" Cookie asks. "You hired a shopper to buy that stuff for me?"

"If I'd bought your clothes, your closet would be filled with black cargo pants, turtlenecks and steel-toed boots for kicking boys in the junk who get too close."

Cookie grins. "You wear a lot of black. Maybe *that's* your favorite color."

"It's practical in my line of work."

Right. Black hides blood. That's why I wear black leggings a couple of days before my period's due, in case I start early.

So glad he doesn't explain that to my eleven-year-old sister.

Before dinner, Angelo takes me and Cookie to the kitchen to introduce us to the housekeeper, cook and maid. All three look at me with a strange kind of awe but are instantly charmed by my little sister's exuberance and frank admission of hunger.

"Smells yummy," Cookie says with an appreciative sniff when the cook promises dinner is ready to bring to the table. "Can't we eat in here?"

The kitchen is industrial sized with a large eating nook at one end. Three men are already sitting at the table there.

"If that's what you want," Angelo easily agrees. "You can meet some of the men who patrol the grounds."

That's how we end up eating a fancy three-course Sunday dinner with a bunch of mafia soldiers at the kitchen table.

At first, the men at the table don't do much talking, but my sister and I are curious people and we ask a lot of questions about the house and what it's like to be on a security detail.

"I am learning to make Polish food as Mr. Caruso requested, but I look forward to getting tips from your mother," the cook tells me as she puts a plate of roasted meat and vegetables in front of me.

"That will make her very happy. Neither Cookie nor I are natural cooks." We learned what we had to so we wouldn't starve, but neither of us ever found the joy in the kitchen mom does.

By the end of the third course, I'm not sure I'll ever eat again and even Cookie doesn't finish the meat on her plate.

"I'll take mom a plate and then call my friends. I want to tell them about the game system in my room. Maybe a couple of them can come home with me after school?" Cookie asks.

Angelo nods. "Fine by me."

"As long as mom plans to stay another night," I tack on.

But we've seen mom this exhausted before. Even with the therapist giving her a massage, she'll need to rest up tomorrow before a car ride back to the apartment.

"Can Mars sleep in my room?" Cookie gives Angelo her best pleading look.

It's not necessary. Of course, he says yes.

"You're going to spoil her." He's going to spoil all of us.

"She deserves to be spoiled, as do you."

"Are you reading my mind again?" I tease as we head upstairs to our bedroom.

Our bedroom. Am I admitting I live here now?

I think I am.

Taking my hair out of the messy bun I put it in earlier when I was in such a hurry to get downstairs and head off my mom calling the cops, I shake it out. I never brushed it out last night either and I don't look forward to what it's going to take to smooth the tangles now.

Angelo makes an approving sound, like the sight of my messy hair is all that. "I'll brush it out for you."

"You want to brush my hair?" Is that a thing men do?

Maybe? He sure seemed to enjoy washing it before and his insistence on doing the conditioner step is the only thing that will make the next thirty minutes even slightly bearable.

"I always want to touch you, whatever form that takes."

"Okay, then." I sit down on the bench in front of the vanity and pull open the drawer with the hair stuff. "I can't believe you thought to get a detangling brush for me."

I'm grateful though.

"You have long hair. Xabat said you'd need it." He reaches past me and pulls out one of the many product containers. "This too."

It's a detangler spray. Of course, Angelo thought of that too. Or rather, consulted the expert who did.

He reads the directions on the side before spritzing a section of my hair. Lifting it, he gently pulls the detangling brush through the strands, his expression intent.

My shoulders relax more with each swipe of the brush. When Angelo hits a gnarly tangle, he doesn't force the brush but adds another spritz of detangler and then pulls the matte apart with his fingers until the brush will go through.

"If I wasn't already falling for you, this would do it right here," I tease.

"Good to know." He doesn't look at me in the mirror when he speaks but keeps hyper focused on his task.

"Who were you on the phone to when mom and Cookie got here earlier?" I ask, curious about his life as much as he is about mine.

Well, maybe not quite as curious. I have no plans to go foraging under beds to see what he treasures. Knowing him, there's nothing under the beds in this place. Not even a dust bunny.

"My boss, Severu. He wanted my version of what happened last night."

"Someone told him about what happened in the alley?" Will Angelo get in trouble for his men killing a capo's soldier?

Angelo shrugs. "I would have but I didn't want to leave to make the report in person."

"Because your guys kidnapped me and were bringing me here."

Angelo's lips quirk, but he doesn't answer.

"Are you in trouble?" Some of the tension that drained away is creeping back into my muscles.

"No."

"But I bet Stefano is mad at you."

"He is, but I'm not the one in trouble," Angelo assures me.

"Who is?" I wonder.

"Bianchi."

"What? Why?"

"His men were sloppy and that's on their capo."

"Oh." Derian and Mario sure hadn't seemed impressed with Freddy and Gino.

"Until recently, Bianchi leaving you and your mom to fend for yourself wouldn't have gotten him in actionable trouble with his don."

"But now?" I ask.

"Miceli will sanction him in some way for creating the clusterfuck from start to finish."

"I wish someone had made him pay my mom support back in the day, for her sake, but I don't want anything from him now."

Angelo runs his fingers through the section of hair he just finished "You don't need him."

"No, I don't."

"But that doesn't change the fact that he abandoned you," Angelo says grimly. "Family is supposed to mean something in the mafia."

"His family does mean something to him. I'm pretty sure they're why he never acknowledged me."

"You're his family too. Things happened to you that should not have happened because he did not watch over you like a father should watch over his daughter."

I can't deny that. "Those things led me to mom and I wouldn't give her or Cookie up for anything."

"Why do you call her Cookie when her name is Diamond?" He spritzes another section of my hair.

"That's my fault. Mommy never used her given name and she called me her Candi girl when I was little. So, when I started dancing, I used Candi as my stage name."

"Everyone calls you Candi now."

"I ask them to. Candi feels more like me than Kathleen, or even Kath." For a while, Bianca called me Kath because she thought I wanted her to, but I don't. "Cookie wanted to be like me, so she asked us to call her Cookie. It stuck."

"Because of the nickname your mom gave you?" he asks, working on another big tangle.

I grimace. "And because Kathleen is the name of my sperm donor's grandmother."

Mommy probably thought naming me after her would make Stefano more likely to show an interest in me. If that was her plan, it failed.

"Asshole," Angelo mutters, like he knows what I'm thinking. Then he cinches it by saying, "I promise you, Candi, I will never abandon you or our children."

"Now we're having children?" I can't help it, there's a thread of panic in my voice.

Everything about this thing with Angelo has gone fast, but kids? I'm not ready for that.

"We don't have to talk about having them right now. We should wait a couple of years anyway. Relationships benefit from time alone as a couple before bringing children into the mix."

He's quoting the book on relationships again, I bet. But I happen to agree with that nugget of wisdom.

"I never really thought about having kids." Before Angelo, I didn't think about having a relationship either.

My life was consumed with caring for mom and Cookie.

"But you'll be such a good mom."

"You think so?" I tease, wondering what kind of dad Angelo will be.

If he's anything like he is with me, my sister and mom, he'll be an amazing dad.

"Loving comes naturally to you." He meets my eyes in the mirror. "You'll never abandon your children."

"No, if I ever have children, the only thing that would take me from them is death."

"Like your mom."

"Mommy never would have abandoned me if she had a choice." I know that the same way I know deep down that I'm Candi, not Kathleen.

Angelo goes back to brushing my hair. The tangles are pretty much gone now, and his long, smooth strokes are hypnotic. "I notice that you call Mira mom and refer to your biological mother as mommy."

"Yes. Mommy preferred to be called that. I was ten when she died, but I never called her anything else." It's my way of keeping her alive in my heart.

"My mother is alive, but she's got no place in my heart," he says grimly.

"She abandoned you."

Angelo nods and shrugs. "Living with nonno and nonna was a huge improvement over life with her and dad. And that's when I met Severu, Miceli and Salvatore."

"How?"

"We went to the same school."

"Mafia school?" I tease.

"St. Catherine's. It's where all the children in the Genovese Family go if they don't attend public school."

"Were you friends then?" Does it bother him that Severu essentially has the life he was born to lead?

"Yes. We clicked right away. None of us showed emotion. They were trained not to, but for me there were no emotions to show."

"Do you mind that Severu is the godfather and Miceli is a don and you'll never be those things?" I ask, a little worried.

What if Angelo *wants* that life? Can a stripper be a don's wife?

"My brothers are welcome to those headaches." Angelo runs his fingers through my now tangle free hair, seemingly mesmerized by it. "They don't show emotion, but they experience more of it than I do. They want what's best for the mafia. I want what's best for the few people I care about."

"And I'm one of those people?" I ask.

"The most important one."

My heart swoons in a ridiculously girly fashion I have no intention of admitting to. "So, no sibling rivalry?"

He called them brothers and I like thinking he has some decent family, so, I'm going with it.

"None. Miceli can be a pain in the ass, Severu wants to control the fucking world and Salvatore's still a little pissed I got to Gino before he did, but we're family."

Of course, Salvatore would want to punish Gino for putting the same pressure on Bianca that he did to me, but honestly? If he hadn't, the capo would never have met my friend.

"Thank you..." I pause. Am I really going to do this? Yes, I am. "For killing Gino. He was a predator and he would have found other women to exploit and hurt if you hadn't."

"Yes, he would." Angelo makes a ponytail with his hand and releases it, letting my hair fall softly to my back. "Can you put your hair in a dancer's bun?"

"Are you telling me that's not one of your many skills?" I ask, only partially joking.

"If you want me to learn, it could be." There's zero joking in his tone. He means it.

"Not necessary." I grab the paddle brush from the drawer and smooth my hair into a high, tight ponytail. "Why a dancer's bun?"

It's a little early for sleep, but I assumed sexy times were on the dessert menu for tonight. Not sure how putting my hair up plays into that.

Does Angelo want to try something kinky?

"I want to show you something and I don't want your hair to get tangled again."

"Tired of brushing it?"

"No, but you'll be too tired to sit here and let me do it."

That sounds promising. I finish creating the tight bun and stand up. "Ready."

"You're going to like this." Angelo's eyes glimmer with sensual promise.

No question this man knows what to do with his body, and mine, in the bedroom department. "I'm sure I will."

"I had it installed just for you." Angelo takes my hand and tugs me out of the bedroom, a palpable air of anticipation around him.

All the soothing calm he bestowed brushing my hair turns into sexual eagerness.

When we get downstairs, we take a right instead of a left and Angelo leads me down a hall and through a door, where we step into a garden of jungle plants. The air is a little humid and it smells like earth and flowers.

"What is this place?" I reach out to touch the broad leaf of a banana plant.

I only know what it is because our dental clinic has one in the waiting room and I asked.

"A conservatory."

"And indoor garden," I breathe.

I chaperoned a school trip for my sister to The New York Botanical Garden. Their conservatory is bigger, but not any more impressive.

There are plants and flowers everywhere, and the sound of rushing water hits my ears. Mom is going to love this place.

Angelo pulls me further along the path. "I had this area designed just for us."

Coming around some large potted tropical trees, we step into a grotto surrounding a small pool fed by a freaking waterfall.

"It's a hot tub," he tells me. "With a special feature just for you."

"Hot water to soak in is pretty great all on its own. You don't know how much I want to be able to just soak after a night of dancing." The bathtub in our apartment is too short to stretch out my legs, even when I'm sitting up.

"We're going to do more than soak, *amate*." Angelo's sensual growl sends a shudder through me.

"We didn't bring swimsuits." And right about now, I'm really regretting that oversight.

"We don't need them." Angelo peels his shirt off, folds it and puts it on a bench tucked behind some foliage.

He does something and a small door opens revealing a cabinet with a black hard plastic case inside. Opening it, he slides the knife sheath from his shoulder into one compartment and follows that with the rest of his weapons.

Watching him take off all of the guns and knives he wears on a regular basis shouldn't turn me on, should it?

The wetness soaking my panties right now is an irrefutable fact though. Knowing he's always *that* ready to do his thing sends a pulse of arousal right to my core.

"What if someone comes in?" I have no desire to put on a show for anyone but Angelo.

Which begs the question: can I keep dancing at Pitiful Princess?

"I locked the door with the remote on my phone. Only yours and my thumbprints will open it when we're in here alone." He unzips his pants and shoves them down his muscular, hairy legs.

Everything about this man is so darn sexy.

"What about the windows?" I wave toward the glass mostly obscured by plants.

Mostly being the operative word.

"It turns opaque at night, or whenever it's programmed to."

It's definitely dark outside. "So no one can see through it?" I ask, just to be sure.

"No one. It's a matter of safety too." He finishes putting his clothes in a neat pile on the bench, leaving his body gloriously naked. "All of the window glass in the house is the highest level of bullet resistance, but we don't take chances."

"Huh? Oh. That's great." My eyes are glued on the rippling muscles of his torso.

The men who dance on ladies night at the club would kill for Angelo's muscle definition. Never mind the size of his dick. Which is drool worthy hard right now. Although I'm not sure that thing ever goes down.

"Are you always hard?" As much as I want to tear my own clothes off and get straight to nakey-times, I force myself to go slow, toeing off my shoes first.

He takes them from me and puts them on the rack under the bench next to his. "When I am around you, yes."

"Seriously?" I pause in the act of removing my socks. "Even at dinner?"

"Not like this." He waves his hand at his erection. "But yes, I'm always at least semi-erect when you're around."

"That's got to be uncomfortable." I slide my leggings down my hips, putting a little wiggle in as I bend down to pull them off over my feet.

Angelo groans.

I hide my smile before I straighten and start tugging up the hem of my top one slow centimeter at a time.

"When you spend so much of your life not feeling much of anything..." His eyes hot on my body, he fists his hands at his side, like he's stopping himself from reaching out to touch. "Having a constant source of emotional stimulation isn't always a comfortable experience, but it's one I revel in."

Wow. Okay, yeah, he's said stuff like this before. But the idea that when he's not around me, he doesn't feel much of anything makes my heart ache.

I pull my top over my head and toss it to him, grinning when he lets it fall at his feet.

"What about you?" he asks in a gravelly voice. "Does being around me keep you on a slow burn of arousal?"

Am I always on the verge of wanting to have sex when he's around? The startling answer after years of having almost no sex drive is, yes. Yes, I am.

"Even when I've been kidnapped and I'm lying on a sofa, trussed up like a mummy."

He steps forward and reaches around me to undo my bra. "You're not going to hurt my feelings if you tell me you're not as excited by my presence as I am by yours."

"I just told you—"

"That during a time of high adrenalin, which can have an amplifying effect on the libido, you were turned on. You don't have to find my presence the same stimulant I do yours. It's okay. Everyone is different."

He's really not getting it. "You read that in your book didn't you?"

"Yes." Tugging my bra straps down my arms, his eyes never once stray from mine.

"You and that book." I let the bra fall. "I'm not sure if I should hug the author or smack them."

"If you hug them, I'll have to smack them, so how about neither?" Dropping to one knee, he presses a kiss to my tummy as he slides my panties off.

"Was that a joke Angelo?"

He smiles that pirate smile I'm coming to love. "Maybe." Then suddenly, Angelo, the enforcer comes over him. "Or was it?"

I shiver but not from fear. "Your death mask shouldn't turn me on so much."

"You mean the mask at the Halloween party at the club?" Lifting my panties to his face, he inhales deeply.

My thighs clench and it's all I can do to remember the question I'm supposed to be answering. "No, that mask on your face you get when you *become* Death.

He frowns. "I'm always Death."

"I know that, but sometimes that part of you eclipses all the other parts."

"Most people think there are no other parts."

"Most people are wrong. And by the way, my adrenaline doesn't spike when you go all *Death* on me because I trust you, but it still makes me wet. So, yeah, being around you is a pretty constant turn on."

His jaw so taut it looks hewn from rock, Angelo sweeps me into his arms and carries me to the pool. He steps into the water without hesitating.

There must be stairs, because I feel the jostle of each step before he sinks down to sit on something. Hot water bubbles around us, not too intense to enjoy but warm enough to relax my muscles.

I moan, and it's not entirely sexual. The water feels so good. "I would spend hours in here if I could."

"The temperature is set at a perfect 98°. You can soak in the water as long as you like." He shifts me so my back is to his front and my legs dangle in the water on either side of his thighs, his erection pressing against my spine.

I let my head fall back against his shoulder. "Good to know."

Angelo presses my thighs further apart so I'm completely open. I expect his hand to slide up my thigh and touch my vulva.

It doesn't. He puts his hand behind him and does something. A second later, a strong stream of water hits me right between my legs.

I cry out in surprise and try to close my legs.

Angelo's hands grip both my thighs, holding me in place. "Relax, *amate*. You're going to like this, I promise."

But it's not his reassurance that stops me trying to close my legs, or even his hold on my thighs. It's the way the water feels pulsing against my intimate flesh, stimulating my clitoris in such an unexpected way.

Of course, a lot of my experiences with Angelo are brand new for me but this is a doozy.

Once I relax, Angelo's hands begin to explore my body, caressing my limbs and finally coming up to cup my breasts and play with my nipples.

My desire grows to epic proportions as he plays my body like a finely tuned instrument only he has the key to. I'm on the verge of coming, so stimulated, I can't think straight.

The water continues to pulse against me. Angelo continues to touch me, but it's not enough.

"I can't," I finally cry in frustration, once again trying to close my legs. "It's torture."

Amazing torture that feels better than pretty much anything, but I can't come.

His calves coming around mine to trap my legs in place, he lifts my hips enough so that his dick can press against my opening.

"Yes," I breathe. "That. I need you inside me."

He lowers my body slowly over his engorged penis. "Water washes away natural lubricants so we have to be careful here. Go slow. I don't want to hurt you."

Do I believe him? Or is this more sexual torture? But he doesn't stop the roll of his hips that push him deeper with each thrust.

"Move your hips but only a little."

My instincts are to ride him like a wild pony, but I do what he says. He helps, his hands guiding me until I find a rhythm that has me moaning with pleasure.

Then his big hands glide up my torso to cup my breasts again, pinching and rolling my nipples under the water.

His engorged erection continuously hits that spot inside me that lights my clitoris up like a strobe spotlight.

Needing something to hold onto, I throw my arms behind me and grab his hair.

It's too much.

It's not enough.

My body is on fire, but I never want it to end. Turning my head into his neck, I kiss the underside of his jaw, lapping at the salty skin like the cat he likes to call me.

His head turns and his lips crash down on mine.

And that's when the cataclysm happens. I explode into sparkly bits all over the place, my body going into a rictus of such pleasure, I can't breathe.

Can a body survive feelings this intense?

Angelo's calves keep my legs trapped so I can't get away from the stimulation to my clitoris as he continues to thrust into me from behind. My climax goes on and on and on.

There's no aftershocks; it just doesn't end. The ecstasy is so intense my vision is going black around the edges. It's the jet of water. The muted pressure against my pleasure center never lets up.

Angelo's breathing speeds up and he swells inside me, his movements losing their smooth rythm. He's about to come and I crave it.

I want to feel him in that moment he is as lost to ecstasy as I am.

But he's not done with me yet. Two of his fingers slip down on either side of my clitoris, rubbing fast as the water continues to jet against it. It's too much. I'm going to pass out.

For real.

And then my second climax hits so hard my muscles contract to the point of pain as Angelo bathes my insides with his heated cum.

CHAPTER 30

ANGELO

C andi and Cookie play with Mars in the yard while I work on my phone nearby in case the young Cane Corsica mastiff needs a training moment.

So far, the dog's training holds. He is as attached to his charges as I am which makes our own bond that much stronger. We both know it's our job to watch over them.

My phone buzzes and initials flash on the screen. CA. It used to be CSB for Capo Stefano Bianchi, but after learning he's Candi's neglectful father, I renamed him Capo Asshole in my head and phone.

I tap my Bluetooth headphone to answer. "What do you want?"

"She's not safe in New York." Bianchi doesn't waste time with formalities either.

My fury is instant. "Are you threatening my woman?"

"No, of course not. She's my daughter. What do you take me for?" He has the gall to sound offended.

"I take you for the absentee sperm donor you are, *stronzo*. Candi doesn't consider you her father."

"That doesn't change the fact that she's my family." The fact he ignores me calling him an asshole is a surprise.

He's a proud capo, used to receiving more than his fair due respect.

"She's 24 years old and you're just acknowledging this now?" I ask with a marked lack of that commodity.

"You know what trouble it would cause me with my wife and her family if I were to admit to a daughter by another woman? It's not as if I was in a relationship with Bonbon. She was a whore, for fuck's sake."

"And you are a criminal." Too many old school mafiosos consider themselves above others because they made a vow. "You think what you do to pay for your designer suits is more *upstanding* than selling sex to desperate men?"

"I was not desperate," he claims, affronted. "There are things a man wants that a proper wife refuses to do for him."

Yeah, I've heard the *whores are for blowjobs* argument before. If Candi doesn't want to take me in her mouth, I won't go looking for it elsewhere. That's for damn sure.

"Considering the fact you got Bonbon pregnant, apparently that includes your wife letting you fuck her," I mock.

"Listen you bastard—"

"Call me that again and you'll wake up to my knife slicing your tongue out of your mouth."

"You can't threaten me!"

"I don't make threats." Threats implies I might not follow through.

"You really think Severu is going to—"

"That's Don De Luca to you."

"Just because the godfather didn't sanction you over Gino's death doesn't mean he'll tolerate your disrespect to a superior. It's his job to protect our way of life."

Sounds like someone missed one of his lessons on mafia hierarchy. "I am the godfather's top enforcer. You are a capo under one of his dons. I outrank you in the chain of command."

Doesn't mean I can order his soldiers to do something, unless it's on behalf of Severu. Like in the military, we have our own spheres of influence, but when push comes to shove? I'll shove Bianchi right off a cliff.

Bored with the conversation, I demand, "Why the hell are you calling me?"

He has to know that I'm not sending Candi out of New York for the sake of his pride and domestic harmony.

"Miceli has ordered me to sign over one of my businesses to each of my sons with a tithe from them to Kathleen for the remainder of her life."

Bianchi probably considers that punishment for not protecting his daughter rather than simply making right his neglect and lack of financial support she was due as his child.

"If you expect me to talk your don out of that plan, you're stupider than I thought." Not that I think Candi will accept the money from her brothers.

Not if it's grudgingly given. I'm going to have to have a little talk with them. I'm more than capable of providing everything Candi needs, but that doesn't mean she doesn't deserve the tithe.

"I don't expect anything from you, you son of a bitch."

That is not the insult he thinks it is and if he knew anything about me, the capo would know that. My mother *is* a bitch.

"We can't keep Kathleen's existence a secret anymore. Even if I could be sure the men in the alley wouldn't talk, once my sons learn about the tithe and who it's to, her life is at risk."

"Cosimo and Renato would try to harm her?" I didn't promise Candi I wouldn't kill her brothers.

They're dead men walking if they pose a threat to her.

"No! Not them, but once my wife and her family find out about Kathleen..." His voice trails off on a sigh. "Why do you think I've kept my distance her whole life? When she was eighteen, I sent a lawyer to her. I offered to pay for her to attend college out of state."

"She refused." Of course she would and this *stronzo* didn't realize that?

"Yes."

"You never paid her mother child support."

"She was a whore," he dismisses for the second time.

"And the fucking mother of your child. She deserved to be taken care of and so did Candi."

"Kathleen didn't want my support."

"You call offering her a bribe to leave New York and save you embarrassment support?"

"You don't?"

"I call it shitty parenting."

"Fuck off, Angelo. I didn't call you to talk about my character."

Or lack the fuck of.

"Get to the point then."

"I could ask the boys not to say anything, but after Kathleen's ill-advised announcement of my paternity in front of witnesses, their silence won't be enough."

"Enough for what exactly?" I need the threat spelled out so I can take the necessary steps to get rid of it.

"My wife is a very proud woman. She will not tolerate the existence of my bastard child in New York for her friends to gossip about."

"I will eliminate any threat to Candi's wellbeing," I promise him.

"You can't murder my wife!"

"Wrong." But Candi will be happier if a warning suffices.

I disconnect the call now that I know the extent of the threat toward *mia amate*.

She doesn't want me killing people on her behalf, unless it's absolutely necessary. She wasn't upset that I killed her old boss, or that Mario killed Gino Bianchi, but she didn't like the kill list I made of her past boyfriends when I thought they'd had sex with her.

Before her, I would not have considered giving a warning, but Candi brings out the better man in me.

With an exaggerated groan, *mia amate* drops into the chair across from me at the outdoor table. "I need a non-sexy soak in your hot tub. My sister and that dog are indefatigable."

"It's your hot tub too. The house and everything in it are as much yours as they are mine."

"Even your armory?" she teases, choosing to make light of it.

But it's not a joke. My life and everything in it is hers. "If you want in my armory, you have to let me teach you how to handle weapons safely."

"I don't really want in your armory." She smiles at me. "But it's nice to know you meant what you said."

"I always mean what I say to you."

Later that night, after making love to my beautiful, precious woman and watching her sleep for over an hour, I drag myself from our bed.

The sooner this is done, the fewer funerals the Gambino don will have to attend.

Bianchi's wife comes from an old lineage in the Gambino Family. Her father was a Gambino capo and now her brother has replaced him.

I take the launch out and head directly to Staten Island. Jumping out, I moor it right on the rocky beach of the capo's home.

"All the exterior guards are neutralized." Derian materializes out of the foggy darkness. "And the security system is feeding false information to the monitoring company."

"He uses a civilian company for the system. Can you believe that shit?" Mario shakes his head.

I don't answer. The faster I get this taken care of, the faster I get back to Candi. Jogging up to the house, I have my plan already mapped out in my head. There are only two interior guards and one is sleeping.

Fuck, if this capo hasn't grown complacent.

This level of laxity is something Severu is going to have to address as godfather. There are too many other players who would be happy to take our territory if we don't make doing so impossible.

I take care of the guard who is supposed to be monitoring the exterior security cameras first. He's watching a rerun of Seinfeld on his phone. I should do the capo a favor and kill him, but that's not what I'm here for.

I was going to drug him with a shot of K, which would leave him insensate quick enough for my purposes and with no memory of my being here. But fuck if I'm giving this piece of shit the gift of amnesia about his dereliction of duty.

Slapping the special strength scrim-backed, pressure sensitive tape my team uses over his mouth, I flip the man on his stomach before he knows what's happening. It takes a few seconds to get his wrists in the reinforced zip tie cuffs. Then, I use the tape on his ankles and knees.

"You should be fucking ashamed," I grind out tossing him up against the wall opposite his security monitors.

I tape him in place with four bands across his torso. They'll have to repaint and texture the walls in here after freeing him. That tape takes plaster with it when it's removed.

He's definitely not going anywhere.

Unwilling to waste any more time on these guys, I drug the sleeping guard, who at least has the training to have a door alarm which I have to disable. He sleeps with a gun under his pillow and knife on the bedside table too.

It's good to know Gambino soldiers aren't a bunch of fuckups.

Nevertheless, I'm not worried about being disturbed while me and the capo have a little chat.

All the guards are neutralized, and he and his wife have bedrooms on opposite sides of the house. She also takes sleeping pills. Unless we make a helluva racket, she's not waking up. Their kids are both away at college and the live-in staff have bedrooms on the basement level.

After turning on a bedside lamp that casts a low glow over the sleeping man, I shake my head. Snoring, he's got no clue Death has come calling.

Giving him the same treatment I did the first guard, I'm disgusted he doesn't wake up until I'm taping his ankles around the legs of his silk pajamas.

His night watchman's lack of attention makes sense. Sloppy leaders make for sloppy soldiers. Show me an efficient soldier with a strong awareness of his surroundings and I'll show you a CO who knows how to train his men.

The capo starts thrashing.

Giving him a not so gentle tap on the cheek to get his attention, I order, "Settle down."

His eyes zero in on my face, or rather the Death mask I wear when I'm working, and he goes completely still.

"Good. You know who I am."

He nods.

"Do you know who Kathleen Brigliano is?" I ask.

His eyes tell me *yes* while his head shakes *no*.

I backhand him. "Try again."

He nods.

"So, you know who her sperm donor is?"

He glares at me defiantly, the stubborn tilt to his jaw telling me he's not going to answer. Considering who's straddling his torso right now, that's some serious aversion to admitting Candi is Bianchi's biological child.

He wasn't exaggerating the reaction of his wife's family to the existence of his unknown daughter.

Pulling my knife, I flip it over my knuckles before gripping it and pressing it against his throat. "You, or someone in your family, might be tempted to try to get rid of her."

Try being the operative word. No one hurts what is mine.

I push the knife just enough to cause pain and cut a thin line as I move it an inch toward his Adam's apple. The capo's eyes widen in fear, his breathing labored and fast through his nose.

"What you need to understand is that who's her sperm donor isn't nearly as important as who she belongs to now."

Shock widens his eyes even further.

"I see you've figured it out. She's mine. Not my sidepiece. Not my girl-friend. *Mine*. And if any of you tries anything, I will kill all of you. Your brothers. Your wives. Your heirs. I will wipe your name from *la famiglia*."

All the color leaches from the capo's face and I know I'm getting my point across.

"This is your only warning. You so much as say something derogatory to her and I will cut out your tongues. You touch her in *any* way and I will cut off your hands before shoving them up your ass. Then I will kill you and dump you in the soup so you can't even have a proper Catholic burial."

I yank the tape from his mouth.

He sucks in air for several seconds before he asks, "Does the godfather know you're threatening a capo?"

"Don De Luca has formally acknowledged my claim on Candi." Married yet, or not, she's mine in the eyes of the Cosa Nostra.

"Everyone knows you don't feel anything. Why would you take the bastard daughter of a whore under your protection?"

I hit him in the mouth with the hilt of my knife, the satisfying crunch of breaking teeth accompanying the blood spurting from his mouth. "If you can't say something nice, don't say anything at all. My nonna taught me that. I guess yours should have taught you too."

"She's safe from us," he lisps from between broken front teeth.

"Give me your vow."

"On my honor as a made man," he adds obediently.

This is too easy. "If your honor is as lax as your security, your desire to live had better be stronger. If you die by my hand, it won't be fast. *Capisce?*"

"*Sì. Capisco.*"

I climb off him. "I want the word to go out tomorrow. Remind your sister and the rest of your family of my nonna's maxim and the consequences if they forget it."

The capo nods fervently, sending droplets of blood and spit flying from his mouth.

"Your guards are alive. This time."

If they worked for Severu, I'd kill them for their incompetence. But can you really blame a poorly trained dog for the deficiencies of his master?

The next day, I get a call from one of Candi's biological brothers. Renato and Cosimo want to get to know the sister they never knew about.

My first instinct is to say no. More people in Candi's inner circle mean more people I have to share her attention with. I'm a jealous bastard where she's concerned, but I agree to meet them anyway.

Unfortunately, they're not much like either of their parents and their desire to know Candi seems sincere.

After warning them what will happen to them, in detail, if they hurt her in any way, I agree to ask her if she wants to meet them.

Go me, being a good boyfriend and putting her needs above my own.

The author on that fucking book about healthy relationships has a lot to answer for.

CHAPTER 31

ANGELO

There's a light tap on my office door when I'm going over intel recently received from Severu regarding my mother and her husband. They're in the US already, having arrived in Boston yesterday.

"Come!" I call, assuming it's one of my men.

But it's Candi. Her hair up in a high ponytail, she's dressed casually in jeans and a sweater that clings to her curves. An instant desire to slide my hand up the naked skin of her stomach under that sweater washes over me.

"Have you got a second?" She tugs nervously at the hem of her sweater, but there's a determined glint in her eyes.

I left her visiting with her mom in the conservatory, Mars laying at their feet. The women and Cookie have stayed the last two nights. Mira seems to enjoy the freedom of the estate. But maybe Candi's going to try to tell me she wants to go back to the apartment.

"For you? Always." Standing, I come around the desk so it's not a barrier between us. But that's not enough, so, I lean back against it and pull her into me. "What do you need, *piccola gatta*?"

"I'm on the schedule to work tomorrow."

I'm not sure which argument I would least like to have. The inevitable one regarding her wanting to go *home* or this one.

Candi's showed I can't predict her responses when she went ballistic over the joint checking account I opened for us. I told her about it when she mentioned paying Cookie's afterschool winter activities fee.

I like having things with both our names on them. Candi, not so much.

She accused me of treating her like a whore and said she wasn't taking money for sharing my bed. I told her it was *our* bed and what's mine is hers.

"How can I see you as a whore?" I asked, genuinely confused. "We're getting married someday."

That really set her off.

When I tried to calm her down by telling her that no man in his right mind would pay a million dollars for two nights of sex, she threatened to castrate me and put my balls in a jar for safe keeping.

The angry sex after was off the charts, but I didn't like her calling herself that.

Which is why I haven't mentioned the other financial arrangements I've made for her. Though maybe since I made them for her mom and sister too, she won't take it the same way.

I have no idea how she's going to react to being told that working right now is a very bad idea.

"It's not safe." Especially with my mother and her as yet to be discovered agenda in Boston.

Her face goes carefully blank. "Are you saying you don't want me to dance?"

Am I? Yeah, probably. But that's not fair. Because I told her I would support her dancing if she wanted to keep doing it.

So, I compromise. "If you stay on the stage, I can protect you but working the crowd is out of the question."

As soon as the words are out of my mouth I realize I should have worded that differently.

"For your safety," I hastily add.

She doesn't like working the floor anyway. Not that I expect that to influence her stance on doing it. Logically, it should, but logic didn't work when I brought up the million dollar payment thing, so I'm not mentioning her lack of enjoyment with that aspect of her job either.

"Okay."

Wait. What? "Okay?" I ask to make sure I wasn't fantasizing that response.

"I don't like working the floor anyway."

Fuck. So, I could have mentioned that.

"But you don't mind if I keep dancing?" she presses, her gaze searching mine.

Should I tell her that the men who look at her with lust will have to die? No. That puts undue influence on her to do what I want.

Maybe I can engineer a fatal dose of food poisoning for them. Or a series of fatal car crashes. Then she won't know it's because they looked at her almost naked body with lust.

Fuck if I'm not a hell of a lot more jealous than I thought. What I could stand before I touched her for the first time no longer applies. Maybe a more evolved man would have no issue with her dancing. And a man capable of empathy would feel badly about considering mass murder.

I'm just trying to figure out a way to prevent Candi getting her feelings hurt by my jealousy.

"It bothers you, doesn't it? Now that we've been together." She lets her body rest against mine, showing no signs of anger.

"Your dancing does not bother me. It's beautiful."

"Thank you, but don't pretend you're okay with me doing it on stage tomorrow. Even if you were before, alright?"

"The idea of other men seeing your beautiful body move like that and picturing themselves touching you makes me homicidal," I admit.

"You know I'm not responsible for what men think when they look at me, right?"

"You're not the one I want to kill."

Her lips tilt wryly and she pats my chest. "Not sure you should be thinking about killing anyone."

"I'm sorry." I feel actual regret for disappointing her.

It's a new sensation and not one I particularly enjoy.

"If I don't dance, how do I support myself? And more than that, how do I save the money for my sister to attend university?" Her head tips forward against my chest and her next words are muffled between us, but I understand them. "Don't bring up the million dollar checking account balance."

I won't mention it, but it's not going anywhere either. Now's as good a time as any to tell her about her brothers.

"Miceli ordered Bianchi to sign over two of his companies to your half-brothers and for Renato and Cosimo to pay you 10% of the profits in perpetuity."

Candi goes rigid and rears back. "What?"

"It's to compensate for his neglect of your welfare as a child." Doing what I wanted to earlier, I slip my hand under her sweater and rub her back in soothing circles. "Your brothers *want* to give you the money. They're furious you weren't brought to live with them when your mom died."

"What? Really?" Candi sounds dazed.

"If you're open to it, they want to get to know you. Mira and Cookie too." Which is how I know they're sincere. "They were respectful about you and your mom without pretending ignorance of either of your professions."

"They weren't mean about mommy?" she asks in a tremulous voice.

"No. I did some digging into them. They check out okay."

She swallows. "They're mafia?"

"Renato was made when he turned twenty-two, after he graduated from university. Cosimo already runs the legit business Miceli is forcing your father to turn over to him."

"Cosimo is not a made man?" Her shock is understandable considering how old school her biological father is.

"No. He was supposed to get made after he got his MBA like his brother, but after he did the interview with Severu, my boss ordered Bianchi to put Cosimo to work in the legit businesses."

"And Stefano was okay with that? He didn't disown Cosimo, or anything?"

"You been talking to Boomer?" I ask.

"His story is so sad. I'm really glad you brought him into your family."

Fuck. Is that what I did? "I thought I just gave him a job."

"Training your dog and looking after us. That sounds like family to me."

Shit. She's right. "He's a good man."

A better one than me because he's always had a conscience.

"What about my sperm donor and Cosimo?"

"Bianchi believes Severu wanted Cosimo to be one of the members of the mafia we keep clean to interact with the FEDs and facilitate our legitimate businesses." He assumes that someday, Cosimo will be forced to get his hands dirty like everyone else.

According to Severu, that's not going to happen. Miceli is Cosimo's don now and he's as committed to keeping the younger Bianchi clean as Severu is.

"Is that true?" Curiosity about her brother infuses Candi's voice.

"Cosimo is not a killer. Miceli will not allow him to be forced to become one."

"That's kind of enlightened for a mafia don, isn't it?"

"It's practical is what it is. You force someone with the wrong mindset to kill and you can't predict the outcome. We thrive by not drawing attention to our business. You get someone unstable in the mix and shit goes sideways fast."

"Oh. I don't think I could kill either, but I'm not nearly bothered enough that you do."

"That's not a deficiency, *amate*. It only makes you perfect for me."

"I want to meet them."

I knew she would say that. "I'll make it happen."

"Good."

"Are you going to argue about taking the money from the companies?"

"No. It's not from Stefano. It's from my brothers because your don saw an injustice and chose to address it. If it was just me, I'd probably donate it to charity regardless. But it's not. The money will allow me to take care of my mom and sister the way I want to."

"With more than a million dollars a year, you can donate plenty to charity and do whatever you want for your mom and sister."

Candi's knees buckle. I have to grab her tightly against me so she doesn't fall.

"This is probably a bad time to tell you I've already set up a trust fund for Cookie's future education." But I'm not going to let her believe she ever has to worry about her sister's future again.

Regardless of what happens with the Bianchi holdings.

"What? Why would you do that?" she asks in a stunned voice.

"Because she's my sister too."

That has Candi straightening her spine. "Not yet, she's not."

"It's just a matter of time." But first I have to figure out how to give Candi the perfect proposal and I have no clue what that should look like.

I am not a romantic guy.

CHAPTER 32

CANDI

I find mom sitting on a wicker chair, her feet up on an ottoman enjoying the fall sunshine in the conservatory.

She smiles. "What do you think? I feel like the Queen of Sheba with the way Boomer follows me around to make sure I can sit where I want and do what I want."

"I'm glad." And even more glad she lets the veteran help her like that.

I didn't get my sense of independence from a stranger.

"If he's not careful, I could fall in love with that kind of attention." Mom winks at me.

"Do I need to have a talk with him?" I ask, only half-jokingly as I sit down in the other wicker chair near mom's. "Warn him about playing with my mom's affections?"

Mom smiles and shakes her head. "He's being paid to do what he does. I'm just kidding, Candi. I know my days of romance are well past. "

"That's only true if you want it to be, mom. You are such a beautiful soul," I say fervently. She's also gorgeous, but mom isn't impressed with compliments about appearance. "Any man would be lucky to have you in his life."

"Well, I love that you see the world that way." She pats my hand, none of her fingers curled in from pain. "Maybe that's why you can see the good in your assassin."

Looking at my mom's more relaxed appearance and her face uncreased with pain is all I need to see the good in Angelo.

He's behind the foundation that brought Petra into our lives. And the new wholistic regime she's got mom following is making a difference. The nurse brought in a dietician, a physical therapist who specializes in joint pain and an acupuncture doctor. All of whom are focused on minimizing mom's joint pain.

It's working.

Six months ago, even mom's indomitable will wouldn't have made it possible for her to show up here, demanding to see me after a car ride from Queens.

"He's more than an assassin," I remind my mom.

He's a man who cares deeply about a select few and I'm one of them. Every day that hits me more deeply.

Angelo doesn't want to own me, he wants to empower me. He wants to make it possible for me to do the things that matter to me. He installed a dance studio in the house. For me.

Because I love to dance.

But it's more than that. When I'm with him, my heart is happy. Do I need a logical reason for that?

I've got them but it's really not logical. It's pure emotion and he calls to my heart like no one else does. Not even mom and Cookie. They're different.

Family and important, but part of my life.

The feelings I have for Angelo are consuming and that's a little scary after such a short period of time actually spent together. No matter how he sees the last few months as *dating*.

"Yes, he is," mom readily agrees. "Whatever he does for a living, he is the man you love."

"I haven't told him that yet."

Mom's brows lift. "Has he told you he loves you?"

"Yes. Sort of. Is claiming he fell in love with me at first sight a genuine admission of love? I don't know what to believe. Angelo's so confident this thing between us is the real deal. But are his feelings love or obsession?"

"Sweetheart, when a man like him feels an emotion he considers to be love, I believe you can trust it to be the real thing," mom says reassuringly.

I wish that were true. "Isn't it the opposite? A man who only feels when he's with me would struggle to identify exactly what he's feeling, right?"

"What is love if it is not the willingness to change your life to accommodate another? The desire to spend time with that one person more than any other. Finding joy in their company."

That describes how I feel about Angelo to a T. "But—"

Mom cuts me off with a raised hand. "Sometimes, you get in your own head and miss what's right in front of you. Your Angelo has made incredible efforts on behalf of me and your sister. Most men would focus on you and the relationship you two have. But because he sees the love you have for us, that obsessive emotion, that need to take care of you spills over onto us. Sweetheart, I'm not sure there's a better example of love than that."

Tears prick my eyes, but I'm not sad. Joy fizzes in my veins like champagne at my mom's words. Because my mom is right. Obsession doesn't explain all that.

"Maybe he does love me," I say with some of that joy bubbling into my voice. "And maybe I need to admit that what I feel for him can't be called anything else either."

"Take a page out of my book of learnings and tell him sooner than later. Jakub and I dated for almost three years before I finally admitted my feelings for him because of my mother's disapproval. That's three years we could've been together as a man and wife. And when I lost him, you can believe I regretted every day of those three years."

My heart kicks a beat. "With the line of work Angelo is in, our time could be limited too."

"Not if he has anything to say about it and sweetheart, I think he does. Have you seen the attention to detail in the security of this place? Your

Angelo is not going to die on you from sloppy mistakes or even unsloppy ones."

"I hope you're right, because I don't want to live without him now that I've experienced life with him." It's a scary thing to admit, but the truth usually is.

"I am so glad to hear that. You deserve a love like that."

"But my happiness doesn't have to come at the cost of yours." I get to the point of the talk I want to have with her. "Cookie doesn't have to live here to have a good life. You two don't have to live here for me to be happy."

Mom's smile is gentle. "I know that, Candi. I raised you to be independent and to spread your wings, but back in the Old Country, it's not uncommon for parents to live with their children."

"The apartment is your home though. It's the home you shared with Jakub. I don't want you feeling like you have to leave just because I am moving in with Angelo."

Mom's smile turns bittersweet. "That apartment holds many dear memories, but I've spent the better part of the past five years practically trapped there."

I open my mouth to respond and then shut it again. This is a time to listen, not talk.

"Even when the elevator works, getting outside is hard." Mom looks around the conservatory. "This place is paradise for a woman with my joints. I can enjoy the sunshine, plants and even a waterfall..."

I duck my head to hide my blush at her mention of the waterfall pool. Some things I will *never* tell my mom about and the special jet in that pool is one of them.

"The apartment is just a place. What matters is the love that existed between its walls. We're taking that with us."

"Are you saying you want to move in here permanently?" I ask, unable to hide my shock.

My mom seems less conflicted about leaving the only home she's known since moving to New York than I am about moving out of our small apartment.

"Yes."

"Wow. Cookie is going to be over the moon."

"I'll be the hero for at least a week, won't I?" Mom adjusts the throw over her legs.

"You'll always be our hero, mom. Don't you know that?"

Mom opens her arms and for the first time in recent memory we share a hug that doesn't make her wince in pain. That's down to Angelo and if I didn't love him already, I would fall fully and forever in this moment.

CHAPTER 33

ANGELO

"That's a new look for you." Miceli leans back in his chair at the large circular table in the private backroom of Nonna Agata's.

The mafia-owned Italian restaurant that has been in New York as long as the Five Families is closer to Pitiful Princess than either Severu or Miceli's office. Since both of their wives are safely at home while Bianca and Candi are catching up at the club, they agreed to have our meeting here.

Salvatore and I would both rather be at the club, watching over our women, but we can't be with them twenty-four-seven.

At least that's what Severu tells me.

Considering the fact he moved his primary office to the penthouse months before he became the godfather so he could spend more time in Catalina's vicinity, I'm not sure his opinion is valid.

But Candi's is and she told me to get lost. She wanted girl time with Bianca.

Ignoring Miceli's comment, I turn to Salvatore. "Why didn't you install cameras in the office at Pitiful Princess?"

I'd feel better if I had a visual on Candi.

"Because I don't stalk my wife," Salvatore drawls.

Big Sal barks out a laugh at his son's words. "That's why you had Pietro install cameras *inside* your home, because you *don't* stalk your wife."

"What's the real reason there are no cameras in the manager's office at Pitiful Princess?" Miceli demands sardonically.

"She told me if I installed cameras in the office at the club, she was moving her stuff back into the guest room," Salvatore admits. "She doesn't want me *nosing into her time with Candi* and that's where they get together."

"That tracks," I mutter, remembering Candi's adamant demand for time alone with Bianca.

They're safe, I remind myself. Both their security teams are at the club. Derian and Pietro are inside, and we have men at the front and back entrances as well.

There's only one access point to the office and their guards are watching it.

But something is making my instincts twitch.

"They'll have to get together at our homes now that Candi won't be dancing," Salvatore says with satisfaction.

"Don't count on it," I warn him. "Candi is going to talk to Bianca about helping her manage the talent."

"Good," Nerissa says from across the table. "I've told Bianca more than once she needs to get someone to help her."

Salvatore frowns. "She takes on too much."

Which torpedoes any hope I had that Bianca won't take Candi up on her offer.

The smell of garlic and basil precedes the soldier from Severu's security team bringing in our food for the lunch meeting. The food isn't from the restaurant kitchen either, but brought in by one of the De Luca cooks. All the tableware is freshly washed and handled only by our people.

This is the new protocol for Severu eating away from home since becoming godfather.

If we can think of using food to get to someone, so can his enemies.

"Seriously, I didn't know your face could make that expression," Miceli says around a bite of crab ravioli in white sauce.

Big Sal looks at me critically. "What expression?"

"He looks worried." Miceli nods toward me, taking a sip of his water.

We don't drink wine with our meals away from home. I don't drink it at all. A second's hesitation caused by a more relaxed demeanor from alcohol could lead to my death, or someone else's.

The consigliere shrugs like he doesn't see my concern.

Miceli knows me better than Big Sal though.

"Are you really that nervous about Candi being at the club?" Salvatore asks. "You watched her dance there for months without intervening."

Yes, I'm fucking worried. "I hadn't claimed her before. Now everyone knows she's mine."

Salvatore nods his understanding. "No one thought a stripper you were probably banging but didn't bother to date would be a way to get to you."

"Now she's living at your house." Big Sal butters a piece of bread, ignoring his plate of steamed broccoli and grilled chicken breast.

His wife has him on a heart-healthy diet, which he apparently isn't impressed by.

"Our home," I correct. "Candi's on the deed."

She still doesn't know that. I'm trying to ease her into things after the whole checking account thing. She took the news about the trust fund for Cookie's education much better, but that might be because she was still in shock over her newfound wealth.

Severu scrutinizes me like he's looking for something. "How's that going?"

He means living with my new family. "Mostly good. Meshing two lives can be a challenge, but compromise is the key to doing it successfully."

"You've been reading that book on relationships again." Nerissa laughs.

Not sure what she finds funny about me reading a book, I say, "I only read it once."

"You keep quoting from it and we're going to think you've gone soft," Big Sal admonishes me. "I never read a book on relationships and my marriage is fine."

Salvatore shakes his head. "Mamma is the reason your marriage is a good one."

"I won't deny that. Your mother knows what it means to be a true mafia wife." Big Sal leans back in his chair and pats his still flat stomach complacently.

This meeting is a strategic counsel of war for family only. Severu and Miceli are brothers. Salvatore and Nerissa are Big Sal's children and their cousins. I'm the only one here not related by blood or formal adoption.

Not even Severu's council of two consiglieres are here.

No security team are in the room with us, and it has been swept for bugs and cameras. As an extra precaution there's a localized signal jammer. The walls are too thick for distance surveillance equipment, which isn't very effective in a busy city like The Big Apple anyway.

"Our women don't make us soft. They make us more determined to stay on top so we can protect them," Severu says, his expression one that would frighten most men.

"True that," Miceli agrees.

"Stop talking like a teenager," Big Sal admonishes. "You are a don now."

Miceli's face goes blank and he stares his uncle down. "Be careful how *you* talk to *me*. I would hate to have to cut out your tongue. It would piss off Aunt Ilaria and make it hard for you to do your job advising me as my consigliere."

Big Sal rolls his eyes, clearly not worried, but he inclines his head in acknowledgment of his don's words.

"Your mother is in New York?" Severu asks me, obviously ready to move onto the reason for the meeting.

How to respond to his Sicilian counterpart's reaction to Severu being named godfather.

"Maybe."

"I thought she wasn't coming for another week," Salvatore sets his fork down without putting the bite of ravioli on it into his mouth.

"I got intelligence flight plans were filed for Don Messino's jet to arrive in Boston yesterday. My mother and her husband are listed as passengers along with a detail of six men."

Miceli frowns. "That's a small security detail for the godfather's daughter and one of his favored dons."

"They may have other soldiers flying commercially," Big Sal says.

I agree. "Manifests for flights into Boston on the days before and morning of their flight are being checked against known members of the don's security force."

"Did she mention coming to Boston before traveling to New York?" Salvatore asks me.

"No." Which doesn't necessarily mean she and the don are there for nefarious purposes. "My mother does not share her plans with me. This is the first time in five years she's bothered to tell me she's coming to the States at all."

That does not mean her plans in Boston *aren't* nefarious either.

"Do you think the Lombardi is sympathetic to Don Messino's point of view?" Nerissa asks Miceli.

Miceli negotiated the peace agreement after the Lombardi's nephews were involved in unsanctioned actions against the Genovese Family while he was still Severu's underboss.

"Even if he is, he's smart enough to know that backing anyone but my brother in this altercation would be the downfall of his mafia."

Miceli is not talking out of his ass. The Lombardi mafia are heavily involved in politics. Backing a Sicilian play over a powerful ally in New York would be stupid. Unlike his nephews, the Boston don isn't that.

Big Sal frowns. "You talk like we're going to war. We haven't exhausted the option of diplomacy."

"We aren't going to war, but diplomacy only works when the other side respects you as an equal."

Whether or not Don Messino sees Severu as his equal, my boss will never see the other godfather as anything but a hidebound fool.

Our plans don't include war though. That would put too many members of the American Cosa Nostra at risk. We'll take care of the problem subtly, but permanently.

Salvatore rubs his chin in thought. "Do we know who they might be visiting in Boston?"

"They both have known associates in the city," Severu replies.

His wife keeps records of the underworld and their connections that the FEDs and Interpol would cream their pants over having access to.

"Do we need to worry?" Big Sal asks with a frown.

He's not thrilled that the intel comes from Catalina. While he loves his nephew's wife, she plays a role he doesn't consider appropriate for a traditional mafia princess.

"They're not big players," I answer for my boss. "The likelihood is they will facilitate plans for my mother and her husband with strategic assets."

Severu steeples his hands. "Domenico's team is compiling a list of properties, weapons access, etc. in case they're gearing up for a violent attack on me."

"They have to know that would fail but would cost many lives. It would be a declaration of war." Big Sal shakes his head.

"Don Messino's arrogance makes him blind to reality sometimes." Severu looks at me pointedly. "He wants to oust me for the same reason he rejected Angelo as his uncle's successor."

"He thinks you're a psychopath too?" I ask drolly.

Severu shakes his head. "Your lack of empathy makes you impossible to control and he never understood your code of honor and loyalty."

"The old dinosaur knows he can't control my brother like he did Don Caruso," Miceli says with satisfaction.

"He didn't control him at the end," I point out.

Don Caruso backed Severu as his choice for the next godfather against my grandfather's wishes.

"How are we going to avoid war?" Nerissa asks, her expression hard. "Don Messino keeps the Sicilian Cosa Nostra in the Dark Ages. He's not spreading that garbage here."

There are no made women like Nerissa in the Sicilian Cosa Nostra. There are still military leaders who don't think women belong in the military either. More the fool them.

Nerissa's a damn good underboss for Salvatore.

Severu tells the rest of the family my plan for taking out my grandfather while I finish my lunch.

"You're okay with this?" Big Sal asks.

"To protect Candi from the risk of mafia war, I would kill the devil himself."

No one has any more questions after that.

CHAPTER 34

CANDI

"So, Angelo?" Bianca rounds her eyes like an anime character.

I roll mine. "Yes."

"You know they call him the Angel of Death."

"And they call me a stripper, but he calls me his soul." I peel back the top on the foil container with the lunch Bianca brought for me and take an appreciative sniff.

Cooked wine and mushrooms. Chicken marsala is one of my favorite meals ever and Bianca brings it for me every time we're able to meet like this.

My best friend gasps, warmth filling her blue eyes. "That's so sweet and I can honestly tell you, I never thought I'd say that about Angelo Caruso. He gives me the heebee jeebees."

"Salvatore isn't exactly warm and cuddly."

"But he's hot." Bianca winks. "And he cuddles me plenty."

"Angelo is surprisingly affectionate too. He's always touching me."

"And it doesn't bother you?" Bianca knows about my reticence with men.

We have a lot in common. I'm sure that's why we bonded so fast when she started working here.

At the time I thought it was because we were close to the same age and in the same place in life. Dancing the pole to support ourselves and trying to finish college part-time.

She was on her own by then because the man who'd stepped in to save her had died. I was supporting the woman who had stepped in to save me.

What I didn't know before last month, when things got real between us, is that we both had asshole mafia men for fathers. And we both had traumatic sexual experiences when we were teens because they didn't protect us.

I consider Bianca as much my sister as Cookie.

I bite into the crusty bread that Bianca brought with lunch. "I'm so not going to miss having to forego carbs so I don't go *too plus size* for the stage."

"Nerissa never said that to you!" Bianca takes an angry bite of her own bread.

I grin. "Back then, she never talked to the dancers at all. No, that was Ugo and Gino. Don't tell me they never gave you a hard time about your curves?"

"Gino was too busy trying to get me to work the backrooms. I guess Ugo used up his asshat tendencies on you." There's a knock on the door and Bianca calls, "Come in."

Nina steps through the portal carrying a tray with a bottle of wine and two glasses.

She doesn't smile, but she's careful when she places the tray on the big desk Bianca and I are using as our table for lunch. "Mr. De Luca sent this with his regards."

Looking at the bottle, I see it's our favorite moscato. We don't usually indulge with lunch, but since I'm not dancing later, I don't mind having a glass today.

Bianca sighs happily. "That man spoils me."

After opening the bottle and pouring each of us a glass, Nina leaves, taking her sulky attitude with her.

"I can't believe she's still not over Gino leaving. It's not like they had a thing." I take a sip of wine and chase it with the perfect bite of chicken marsala. "She wasn't even the only one he had sucking him off for a better schedule."

"She had a crush on him for sure." Bianca makes a face. "I guess it takes all kinds."

"Well, he's not coming back so she needs to move on."

Bianca waggles her eyebrows. "What do you know?"

"According to a source I can't name, but he kidnapped me and drug me back to his boss's lair, Gino died choking on his own dick after having his hands cut off."

"Eww. Gruesome. Did Angelo do it?"

"Not saying he did. Not saying he didn't."

Bianca laughs. "You just did."

"There's probably something wrong with me that I don't feel pity for him."

"Are you kidding? Do you know how many dancers came to me and told me he molested them after he was gone and I took over as talent liaison? He had power over them, and he abused it." She takes a big gulp of her wine. "He deserved what he got."

"Correction, there's probably something wrong with both of us."

"If there is it's because men like Gino destroyed any pity we might feel toward them." She lifts her glass.

I clink mine against hers. "Truth."

"I don't know what I want to hear first, the whole Stefano Bianchi being your father thing, or more details about Angelo, the love angel."

We laugh together, loudly. I reach for my fork and miss it and laugh again. "Clumsy today."

"So, spill."

I tell her about my brothers and my new wealth. "It's so weird not to have to worry about money anymore."

"Pretty sure once Angelo set his sights on you, that became a thing of the past."

"He's behind the foundation. Did I tell you that?" Of course, I called my best friend on Monday and told her all about the kidnapping and my first time having sex.

Now we're talking about everything else that's happened in the last few days.

"That doesn't surprise me. Salvatore would have done the same thing."

I didn't think so the first time I met him, but now I agree with a nod. "Shal...Sal...your husband is pretty cool."

"Something's wrong." Bianca tries to pick up her phone, but can't get her fingers around it.

Clinging to the desk, I stand up. "The wine."

That bitch, Nina. She put something in the wine.

"Get P..." Bianca's voice peters out as she slumps forward on the desk.

I will my body to turn toward the door but my muscles won't listen to me. My vision goes fuzzy and I start hallucinating because I see the wall behind the manager's desk open.

Then everything goes black.

CHAPTER 35

ANGELO

"Candi asked me if I would kill you if Bianca needed me to." I smirk at Salvatore, who is sharing the back seat of the SUV with me. He left his at the club when we went to lunch after making sure the women were safely tucked away in the manager's office.

"The fuck. Bianca loves me."

"That's why I felt safe telling her *yes*."

"You asshole. I bet you meant it too." Salvatore doesn't sound too broken up by the prospect.

"I did."

"Good. Bianca deserves a friend who watches out for her like that and Candi deserves a man who would make that promise."

"Fuck, listen to you sounding all philosophical."

Salvatore shrugs, unembarrassed by his feelings.

Feelings I would have said he didn't have before he met Bianca. Just like me.

Sure, he showed more affection for his mom and sister, but at the end of the day, Salvatore was capo first, son and brother second. With Bianca, he is husband first, everything else comes after.

It's the way it has to be when you meet your soulmate.

At the club, we find Pietro in the main club area surveilling from one corner. Pitiful Princess doesn't open until later, so the only people around are staff. Derian is in the hall outside the manager's office, looking frosty.

He nods to me and Salvatore and steps back from the office door.

Salvatore shoves it open. "Hey, Candi I hear Death promi..." With a wordless shout, Salvatore rushes forward.

I'm right on his heels.

At first glance, what I see makes no sense to me. Bianca is slumped over the desk, unmoving. And Candi is nowhere to be seen.

Where is she? Did she go into the bathroom to get something to help Salvatore's wife? Why not call Derian in to help?

I rush to the attached bathroom and fling open the door, but there's no one inside the small space.

Coming out, I see that Derian has the door to a storage closet open. "No one's in here, boss."

"Candi!" I yell loud enough to be heard out in the main club.

There's no answer. Grabbing my second by his throat, I throw him up against the wall. "Where is my soul?"

"She was in here, boss," he chokes out. "I never took my eyes off the hall."

"How the fuck is that possible?"

Derian can't answer. My hold on his throat is too tight.

Releasing him, I step back trying to think, but the thoughts in my brain are spinning like chopper blades.

"She didn't come out, Death. That door didn't open," Derian croaks out as he scoots around the desk to look underneath like maybe Candi is hiding there.

Salvatore shoved everything off the desk and laid his wife on top in the few seconds it took me to check the bathroom.

His fingers are on her pulse at her wrist. "It's sluggish."

Fuck. What the hell is going on?

He lifts her eyelids.

"What's wrong with Mrs. De Luca?" Derian asks.

Salvatore lifts Bianca's eyelids and curses. "She's been drugged."

"I called medical." Pietro steps into the room. "ETA seven minutes."

Salvatore doesn't answer. He's trying to get his wife to respond, but she's out for the count. Not dead though.

And not fucking missing.

The same cook who made our meal made the one now strewn all over the floor around the desk. "The food wasn't drugged."

What chills me is how much of the food there is. Whatever happened occurred soon after the ladies sat down to eat lunch.

"What about the bottle of wine?" Derian points to a bottle of Candi's favorite Moscato.

It hits a discordant note in the already cacophonous absence of *mia amate*. Candi doesn't drink when she and Bianca get together because she has to be ready to dance. Not tonight though.

Maybe they ordered a bottle of wine to celebrate.

"Who served it to them?" I demand at the same time as Salvatore asks that question.

"Nina brought it in," Derian answers grimly. "She said the capo called and ordered it for Mrs. De Luca."

Spiders crawl up my spine like they used to when I knew the enemy had a bead on me. "Send someone to pick her up."

Salvatore makes the same order of Pietro simultaneously. Again.

I look at him.

He stares right back. "You find your woman. I'll take care of Nina."

I jerk my head in acknowledgment and grab my phone, going immediately to the app for Candi's tracker.

As soon as Bianca made sure all the dancers got medical and dental insurance through the club, Candi scheduled herself a cleaning appointment with the dentist she'd gone to while on the state's insurance as a foster child.

When I found that out, I bribed her dentist to tell her she had the beginning of a cavity, and that if she got it fixed then to prevent further tooth decay, it would cost less. Instead of fixing a cavity the dentist implanted a tracking device in her tooth.

Until I installed the cameras in her apartment, I spent a lot of time watching the little dot that showed her location.

It gave me peace. Now it keeps me sane.

I will not lose my soul.

She's northeast of New York, in Massachusetts, but nowhere near Boston. The good news is that the dot indicating her location is stationary. Her kidnappers had to have used a helicopter to be there this quickly.

"Assemble a team and have them meet us on the roof of the Oscuro building in fifteen minutes," I order Derian.

I text Mario a Code Red alert for Mira and Cookie's protection. He'll make sure they get to one of the house's saferooms and stay there until I bring Candi home.

Then I call Severu.

He picks up on the first ring. "Salvatore texted Nerissa. What do you need?"

"The ten-person helicopter ready to fly in fifteen minutes. This is a Code Red, Severu. Get Catalina and your mom to the saferoom and stay there with them."

"Their security teams are already on it."

When we arrive on the roof of the Oscuro Building, I'm not surprised to find my boss waiting. I'm shaking my head at him before I realize that Miceli is already on the helicopter.

"You are the fucking godfather, Severu. This whole thing is about getting to you through me." Because there's no question in my mind who is responsible for Candi's disappearance.

My mother working on behalf of my grandfather.

They think they'll use Candi for leverage.

But what they've really done is bring down the wrath of Death on their heads and everyone involved with helping them.

I am Death and I have no mercy for my enemies.

"You are family, Angelo and that means Candi is too." Severu jumps into the helicopter and jerks his thumb for me to follow. "You're fucking right, she was kidnapped to get at me and I'll be there to break the necks of the men who took her."

Severu gives the pilot the signal to go and the helicopter lifts off the roof.

"Coms on," I tell my team and then reach my hand out toward Severu and Miceli. "Give me your phones to activate our com channel."

After that's done, Severu says, "Our intel shows a vacation home near Plainville owned by one of Barone's business associates."

My phone pings with the address and I add it to Candi's tracker app.

Bingo. "That's our target." I check my other messages and forward the info on our secure channel. "There are twelve Barone soldiers total. Six flew in with Perla and the don. Six arrived two days prior."

Which means she was planning this kidnapping before she called me on Saturday night. She saw Candi as leverage before I told the world she was mine.

"Domenico says there are four private security guards assigned to the house," Severu says.

I nod my acknowledgment and tell my men, "Study the pictures I sent."

"Why?" Miceli asks.

"We don't kill civilians," Derian answers while I read through the other information our team has gathered. "The private security team didn't sign on for war with the mafia. They're there to protect some rich man's property."

"We incapacitate and warn. If they cross our paths again, they get no mercy." I don't look up from the glowing dot that represents my woman.

"Incapacitation presents more of a challenge," Miceli says with relish.

Not going to lie. That's one of the reasons we have the rule. It makes things more interesting.

Suddenly, *Right Place, Wrong Time* by Dr. John starts playing in my earbud. I look up and Miceli is grinning.

"Let's do this." Derian slams his fist against his chest.

I flip my knife up toward the ceiling of the helicopter and catch it before hitting my chest with the fist gripping it. "The Sicilians die."

My men shout *sì la morte* in unison.

Yes, Death.

"I want a saying like that for my men," Miceli complains. "*Sì don* isn't as cool."

He might be joking, but the deadly look in the don's eyes says he's ready to kill some Sicilian soldiers.

Good. Because tonight, twelve of them die with their don. But not their dona. I still have plans for Perla.

She will be my grandfather's downfall and after tonight, they both deserve nothing less.

CHAPTER 36

CANDI

The first thing I'm aware of is a pounding ache in my head. My throat is thick and tastes like I sucked on someone's dirty sweat socks.

My eyelids feel glued shut and it takes a concentrated effort to force them open. At first, I can't see anything, but my eyes slowly come back into focus and the moonlight through the window allows me to make out most of my surroundings.

I'm in a bedroom with huge windows and no drapes. The walls are naked logs meant to look rustic, but too polished to be anything but part of some rich person's vacation home. Thick trees obscure the skyline out the window.

We're definitely not in the city. I don't know much about Long Island, but those trees look too thick for anything I've seen on the island.

So, where am I? One thing I know: I'm not going to figure it out lying here.

Groaning, I force myself to sit up. The pounding in my head gets exponentially worse. I'm pressing on both sides of my temples in a vain attempt to alleviate it when the door swings open and bright light from the hall spills into the room.

"Good. You're awake." The woman in the doorway is beautiful in that cold, cruel villainess sort of way.

Or maybe that's just my circumstances talking. "You'd make a great stand-in for Cruella De Ville."

Oops. Brain to mouth filter offline. Is that a result of the drugs that knocked me out, or the fury roiling inside me at being kidnapped. Again. Only this time there's no Angelo waiting for me to arrive with his obsessive certainty we belong together.

Whoever this woman is, she doesn't work for him.

He would never let someone who works for him drug me and give me such a terrible headache.

The woman's perfectly painted lips twist in a moue of distaste. "Don't try to be clever, dear. It doesn't suit you."

"I'm not your dear and you don't get a vote. At least I'm smart enough to know what a huge mistake it is to kidnap the Angel of Death's beloved."

"Beloved?" she scoffs. "Angelo is no more capable of love than a dog can speak."

"I'd rather listen to Mars bark than your ugly voice."

There is something familiar about the woman's gray eyes and then it hits me. "You're the sorry excuse for a mother that gave birth to *my beloved*."

Perla Caruso, or whatever her last name is now that she's on husband number three, wrinkles her nose like she smells something bad. "Pregnancy and giving birth was the worst experience of my life, but it was supposed to lead to my offspring becoming a don and eventually a godfather."

"Yeah, nothing like pinning all your expectations on the next generation, instead of making something of your own life. Too bad it didn't work out for you. *Or not*." Swallowing back nausea, I scoot toward the edge of the bed an inch at a time.

"My fortunes are changing. All my son has to do is his duty."

And that family thinks Angelo's the psychopath? "Maybe with enough fortune you can buy a better personality. Or even a conscience."

I swing my legs over the side of the bed and try to stand. But woozy, I fall back on my butt. I need a glass of water or something, but I'm not asking his awful woman for anything. Besides, I couldn't trust her not to poison it.

I stand again and manage to stay upright, even if I'm swaying a little. "Where's the bathroom?"

"Through that door." Angelo's mother points toward a door in the wall opposite the bed.

I head where she's pointing one slow footstep at a time. When I reach it, I step inside, find the light switch and turn it on before shutting the door.

It's less fancy than I expect based on the bedroom, with a single sink vanity, toilet and shower cubicle. And no window.

I'm pretty sure I couldn't manage to climb out one right now anyway.

I splash my face with cold water before drinking several gulps straight from the tap. I have to breathe through my nose for almost a full minute before I'm sure it's going to stay down.

After I pee and wash my hands in water that has turned more and more frigid the longer it runs, I splash my face again.

Finally, I can stand without swaying. I start searching the bathroom for something to use as a weapon. There's a comb, but no hairbrush in the vanity. No razor, though how I'd use one as a weapon is unclear to me. There's a manicure kit, but the nailfile inside is a blunt emery board.

I might be able to give her a good gouge with the toenail scissors, but I'm not going to incapacitate her.

The lid on the toilet tank has some heft but would make a very awkward weapon, no matter how they show it on T.V. Still, if that's all there is, I'll take it.

Do I know Angelo is coming? Without doubt, but Queen Bitch kidnapped me for a reason, and I have an ugly suspicion it's to use me as leverage against her son. Little does she know how well that could work.

No matter what she thinks, Angelo loves me and he's not going to risk me being hurt. Which means I need to get away from the bad guys before they can use me as bait to kidnap *him*.

My eyes land on the shower cubicle again. Instead of a door, there's a fabric curtain with a plastic liner trying a little too hard to be casually rustic.

The curtain is useless, but the rod it's hanging from looks like a peeled and smoothed branch.

I turn the water on full blast and flush the toilet just before I knock it from its brackets. It comes down pretty easily, which makes sense since the curtain has to be easily removable for washing and liner replacement.

Dropping the curtain into the bottom of the shower cubicle I heft the wooden stick. It's solid but not too heavy and only about three feet long.

A peremptory knock sounds on the door. "Come out, Kathleen. I do not have all night."

I turn off the water and place the rod to the right of the door, out of sight of the opening but easy to reach if I leave the door open and stay close to the bathroom.

Perla is pacing the room impatiently when I come out.

Pretending I'm still woozy, I lean against the wall beside the bathroom doorway. "What do you want?"

"You're going to call Angelo and tell him to do as he's told if he wants to see you alive again."

Yeah, no. I pretend compliance with a grimace and a nod though. I'm not pissing away a chance to talk to Angelo on the phone.

"Good." Perla lifts a burner phone and taps on the screen twice.

At least I assume the cheap phone isn't her personal device.

There's a single ring at the other end and then Angelo's voice. "Speak."

There's loud music in the background and something else. Is he still at the club?

Somehow, I doubt that very much.

"Angelo. It's me," Perla says like he should recognize her voice.

"I'm here too and I'm okay," I say quickly.

The older woman glares at me. "Shut up, Kathleen. You will not speak until you are told to."

"Talk to her like that again and I'll cut your tongue out." His tone sends a shiver down my spine.

Perla blanches before glaring at me threateningly. "Talk, Kathleen. You know what to say."

"Your mom is the real psycho in your family," I inform my guardian angel.

Perla raises her hand to strike me.

I shake my head at her. "The last person who touched me without my permission lost a hand to your son's knife. I don't know, but I feel like you're not someone who would handle that very well."

"If you don't want your mouthy whore's tongue cut out, you will hear me out," Perla threatens. "The only reason she's unharmed is her value to you, but I'm losing patience with her."

The only sound at Angelo's end is the loud music blaring in the background. That song isn't on any of the playlists at the club.

"Did you hear me?" Perla demands.

"I heard you begging me to cut off every appendage on your body before I kill you." There's no emotion in Angelo's voice now.

He almost sounds bored.

But the effect on his mother is the opposite of boredom. Her eyes go wide with fear and nothing comes out of her mouth when she tries to talk.

"I think someone is regretting their life's choices right now, stalker angel."

"Stalker angel?" he asks.

"Too much? How about hot stuff? Oh, I know, Iron Man. Because you're my morally gray superhero who actually kills people."

"That would be Deadpool," Angelo says.

My heart settles in my chest because he sounds like himself again. I really don't want to witness him cutting off all his mother's body parts.

"Yeah, no. What about babe? Or my beloved dark angel...but that feels too long."

"Beloved?" he asks, picking that word out of all the others I'm throwing to de-escalate the situation.

Wherever Angelo is, he's on his way to get me. If he weren't he'd have asked where I am. He didn't because he already knows and I'm also hoping my little show about endearments will have sidetracked his mother enough not to notice that.

He would also sound more worried. Maybe not for anyone else, but for me?

Definitely.

Shrieking, Perla spins on her heel and storms out of the room. Coming away from the wall, I go to follow her, only to be stopped by a man standing in the doorway.

Leaning around him, I yell, "How do you like stud muffin?"

My guard gently, but firmly pushes me back into the room and then shuts the door in my face. I don't bother banging on it. I got what I wanted, a glimpse of my prison outside the bedroom I'm in.

The hall outside my door is open on one side with a view of the first floor, where I saw a bunch of guys sitting around a table playing cards. Do they really think Angelo won't find me?

They must. Which gives me pause. I'm assuming my phone and whatever tracking app Angelo no doubt has on it got left at the club.

How *is* he going to find me? Maybe he didn't ask because he assumes I don't know anything about where I am, which is mostly true.

But he didn't sound worried.

Whether he's coming sooner, or later, I'm not sticking around to see what plans that evil bitch has for me.

She wants to use me as leverage against her son, but she can't do that if I'm not here.

My brief glimpse into the hall told me that this room is at the far end of the hall, away from the stairs.

Even if I could incapacitate Mr. Personality out there, the chances for me making it to the stairs down the open hallway and sneaking out the front door without alerting the guys downstairs are slim to none.

That leaves escape from within the room.

Peering through the window, I'm delighted to see the exposed beam motif from inside extended outside. Suspended by other beams, one runs the length of the eaves. About five feet from the wall of the house and open at the top, it is even with the bottom slope of the roof putting it only a couple of feet above the top of the window.

I don't know if the beams are structural or decorative. They're there and that's all that matters to me. If I can MacGyver some kind of rope, I can try to throw it up and over the beam.

Then I'll shimmy down and run like hell. Dancing the pole has developed my core strength so I could scale the side of a building as long as there's something to hold onto.

Like a shower curtain tied into a rope with the sheets from the bed. Which answers one how, but it's still a plan with a lot of ifs and not a lot of strategy.

Before anything, I need to see if the windows open and if they are wired to an alarm.

For that, I come up with a pretty decent strategy if I do say so myself. But it requires hanging the curtain back up in the shower. I check the closet and drawers in the dresser and bedside table first.

There are two wire hangers and six flocked ones on the empty closet rail. An extra pillow and blanket are the only things on the shelf above it. There's nothing in the nightstand, but there's a dark sweater in the bottom drawer of the dresser.

As my mind flips through the possibilities of how to use what I found, I open one of the windows. Then I wait.

It takes nearly five minutes for the door to slam open. My guard rushes in, but stops when he sees me on the bed, doing my best to look pathetic.

"What?" I pretend to hold back being sick.

His mean glare morphs into a grimace and he looks away. "Close the window."

"No."

Still not looking at me, he marches toward the window, like he's going to do it himself.

"I need the fresh air." I whine pitifully, which is so not me, but he doesn't know that. "Whatever you people drugged me with is making me nauseous."

"You're going to have to deal," he says unsympathetically.

While he's closing and relocking the window, I shove a finger down my throat, making myself retch. I don't try to hold back and manage to throw up a little bile onto the floor beside the bed.

Turning back to me and looking pretty green himself, the guard says something Italian in a nasty tone.

"I'm not cleaning that up. It will just make me throw up more." I turn over, like I'm trying to get away from the smell.

I feel the renewed breeze from the open window and cheer inside, but I don't turn over. Grinning inside, I enjoy every second of the guard's huffing and puffing while he gets something from the bathroom to clean up the mess. When he makes gagging noises, I'm positively gleeful.

He says something else in Italian and drops something wet on the carpet.

"Stay away from the windows," he orders, like I'm going to listen to him.

Even if I didn't think he was an asshole for being part of my kidnapping entourage, I wouldn't let him boss me around.

I'm off the bed as soon as the door shuts again. He left a sopping hand towel over the place I threw up.

Whimp. I guess he's never had to nurse a little sister through the flu or helped his mom clean up after new meds gave her diarrhea.

At this point, my stomach is pretty much made of cast iron.

I rush to pull the sheets from the bed and toss them into the bathroom before stacking the pillows neatly and putting the comforter back on.

It only takes a minute to retrieve my weapon and free the shower curtain from it. The nail scissors come in handy making snips so I can tear the curtain, sheets and spare blanket into strips. If anyone comes into the bedroom, I'll pretend to be washing up after being sick again.

In the time it takes me to twist the fabric strips and tie knots, no one comes to check on their nauseated captive.

After attaching the shower curtain rod to one end, I dismantle the two wire coat hangers and twist them together to make a long wire with a hook at the end.

Once everything is assembled, I tiptoe to the bedroom door and press my ear against it. No one is talking, or walking by.

I'm sure my weak-stomached guard is still out there, but it doesn't sound like anyone else is.

It's now, or never.

Being as quiet as I can, I climb onto the windowsill and lean out with one hand holding onto the window. You can't dance a pole if you have a fear of heights, but even I'm nervously aware that one slip and I'm a pancake on the ground below.

Relief floods me when I manage to get the end of the shower rod to sit on the eave. Despite the hours of throwing balls for Mars with Cookie, my aim is not that great. If I had to toss it javelin style, I would probably miss and make enough racket to expose my escape attempt.

But this way, I just have to shove and the wood acts like a needle guiding the rope over the eave. It takes me longer than I'd like to catch the rod with the hanger hook, but eventually I do and I'm able to pull it back to me.

After removing the stick from the end of my makeshift rope, I tie it around the other part of the rope. Then I reattach the stick. It could still come in handy as a weapon.

Hoping for the best, I swing out on the rope and flip upside down to see what's below my room.

Light blazes from a window that looks into some kind of office. An older man is sitting at a desk facing the window. He's not looking up, but that could change any second.

Okay. Plan B.

Wrapping the rope around my knee, I flip back upward and quickly shimmy up the rope instead of down. Once I can reach the exposed beam under the eave, I climb onto it on my belly and check out the rest of the house on this side.

There's no light coming from the window on the first floor at the other end of the house. Of course, it's going to be as far away from me as possible.

Untying the rope, I draw it upward, looping it over my arm until I can scoot along the beam to the other end. Once I get it tied back onto the beam, the stick at the bottom of the rope, I shimmy down, remove the stick and proceed with the second part of my plan.

Running toward the forest as fast as my dancer's legs will carry me.

CHAPTER 37

ANGELO

As soon as I end the call with Perla, Miceli whistles. "Candi's right. Your mom is the one swimming in the bonkers end of the gene pool."

I had the call on speaker phone so Severu and Miceli could hear what Perla wanted. They heard Candi call me beloved too.

That's the only part of the phone call that means anything to me.

I'm not leaving my soul in Perla's clutches long enough for any harm to come to her.

"*Se rat kay k ap manje kay.*" Derian intones.

Severu asks, "What does that mean?"

"It's the house rat that eats the house." Derian gives me a look of commiseration. "Your mother is one foul house rat."

"She's not from my house." Not anymore.

"She's a rat though," Miceli says with disgust.

While trying to convince me that I should kill Severu and make it look like a rival faction did it, Perla kept harping on the importance of family.

Too bad for her, I don't consider her or my grandfather family. Because I'm fucking loyal to family.

"It's time to deal with Don Messino," Severu grits out.

"The final step is already in place," I assure my boss.

And if my mother wasn't the catalyst for it, she would die tonight.

Thirty minutes out from our target, we pull on our masks. I dig in the weapons go bag I brought with me. We keep one in the hidden compartment of all the work SUVs. This one is from the SUV Derian drove into Manhattan earlier today.

I pull out two extra skull masks. Every weapons go bag for my team has them.

"Here, put these on." I hand the nitrile masks to Severu and Miceli. They're imprinted with skulls like ours, but are disposable. "The skull pattern prevents facial recognition from nodal points."

"That's why your team wear skull masks?" Miceli asks.

I nod.

"Huh. I thought it was because everyone calls you Death."

Derian pulls on his mask. "Scares the hell out of targets and that's always a plus."

"I'm keeping this one," Miceli informs me.

I shake my head. "It's disposable. I'll have one made for you like ours."

"Cool."

Severu shakes his head. "If I didn't know any better, I'd believe you two were the ones that shared genes."

"That's why Angelo is our brother. He fits."

Severu grunts, but he doesn't deny it.

This is the family I am loyal to. My family by choice, the De Lucas. My team who are also my brothers in arms. My soul, Candi, and the mom and sister she brought into my life. Not the fucking Messinos.

I never fit with them and I never will.

Perla tried to tell me that killing Severu wouldn't come back on me. That my grandfather would make me a don.

But the sickly old man isn't a kingmaker anymore. And even if he was, he wouldn't be making me one. He'd sacrifice me for his plans, not put me in the center of them.

The pilot kills the lights ten klicks out. When he reaches the clearing a klick away from the house, he drops altitude and hovers.

There's no way to mask the sound of a helicopter out here, so our only option is to do the drop far enough out it won't draw too much attention. Once it flies overhead on the way to the municipal airport, with the lights back on, our helicopter will be unremarkable.

Putting on low profile night vision goggles that slide right over the skull eye sockets on our masks, eight of us prepare to rappel down two ropes hanging off the side of the helicopter. One of my men will stay onboard to pull the ropes in before the pilot takes the bird back up to altitude and turns back on the lights.

I go first, landing with a soft thud, my knees bent for impact. Seven more thumps follow, Severu, Miceli and my team landing around me in quick succession.

As one, we jog toward the target property.

I slow to a stop and put my fist up to indicate we are 100 yards out. The rest of the team takes up a wedge formation behind me. Derian drops to one knee and holds up the heat signature scanner to read the location of bodies on the property.

I take the moment to check Candi's location app. Her dot is moving, but not fast enough to be in a car.

Are they moving her from the house to a more secure location? There's a small guardhouse on the property where the security team in charge of protecting the property stay full-time. Maybe it has a basement.

Perhaps the sound of the helicopter made them wary but why not move her to the saferoom inside the house? It's a given there's a panic room there somewhere. However, Candi's not in it if she's moving.

"Two in the guardhouse," Derian says quietly. "One moving through the forest." He sucks in a breath.

"What is it?"

"There's a mass exiting the back of the house."

I don't ask for numbers. It's impossible to distinguish between heat signatures when they're close together.

"They're fanning out and running this way. I count six heat signatures."

Derian's update makes my gut clench. Candi escaped and she's being chased.

"The single runner is not a scout," I inform everyone quietly over the com units. "It's Candi."

"Roger that," is repeated back to me five times.

Severu says, "Heard."

"Got it," Miceli acknowledges.

"We reach her before they do." I lift my fist, signal *go* and start sprinting toward the location Candi's locator dot says she is.

The men chasing her are yelling shit at her in Italian I'm glad she can't understand. Some are shouting her name.

Do they think she's going to stop because they're yelling for her?

I hear her before I see her. Branches crackle then a heavy thump and Candi's voice. "Damn it!"

She fell.

Changing my trajectory slightly, I run toward the sound of her voice. Then I see her. She's still running, but she's limping.

Fuck.

I say her name just before I reach her. "Candi. *Amate*, it's me."

"Hot stuff?" She looks up and around, but the moon hasn't risen and the dark is nearly impenetrable without night vision goggles.

No wonder she tripped and fell.

When I reach her, I touch her lightly with my hand.

Gasping, she grabs my arm in a hard grip. "Angelo. I knew you'd come for me."

"If you knew I'd come for you what the fuck are you doing out here in the forest? You could've broken something running in the dark." I need to find out what's making her limp.

Behind me, Miceli laughs.

"From what Derian told us about how she responded in the alley, are you really that surprised?" Severu asks.

My men need to stop gossiping with my boss.

"Get over yourself, babe. I wasn't about to let them use me as leverage against you."

"I prefer beloved," I inform her.

She huffs a slightly hysterical laugh. "It's a little old fashioned, isn't it?"

"What do you think *amate* means?"

"You've been calling me beloved? I thought it was sweetheart, or something."

"No."

"Now you really can't make me believe you wouldn't have given yourself up for me."

"They don't want me," I inform her. "They want me to kill Severu."

She clutches more tightly to me. "That's stupid. Don't they realize how loyal you are? Not to mention superhero resourceful. How did they not realize you were never going to choose Option A?"

"Yeah, his birth family lost the lottery in the intelligence department," Miceli drawls. "Not to mention that whole cray-cray thing."

"You're telling me?" Candi sounds about as impressed with my mother and grandfather as I am.

"They don't know me like you do." The sound of the soldiers getting closer reminds me we have a job to do. "I need you to go with Derian."

Saying the words is harder than I expect. I don't want to leave her. But I don't want her to watch me become Death either.

"No." Her tough exterior cracks, letting the trauma she's experienced bleed through. "I don't want to be away from you."

"*Amate*, you cannot participate in this fight."

"No, duh. But can't I just go and be off to the side somewhere?" she asks in that pleading tone I hate to hear from her lips.

The fact that in her fear and stress, she wants to be near me does things to the heart I never thought I had before her, but I shake my head. "Too risky."

Candi takes a deep breath and lets it out. Twice.

"Okay." Releasing me, she steps back. "I know this is the way this has to go down. I'll be fine."

I have never been in a situation where what I knew I should do is so at war with what I want to do. I want to stay with her and make her feel safe, but for her to genuinely be safe, she needs to go with Derian.

Fury at the situation my mother has caused rolls through me. I pull Candi to me, pull my mask up above my mouth and kiss her like she's my world. Because she is.

"Stay safe," she whispers and steps back. "Which one of your Death lookalikes is Derian?"

"Me." Derian puts his hand up. "I'm wounded you didn't recognize my manly stance."

"We'll talk about your dip into toxic masculinity when we're out of the way," she sasses and lets Derian lead her away.

I lift my fist. "Now, we hunt."

I'm running toward my first target as I make the sign to move.

The battle goes quickly. Too quickly to sate my fury and bloodlust. I kill two men in the forest and four of the mafia soldiers left to guard the house. Blood soaks my clothes and my knife drips with it.

"All targets down or accounted for," Derian's voice sounds over the com units.

He's back at the original recon point with Candi and monitoring with the heat signature scanner.

"Order a cleanup and disposal crew." None of these *stronzos* are making it back to Italy for burial.

Miceli handled the four civilians, leaving them drugged with Special-K and in their beds at the guardhouse. They'll wake up tomorrow with little or no memory of today.

All sixteen of the mafia soldiers are dead, including the one stationed outside my mother's bedroom. I left her inside, none the wiser.

"Wait ten minutes and then bring Candi to the house." By then we'll be done doing what needs to be done.

CHAPTER 38

ANGELO

Don Barone hasn't moved from where Candi saw him last. He's still sitting in the office, drinking a glass of wine and listening to fucking opera.

"That's pretty cliché," I judge, stepping into the room.

He jumps to his feet. "How did you get in here? You know you aren't getting out alive," he threatens. "I have twenty men guarding this place."

"Yeah. It felt like overkill, eight of us against only twenty of them." Miceli sidles up to stand beside me. "I only got to kill two."

"Stop complaining." Severu walks past both of us to face Don Barone. "You got to play drug-the-security-guards and get them to fall in their own beds."

"What can I say? I like a challenge."

"Who are you people? If it's money you want—"

I don't let the bastard finish his sentence, punching him so hard, his head snaps back and his body goes with it. Don Barone collapses to the ground, knocked out.

"Well, that was anticlimactic," Miceli bitches.

Severu prods Don Barone with his booted foot. "Wake up, *stronzo*. You don't want to miss the finale, considering you've got a starring role."

The Sicilian don groans.

"Have they found her?" Perla stops two feet into the room, her eyes going wide with fear.

She spins to run right back out, but Miceli is already blocking the doorway behind her.

"Who are you?" she demands with more arrogance than bravado.

I laugh, the sound hollow and without humor. "Don't you recognize your son?"

"Take that silly mask off, Angelo. Don't think this little display changes anything." She waves toward my mask and the other two men wearing skulls for faces. "Even if you find Candi before our men, she's at risk until you kill Severu De Luca."

I don't take off my mask, but Severu takes his off. "That is not going to happen."

Grabbing Don Barone by the scruff of his neck, he lifts him and shakes him until the other man groggily says, "Whaaa... "

"Stop that! You can't treat a don that way."

"Looks like I can," Severu says sardonically.

"I am the daughter of the Sicilian godfather. That is his son-in-law. You don't dare do anything to us."

Severu's eyes go glacially cool. "You thought you could come into my territory and conspire to have me assassinated, but believe I can't do anything to you *in my own fucking territory?*"

Perla's mouth opens and closes without a single word coming out.

Unamused by the tableau, I ask her, "Where is your phone?"

"In the bedroom." She crosses her arms over her chest and glares at me. "The least you can do is take that macabre thing off your head."

"The least I can do is *not* kill you. Get your fucking phone. Miceli will go with you."

"Don't try to run," Miceli warns. "You won't like the consequences."

"I know your mother and how she raised you," Perla scoffed.

"She taught me to respect women, but you're a rat and my father taught me to exterminate those."

Perla tilts her chin, like she's above the threat, but her nervous breathing shows she took him seriously.

They're back in a couple of minutes, Miceli looking disgruntled. "She walked right by a door to the outside and didn't even try to open it. I mean, Candi climbed out a second-story window to escape."

"My mother is not in the same league as *mia amate*."

Miceli peels off his mask and tucks it into his pocket, then shakes the sweaty hair away from his forehead. "I'm rethinking wanting one of my own."

I shrug. "You get used to it."

With a shake of his head for our byplay, Severu orders my mom to make a video call to my grandfather.

Glaring with impotent defiance, Perla swipes across the screen. I move next to her so I can watch to make sure she's doing what Severu tells her to. But she taps her number one contact and hits video call.

It rings four times before Don Messino answers.

"Is it done? I thought the plan wasn't to talk to Angelo until tomorrow."

I grab the phone from my mom before she he has a chance to answer and let my grandfather see me as I am. Death. His future.

"It's not done, but it will be soon." I tap the icon to flip the camera so he can see the other side of the room where Severu has Don Barone kneeling in front of him.

"Your don has been found guilty of conspiracy to assassinate the godfather," Severu intones.

My grandfather's mouth works but he holds back his invectives. He knows he's caught and he's trying to work out how to get out of this without losing face.

It's not going to happen.

Severu looks to me with a question. I nod my head.

He leans down, whispers something in Don Barone's ear and then snaps his neck, dropping his body to the floor like the piece of trash it is.

"What the hell do you think you're doing?" Don Messino screams. "You can't kill my men. This is war."

Severu walks around the dead don and glares straight into the phone's camera. "You declared war the minute you tried to arrange my assassination."

"Fuck you, Severu!"

"Eloquent," Severu mocks, but his tone is as deadly as anthrax when he says, "Barone acted against *me* and I am the fucking godfather of the Cosa Nostra in America. The five Families answer to *me*. Boston answers to *me*. Chicago answers to *me*. Nevada answers to *me*. New England answers to *me*. Detroit answers to *me*. None of those dons answer to you and they never will."

"They don't know what you're really like."

"Don't they? Those dons would all expect what I'm going to say next. I wonder if you do?"

"What are you talking about?"

"I have men in place ready to take you and all of your top lieutenants out," my brother from another much better mother says. "You have one chance to avoid that."

You've got to love the quality of a good video call. I can see the color leach from my grandfather's face.

"I don't believe you," he tries to bluff, but his voice lacks any conviction.

"Declare a truce right now. You tell your other dons that Barone made the grave mistake of trying to kill the American godfather and out of abject remorse, he killed himself. Unfortunately, you have nobody to bury because he jumped from a cliff into the ocean."

"Róise would say that has pathos," Miceli approves.

"Why the—"

"Don't. I have no fucking patience for your bluster. You have no honor and I afford you no respect. You tried to have another godfather killed in a vain attempt to hold onto power that you lost when Don Caruso decided to back me instead of your choice for the next godfather."

"You're an upstart! The De Lucas never even had a don in their family before your grandfather."

"But he *was* made don and I *am* godfather, old man."

"Only because you killed your own men that opposed you."

This is new. "What the fuck are you talking about?" I demand.

"Everyone knows Severu killed his loyal consigliere when the man tried to put a brake on his grasp for power," Perla says contemptuously.

"That's not even close to what happened," I tell my mother with a frown, but I'm not about to tell her what really went down.

That was Genovese Family business.

"Where did you hear that fairytale?" Miceli asks silkily.

Perla presses her lips together firmly in mute denial.

"Let me guess. Lora Revello. I knew letting her live was going to come back to bite us in the ass." Miceli shakes his head.

"And we're not going to off her now. She is my wife's aunt and Catalina cares about the old bitch."

"Sounds like her retirement solution needs to be addressed," I say.

Whatever they decide to do with Lora is probably what we should do with Perla once my grandfather is dead.

"Lora is part of our mafia now. You have no jurisdiction over her." Don Messino is as deluded and arrogant as his daughter.

Severu's patience snaps at that arrogant claim. "Like you have no jurisdiction *anywhere* in North America?"

"I was attempting to right a wrong. You had Henrico killed to get rid of your competition and killed your own godfather to take his place."

Severu doesn't dignify the ridiculous accusation with a reply, but asks, "If you had succeeded in having me killed, what do you think would have happened?"

"A better godfather would take your place."

"Maybe, but his name would be De Luca too."

"You're not roping me into that headache," Miceli mutters sotto voce.

"And my brothers would have destroyed you and obliterated the Sicilian Cosa Nostra to extinction," Severu finishes.

"You only have one brother unless there are more skeletons in the De Luca closet than we know about." There's a snide twist to my grandfather's lips lost on Severu because he can't see the screen.

"Wrong. Miceli is my brother by blood. Rafael Mancini is my brother by marriage. And Angelo Caruso is my brother by choice. Both his and mine."

"What do you want?"

"I already told you. Promise a truce on your vow as a godfather and I will send your daughter home alive."

"You can have your truce but we are not allies."

"Not as long as you are godfather of the Cosa Nostra in Sicily."

Don Messino doesn't look worried enough to have taken that as the warning it is.

Severu makes a cutting motion with his hand and I end the call.

We both turn to Perla, who is staring at her dead husband, not with grief, but with shock and more than a little dismay.

"You return to Sicily tomorrow," Severu tells her. "You do not return to the United States ever."

Her return to Sicily is key to the plan that's been in the making since we first learned about Messino's disapproval of Severu becoming the next godfather.

CHAPTER 39

CANDI

His hand on my arm to make sure I don't trip again, Derian and I jog back to the house I escaped from.

"This is not necessary." I tug on my arm a little.

He doesn't let go. "I already fucked up once today protecting you. Nothing else is happening to you on my watch."

"Unless you gave Nina the drugged wine, it wasn't your screw up," I pant.

My cardio capacity is high, but after the last few hours, even I'm getting a little breathless from running again. I'm not slowing down though.

Angelo is at the end of this little jaunt, so that is where I want to be.

"I should have known about the secret egress point in the office." Derian sounds like he's walking in the park, not running through a dark forest.

"Pretty sure no one knew about it if you didn't."

Breaking out of the trees, we're confronted with a yard full of activity. Light blazes from every window in the house and men wearing skull masks carry bodies between them.

"Is everyone on our side okay?" I ask, feeling guilty I hadn't sooner.

Derian slows to a walk. "No injuries were reported." Then he asks, "All safe boss?"

And I know he's not talking to me. First, I'm not his boss. Second, he's wearing some kind of hands-free communicator because he's been having a conversation with Angelo and the others since we separated from them earlier.

"I thought he already said it was safe to come." That's the impression I got from the one side of the conversation I could hear, anyway.

Derian shrugs. "Just double checking."

I frown. If Derian is this overprotective, what is Angelo going to be like now that I've been kidnapped from under their noses?

He must've got an affirmative because he leads me through the house. An overturned chair near a pool of blood catches my eye. Wincing, I take in the other signs of violence. One of the windows in the great room has a bullet hole with spiderweb cracks all around it. There's another pool of blood near the fireplace.

The table the men were playing cards at earlier is littered with debris from some kind of altercation.

We reach the doorway to the room I saw the older man in earlier and my focus zeroes in on what I can see through it.

The first thing I see is the man passed out on the carpet. With his head at that weird angle, he might be dead. Probability is high.

There are two unmasked men in the room, Severu and Miceli De Luca. OMG. The freakin' godfather and Genovese don are here? Their sweat matted hair indicates they were two of the men wearing skull masks in the forest.

Wow. Just wow. Angelo had them on his Death crew?

Even two men so high up in the mafia can't hold my attention though. It's too caught by the man wearing a familiar skull mask.

Angelo.

The second I see him, the stress thrumming through my body goes down about a hundred levels and I take my first full breath since parting from him in the forest.

Huh, maybe it wasn't the cardio after all.

"I'll go help with cleanup," Derian tells his boss.

Angelo jerks his head in a single affirmative.

Derian leaves but I can't stop looking at Angelo long enough to tell him goodbye, or even thank you. Later. I'll do that later. Right now, I just want to soak in being near my beloved.

Harsh laughter from my left grates on my eardrums and I turn my head to see Queen Bitch.

Her expression is filled with condescending pity. "Look at the two of you. It's ridiculous."

"I don't know what you think is ridiculous, much less why you're laughing. Maybe it escaped your notice, but your husband is lying dead on the floor."

If that were Angelo, I sure as heck would not be laughing.

"You are here because of my callous son and that is laughable. That we thought we could use you as leverage and that you so clearly think he has feelings for you. *He has no feelings*," she sneers. "Tonight proves he has no honor or loyalty either."

Anger at her absolute lack of knowledge of her own son bursts out of me. "The only thing tonight proves is that it's a miracle he's turned out to be such a decent person considering the gene pool he swam out of."

"You think telling me my son is not like me is an insult? It's not. That you consider him a decent person is even more laughable than my deluded belief he cared enough about your safety to be swayed by your loss."

"Uh, is it just me, or haven't you noticed that I'm safe and your men are dead?" Deluded is right.

Perla crosses her legs, leans back on the couch and waives her hand dismissively. "That's mafia politics. He could have gotten you killed as easily as saved you with his so-called rescue attempt."

"Yeah, I don't think so." Angelo knows what he's doing and he would never have put me at risk.

Angelo's black glove covered hands fist at his sides. "Our egress would have happened differently if you hadn't escaped."

He doesn't look at his mother, just at me.

I smile. "Don't think for a second I'm listening to the Wicked Witch of the West over there. Her passport lists Delulu Land as her country of origin because she doesn't live anywhere near reality."

"Good one," Miceli-freakin'-De Luca says admiringly.

"You're a stupid little girl who will learn she trusted the wrong man too late," Perla gibes.

Yeah. No. I will never regret trusting Angelo. "That sounds more like you regretting your choices than an omen for my future."

Despite her attempt to look casual and unconcerned, Perla's hands have a fine tremor and her eyes reflect her own bitter disappointment. Whatever happened in here shook the arrogance I noticed earlier to the very core.

"The only thing I regret," I add, "is that I can't hate you because you gave birth to the most amazing man I know." I turn my smile to Angelo. "The man I love."

Is this a weird moment to tell him I love him? Maybe, but if this whole kidnapping debacle taught me anything, it's that there's no way of knowing what tomorrow will bring.

That wine could have been poisoned, not drugged. There are no guarantees in life, so I'm not waiting around for my feelings to make sense based on society's timeline. And if I want to say I love him in a room full of people that he deserves to have know that? Well, that's okay too.

Angelo makes a strangled sound.

Miceli says, "Aww. Róise owes me a BJ because I told her you two would be an item by Halloween. She thought Christmas."

They've been talking about me and Angelo becoming a couple? That's a little creepy considering I didn't know we were in a relationship, but also cool. Mostly cool. Knowing his family is aware of me makes this thing between me and Angelo feel more solid.

Like my *I love you* means something real to him like it does to me.

"Róise doesn't realize how fast the men in our family fall for their women," Severu says. "Because you were a little slow on the uptake. You let months pass between your first meeting and signing the marriage contract."

"At least I didn't get engaged to her sister," Miceli shoots back. "Don't tell me Catalina had a single clue you loved her in the beginning."

"Hell, I didn't have a clue." Severu's eyes warm, like he's remembering something.

This moment hits an epic level of surreal as I witness the Godfather of the Cosa Nostra and his little brother, the Don of the Genovese, ribbing each other.

"Angelo knew he loved me from the first night he saw me," I say with wonder.

Maybe for men like this, who live life so intensely, that love at first sight thing isn't such a stretch.

"Looks like you got the smart one in the family," Miceli quips.

"Love? He doesn't know the meaning of the word," Perla snipes.

Grr. This woman is getting on my last nerve.

I smile at her, oh so sweetly. "Again, it sounds like you're doing some self-reflection there. The only person I see in this room with a defective ability to love is you."

"How dare yo—"

"Whatever your plans were for Angelo," I say, cutting her off. I am so done interacting with her, but I have one last thing to say to her. "Understand this: if you ever try to hurt him again, I will hunt you down and I will stab you through your cold heart. Then I'll twist the blade until it's as damaged as your sense of morality."

Miceli whistles. "Damn, Candi's got some backbone."

Ignoring the compliment, even though it makes me preen a little on the inside, I turn and face Angelo. "So, everything's okay now?"

"Yes."

"Did you get hurt?" Wanting to run to him and hold on tight, I can't help taking a single step closer.

I force myself to stop though. There's something off about Angelo. Why isn't *he* crossing the distance between us?

Scoffing sounds come from the mafia elite peanut gallery.

But Angelo just shakes his head.

What is it with him staying over there giving off that don't-touch-me vibe? Doesn't he realize how I crave his arms around me? Mom always says, *start as you mean to go on* and I mean to have a good relationship with Angelo.

His book is right about one thing for sure. Open communication is key to a good relationship.

"I need you to hold me right now." I lay it out there for him. No dressing it up, or trying to hedge to protect my pride.

He takes a step forward and then back again. His fists bang against the side of his hips. "I'm covered in blood. I'm Death right now."

"Remember, you told me you're always Death? And I told you I know that. Do you think seeing the evidence with my own eyes makes it different for me? It doesn't, beloved. Not even a little." And if that puts my moral compass in grayscale, I can live with it.

"She's right." He indicates Perla with his chin.

"Pretty sure she's not." I have a hard time believing Perla is right about anything, but especially anything to do with her son.

"I *am* a monster."

Severu grunts. "Aren't we all?"

"I'm not disgusted by you or scared of you. You're my beloved, monster tendencies and all." I smile a little. "Besides, isn't this the time of year for monsters to find love?"

Tomorrow night is Halloween and I'm going to make sure it's the best one my monster has ever experienced.

Angelo peels his gloves off and shoves them in one of the pockets of his cargo pants. Then he reaches for me. I don't wait for any more of an invitation and rush forward, throwing myself against him. Wrapping my arms around him, I press my cheek to his chest over his heart.

Hearing the steady, thump-thump-thump, I soak in the safety I find there.

The tangy scent of copper tells me his black clothes are probably soaked in blood and it's no doubt getting on my clothes right now too. I don't care.

Angelo holds me tight, rocking me side to side and whispers a bunch of Italian, I don't understand, but I know what the words *mean*. They mean he loves me.

He cares about me. He can't live without me.

He's going to stalk me forever.

Okay, I'm not sure about the last one, but the rest rolls off him in heady waves that wrap around my heart.

"That's our cue to leave you two lovebirds alone," one of the two De Luca brothers says. "We'll put men on this rat to make sure she goes straight to the airport without passing go and right back to Sicily, never to darken our shores again."

That's definitely Miceli, but I don't look to see if I'm right. I'm too busy soaking up the comfort of Angelo's arms around me.

There's a scuffle and Perla yells, "Take your hands off me!"

"The passenger helicopter will land in the street in front of the house in thirty minutes to take you and Candi back to Long Island." That bossy tone must be Severu.

And then there's silence and I sigh happily. We're alone. Finally.

Except for the dead body.

"So, that's your stepfather?" I mumble against Angelo's chest.

"My mother's husband. Yes."

"Did you kill him?" I'm trying to figure out what has Angelo so reticent about touching me right now.

Yes, he's holding me, but there's an unfamiliar tension in his body, like he's holding part of himself back from me.

"No. That was Severu's right as both the godfather and the person Barone was conspiring to murder."

"Sounds like he deserved what he got."

"He deserved death for taking you," Angelo grinds out. "I killed the men who kidnapped you. "

"Were there a lot of them?" I ask.

"Sixteen men earned their death participating in your kidnapping and the conspiracy to murder our godfather." Angelo takes a deep breath and lets it out in a gust. "I killed six of them, including the man who guarded your room and the man who made my mother feel safe by guarding hers."

"You don't want her feeling safe?"

"She doesn't deserve to after making you afraid. I'll make sure she doesn't ever feel completely safe again for the rest of her miserable life."

"And will that be a very long life?" Maybe he's upset because she has to die.

Angelo shrugs.

"But you're not planning to kill her?" I press. "Miceli said she's going back to Sicily soon."

"Tomorrow. She has a job to do."

"Yeah? What's that?"

"Administer her father's final dose of poison."

"She agreed to do that?" I ask, shocked. "Isn't that signing her own death warrant?"

"She's unaware of what she's about to do."

I lean back so I can see Angelo's gorgeous face, only to remember he's still wearing the mask.

He goes to take it off, but I stay his hand. "Will you wear it for me again? It's really kind of sexy. I thought it was a huge turn on at the club. You would've gotten lucky that night if you hadn't been so sure I was drugged."

"I thought you didn't know it was me. I couldn't believe you would take another man to the backroom, and you being drugged was the only explanation I could think of."

"Well, you were right about that, at least. I would never have taken another man back there. I would never have entered the VIP area for another man either. But Angelo, I always know it's you." I lift my hand to help him remove the mask. "Even when you're wearing this."

Together, we pull it off of him.

Hair plastered with sweat to his forehead and temples and his mouth is set in a firm line, he's as much Death as he is with the mask on.

But his eyes are filled with emotion. For me.

I touch his cheek. "Explain about your mom poisoning your grandfather."

"My uncle, Don Caruso, sent a New York cheesecake from his favorite bakery to my grandfather once a month."

"Okay..." Not sure where he's going with this, but I don't interrupt.

"My mother purchased the dessert to take back to her father in celebration after Severu was dead. Now she'll give it to him as an apology for her failure."

"You sound pretty sure of yourself."

"My mother might not know anything about the real me, but I know everything there is to know about her and my grandfather."

"Knowledge is power," I quip.

"Exactly."

Then it clicks. "Somehow, you poisoned the cheesecake. But what if someone else eats some?"

I'm not going to mourn the men who died today, but the thought of someone innocent sharing in the evil godfather's fate upsets me.

"Don't worry, *mia amate*." It's Angelo's turn to brush his hand down my cheek. "My grandfather is an abjectly selfish man. No one is allowed to have even the tiniest slice."

"Sounds excessive and also hard to predict. How would he know?"

"Trust me, he would. Don Messino had a cook killed ten years ago who was discovered eating a tiny slice shaved off the cake. She wanted to duplicate the recipe."

"And he had her killed for it?" Appalled isn't a big enough word for how I feel.

Angelo nods. "In front of his men and other staff as a lesson."

"So, for real, no one is going to eat that cake but him." I'm glad.

"Exactly."

"What's in it?"

"Thallium. It's a tried-and-true method for poisoning someone without detection."

"Can't they find it in an autopsy?"

"There won't be one. Without unquestionable cause, there is no justification for disturbing the corpse of a dead godfather with something like that."

"You really think no one will suspect?" I worry.

"My grandfather has been suffering from gastric and intestinal trouble for years. His doctors tried to tell him he's allergic to tomatoes, but he refuses to believe them and continues to eat sauces made with them daily."

"Is that why you chose thallium to begin with?"

"That and the fact it is colorless, odorless and tasteless when mixed with food. When he starts showing gastrointestinal distress about eight hours after eating the first slice of cheesecake, it will be chalked up to the same complaint."

"Really? It's that easy?"

"We've been administering low doses of thallium in his food for the past three months which have been steadily increasing his gastric problem, but without raising suspicion with his doctors."

"You said your mom would be administering the fatal dose. How does that work?" I ask.

"Don Messino will be dead within seven days of eating the second slice of cake. Eating more will only make his reaction more acute."

"You're so sure he'll eat two pieces?" Though from the sound of him, Don Messino doesn't give up what he likes to eat for the sake of a stomachache.

"Yes."

"What happens when he dies?"

"My uncle takes over as godfather."

"Won't he cause trouble for Severu too?" I worry.

I don't want anyone coming for Angelo again.

"No. He wants to take the mafia in Sicily and Southern Italy into the twenty-first century. He wouldn't do anything to hasten his father's death, but he'll be relieved by it. He's already let Severu know that when he becomes godfather, he'll honor the old alliances."

The sound of a helicopter landing outside cuts off what I was going to say next.

"Time to go home."

"Good, I'm ready to see the back of this place."

"It won't be here to see tomorrow. The cleanup team will burn it to the ground."

"That's one way to destroy evidence."

Angelo keeps his arm around my shoulder as we head to the front door. "It's also a good way to get a message across. The owners of this property allowed Barone its use. If they were unwitting accomplices, losing the house will be their punishment."

"And if they're not?"

"Then Death will pay them a visit."

CHAPTER 40

ANGELO

Once we're on the helicopter, the pilot offers me and Candi a headset so we can talk and hear each other.

Usually, I wouldn't wear someone else's equipment. There's no way to know what the cleaning protocols are, but I want to be able to hear anything *mia amate* wants to say.

I take the headsets and clean one with a disinfectant wipe before handing it to Candi and doing the same for my own.

"Is it really that loud?" she asks, her voice coming through clearly on the earphones.

"It can be." We could probably hold a conversation because the cabin is insulated for sound, but we'd still have to raise our voices to be heard.

The noise inside the cabin increases as we lift off.

Candi grimaces. "Oh, that *is* loud."

"Like being at the club." Where you have to be within a couple of feet to hear another person speak.

"What was that loud music I heard on the phone when Queen Bitch called you?"

"I had Miceli send his music to the cabin sound system before I answered so the sounds of helicopter flight wouldn't be obvious."

"It worked. I thought you were at the club for a second and then I realized you were probably already on your way to me."

"I was." Her faith in me reminds me that she does not only see me as the monster, Death. "But you still decided to run."

"I told you why."

I don't mention how illogical her conclusion was because it was born of concern for me. "I don't want you taking risks like that."

"I don't like that you take risks either. I guess we'll both have to be careful."

"You didn't even have a weapon." I try not to allow the frustration I feel at that fact bleed into my voice.

"I had a stick, but I dropped it so I could run faster when I realized they had followed me into the forest." She plucks at the dark sweater she's wearing. "At least I had this. They didn't bring my coat when they kidnapped me."

"Inconsiderate."

"At least Derian and Mario kept me in my hoodie," she jokes.

But I'm not ready to laugh. "Tell me how you got away."

I can't stop looking at the smears of blood on her borrowed sweater. Blood from my kills tainting her.

"All I had to do was fake a little nausea to get them to leave one of the windows in my room open for me." She describes her escape like a big adventure.

Of course Candi would try to run. She doesn't take anything lying down. When she talks about untying the makeshift rope and carrying it along a beam two stories off the ground, so she can climb down unnoticed, I about lose my shit.

I pull my knife out and start flipping it over my knuckles. Flip. Flip. Flip.

"Uh, are you okay, Angelo?" She looks at me with concern.

Forgetting my desire to keep Candi from getting any more blood on her, I slide the knife back into its sheath and pull her close. "I'm proud of you."

"This feels more like worry than pride." Her voice is muffled by my chest.

I kiss the top of her head because I can. "I'll have to brush your hair out again tonight."

"I like when you do that," she says softly.

"I do too."

She snuggles into me, molding her body as close as she can get with the safety belt on.

"I want you to know I never doubted my ultimate safety, Angelo. I didn't just know you would come for me. I knew you would succeed."

"There will never be a time I don't come for you. Even after death I will come back to protect you."

"That's not morbid at all." She tries to sound snarky, but even I can distinguish the underlying emotion in her voice.

"What's morbid about spending eternity together?"

She huffs out a sigh. "When you put it that way, nothing. But I thought you weren't religious."

"How can I not believe in the afterlife when I know I will spend it with you?"

"The things you say." She moves restlessly against me. "It's not that cold in here, right? I mean I don't need the sweater anymore."

"You want to get the blood off." I'm not surprised.

Candi is not meant to be marked by Death.

"It stinks." She sits up, her nose wrinkled in distaste. "Haven't you noticed? It's like fake lavender or something. I mean lavender isn't my favorite fragrance to begin with, but add a chemical component in and it's nauseating."

She pulls the sweater off and tosses it onto the floor before taking a big breath. "That's better but I can still smell it."

I grab the sweater, open the door and toss it into the rushing wind before shutting it again.

"You can't do that! It's littering."

"Birds will find it and pick it apart to make nests." I don't know if that's true, but I wasn't keeping the offending garment in the cabin when it bothered her.

"Only if they can get past that awful smell." She sighs. "Why did you think it was the blood?"

I shrug.

She shakes her head at me, the smooth ponytail she left the house in earlier today long gone. "Don't hide yourself from me. I love all of you, Angelo."

"How can you love me as I am?"

"It's easy, just like it was for your nonno and nonna. Severu and Miceli will probably never say the words, but it's clear they love you like family. Your men who trust you and follow you wherever you go, they love you."

"You see my world through rose colored glasses." As much as I enjoy her interpretation, it's not fair to let her keep believing that. "My men are loyal because I pay them well and they know they can trust my leadership to keep them alive."

"Yeah, you keep telling yourself that. Derian told me how many men in your Special Forces unit joined the mafia so they could work for you. Not because they were looking for a big payday."

"Derian has a tendency to romanticize."

She cocks her head to one side like she's considering my words and then shakes it. "Nah. I don't see it. He said the mafia often uses the military to train their men, and sometimes recruits people who serve with them."

"True."

"But no other made man has ever brought as many men he served with into the Cosa Nostra as you."

"I knew I could trust them." They'd proven they had my back and knew I had theirs.

"Angelo, you might lack empathy. You don't always get social or emotional cues and I'll have to remember that. But your loyalty is absolute. You will kill and die for those you care for. You may not call that love, but I do."

"Now who's being morbid?" I ask because other words fail me.

She sees me like that?

"I love you, Angelo, with my whole heart. And I *know* you love me. Your mother is so wrong about that. You are capable of love and if she'd been a decent parent who treated you with care, she would have known what that feels like too."

"Probably not. I don't even like Perla."

"Neither do I, but the issue isn't with you. It's a her problem."

"What if what I call love isn't enough for you? I'll never be *normal*, Candi." My obsession with her didn't suddenly give me a new set of emotions toward the world.

Only her. And her mom and sister.

"And you're not as different as you think. You love my mom and you love my sister, and I believe you love the De Lucas and the men on your crew. It just doesn't look like love to everyone else. But it *is* enough for me because your brand of love is exactly what I need," she says fiercely.

I'll never get used to the look in Candi's beautiful eyes that says I'm the hero in the story.

Death is never the hero. People look at me with caution. But not *mia amate* or her sister. Mira is still cautious, but *that* I understand.

"I didn't realize how much I would like having a little sister," I say. "She looks at me like a hero just like you do."

I will never damage that. Every child deserves to believe that the important adults in their life are their ultimate protectors, that they care about them.

"She'll never know the neglect and insecurity we did," Candi says with deep conviction.

"No, she won't."

"That's one of the things I love about you, Death. My beloved. *You* are everything I want."

Fuck.

She *does* understand that me and Death are one in the same and she loves me anyway. "And you are everything I need, *mia amate*."

I lean down and she meets me halfway.

The kiss we share is not incendiary. There are no biting lips or thrusting tongues. It's a benediction of the love we share. It goes from her lips straight to my beating heart.

She is this dark angel's salvation.

Candi withdraws her mouth just far enough to whisper against my lips. "I'm your soul. And you're my safety."

"I am your future, and you are mine," I agree reverently.

"My sexy stalker. Don't ever stop watching me. I think it would break my heart."

"That is one thing I will never do."

We kiss for long moments before she ends up cuddling against my chest again.

Thinking about what Salvatore said at the lunch table, I admit, "I have cameras all over the house and I watch you when you're not with me."

"Even in my mom and sister's rooms?" she asks worriedly.

"No. Not in the staff quarters either. But in all of the public rooms, and the conservatory, especially because..." Is this something she's ready to hear?

She pats my chest. "Don't be a scaredy cat. Tell me."

"No one has ever called me that before."

Shrugging, she nuzzles my neck, sending sensation straight to my cock. "I recorded us in there." Will this be the obsession one step too far?

"With anyone else that would scare me." Her hand drops into my lap, lightly massaging my dick. "I would worry about revenge porn or something, but not with you. You will always protect me, even from yourself."

"I will."

"I want to watch it." She gives my cock a firm squeeze. "I spent most of that time in the hot tub facing away from you. I want to see what you looked like."

Not what we looked like together, but what I looked like, because my Candi is almost as obsessed with me as I am with her.

She unzips my fly and slides her hand inside, molding my steadily growing erection with her fingers. Humming, she rubs her hand up and down. "I want to taste you."

"Not here!"

Her laugh is sultry. "Don't make so much noise. You don't want the pilot turning around to find out what's wrong."

"Won't happen." And I make sure of it by ordering them in Italian to keep their eyes forward unless they want me to gouge them from their heads.

Their com units are already on a different channel because I didn't want them listening to my conversation with Candi.

Candi slips her hand under my boxers, her hot skin against my cock so fucking arousing, I groan.

She speeds up her movements telling me how sexy I am, how much she loves touching me, but when she says those three little words, "I love you," I come so hard my vision goes white for a second.

Rubbing my cum up and down my shaft, she kisses the underside of my jaw. "I like doing that."

Then before I can get my brain to mouth signals working enough to tell her I fucking adore it, she pulls her hand away and lifts it to her lips. Our gazes locked, she licks at the spend coating her hand.

"It tastes better than I expected."

"Does it?"

"Lots of the dancers say it's awful, but I like it. Maybe that's just because it's yours."

Watching her clean her hand with her pretty pink tongue, I'm rendered speechless.

CHAPTER 41

CANDI

Cookie is thrilled with the experience in the saferoom. She talks a mile a minute about the stuff she and mom did with Mario and Boomer. "We played Monopoly and mom won, like she always does, but I think sometimes Boomer sold her properties he shouldn't have. He lost pretty fast. And Mars was the best dog ever. Did you know he has his own potty room in the saferoom? Boomer trained him to use it."

"I'm glad you weren't scared."

"I knew Angelo would keep everybody safe."

Smiling, I nod. "I did too."

"Alright, you've been up for two hours past bedtime already. I think we're going to have to call in an absence for you tomorrow," mom says.

Angelo, who has been talking quietly with Boomer and Maria, looks up. "Would you mind keeping her out until the weekend? We need to come up with a security plan going forward. Keeping her safe in a public place, like school is harder."

Not impossible. Because nothing is when it comes to our wellbeing for my mafia assassin.

Mom shocks me by nodding readily. "Boomer explained that Cookie's schooling might have to change. Doing it midyear isn't ideal, but keeping my daughter safe is the most important thing. Both of my daughters."

The look she gives Angelo is both a warning and approval. It's strange, but I'll take it over open hostility, which is what I expected.

"Will you tuck me in tonight?" Cookie asks me.

That's her code for mom is too tired but won't admit it.

I nod quickly and smile. "You bet. Come on, you need to brush your teeth. I'm not even going to ask what kind of snacks Mario let you have while mom wasn't looking."

Cookie grins unrepentantly, but Mario dips his head in embarrassment. "She's hard to say no to, Ms. Candi."

"I'll keep that in mind, but if she starts bouncing off the walls from a sugar rush, you're the one staying up to play Mario Kart with her."

"Yes!" Cookie fist pumps the air.

Mario's eyes widen with near comic concern. Hiding my grin, I take my sister to her room to tuck her in.

"You're really okay, right, Candi? You'd tell me if they hurt you?" she asks.

"They didn't hurt me. I promise."

"I didn't think Angelo would let them." She yawns wide and I shoo her off to brush her teeth and wash her face.

Tomorrow is Halloween and if she can't go to school, there's no way Angelo is going to be okay with her trick-or-treating.

I wonder how he's going to feel about having a couple dozen eleven-year-olds running around his...our home for an impromptu Halloween party?

Between me, mom and Bianca, I have no doubt we can pull this off.

Oh, crap. I didn't call Bianca. Mostly because I still don't have my phone, but also because I forgot.

"Hey, Cookie, can I use your phone to call Auntie Bianca?"

"Sure," she yells around a mouth of toothpaste from the bathroom.

Shaking my head, I grab her new and improved phone just like mine. Using the parental override password, I open it and dial Bianca's number.

"Cookie? Is everything okay?" Bianca's worried tone makes me feel six layers of guilt.

"It's me, Bianca. I'm sorry I didn't call right away."

"Candi! I'm so glad to hear your voice. Salvatore told me you were okay, but sometimes he tries to protect me and I wasn't sure if I was getting the full story. His mom is my usual ally, but she didn't have any deets either."

"Well, after I woke up with a nasty headache, I escaped out a window." I gloss over some stuff as I tell my best friend and eager eavesdropper sister, but share enough so they both know I really am okay.

"What about you? Whatever was in the wine left me really woozy and that headache..."

"It was bad, but you know Salvatore. I had two different doctors running blood panels to try to figure it out."

"Bet they were both women," I tease.

Salvatore is like pathological about another man touching her. After her past, she doesn't like men touching her except him, so it works.

Kind of like with me and Angelo.

She about peed herself laughing when I told her Angelo said he wouldn't try to stop me dancing. Turns out he's got a possessive bone as deeply embedded as any of the De Luca men.

After the phone call with Bianca and tucking my sister in, I cross the hall and knock on mom's door.

"Come in," she calls.

I open the door to find her sitting in her lift recliner watching one of her shows.

"Since when do you knock on the door?" she asks with raised eyebrows.

"Well, this is your room."

"Which you are always welcome to come into. If the door to the bedroom is shut, you may want to knock just in case..." She winks at me.

What? "I know Boomer spent the time in the saferoom with you and Cookie. Are you saying a flirtation developed?"

I mean, I'm not against it, but really? This fast?

"Let's just say that you might have been right about me not being too old for a little romance in my life."

"Is that why you're taking all this so calmly? I thought you were going to demand I stop seeing Angelo and for us all to move back into the apartment." And I am so, so grateful that's not what is happening.

Is it? Maybe she's lulling me into a false sense of security to swoop in and get all logical on me. Moms are known to do that. At least mine is.

"Sweetheart, the identity of your sperm donor always meant that there was a risk you would get pulled into mafia politics. I admit I thought that if something like this happened, it would be because of Mr. Bianchi. At least with Angelo, I know you will be protected. He moved heaven and earth—"

"And rappelled out of a helicopter." After I gave him a hand job that we both thoroughly enjoyed, I made him tell me the details of his side of the night.

Mom smiles and finishes, "To get to you."

"There was never a moment when I didn't believe he would come for me."

"Maybe it's because I see him through your eyes, but I believe you will always be his priority. I never doubted he would bring you home safe."

I look around mom's living room that Angelo had designed specifically for her needs. "This is our home now, isn't it?"

"Yes," mom says firmly.

"Do you resent being pulled into the mafia world because of me?" I have to ask.

Mom shakes her head. "You are my daughter. Whatever world that means touches mine, that fact never changes."

I bite my lip, blinking back tears. "You're such a good mom, you know that?"

"I'm aware," she teases. "Now tell me everything."

It's different telling my mom. I don't leave out the parts where I was afraid, or in pain. Because it's my mom.

"You should not have risked falling and cracking your head open when you knew Angelo would come for you." She tsks at me.

I shrug. "Maybe, but I didn't realize they were trying to use me to force Angelo to do something. I thought they were trying to get their hands on him. And if I was around they could use me as the bait."

"Don't you think they could have figured out a much simpler way to get him if that were the case?" she asks me gently with that mom logic I was expecting earlier.

"Maybe I wasn't thinking all that clearly. I'd like to blame the drugs they gave me, but the truth is, logic went out the window when I got worried about Angelo's safety." Which is silly. Right?

Death can take care of himself.

But that doesn't mean it isn't still my job to take care of him.

"I guess that means you really do love him."

"Is that what it means?"

"A woman as smart as you doesn't get stupid for anything less than true love."

CHAPTER 42

ANGELO

There are twenty-two children in Halloween costumes from the macabre to the ridiculous running around our home.

From the amount of gore on some of these costumes, I think we have some mafia soldiers in the making.

Cookie is dressed as Super Mario. She had Mars with her earlier, when it was just her and her three best friends. My dog was dressed as the green dinosaur sidekick and he took it like a champ, but when the guests started arriving, Boomer took him to the barracks.

Boomer, Derian and Mario conscripted six more mafia soldiers and turned the basement level into a haunted house, the dining room into a mummy room with games and the movie room into a haunted theater screening age appropriate Halloween movies.

I got caught up watching *The Addams Family* and Candi teased me about having a crush on Morticia.

I informed her the only woman I have a crush on is *la mia piccolo gatta*.

But now there are four girls hopped up on sugar having a sleepover in Cookie's bedroom and Candi told me to meet her in the basement.

Wearing the same costume I was when she gave me a lap dance, mask included.

The Angel of Death. Only the mask isn't a costume. It's part of me.

When I get to the bottom of the stairs, Candi is there. However, instead of the Princess Peach costume she was wearing for Cookie's party, she's got her angel costume on without the tiny toga she'd stripped out of onstage.

This time there are no pasties under the sheer bra and her dark pink nipples poke against the gossamer fabric. My mouth goes dry.

Dark hair, brushed to silky perfection and shining with some kind of glitter cascades down her back, bisecting the small iridescent wings. Her G-string covers her pussy, but that doesn't stop me fantasizing about the puffy lips that stretch so perfectly around my cock.

She's holding something in her left hand, but I can't focus on it with her luscious curves on display for me.

"The k..." I have to clear my throat to continue. "The kids."

"Are fine. Mom and Boomer are supervising the sleepover. This is our time."

"Our time?" My voice breaks like a pubescent boy and I grimace.

She grins. "Yes. I want to play a game with my sexy Angel of Death."

"What kind of game?"

"Hide and seek."

The predator in me rises to the surface. "You're hiding." It's not a question.

I will always be the hunter.

"I am."

My muscles tense with anticipation. "What happens when I find you?"

"Whatever I want."

"Shouldn't it be whatever *I* want if I catch you?"

She blows me a sultry kiss. "My game. My rules."

Fuck.

The lights go out and I hear her giggle in the near pitch black.

Then the clip of heels as she runs away. "Come and find me, Death. I'll be waiting!"

How is she moving so fast in the dark? Then the shape of what she had in her hand clicks. Night vision goggles.

Anticipation thrumming through my veins, I follow the scuffs of her footsteps in the dark. There, she turned into the large storage room.

When I reach it, she's not there but her shoes are.

She's barefoot making it easier for her to move quietly.

Good job, *piccola gatta*, I silently praise her as I stop moving entirely to listen. I moderate my heartrate and breathing and wait.

There. It's a soft brush of something further down the hall, near the saferoom. Maybe in it. The door to the room was closed during the party. Is it now?

I move swiftly and silently down the hall, my predator's instincts aroused like the rest of me.

The saferoom door is cracked in invitation. One I'm only too eager to take.

Pushing it open, the only thing I can see in the dark room is the gray couch sectional glowing purple.

Fabric rustles, landing against the floor with a whisper of sound.

Mia amate floats in midair. Her head thrown back, her back arched, one leg is bent and the other sticking straight out from her body. Just like at the club, the UV light reveals her entire body, but the white angel costume glows, highlighting her tits and pussy. The glitter in her hair glows too, making it look like a shimmering curtain falling toward the floor.

Fuck.

Candi had my men busy with more than decorating for Cookie's party today.

This setup took planning. She must be on a newly installed matte black dance pole for it to disappear as if it's not there in the ultraviolet light. Everything in the room has to be draped in black too.

And she did it all for *me*.

I pound my fist against my chest, trying to dislodge the weird feeling there only to realize a second later, it's that emotion only she evokes. Happiness.

She points toward the couch. "Sit down, my beloved Death. I want to give you a show."

Turned on to the point of discomfort, I have to adjust the log in my pants so I can do as she says. Gripping my cock through the leather, I squeeze and let my groan of pleasure free.

"Save some of that for later," she purrs like the sweet little cat she is. "We're just getting started."

The familiar beat of *Closer* begins to play over the saferoom's speaker system and Candi starts the routine I first saw five nights ago. Twirling around the pole, her gorgeous breasts jiggle more than usual and I realize her bralette isn't as tight over the fleshy mounds.

Fuck. Me.

This is her putting on a show, like she said. For me.

More sensual and more arousing than anything she ever did at the club, there's a sexual energy around *mia amate* that is only there when we are alone together.

She does a scissor split on the pole and tosses her head back. "You were the one I was dancing for on Saturday."

"Thank you." She just saved a lot of men's lives saying that and I didn't even realize I was planning their demise. "You're the only one I watch on those stages."

"I know. I could feel it. Your eyes on me. When you were at the club, I only ever danced for you."

We both digest that truth. She is mine and I am hers. The pulse in my cock thrums with the beat of the music.

"It made me wet. Every time. It's making me wet now." She hangs from the poll by her hands, her body on display for me and spreads her thighs into a wide split, revealing a dark patch in the white silk of her thong right over her slit.

Gritting my teeth against the need to touch, my fingers curl into fists.

"Stay where you are, beloved," she orders me. "Remember, it's whatever I say goes right now. It's the least I deserve for making it so easy for you to find me."

"It's the least you deserve for setting this up at all, *mia amate.*" I will never grow tired of hearing her call me beloved.

That she calls me, beloved Death blows my mind.

Her body undulates up the pole that I cannot see. My ephemeral angel, who can float with the heavenly bodies.

When she's near the top, she flips her body back, hanging by her legs only and does a dizzying spin downward, stopping just as her hair brushes the floor.

Gasping, I'm half off the couch and have to force myself to sit back down.

Moving with sinuous grace, she dismounts from the pole and dances toward me. "I want to play another game."

"Whatever you want." The words come out strangled, but she understands them.

"Have you ever played Simon Says?"

"No. I didn't play a lot of games as a child."

"Is that a mafia thing? Or was that a *your parents really sucked* thing?" Swooping down, she shakes her tits right in front of my face.

I have to force myself to remember her question and dig through my brain because I'm sure as hell not thinking about my past right now. "Probably a little bit of both."

Her hands land on my shoulders, and she knee walks onto the couch, her thighs spread wide over mine. "You know those kids you say we're going to have some day?"

"Yeah?"

"They're going to play games."

"Whatever you say." With a mom like Candi, their childhood will be amazing.

"In Simon Says, the person who is Simon tells the other players what to do. If Simon doesn't say *Simon Says*, but you still do the action, you lose the game."

"What if I don't do it?" I ask.

"We keep playing."

"So, we both win," I say gutturally.

"Yes."

"Okay. Let's play." I have never given another human being this kind of power over me.

But I trust Candi like I don't trust anyone else. She can tell me what she wants me to do anytime.

She leans down so air from her mouth brushes my lips as she speaks. "Instead of *Simon Says*, I'm going to say *Candi Says*. Alright?"

"Yes," I breathe against her lips.

Giving me a soft kiss, she straightens. "Candi says put your hands flat on the couch."

I press my hands against the sofa cushion without hesitation.

Testing my resolve, she leans forward, so her breasts brush side to side against my chest and it is all I can do to keep my hands where she told me to.

"Beloved Death, you are so good at this game." She gyrates her hips, giving me the kind of lap dance she never gave a man at the club.

Every incredible, angelic inch of this gorgeous woman is mine. Every move of her body is for me and me alone.

Candi rubs her silk covered pussy against my erection while moving her body in time to the music making my heart beat a fast drum in my chest.

Leaning down, she whispers breathily into my ear, sending shivers of sensation through me. "Candi says take off your gloves."

That's an easy one with her. I'm only wearing them because she told me to dress exactly as I had on Saturday night.

She is the only person I automatically remove my gloves around when we are alone. If I'm in the house, I don't wear them now. Because there's always a chance I could be touching her and I don't want the barrier between us that I need with the rest of the world.

Taking advantage of her order, I reach around her back, and peel them off, dropping them to the side of me on the couch.

Then, because I cannot fucking help myself, I brush my hands up and down her back, reveling in soft skin. She shudders, as moved by the skin-on-skin contact as I am.

Then, in a move I neither expect, nor want, Candi scoots backward off of my lap.

Did I break the rules by touching her?

She shimmies backward three steps. "Candi says take off your coat."

Standing fast, I pull the black duster off, relief at one more layer being removed between us flowing over me. I want to rip the rest of my clothes off, but force myself not to.

Candi didn't say to.

"Candi says take off your boots."

"May I take my socks off at the same time *piccola gatta*?" I ask.

She laughs softly. "Candi says you may."

I remove my boots and socks, stacking them neatly to the side, aware that my hands tremble.

"Candi says take off your shirt." She kicks her leg up and holds the split, giving me a scintillating view of her white silk covered pussy.

I rip my shirt off over my head and drop it on top of my boots without bothering to fold it.

Candi glides forward and leans in to brush her mouth along my collarbone. Sparks of sensation light up my nerve ending.

When she sucks up a love bite at the base of my throat, the primitive man in me is delighted to have a mark that will show I am hers. I won't be wearing buttoned collars for a couple of days so everyone else can see it too. My beautiful woman wants to claim me as hers.

She leans back, her beautiful eyes dark with desire. "Candi says you can touch my breasts through the bralette, but don't unhook it."

She's really dragging this out and I'm so fucking here for it. I cup her breasts, squeezing the generous mounds. My mouth salivates in anticipation of tasting the sweet peaks.

Candi's hands land on my shoulders and rub down my chest playing over my nipples and sending zings a pleasure to my cock.

"I like that," I say with surprise.

"None of your past lovers did this?" She scrapes her nails over the small bits of flesh.

"Fuck," I gasp. "No."

"Good. I like knowing there are parts of you that no one has ever experienced the way I do. "

"No one has ever experienced anything of me the way you do, *mia amate*. You make me feel things inside, not just my body's physical reaction. I belong to you, my lover. There is no comparison with previous sex partners."

Candi kisses my chest, sucking up love bites along the way. My arousal grows to such a high-level it's nearly uncontrollable. My cock is ready to burst out of my leather pants.

Candi moans. "You're so hard right now."

"Yeah."

"Does it hurt?"

"Only in the best way."

Reaching down between us, she undoes my fly and waistband. Her hand delves inside and grips my cock like in the helicopter.

And it feels just as fucking fantastic as that day.

But I don't want a hand job. I want more. I want all of her. "Let me take them off."

"Candi says take off the sexy leather pants." After giving my dick a final squeeze, she releases me and steps back.

I waste no time shimmying out of the tight leather and silk briefs I wear beneath it.

My cock springs free, the tip already drooling for her. I kick the leather and silk aside.

"I know you're really turned on when you stop folding your clothes," she breathes against my chest.

"That's what your touch does to me." Almost every time we have sex, there's a pile of clothes to pick up after.

Pressing against my chest, she purrs, "Candi says sit down."

I drop to the couch with alacrity.

Kicking off her shoes, she cups her tits, offering them to me, but standing too far back for me to actually touch. My dick jerks in appreciation. Even her teasing is perfect.

She drops to her knees and everything inside me stills. She's going to take me in her mouth. Fuck, I want that.

I grab the thick seat cushion to my left and pull it off the couch. "Here."

"Always thinking of me." Smiling, she scoots back and lets it drop to the floor in front of my feet. "Spread your legs, Angelo."

Fuck. What do I do? Are we still playing the game.

Cocking her head in question, she asks, "Don't you want this?"

"Fuck, yes."

"Then..."

"You didn't say, *Candi says* and I don't want it to stop."

Her sexy laughter tinkles between us. "Oh, you really are good at this. I forgot we were playing."

"Are we done playing the game?" I ask, to make sure.

"Not yet." She presses on my knees. "Candi says, spread your legs wide."

I do what she says, picturing us in a reverse position and liking that image too much not to have another *date* with *mia amate* in the saferoom.

"Now, scoot your butt down a little." She shifts her own body closer. "Candi says," she tacks on when I don't move.

I slide my ass forward so my cock juts straight up.

Candi licks her lips. "I've never done this before. You know that right?"

"I've never had a mouth on my cock that mattered before."

She smiles and then swoops down, licking my precum right off my weeping slit. Humming her approval, she does it again. And again. And again.

Bathing my dick with her tongue, she gives every inch of it the same level of attention. "Fuck, please. *Mia amate* I need your mouth on me."

"You have my mouth on you."

"Suck me," I demand.

After a little look that says, *will she or won't she*, she lavishly licks her lips and then takes me into her mouth, her slick lips sliding over my cockhead and an inch down my shaft.

Pulling back, she keeps the suction tight and then takes me deeper than before. I hit the back of her throat, but she doesn't gag. She hums with pleasure and swallows.

My cock slides into her throat and my muscles go rigid with the effort it takes not to thrust deeper.

Pulling back, she inhales through her nose and drops forward again on the exhale.

Three more times she swallows, sucks and then pulls back to breathe. But on the fourth I stop her and lift her head. "I'm going to come."

"That's the idea, isn't it?"

"Not in your mouth the first time."

"Why not?"

There's a good reason, but my brain's not throwing it up right now. That's it. "I don't want you to vomit."

"Won't happen. I already tasted you. Your cum won't nauseate me. I like it."

"Next time. I want you to ride me so I can play with your gorgeous tits."

"You've got a fixation for my boobs." She doesn't sound like she's complaining.

"They're perfect, like the rest of you."

CHAPTER 43

CANDI

C an a woman ever get tired of being called perfect? Doubtful. At least not this woman.

Angelo doesn't see me as a stripper first, woman second. He sees me as his beloved first, last and always.

I stand up and slip my fingers under the waistband on both sides of my G-string. "Perfect for you, like you're perfect for me and that's all that matters."

His heated gaze zeroes in on the juncture of my thighs and stays there as I slide my G-string down my hips. Kicking it away, I do a little shimmy and his eyes snap to my boobs.

See? Fixated.

I draw out taking off my wings before unhooking the halter clasp of the bralette at the back of my neck. Smiling, I slowly pull the shimmery white fabric from my body until my heavy breasts bounce free.

The music doesn't mask Angelo's sharply indrawn breath.

Massaging my breasts, I tease my beloved. "Do you want to touch them?"

"Yes."

I climb over his lap so my slit is right above his delicious erection. "Candi says..." I drop down a little and rub over the bulbous tip, my core contracting involuntarily. "Candi says..." I breathe against his lips. "Make love to me, my beloved Death."

He reaches between us and positions himself at my entrance. Then he surges up at the same time I let my hips drop down. His thick shaft spears me, stretching my tender flesh and filling me.

Connecting us.

Rocking my hips, shards of pleasure pierce my tender flesh.

Angelo circles me with his arms, his hands pressing against my shoulder blades. "Lean back."

I do and it changes the angle so his hard-as-iron penis presses against that spot inside me that makes me see stars.

Then his mouth is on my nipple. Biting and sucking, he amps my arousal higher and higher.

But then he pulls off my nipple with a pop. "Touch yourself, *mia amate*. Give me your pleasure."

I slide my hand between my legs, scissoring my fingers on either side of my clitoris the way I like to start. But I can only do that for a few seconds before I'm circling the pleasure nub and rocking my hips as fast as I can.

My climax slams into me without warning and I cry out my pleasure as Angelo surges upward with a harsh shout and fills me with his heat.

"I love you!" I sob, the pleasure consuming. "Death. Angelo. My beloved."

He pulls me in so my breasts pillow against his chest and kisses me, the connection of our lips soft in contrast to the harsh ecstasy still rocketing through my body.

"*Sei il grande amore della mia vita*. You are the love of my life. *Il mio tutto*. My everything. *La mia anima gemella*. My soulmate." He intersperses English with Italian, making sure I get his every word.

"Say you'll stalk me forever in Italian," I demand, wanting the mafioso deep inside him to make the vow too. "Promise me."

"*Ti perseguiterò per sempre. Prometto.*" He kisses me fiercely, all gentleness gone and then says, "Even if I die, I will haunt you like the wraith I am. *Ti amo.*"

"*Ti amo,*" I say back, reveling in the intensity of his promise. "Forever."

EPILOGUE

Comeuppance

S alvatore did as promised.

Nina sits strapped to a metal chair in the box, eyes defiant despite the chapped lips, messy hair and snot dried onto her face.

Her time as a guest of the mafia hasn't been pleasant, but she's not dead and that's what Salvatore promised.

Her defiance turns to hatred when her gaze lands on me. "You can take the mask off. I know who you are, Angelo Caruso."

"You think I care if you know who I am?" I guess that piece of wisdom from my book on relationships is true too.

Every situation reads differently to the person experiencing it.

I didn't believe it because Candi and I see things in the same way if not for the same reasons.

It's weird, but it works.

"Don't you?" she sneers. "You think I won't go to the cops after this? Tell them what you did?"

"What exactly did I do?" I ask. There are so many things.

"I hear things working at the club."

"This is new." Salvatore pushes himself off the stainless steel wall with torture implements on it. "She hasn't said a word about knowing things before now."

Nina's gaze slides to him. "I know you own the club and that you're a mafia capo."

"You sound like you think that's some big secret." Salvatore pulls out his phone and taps the screen.

The tune for Candy Crush plays as he slides his finger over the screen.

"It is!" Nina glares. "You don't want the cops knowing the mafia owns the place."

"You mean the cops on our payroll, or the cops not on our payroll?" I ask.

"Right. This isn't a movie," she derides. "You don't have cops on your payroll."

"In a movie I'd spare you to show my humanity. In real life, I'm Death and today I end yours."

She gasps and stares up at me. "You can't kill me. I'm a woman. Everybody knows you have rules."

Ignoring her claim to know my rules, which do not apply in her favor, I ask, "Did you know Perla's plans for Candi when she bribed you to help them?"

Showing intelligence for the first time since I came into The Box, she refuses to answer. Because she knows the truth is *not* going to set her free.

"She did not. She didn't even know what they drugged the wine with," Salvatore says, his fury at Nina's actions bleeding into his voice. "For all she knew, it was poison, not a knockout drug."

"You did know Salvatore owned the club though."

Nina nods, clearly not as proud of that fact now as she was a minute ago.

"So, you knew you sold information on how to access one of the mafia's properties to our enemies?" That would be an offense punishable by death in our world.

That she facilitated Candi's kidnapping only guarantees her demise at my hands.

When Salvatore questioned her earlier, Nina admitted that Gino showed her an access panel to a hallway that runs between Pitiful Princess and the business next to it. There's a stairway that leads to a passage that eventually connects up with one of New York's underground tunnels.

After looking into the history of the building, we learned that back in the thirties, the same man owned both business sites and ran an illegal gambling den in the back of both. We've got people checking the walls in the dressing room for access to the other backroom.

I don't know how Gino knew about the panel in the office and I never will, because he's dead and gone.

"How was I supposed to know they weren't your friends?" Nina asks truculently. "They're mafia too, right?"

"The fact they bribed you to give drugged wine to my wife and Death's woman should have been a big fucking clue," Salvatore bites out.

Nina's mouth twists into a pout. "They didn't tell me the wine was drugged."

"You lied to get Candi and Bianca to drink it. You knew." I pull out my knife and start flipping it over my knuckles.

Death is ready to claim another soul.

"So what if I did know? Bianca's fine. Candi's fine," Nina spits. "You'd be throwing it in my face if she wasn't."

"They fucking kidnapped her." My voice sounds loud. I never noticed the acoustics magnifying sound in here before.

Nina tries to rear back in the chair.

Salvatore lays a hand on my shoulder. "You alright, brother?"

"Why wouldn't I be?" I ask. This is what I do.

"I've never heard you shout before."

"Because I don't shout," I say dismissively.

His raised brows mock my words. "Looks like you do now."

Huh. I guess I do.

"You put Candi and Bianca's life at risk." I carefully modulated my voice this time, keeping the emotion out of it.

The only person who gets my unfiltered emotion is Candi. Even when I'm furious, I act on it, but I don't express it by yelling.

Nina eyes Salvatore like he's the dangerous one in the room. "They said they wouldn't hurt Bianca."

"But *mia amate* was fair game in your eyes?" I ask.

"Candi deserves what she got. I know you did something to Gino because of her. Because she thought she was too good to sell her ass like the rest of us."

"Candi is better than you." It's got nothing to do with whether or not she sells her body for sex. "Because she's a decent human being and you're not."

Candi would never take money to set someone else up to be harmed. She's got me to protect her soft spots.

"You're a rat." The disgust he feels toward Nina infuses Salvatore's voice. "You sold our secrets. You were willing to risk *my wife's* life in order to get some petty revenge for a *stronzo* I would have killed if Angelo hadn't."

And if I had killed Gino earlier when he first leered at Candi like she was a commodity, he would not have been able to cause Candi and Bianca so much stress. That's a lesson for another day.

"I knew you killed him. I knew he was dead because of her." Nina spits at me.

The globule of mucus lands on the floor a good two feet away and I roll my eyes behind the skull mask.

"I'm not cleaning that up," Salvatore bitches.

"The sanitization process will take care of it." And any other DNA left in the room.

I jerk my head toward the panel that opens the floor. Salvatore gets my meaning immediately and walks over to activate it. The floor drops and starts sliding away from where Nina is sitting.

On the last flip over my forefinger, I grip my knife instead of flipping it again. "You've got such a hard on for Gino, you can spend the rest of eternity with him."

"No! You can't throw me in some pit to starve to death. You can't do that!"

"Don't worry. I won't."

"I knew you had a rule about killing women," she says smugly.

"Wrong." I step up behind her and pierce her jugular, pulling out the knife immediately. "My rule is about torturing them."

Her blood sprays in an ark into the soup and she bleeds out in seconds. When she's dead, I unstrap her and toss her body in.

"I wondered if you had a rule about women too when your mom survived kidnapping your woman." Salvatore remarks.

I shrug. "Killing her would have made the role she's going to play in her father's death impossible."

I'm strangely reluctant to kill Perla. When I mentioned this to Candi, she told me not to worry. If Perla ever came for me again, I wouldn't have to be the one to take her out.

Candi's not a killer, but she's right. My men will kill Perla without hesitation if she poses a threat to me.

"You're a cold bastard, Angelo. That's one of the things I like most about you." Salvatore's grin is a little unhinged.

And I know what people mean when they say I look like I have a demon in my soul. And that's probably one of the things I like best about him too.

Don Messino Dies

The call comes from my uncle a week later. His father's condition has deteriorated rapidly. The doctors are blaming his emphazyma and lifelong gastric trouble like expected.

"I'd like to come to say goodbye," I tell my uncle.

"You are family, Angelo. You are welcome."

"Perla might not agree with you."

"My sister gives her loyalty to the wrong people." The soon to be new godfather of Sicily never liked Perla's husbands.

Including my father.

When I arrive in Sicily, my uncle has a ride waiting to take me to the Messino estate from the private airfield Severu's jet landed at.

There's a hush over the household. They're all waiting for the Grim Reaper to come for my grandfather's soul.

What they don't know is that Don Messino doesn't have a soul and Death is already here.

My uncle greets me with a somber handshake. "Thank you for coming, Angelo. I know the family has not always treated you like we should, but know that once I become godfather, you will always be welcome here."

"Thank you. My life is in New York with my family there."

My uncle nods. "I heard you are engaged to a lovely young woman. The daughter of a capo."

Severu would have told him that. Perla wouldn't have said anything so complimentary.

"He doesn't acknowledge her," I say grimly.

"But her brother's do. One day Renato will be capo in his father's place and things will change in that family."

"Like they're changing in this one." I don't call it my family, but I acknowledge that my uncle has a plan for the future that is very different than my hidebound grandfather's.

"Yes."

Death has a smell I'm very familiar with and it clings to the opulent bedroom as my grandfather gasps his last breaths.

Perla jumps up when I enter the room. "What are you doing here?"

"I came to say goodbye."

She shakes her head and starts to speak, but at a look from her brother subsides back into the chair beside the bed. "Say your goodbyes then."

"I will leave you to it," my uncle says before turning to go.

"You don't mean to leave this killer with our father?" Perla demands.

"He is your son, Perla. Remember the importance of family. He is here to pay his last respects. There is nothing to criticize in that."

"He's a..." This time her voice trails off after a look from me.

"There are guards right outside the door. Invite one of them in if you feel the need," my uncle says like he's pacifying a hysterical woman.

"Yes, invite a guard in," I tell her and then say quietly so only she can hear. "I'm sure he'll be very interested in my final words to my grandfather."

My mother is not always stupid. This time she realizes whatever I have to say, *she* doesn't want a mafia soldier overhearing.

She's right.

After my uncle shuts the door, I activate the handheld scrambler that will prevent any audio or video feeds from sending a signal while it is on.

Then I stand at the end of the bed and inform my grandfather and mother the truth about why he is dying. "Try to tell someone," I say to my grandfather, who frankly isn't telling anyone anything despite the venom in his eyes. "Have an autopsy performed and it comes back on you, mother dearest."

"That's not possible," Perla denies. "I didn't do anything the Sicilian mafia would blame me for."

"Only the American Cosa Nostra considers you an enemy, Perla. It's in your best interest to keep it that way."

"I'm loyal to this family even if my spawn isn't."

I shrug. Spawn. It's not a bad word. "If you attempt any more interference in the American Cosa Nostra, your part in the death of your father will be revealed."

"I had no part."

"You did. In fact, you've been poisoning him with thallium for months. Analysis of his fingernails will show the longevity of the use."

"No one will believe that."

"The fact the fatal dose was administered in the cheesecake you bought him is very compelling."

"There's no way to prove that."

"This is the mafia, Perla. Not a court of law. One whisper of the truth becomes fifty and you are tried and convicted before Sunday dinner. You were very protective of the cake after all, not allowing anyone to have a slice but him."

"That's because of his rule. They all know that."

"But will it look that way when his autopsy proves he's been imbibing thallium for months? Your husband was ambitious, after all. He wanted to be the next godfather."

"He's dead!"

"Yes, but that doesn't change his ambition before he died. Does my uncle know that you supported Barone's delusion of taking your father's place?"

"I don't...how did..."

"You and Lora Revello will be moving to Elba to grieve the losses of your husbands in your shared widowhood."

"I'm not moving away from my home," Perla hisses.

"It's fitting, isn't it? Napolean was exiled to Elba for trying to claim territory that was not his. You and Barone were doing the same and it started with trying to kill Severu, but it wouldn't have ended there, would it?"

My grandfather is looking at my mother like she's the devil in the room now.

"You planned to get rid of my uncle after your father died to clear the way for Barone to be godfather."

I look at my grandfather. "If you had left Severu alone, you would not be dying right now. But I protect my people. I guess you could see this as me protecting my uncle too, the only member of this cancerous family worth it."

I'm on a video call with Severu when Don Messino passes. The last voice my grandfather hears is my brother telling him to rot in hell.

END

*I*f you enjoyed *ASSASSIN'S OBSESSION, please consider leaving a review, or rating. Thank you!*

I'll be posting an extra scene for Angelo & Candi to the bonus content page for newsletter subscribers in November. Make sure you're subscribed if you want to read more about these two. To access this scene and all my free bonus content, sign up on my website:

https://www.lucymonroe.com/

If you can't get enough of the De Lucas, watch for my story *A De Luca Family Christmas Carol* in the coming exclusive to Kindle & Kindle Unlimited Dec 5th for a limited time.

With more than 10 million copies of my books in print worldwide (Isn't that wild?), I'm an award winning and USA Today bestselling author with over 90 published books. My stories have been translated for sale all over the world and after a long career in traditional publishing, I've gone indie. I am loving the freedom to write the stories both me and my readers enjoy the most. My new steamy mafia romance series, Syndicate Rules features the morally gray alpha heroes and spice I love to write. I write contemporary, historical and paranormal romance. Some of my books have action adventure and intrigue. All of them are spicy and deeply emotional. I'm a voracious reader and love to talk about both my books and those I've read (or should read...good recs are always welcome) on social media. Welcome to my world where love conquers all, but not easily!

For info on my books and series extras, visit my website:
www.lucymonroe.com

Follow me on Social Media:
Facebook: LucyMonroe.Romance
Instagram: lucymonroeromance
Pinterest: lucymonroebooks
goodreads: Lucy Monroe
YouTube: @LucyMonroeBooks
TikTok: lucymonroeauthor

ITALIAN & SICILIAN GLOSSARY

Note: certain words are not italicized in the book because of their common use in American English. Also, these translations are not literal. They are the more common vernacular. Italian as it is used in Northern or Southern Italy (and Sicily) as the case may be.

accidenti – (positive) wow, gosh, my goodness (negative) darn, drat

alla famiglia – to the family

amati/amate – beloved (m/f)

amore mio – my love

amorina – little love

amicu/amica – friend (m/f – Sicilian)

anima gemella – soul mate (no masculine form/same for either)

basta – stop, that's enough

bastardo – bastard

bèdda – beautiful (Sicilian)

biddùzza – beautiful (more endearing form Sicilian)

bella mia – you are my beautiful one, or listen to me i.e. in an argument to get the person's attention (alternate uses from Southern Italy)

bella ragazza – beautiful girl

bellissima - gorgeous
bisnonna – great grandmother
bisnonno – great grandfather
brava ragazza – good girl
bravo – well done
cara/o – darling
carina/o – cutie or pretty one
carissimo/a – very dear
cazzate – bullshit
cazzo – dick/fuck equivalent
caspita – yikes/wow
che bella – how beautiful
che bello – how handsome/how nice
che buono – how tasty
che palle – oh balls/fuck it equivalent
codardo – coward
dannazione – god damn it
delizia – when someone or something is yummy
Dio mio – my god
dolce fiore – sweet flower
dolce ragazza – sweet girl
dolcezza – sweetheart, honey (literally sweetness)
mamma – mom or mother
fottuto stronzo – fucking asshole (see also *stronzo del cazzo*)
fratello - brother
giamope – fool (Sicilian and credited with being the basis for *jamook/gi-amoke*)
gioia ru me core – joy of my heart (Sicilian)
goomah – mistress or side piece
grazie a Dio – thank God
il mia lei – my her (possessive endearment for a woman)
il mio lui – my him (possessive endearment for a man)
la mia dia – my goddess
il mio tutto – my everything

ma va' – no way

ma va? – really?

magari – I wish

mamma mia – oh, man

managgia – damn

managgia la miseria – damn it (literally misery or poverty)

manaja – damn (variant from Southern Italy)

marito – husband

meno male – thank goodness

mi vitù – my life (Sicilian)

moglie – wife

nonna – grandma/grandmother

nonno – grandpa/grandfather

oh merda – oh crap/shit

patatina – a small potato (it's a beautiful thing not like in English)

per favore – please

piccolo gatto – little cat

porca miseria – damn it

puffetta – it means a female Smurf

puttana – bitch

saluti – cheers (Sicilian)

sempre – always

sempre e per sempre – always and forever

stronzo/a – asshole (also another way to say bitch)

stronzo del cazzo – fucking asshole (see also *fottuto stronzo*)

tesoro – treasure

tesoro mio – my treasure

vaffanculo - fuck

vita mia – my life

vitù – (my) life in Sicilian

Phrases:

A accidenti. – (teasing or serious) darn him/her/you

Dammi il tuo cazzo. - give me your cock

Ho detto basta - that's enough, I said enough

Ho bisogno di te. – I need you.

Ho bisogno del tuo cazzo. – I need your cock.

Io sono tua. – I am yours.

Oh, sono qui! - Hey, I'm here.

Non fermarti! – Don't stop!

Prometto. – I promise.

Tu sei mia! –You are mine. (jealous: another man or woman involved)

Sei fuori! - Are you out of your mind?

Sei la mia anima gemelli. – You are my soul mate. (no masculine form – same for either)

Sei mio. – You are mine.

T'amu. – I love you. (Sicilian)

Ti amo. – I love you.

Ti perseguiterò per sempre. – I'll stalk you forever.

Uscire. - Get out.

Voglio il tuo cazzo. - I want your cock.

Zitto. - Shut up.

Sei il grande amore della mia vita. You are the love of my life.

ACKNOWLEDGMENTS

I'm feeling especially grateful to the people that help me get my book to publication. The turn around time on this one was tight, but their willingness to "get right on it" made it possible for me to get the book out to you all the original release date.

My husband, Tom, who listens to endless ideas, scene snippets and character revelations as I write and *still* reads the complete book from start to finish when it is done.

Andie, my amazing editor at Beyond the Proof who excels at catching dangling threads and inconsistencies. Her insights make my books better. Full stop. Her ability to catch timeline inconsistencies is her secret superpower. Thanks, Andie!

Josephine Caporetto for her invaluable help on Italian phrases.

Two very special ARC readers who take the time to proofread after the copyedits are done before writing their reviews, Dee Dee & Haley. Massive hugs to you both! With special thanks to Dee Dee for writing such a wonderful book on mastiffs and inspiring Mars.

Any remaining typos, mistakes, or translation errors are my fault and mine alone.

ALSO BY LUCY MONROE

Syndicate Rules

CONVENIENT MAFIA WIFE
URGENT VOWS
DEMANDING MOB BOSS
RUTHLESS ENFORCER
BRUTAL CAPO
FORCED VOWS
ASSASSIN'S OBSESSION

Mercenaries & Spies

READY, WILLING & AND ABLE
SATISFACTION GUARANTEED
DEAL WITH THIS
THE SPY WHO WANTS ME
WATCH OVER ME
CLOSE QUARTERS
HEAT SEEKER

CHANGE THE GAME
WIN THE GAME

Passionate Billionaires & Royalty

THE MAHARAJAH'S BILLIONAIRE HEIR
BLACKMAILED BY THE BILLIONAIRE
HER OFF LIMITS PRINCE
CINDERELLA'S JILTED BILLIONAIRE
HER GREEK BILLIONAIRE

SCORSOLINI BABY SCANDAL
THE REAL DEAL
WILD HEAT (Connected to Hot Alaska Nights - Not a Billionaire)
HOT ALASKA NIGHTS
3 Brides for 3 Bad Boys Trilogy
RAND, COLTON & CARTER

Harlequin Presents

THE GREEK TYCOON'S ULTIMATUM
THE ITALIAN'S SUITABLE WIFE
THE BILLIONAIRE'S PREGNANT MISTRESS
THE SHEIKH'S BARTERED BRIDE
THE GREEK'S INNOCENT VIRGIN
BLACKMAILED INTO MARRIAGE
THE GREEK'S CHRISTMAS BABY
WEDDING VOW OF REVENGE
THE PRINCE'S VIRGIN WIFE
HIS ROYAL LOVE-CHILD
THE SCORSOLINI MARRIAGE BARGAIN
THE PLAYBOY'S SEDUCTION
PREGNANCY OF PASSION
THE SICILIAN'S MARRIAGE ARRANGEMENT
BOUGHT: THE GREEK'S BRIDE
TAKEN: THE SPANIARD'S VIRGIN
HOT DESERT NIGHTS
THE RANCHER'S RULES
FORBIDDEN: THE BILLIONAIRE'S
VIRGIN PRINCESS
HOUSEKEEPER TO THE MILLIONAIRE
HIRED: THE SHEIKH'S SECRETARY MISTRESS
VALENTINO'S LOVE-CHILD
THE LATIN LOVER 2-IN-1 with
THE GREEK TYCOON'S INHERITED BRIDE

THE SHY BRIDE
THE GREEK'S PREGNANT LOVER
FOR DUTY'S SAKE
HEART OF A DESERT WARRIOR
NOT JUST THE GREEK'S WIFE
ONE NIGHT HEIR
PRINCE OF SECRETS
MILLION DOLLAR CHRISTMAS PROPOSAL
SHEIKH'S SCANDAL
AN HEIRESS FOR HIS EMPIRE
A VIRGIN FOR HIS PRIZE
2017 CHRISTMAS CODA: The Greek Tycoons
KOSTA'S CONVENIENT BRIDE
THE SPANIARD'S PLEASURABLE VENGEANCE
AFTER THE BILLIONAIRE'S WEDDING VOWS
QUEEN BY ROYAL APPOINTMENT
HIS MAJESTY'S HIDDEN HEIR
THE COST OF THEIR ROYAL FLING

Anthologies & Novellas

SILVER BELLA
DELICIOUS: Moon Magnetism
by Lori Foster, et. al.
HE'S THE ONE: Seducing Tabby
by Linda Lael Miller, et. al.
THE POWER OF LOVE: No Angel
by Lori Foster, et. al.
BODYGUARDS IN BED:
Who's Been Sleeping in my Brother's Bed?
by Lucy Monroe et. al.

Historical Romance

ANNABELLE'S COURTSHIP
The Langley Family Trilogy
TOUCH ME, TEMPT ME & TAKE ME
MASQUERADE IN EGYPT

Paranormal Romance

Children of the Moon Novels
MOON AWAKENING
MOON CRAVING
MOON BURNING
DRAGON'S MOON
ENTHRALLED anthology: Ecstasy Under the Moon
WARRIOR'S MOON
VIKING'S MOON
DESERT MOON
HIGHLANDER'S MOON

Montana Wolves
COME MOONRISE
MONTANA MOON

Made in the USA
Las Vegas, NV
06 December 2024

13518718R00207